About th

C000178233

Auriel Roe is an artist and head of art in an international school. She has spent most of her working life teaching abroad, in addition to being an art examiner for schools around the world. Auriel has lived in six countries and her favourite, at the time of writing, is Egypt.

A BLINDEFELLOWS CHRONICLE

A BLINDEFELLOWS CHRONICLE

AURIEL ROE

This edition first published in 2017

Unbound

6th Floor Mutual House, 70 Conduit Street,
London W1S 2GF

www.unbound.com

All rights reserved
© Auriel Roe, 2017

The right of Auriel Roe to be identified as the author of this work has been
asserted in accordance with Section 77 of the Copyright, Designs and
Patents Act 1988. No part of this publication may be copied, reproduced,
stored in a retrieval system, or transmitted, in any form or by any means
without the prior permission of the publisher, nor be otherwise circulated in
any form of binding or cover other than that in which it is published and
without a similar condition being imposed on the subsequent purchaser.

ISBN (eBook): 978-1911586319
ISBN (Paperback): 978-1911586326

Design & illustration by Mecob
based on images from:
© Shutterstock.com

To James Bloom, and all who sail in his editorial brilliance.

Dear Reader,

The book you are holding came about in a rather different way to most others. It was funded directly by readers through a new website: Unbound.

Unbound is the creation of three writers. We started the company because we believed there had to be a better deal for both writers and readers. On the Unbound website, authors share the ideas for the books they want to write directly with readers. If enough of you support the book by pledging for it in advance, we produce a beautifully bound special subscribers' edition and distribute a regular edition and e-book wherever books are sold, in shops and online.

This new way of publishing is actually a very old idea (Samuel Johnson funded his dictionary this way). We're just using the internet to build each writer a network of patrons. Here, at the back of this book, you'll find the names of all the people who made it happen.

Publishing in this way means readers are no longer just passive consumers of the books they buy, and authors are free to write the books they really want. They get a much fairer return too – half the profits their books generate, rather than a tiny percentage of the cover price.

If you're not yet a subscriber, we hope that you'll want to join our publishing revolution and have your name listed in one of our books in the future. To get you started, here is a £5 discount on your first pledge. Just visit unbound.com, make your pledge and type JAPES17 in the promo code box when you check out.

Thank you for your support,

Dan, Justin and John
Founders, Unbound

Super Patrons

Omar Abbassi
Elizabeth Abdelaziz
Omar Amr Abdellatif
Anne Akay
Omar Badawy
Louise Barry
Claire Berlin
Owain Bevan
Nigel Bevan
Dianne & Nigel Bevan
Catalina Bingham
Circe Bloom
Asa Bloom
James Bloom
Leland Brandt
Grace Brandt
Georgina Chakos
Sean Colins
Matthew Cooper
Narelle Daffurn
Clinton Davis
Joy De La Vie
Timur Drachko
Ilkcan Duzel
Mervat El-Mahdy
Amy Ellery
Amina Ferrara
Rufus T Flycatcher
Mary Fullerton
Jane Gatley
Alex Geikie

Gar Green
Carol Hamilton
Mohamed Hassan
Mahmoud Hassan
Jonathan Himoff
Sarah Hodgson
Allan Hodgson
Leon Hwacha
Charlie Hykel
Matthew Inwood
Dave Johns
Karim Kadry
Ahmed Kady
Rosheen Kamel
Elan Kattsir
Ayse Kazova
Rachel Kenmare
Geoff Kidson
Dan Kieran
Flo Lead
Vanessa LeFever
Wendy Lightfoot
Joel Mansell
Jonathan Mellor
Suzanne Mills
John Mitchinson
Stephen Mooney
Holly Moy
Daniel Nakhla
Shirley Beth Newbery
Peter Newman
Richard Pairaudeau
Rosie Pinnington
Justin Pollard
Mustafa Ramadan

Tineke Regan
Laura Reilly
Carolyn Rennie
Rowena Isabel Delos Reyes
Jenny Robinson
Brenda Roe
Alan Roe
Marion Roe-bennett
Felicity Salter
Andrew Sartain
Zein Selim
Rosy Sieira-Gonzalez
Darka Soloducha
Lawrence Sporn
Gareth Taylor
Georgette Taylor
Jen Davidson Tegg
Christine Topal
Brian Trenchard-Smith
Louise Tripp
Lisa Waldman
Victoria Walker
James Wallenstein
Siobhan Watson
Jade Weeks
John West
Richard Westcott
Louisa White
Moray Whyte
Leonard Wilson
Leonard Wilson
Adam Wood
Karen Zagor

With grateful thanks to Grace Brandt, who helped to make this book happen.

'I'm going to make an animal out of you, my boy!'

— Kenneth Grahame, *The Wind in the Willows*

Contents

1. The Fair Filles of France   1
2. Guardians of the Flock   23
3. Of Art and Cheese   49
4. A Blindefellows Chronicle   73
5. The Man in the Brown Suit   99
6. Toby and The Tree People   113
7. Cold Foot Farm   137
8. The Fräulein of Ravensbrück   153
9. Randolph in the Underworld   171
10. Gone with the East Wind   191
11. A Farewell from Fairchild   205
12. Japes Abroad   227
13. A Droplet of Cream   247

    Acknowledgements   261
    Patrons   263

1

The Fair Filles of France

It was midday on 31 August, and the new history master had arrived at Blindefellows, a former charity school for poor blind boys, now a second-division private school for anyone who could pay. Twenty-six-year-old Charles Sedgewick gingerly carried one little cardboard box at a time into his assigned rooms in Loaghtan Wing, nervously avoiding the oddly prominent incisors of a flock of a few dozen miniature black sheep that jostled around him. A flock had been there for generations, deployed by the school's founder to crop the grass of the grounds, and were now trotting along baa-ing for a possible treat. Sedgewick, who sported tortoiseshell-rimmed glasses and unkempt wavy black hair, had selected a casual outfit suitable for heavy lifting on his arrival: Bermuda shorts, buckled sandals and an orange T-shirt he'd grown out of, which rode up as he carried the boxes, revealing the loose musculature of his midriff.

The deputy head, Reverend Beaulieu 'Bunny' Hareton, and William Japes, the physics master, watched from one of the neo-Gothic leaded-glass windows of the Oak Room as Sedgewick – assisted by a middle-aged couple, the female of which kept referring to him as 'Charl', omitting the 'es' – ponderously unpacked a purple Austin Allegro Estate.

'Are those his parents he's brought with him? Are you sure about this one, Bunny?' Japes asked.

'Yes, I believe those are his parents,' Bunny replied. 'And, yes, I am quite sure about Sedgewick. He lives and breathes history; it's his life.'

'Mm, I can tell, and that's precisely the problem.' Japes sighed. 'I'll go and see him tomorrow. Help him to get settled.'

'Settled?' Bunny glanced down at him, revealing a tinge of anxiety. There was nothing settled about Japes. With his receding sandy Brylcreemed hair, a mischievous twinkle in his hazel eyes and an ironic smile ever-playing about his lips, he had the look of a vampiric sprite. An ex-military man, he was always dapper, with a silk handkerchief in the breast pocket of his brass-buttoned blazer, which showed off his still-powerful torso. Despite having now turned 40, his circle of lady friends was ever-growing and he displayed not the faintest flicker of ever settling down himself. 'They really have brought absolutely everything for the lad,' Bunny remarked as he observed Sedgewick's parents carrying in groceries, tea towels and an ironing board. 'You'd think at twenty-six he'd be making a move like this for himself. Well, I trust he'll become a man of the world with your expert guidance, Japes.'

The next evening, Japes walked up the hill to Blindefellows from his house in Travistock town centre and called on Sedgewick with a bottle of Rioja, a gardening trowel and a young passion fruit vine in a pot. Before they had left, Sedgewick's parents had set up his rooms for him in an eclectic mix of clashing boiled-sweet hues while he'd been sent to his bedroom to do prep for his classes. His mother had ironed all his clothes and hung them in the wardrobe. His father had polished his shoes mirror-bright and lined them up by the door. The bookcase was neatly arranged with history books – British historians only: Trevelyan, Trevor-Roper, Carr, Elton and Churchill, of course. Popped in at the end of a shelf was the obligatory copy of *The Complete Works of Shakespeare*. Sedgewick had left the door ajar since the wing was empty and Japes, as was his wont, strolled straight in without bothering to knock.

Sedgewick, who was standing at the kitchenette counter, turned around, looking discomposed, as if he were a boy who'd just been caught breaking school rules. 'Uh, I was doing beans on toast,' he stammered. 'Rather more complicated than I'd expected.'

'Great meal in the field,' pronounced Japes. 'Heat up the can in the coals and do the toast over the flames on your bayonet – if there's any bread to be had, that is.'

Sedgewick's eyes widened, looking huge through his magnified lenses. 'You were in the Forces?'

'Fifteen years in the sappers. Got out in 1970. Been teaching here since for my sins and follies.' The older man held out his hand. 'Japes: physics.'

The younger veritably leapt forward to take it. 'Sedgewick: history. Or will be from next week once the boys arrive. It's my first post.'

'Really? You'd never guess it,' Japes lied, registering the flimsy, kitchenette breakfast table covered in an ochre-and-taupe checked cloth, fringed with white tassels and weighted with a limp aspidistra in a pink plastic pot. Japes shuddered, hoping this was the parents' style, not their offspring's.

He noted that the pictures newly hung on the walls were somewhat at odds with this – all images illustrating legendary moments in British military history: the Lionheart at Arsuf, the Duke of Marlborough at Ramillies, the Marquis (later the Duke) of Wellington at Vitoria, General Slim at Mandalay.

Japes waved at the latter, thinking to run with Sedgewick's interests. 'He presided when my class passed out at Sandhurst. Shook his hand, same as I just did yours. Didn't quite anticipate what he was letting me in for though. I was in Suez six months later, in command of a unit, with Egyptians swarming around trying to kill us.'

He now turned his attention to the delightful terrace, which Sedgewick hadn't even noticed yet. 'That'll be perfect for wining and dining when you get your first lady friend up here.'

Japes flung open the French doors and suggested they go out and plant the passion fruit, instructing Sedgewick that, with just a bit of care, there'd be a good harvest of smooth and succulent orange ovals and flowers that would imbue the air around with their exotic fragrance on romantic West Country summer evenings.

As Japes had rightly recalled, there were large planters at either end of the terrace, neither of them with anything in but a few weeds. While he dug the hole for the vine, he briefed Sedgewick on the World War sites trip to France that would be taking place under his supervision after half-term, in the run up to Armistice Day.

'We've taken the final-year O-level history group every autumn since I started here,' Japes enthused. 'Fantastic fun and great respite from noses to the grindstone. Gives the boys a chance to let off steam. Let Lindsay Anderson's *if...* be a lesson to all of us in private education today! We stay at the same *pension* every time: Suzette's in Bayeux, so named for its lovely proprietress, a great friend of mine. I get a perk or two and the boys see a bit of the world and come back much the better for it.'

After a few moments of thought, Sedgewick had an idea as to how the trip might be enhanced. 'How about we all deck ourselves out in appropriate kit from the Army and Navy Stores and wear it over there to get in the right frame of mind? We can even do some realistic manoeuvres on the D-Day beaches. Bring history to life – you know.'

'What a grand idea, Sedgewick! The boys will be thrilled to be out of their Blindefellows uniforms for a week. I'm afraid I won't take part though. Had more than my fill of the real thing, if you know what I mean.'

Japes followed this by spending the remainder of the evening consuming most of the Rioja he had brought along while enlarging upon 'the real thing' in Her Majesty's Forces during their ill-starred twilight years in the Middle East.

For his part, Sedgewick explained that, much to the relief of his mother, his dreadful eyesight had proven a stumbling block when he'd toyed with the idea of the army after university. Instead, he had followed in his father's footsteps and joined K

Shoes on their graduate trainee scheme as a regional manager for Shropshire, which had mainly consisted of introducing the new shoes to the shop girls and helping them to develop as saleswomen, integrating into their sales pitches such enticing stock phrases as 'comfortably malleable uppers' and 'wonderfully durable vulcanised soles', patter they would jot down in their palm-sized K Shoes notebooks.

Living at home again for two years had allowed Sedgewick to save a pot of money within a few months, but his life had lacked something – and that something was history. Every time he travelled to a new town, he'd make sure to set aside an hour or two for the museum or the cathedral, or to seek out the remnants of the odd medieval burgage plot.

Then, one day, musing by chance through *The Times* jobs pages, the post of history master with boarding duties at Blindefellows had jumped out at him. He'd promptly drafted the most impassioned letter of his life to the deputy head, Reverend Hareton, who'd been sufficiently impressed to call him down for interview, where his spirited defence of the destruction of the Garden of Perfect Brightness and Garden of Eternal Spring by the joint Franco–British Expeditionary Force, under Lord Elgin in the Second Opium War, had so struck Major Cowerd, the headmaster, that Sedgewick had pipped the candidates from Oxbridge at the post – and now here he was.

Ten weeks later, with the new history master already surprisingly firm on his feet in the classroom (if not quite so much so in the boarding wing), the day of the Fifth Form history trip to France arrived. A sage-green-and-cream Bedford VAL Plaxton bus, owned and operated by Wilfred, a cantankerous man in his sixties, pulled up in front of the Disraeli Chapel, before which a khaki-costumed cluster of 15-year-old boys in Army and Navy surplus waited with their canvas knapsacks. Wilfred glowered through the window of the bus for some time before pulling the door-lever with a truculent flourish.

Japes, who had in the course of the previous four trips come to feel a fondness for the taciturn old Devonian, bounded up the bus steps to greet him.

'Wiff, my man, splendid to see you again! Another year passed since November last and both of us still above ground and in fine fettle, eh?'

But Wilfred only returned to staring stonily at Japes for a further half-a-minute before asking in his Devonshire growl, 'Why are the boys dressed up like that, Mr Japes?'

Japes, who fancied he had served with a few NCOs of the Wilfred type, and could see things from their point of view, laid a reassuring hand firmly on the old boy's shoulder and answered, 'Just a whim of the new history master to help get the lads into the spirit of the trip. Don't think twice about it, Wiff. They belong to a different generation that's at quite a distance from you or me.'

Wilfred was glaring out the VAL's window again, this time at Sedgewick, who had just come into view lugging an overstuffed army surplus duffle bag and was presently wagging a finger at a couple of boys, Jonathan Peachum and Tighe Brown, as if he were trying – and failing – to give them something like an order.

'Is that him?' Wilfred snorted.

'Yes, that's Mr Sedgewick... Do try to be civil to him, Wiff. It'll undermine his authority with the boys if you're not.'

'There's some don't know they've been born.'

'Precisely, which is why it's on our shoulders to guide them on this trip.'

Sedgewick himself now stood at the bus door, wielding a clipboard. 'Shall we stow the kit and board the men, Japes?' he asked his mentor anxiously.

Japes nodded in assent, while Wilfred rolled his eyes as he unscrewed his Thermos and poured himself some unidentified steaming beverage. Once the boys and their baggage were on the bus, Sedgewick turned to Japes.

'I'd better take the register, or at least count them before we drive off.'

'But you just did the register out on the pavement, Sedgewick.'

'You never know, one of them may have nipped off to the lavatory, unbeknown to us.'

'Very well, I'll count them for you,' said Japes with relish, and he went down the bus, heartily slapping each boy on the top of the head.

Sedgewick, thunderstruck at the front, marvelled at how this was all a big laugh as the boys ducked to fend off Japes's descending palm.

'All present and correct, Sedgers.'

'Are you sure, Japes? Some of them were ducking when you did the count so it may not have been wholly accurate.'

Japes smiled broadly at his green colleague, then turned around sharply and barked out, 'Is anybody *not* here?'

Brown and Peachum shouted gleefully, 'We're not, sir!'

'If only!' Japes retorted. 'Better count you two again just to make sure,' and he gave the boys in question another head-slap.

'Do you two be thinking we might be moving off?' Wilfred grunted from behind the VAL's vast steering wheel.

'Chocks away, Wiff!' Japes called back as he thrust Sedgewick into the nearest pair of empty seats, then almost fell on top of him with the force of take-off from the old Bedford bus.

'Wilfred drives us over to France every year, Sedgewick. Won't get out of his bus, even though it's his old stomping ground. He was with the 43rd Wessex Recce at Normandy. Went right across northern France, through Holland and on into Germany. Hell's Highway, as they called it.' Sedgewick craned his neck to peer reverently at Wilfred's lined face reflected in the rear-view mirror; the bus driver noticed this and looked away.

To put the boys in the right frame of mind, Sedgewick had taught them a medley of wartime songs to sing on the bus and they now struck up 'Run, Rabbit, Run'. Wilfred pulled a pair of cotton wool wads from his shirt-front and plugged his ears.

On the ferry, the boys mooned around the games room and played cards. Wilfred had a spot of shut-eye on the back seat of the bus while Japes and Sedgewick alternately sat in the lounge or strolled on deck in the brisk November breeze.

'So, how are you finding Blindefellows thus far, Sedgewick?'

'Well, apart from the odd rumbustious tyke I've mentioned to you already, Japes, it's all good – very good, in fact. I've realised I'm at my happiest in an educational environment. Once I'd won my scholarship to Adams' Grammar I was away boarding, then it was straight into halls at Warwick seven years later. I tried living out in digs in my second year but I didn't enjoy it so I went back into halls for the last years of the degree and then my MA. Much easier with meals done for you and no cleaning – more time for reading, you know.'

'And then you returned to *mater* and *pater*?'

'Yes, in Bridgnorth: fantastic little town with a funicular. I knew in my heart I didn't share my father's enthusiasm for footwear but I gave it my best shot and he's proud of me for that.'

'But doesn't the Shropshire lad mind not having any sort of adventure in his life?'

'But I do, Japes: the past is my adventure. When I get stuck into a riveting history book, peer into a microfiche reader at centuries-old pamphlets or sit back and watch an old newsreel, I am transported to those dramas of the past. And tomorrow we're going to relive one of the greatest dramas of our century, right there on the beaches of Normandy! I know it's not your cup of tea because you've experienced the real McCoy with your desert skirmishes and so on, but to me it's thrilling.'

Japes accepted that Sedgewick would never be propelled into anything beyond the quotidian, but hoped, when they returned to Blindefellows, he'd at least dip his toe into an extra-curricular romance. He was thinking he knew just the girl to introduce him to: Sheila from the flower shop – bookish like Sedgewick but with a sense of fun that he felt would benefit him.

From Cherbourg they drove straight on to Bayeux so they could settle into their rooms and relax before the next day's mock military manoeuvres. Suzette's *maison d'hôtes*, with the bedrooms looking out onto the River Aure at the back, was a pale greystone building covered in a vine in an autumnal red. Suzette herself was at the door to greet them, her hair, of a similar hue to the vine, teased into short, devilish curls. She wore a periwinkle-blue crocheted knee-length dress that she had plainly picked to match her eyes, which were framed by Arabian Nights-style black eyeliner.

'Monsieur Japes, *mon ami!*' she cried, and hugged him tightly for rather longer than Sedgewick thought proper in front of the boys – but then, this was France and they all needed to adjust.

The room Sedgewick shared with Japes was neat and simple. The boys' rooms were identical to theirs and spread over the two upper floors. Wilfred was staying in the economy basement rooms, which were a sort of British-working-men's club with linoleum floors and lopsided orange curtains, reserved for long-haul lorry drivers and the occasional busman like himself.

Dinner that evening in the hotel dining room was a three-course set menu of *escargots* in a green parsley-and-garlic butter, *magret de canard* and *tarte Tatin*. Japes led the boys in devouring the *escargots* appetiser with such gusto that the butter left shiny trails down their chins.

'Observe, Sedgewick,' Japes whispered in his ear. 'Their puritanical English taste buds are, before our very eyes, losing their gustatory virginity.'

Sedgewick reddened slightly at his friend's diction but the food certainly smelled astonishing compared to the bland pap of Blindefellows.

'French food, like French women, Sedgewick, is full of startling little surprises that burst on the palate, whereas English food, like English women, is warm, comforting and plentiful.'

Sedgewick said his apologies and declined the *escargots*. When the *magret de canard* was set in front of him he was more hopeful... until he punctured the duck breast with his fork and a rivulet of fragrant juices seeped out, which confused him. He bashfully put down his knife and fork and attempted to place his napkin modestly over the duck, but it soaked up the moisture, which only drew attention to it.

'Ooh la la, Monsieur Sage-weak, what is wrong?' Suzette consoled him, putting her arm around him and pushing her bosom into his back.

'I'm so, so sorry, Madame Suz… Suzette,' Sedgewick stuttered. 'It… It all just seems a little rich for my plain old English palate. Do you have something simple, like a cheese omelette, perhaps?'

'Oh, I 'ave just ze sing for you – a nice slice of quiche Lorraine *avec croquettes.*'

Within five minutes, the plain and simple meal was set down in front of Sedgewick. Wilfred, he noticed, had the same in front him as he sat alone and as saturnine as ever at a little table by the window. He decided that he really must talk to him about the Wessexes at Normandy when the moment was ripe.

Sedgewick noticed that the two teenage waitresses appeared to be holding Brown and Peachum spellbound as the boys looked up at them, mouthing their luscious Gallic delicacies. Suzette had mentioned to him and Japes that the girls had come to her in the spring from the Massif Central, where there was no work at all for young women, other than as dairy maids, and they 'wanted to grasp 'old of life, not cows' udders'. Here, in Bayeux, which was a metropolis to them, they worked for Suzette as waitresses-cum-*femmes de chambre*. 'Ah, but zey are very 'appy today, 'aving your boys 'ee-ur – normally we 'ave only ze travelling salesmen, who are all far too ole for zem, poor sings.'

Sedgewick watched aghast as the girls leaned over – displaying their wares in crimson lace undergarments beneath their low-cut tops – to top up the boys' glasses. 'Japes, did you see that? It's illegal! They're giving them more alcohol!'

'It's not illegal here in France, Sedgers.' Japes patted his arm. 'Don't worry, I've given Suzette strict instructions to limit them to three glasses each, and thereafter they'll only get re-filled with *l'eau de Normandie*. It's how we do it every year; she knows the ropes.'

Three glasses, thought Sedgewick. That would entirely finish him. What would it do to them?

'And now for ze tarts!' Suzette announced as the girls brought in trayfuls of individual *tartes Tatin*, each with a globule of *crème Anglaise* on the top, which the boys were very keen to indulge in.

After coffee, the boys were permitted to go out for an after-dinner walk around the picturesque old town, shepherded by Sedgewick, while Japes moved into the *salon* to round off the evening indulging in after-dinner sweet liqueurs with Suzette.

Sedgewick brought all the boys back around eight and, having checked everyone in for the evening, stretched out, still dressed, on his bed. Several hours later, he awoke in the dead of night and had to recall his whereabouts in the darkness for a moment or two, going over his last known movements in a hurried whisper before he remembered where he was. He stumbled about and groped for the light switch on the wall. Japes wasn't in his bed and it hadn't been slept in. He reached for his glasses and looked at his wristwatch – 3am. Must be quite some round of sweet liqueurs Japes is having with Madame Suzette, he thought.

Putting on his carpet slippers, he crept quietly as best as he could over the creaky floorboards to the shared bathroom on the landing, to relieve himself of the evening's ample intake of wine and water. He was embarrassed by the noise of the deluge but couldn't manage the exercise any more quietly, despite aiming for the side of the bowl. *Two glasses of Sauvignon was clearly pushing the boat out*, he thought.

Coming out of the bathroom, he noticed a light from the gap under the door of Peachum and Brown's room. He pushed it open a crack with his fingertips. Two more unoccupied beds. What kind of house of ill repute had Japes brought him to? He peered down the pitch-black chasm of a stairwell for any sign of Japes but all was still and quiet. Returning to his room, he changed into his pyjamas and lay beneath the counterpane, worrying about what kind of trouble he could get into back at school for allowing boys to go missing. Finally, wishing to be fresh for the manoeuvres on the beach the next day, he told himself he would sort it all out in the morning as he was powerless to do anything now and, repeating this mollifying advice, gradually lulled himself back to sleep.

In the wake of his late-night excitement, Sedgewick had slept through his alarm, and by the time he was decked out in his uniform of khaki britches with olive drab knee-socks, army surplus shirt to match the former and woolly jumper the latter, all topped off by a Home Front Command orange beret (which was a tad constricting on his forehead), he found that breakfast was already in full swing. Japes was tapping the top of his boiled egg, with Suzette sitting opposite him, her stilettos abandoned on the carpet and her stockinged toes gliding over his polished brogues.

'Ah, bonjour, Monsieur Saige-weak!' She got up, slipped on her shoes and invited him to sit in her vacated place. '*Voila*, I've been keeping your shair warm for you. Would you like ze full Engleesh or just ze *croissant au confiture et un oeuf à la coq*, like Monsieur Japes?'

'Oh, the full English, please, Madame Suzette!' he lowed and sat opposite Japes in the chair warmed so beautifully by Suzette.

One of the waitresses, looking rather bleary-eyed, set down a proper plateful before him. He dunked his sausage in his fried egg and, as he chewed, counted up the breakfasting boys in his head. 'All eighteen, present and correct,' he declared.

'Heavens, you're not counting them again, are you, Sedgers?'

'Well, two were AWOL last night: Peachum and Brown.'

'Splendid! With any luck, by the time we depart it'll be more than their taste buds that'll have lost their virginity.' Japes winked.

Sedgewick dropped his fork.

'Not for nothing is the region Madame Suzette's fair minions hail from known as the Massif Central, Sedgers my boy.'

'Good Lord! Should we inform the head? Do you think their parents ought to know?'

'Certainly not! Why else have we journeyed to these fair *filles* of France if not to upraise the British flag?'

Sedgewick choked slightly and sputtered toast crumbs onto the tablecloth.

'How would you have liked someone tattling to your parents when you were campaigning to lose your virginity?'

'I did tell my parents… Well, I mean, I told Mother, and I was twenty, certainly not fifteen!'

Japes held his egg spoon aloft in wonder, frozen midway

between mouth and egg cup, as if in momentary suspended animation. 'And since then?'

'Well, I haven't found the right girl. Once bitten, twice shy, as they say.'

'Ah, she was a biter, was she?'

'Who? Phoebe? Oh, no, at least I don't think so. Though possibly. Perhaps. I can't really recall.'

'Didn't stick around long enough for you to find out?'

'No, I never even had the opportunity to introduce her to Mother.'

Japes nodded compassionately. He was determined to get Sedgewick's love life up and running as soon as they returned home. It was the closest he'd get to any kind of adventure.

Following breakfast, they all spent a couple of hours in the D-Day Museum at Arromanches, then ate sandwiches looking out onto Mulberry Harbour. After lunch, they drove over to Sword Beach for the manoeuvres. Sedgewick led them down through the dunes and over the strand to the water's edge, taking care not to get his boots wet.

'Now, boys, you have to imagine how these men would've been feeling when they first landed, he declaimed above the whipping wind. 'Some came off those boats feeling pretty rough already as they'd had dreadful seasickness throughout the choppy crossing. As they approached the shore in the landing craft, they began to come under terrifyingly heavy bombardment. They could see their comrades floating down in parachutes behind enemy lines, and watched as many of them were shot before they reached the ground.

They'd have had quite a bit less ground to cover than you do today, however, because at midnight on 6 June 1944, during the first wave of landings, it was high tide, such was the timely planned operation. Their initial brief was, of course, to secure the beachhead, but as soon as they set foot on dry land they had to dive for the first natural cover they came across and establish the exact location of enemy fire. Many were killed or seriously wounded and out of action before they'd advanced so much as a furlong. Of course, a few of them had the great good luck to be sheltered by Major Hobart's Funnies – Brown and Peachum, you're probably laughing now because you weren't listening in class. Babcock, can you remind them about the Funnies?'

'They were flame-throwing tanks, sir, specially designed to negotiate the uneven terrain,' said Babcock, droning out his usual textbook answer.

'Thank you, Babcock... So, what I want you to do now, in twos and threes, is to imagine a scenario like the one I've just described and then to make your way accordingly up the beach. With caution, mind you: you need to look out incessantly for mines, razor wire and enemy fire. Mr Japes and I will be waiting at the old German bunker over there, which is to be your target, as you want to neutralise the machine gunners stationed within. We will observe your progress and I will award bars of Belgian chocolate to those who are the most convincing.'

Sedgewick withdrew to the grassy dunes, where Japes had erected a camp stool on a level section of roof slab from what remained of the shattered bunker, half filled with sand. As Sedgewick watched the boys' advance through genuine Second World War field glasses, he saw plenty of throwing-down prone then rolling and crawling on bellies.

'Good show, Sedgers, they're really enjoying it,' Japes commented, looking up from a booklet of logic puzzles he'd found abandoned at Suzette's and patting his younger colleague on the back. 'Your predecessor certainly never did anything this exciting, believe me. What with a stomach the size of a Galapagos tortoise, he wasn't up to much at all.'

Twenty minutes later, most of the boys had arrived at the bunker and Sedgewick presented chocolate bars to all of them in recognition of their uniformly sterling performances. He scanned the beach for the final three and saw smoke rising from a lone dune further down the beach.

'Just a moment, lads; I believe I've spotted a lingering pocket of enemy fire,' he called out as he marched off towards it.

As expected, he discovered Brown and Peachum, accompanied by a greenish new boy, Grenville, whom the other two were sniggering at as he attempted to join them in smoking Café Crème cigarillos, as favoured by – and presumably pinched from – Madame Suzette. As soon as they realised Sedgewick was upon them, all three boys sought to conceal their crime in the sand and stood to attention. 'I could send all three of you home for this, you know,' Sedgewick said, surprising himself at the calm authority in his voice, although inside he felt furious that these miscreants had attempted to sabotage what was a tour de force of teaching. Their chorus of, 'Sorry, sir,' and, 'Please give us one last chance, sir,' placated him somewhat.

'Very well,' Sedgwick said, 'but now you're going to move up the beach as if your lives depended upon it, bombarded all the while by truly dreadful enemy fire, with me as your commanding officer.' They did as he bid and slithered along behind him, propelling themselves by their elbows, rolling into natural foxholes and curtly signalling to each other. Through the binoculars, Japes watched Sedgewick joining in with the three boys and occasionally jabbing a plump finger in the air toward the imaginary enemy. He thought how completely in his element the poor chap was in his make-believe battle. How Sedgewick would fare under real fire, Japes didn't like to imagine.

When the VAL Plaxton drew up at the graveyard in Bayeux, at the spot Japes had specifically recommended, Sedgewick stood up and spoke to the boys before they got out.

'Now, lads, we've had our fun for the day. I expect you to maintain a serious demeanour at this powerfully poignant resting place for thousands of valiant young Britons, many of them only a few years older than yourselves at the time they gave up their lives to free Europe from the vilest and most pitiless tyranny the world has yet known.'

Chastened by their teacher's brief snippet of faux-Churchillian rhetoric, the Blindefellows Fifth Form disembarked in an orderly fashion and followed Japes to a little clearing in the graveyard. Here Donald Drake, an earnest boy with literary aspirations and teased as much for his lack of sporting prowess as for his unfortunate name, began to read Charles Causley's 'At the British War Cemetery, Bayeux', which he'd rehearsed repeatedly at school with Sedgewick, who was hoping thereby to raise Drake's credibility among his peers.

A meditative atmosphere descended and Sedgewick felt he had finally touched a nerve even with Brown and Peachum, whose heads were now bowed in contemplation. He caught sight of Wilfred, 100 metres away, out of his bus and looking out, scanning the interminable rows of headstones. There then followed a minute's silence, which wasn't broken by so much as a second of boyish silliness, and Sedgewick felt as if he had found and fulfilled his destiny.

When the minute was over, Japes cleared his throat and began to speak.

'While we're standing in this hallowed spot, boys, I'd like to draw your attention to a grave that's very special to me. On the second row, far left, you'll see the final resting place of my father, Major Thomas Japes, fourth County of London Yeomanry. He served under Viscount Cranley in the Sharpshooters, as they called them. The last time I saw him was in the autumn of 1943, when I wasn't much younger than you are now. I got home from school and he was packing his kit bag, my mother weeping in an armchair. I asked him where he was going, to which he replied he couldn't tell me but, with a wink, he said he thought he might be needing a bucket and spade. A few months later we heard about the D-Day landings on the wireless. Then came the telegraph. He'd made it up the beaches, but had been killed in action during the terrible siege of Caen. A brave, brave fellow.'

All were struck dumb by Japes's revelation and plunged into a second, now involuntary, silence. At last, Sedgewick felt he must speak.

'Mr Japes, thank you for allowing us to share in your poignant reverie. I imagine it must still be painful for you, thirty years later, to recount your final day with your father, and I am sure that everyone present must feel as honoured as I that you have done this before us today.'

'No, it's not painful at all,' Japes replied, and the next moment his hitherto solemn face suddenly burst into a broad grin. 'It's not painful because I don't know who the hell Major Thomas Japes was. My father was over forty when Hitler came to power and spent the war in his dental practice, fighting tooth decay in Clacton-on-Sea.'

Sedgewick's jaw dropped. This was a jape too far. One by one, the astonished boys cottoned on and a wave of uncertain laughter gathered and rolled around the epicentre of the graveyard. Sedgewick tried to hush them in this most solemn of places.

'He's done that every year!' Wilfred was suddenly among them, pointing a leather-gloved finger at Japes. The boys were silenced; he looked as if he might bayonet someone at any moment. 'I've watched them from my bus, Mr Sedgewick, every year, suddenly falling about at something Mr Japes has said. This year, I thought, *I'll come down and find out what the great joke could possibly be in a place like this*, even though it's difficult for me to be among my former comrades. Well, Mr Japes, it isn't funny, what you just did. You may not know who the hell Major Thomas Japes was but you can be damned sure someone else did. Your battles may have been fought elsewhere but mine happened here and I served with dozens of men laid to rest in this very cemetery.'

Several boys were nodding, their mouths downturned in dismay. Donald Drake gazed at Wilfred with moist eyes, his lips compressed. Brown and Peachum stared at their feet in shame, though they were, for once, entirely innocent.

'I'm sorry, Wilfred. You're right,' Japes said, and Sedgewick saw that he looked genuinely remorseful. 'Schoolboy humour from a grown man is not appropriate, especially here.'

Wilfred ignored him. 'With your permission, Mr Sedgewick, could I tell these boys a real story about the war?'

'By... by all means, Wilfred.' Sedgewick bowed his head humbly.

'We were lost in the dark when we arrived in Normandy, boys, with useless maps cobbled together from information from holiday snaps people had sent in. Many of us had never even made it up the beach.

'The Germans surrounded us in Mouen. They had machine guns and heavy artillery. A handful of us made it out of that one and went on to Caen. You couldn't see the pavement in the streets for the dead men there. Yes, I was in Caen, Mr Japes. I lost my best buddy, Cyril, there. He's buried here somewhere – hello, Cyril, sorry it's taken me so long to come round. We joined up as soon as the war started, Cyril and I. We'd worked together in a greengrocer's in Exeter for ten years since we'd left school at fourteen.

'Anyway, those who survived Caen moved on to The Perrier Ridge. We were low on ammunition and so were the Germans. There was heavy hand-to-hand combat with bayonets, rifle-butts, bricks, broken bits of metal. I must have been quite good at it because I came through, but my mates from school, Ronnie and Stan, didn't. Their bodies were never identified but their names are on a cenotaph about twenty miles east of here…

'The French cheered us in the streets each time we drove the Nazis back. It was all that gave us the strength to keep going. These beautiful French girls would take us home with them. They'd boil up water and bathe us, and we'd sleep with them in feather beds. I'd never felt so grateful to be alive.

'So, I'd just like to thank Cyril, Ronnie and Stanley and all the other tens of thousands for fighting to the death, for being good friends and saving my life more than once. I shouldn't have waited thirty years to do it, but it took this old soldier a lot of courage to walk down here today.'

In silence, they all watched as Wilfred turned and walked back to his bus, threading a path among the graves, leaning over a little to run his fingertips over the tops of the low headstones. Then the rest of them began to follow slowly, keeping to the main path at a respect-ful distance, the November late-afternoon sun hovering low and red above the horizon. Sedgewick stood at the door of the VAL Plaxton, counting off the boys as they filed in. Japes followed last and mum-bled as he passed, 'I'd best take a seat at the back for the time being.'

At dinner that evening, Wilfred asked Sedgewick if he'd like to join him at his table. Sedgewick answered that he'd be honoured. Tonight, the menu was more traditional, French country fare: some sort of grilled sprats to start, followed by *boeuf bourguignon*, with the wine supplanted by brown pint-bottles of warm dark Belgian beer, which the boys were downing like cola after being out all day in the autumn air.

Sedgewick noticed that the Massif Central maidens were brushing up against Peachum and Brown more than accidentally as they served them, and that neither their mistress nor her man were to be seen in the dining room. As the dessert – large cream-horns drizzled with caramel – was being cleared, and the weary boys were staggering off to their rooms, Japes appeared in the dining room doorway with a glass of brandy in one hand, the other hand behind his back. Sedgewick, who was facing in that direction, could see him but Wilfred, sitting on the opposite side of the table, could not.

'I see Mr Japes has come down,' Sedgwick said quietly. 'Do you think I should invite him over to our table?'

Wilfred, who was polishing off his second bottle of the Belgian beer, took a long breath in, breathed it out, and replied, 'Why not? Life's too short to hold grudges.'

Sedgewick gave a small wave and nod to Japes, who lingered a few seconds then approached. Between the fingers of the hand he now brought from behind his back were two empty glasses, to match his own, which he now placed before Sedgewick and Wilfred. Placing his glass at the table end, he sat down at a right angle to the older man and the younger. He glanced at each of them, and from his blazer's inside pocket produced a small bottle of Rémy-Martin. He unscrewed it, half-filled the two empty snifters, sat back, crossed his legs and paused.

'I got what I deserved in the cemetery today, didn't I?' he declared. 'I can take my humour a bit too far sometimes, but as you pointed out this afternoon, Wiff, mine were other battles. Ones that weren't something to proud be of, like yours. Generally fought against crowds of poor, ragged Arabs armed with vintage rifles that didn't shoot straight, petrol bombs in old pop bottles or frequently nothing more than sticks and stones – but plenty of words that hurt me, largely because I knew they were true.'

'It hasn't been a pretty sight, has it, Mr Japes?' Wilfred affirmed. 'The decline and fall of our empire in the East?'

'I'm not convinced that the history books would agree with that!' Sedgewick piped up, his naivety causing him to furrow his young brow at this aspersion cast upon the homeland's glory.

'Then I'm convinced I can never agree with the history books,' Japes mused. 'Which brings me to the one reason I don't entirely regret my stupid prank: if I hadn't done it, you couldn't have called me out on it, Wiff – and wasn't it just marvellous for those boys to hear about the War first hand from you like that!'

Japes picked up his glass, held it out towards Wilfred and drank off his remaining cognac in one, like a shot of whiskey.

'I fancy that forty years from now, when Sedgewick here is your age, Wiff, and you and I, most likely, are faded into oblivion, that more than a few of those boys will remember standing in that cemetery in Bayeux today and listening to what you told them.'

Oh, lucky, lucky man, Sedgewick thought of himself, to have fallen into the teaching post at Blindefellows, to have become friends with someone like Japes, to have wound up on this trip to France with him, to have happened to be driven by Wilfred, and to have heard him say what he had in the Bayeux cemetery earlier. He felt a lump rising in his throat, and not wanting to embarrass himself in front of the two old soldiers, imitated Japes's gesture and drank off the rest of his cognac in one... at which he fell into a spasm of coughing like a boy taking his first drag on a cigarette.

'Easy does it, Mr Sedgewick!' chuckled Wilfred, slapping him firmly between the shoulder blades.

'Tenth of November tomorrow, and on to the Somme battlefields in the VAL,' announced Japes. 'Then to Thiepval for the Armistice Memorial Service on the eleventh... Now you've broken the ice, Wiff, I was hoping you'd go on with a good thing and join us? No more unbecoming larks from me: that's a promise.'

Then Wilfred, too, lifted his snifter and drank off the last of his cognac. 'Alright lads,' he assented. 'I suppose I might as well.'

2

Guardians of the Flock

Michaelmas 1977

With two weeks of the summer holidays still left, Japes was none too pleased to find himself walking up the hill to Blindefellows. Major V. Cowerd OBE, now headmaster for the past quarter-of-a-century, had rung Japes earlier in the afternoon when he was in bed, trying to sleep off the effects of a tempestuous four-week stay with an old flame on the Leeward Island of Montserrat in the Caribbean.

'I don't know if you've heard, Japes, but Blythe had a funny turn at the start of the holidays and has headed out to pasture.'

'What, he died?'

'No, no. He's taken early retirement.'

Blythe, the school doctor, was 67, but 70 was the usual age at which Blindefellows masters, who attained such advanced years, tended to retire.

'Anyway, to cut a long story short, I got in touch with an agency, who've found me a replacement – a lieutenant commander, no less.'

The lieutenant commander had, it seemed, already been installed in Blythe's former flat by Birdwhistle, Blindefellows' venerable groundsman. Japes wondered whether Major Cowerd, ever an upholder of the maxim that a penny saved is a penny earned, had gone to the trouble of having the flat cleaned, given that Blythe, hardly a model practitioner of his profession, was reputed not to have done so for many a year.

Under normal circumstances, settling a new member of staff

would have fallen to Bunny but Bunny was unavailable. He was still away on his missionary work among the Jivaro people in the depths of the Ecuadorian rainforest, the provenance, via Bunny, of Japes's most prized possession: the shrunken head of a brown-throated sloth which – so the Jivaro chief who had made a present of it to Bunny had informed him – had been blow-piped and speared in lieu of the missionary to whom he had taken a rare liking. The nature of this exotic relationship with the chief had since become a standing private joke between the two old friends, to which Bunny would invariably respond, 'Japesy, please: he's a happily married man with five wives and four surviving children!'

Major Cowerd, who took no interest whatsoever in the private lives of his faculty, was equally diligent in never having anything to do with what he considered the donkey work of getting new people settled. Japes, as a gregarious bachelor of military background, had seemed to the head to be the obvious choice for the task.

Obliging as ever, Japes set off to welcome the lieutenant commander, bringing along one of the flasks of moonshine rum he had carried home from his visit to an ad hoc distillery in central Guadeloupe – the better, he mused, to welcome his fellow veteran, in the fond hope that the chap would be so blotto by sundown that he could retreat back down the hill to his bed. As he passed through the ornamental wrought-iron school gates, the Blindefellows flock of a few dozen knee-high sheep, West Country Pygmy Bearded Blacks, galloped over to him as a single woolly body. Descended from the very first Blindefellows flock, they were subject to an unfortunate trait of inbreeding in the form of prominent piano-key teeth, which had taken root due to paltry attempts at animal husbandry in recent decades.

Hezekiah Lambton, founder of Blindefellows, had started out as a humble sheep shearer but had developed a method (now lost) of fine-spinning the delicate fleece of these little sheep that had allowed him to prosper. Father to a blind boy, he had built the school as a charitable institution for those who shared his son's affliction. The pupils were taught the practical skills of yarn-spinning and sheep-keeping, thus sharpening their functioning senses and giving them a fall-back career upon leaving the school. In Latin prayer, Major Cowerd relished using the old address 'Ye sightless guardians of the flock' when referring to the boys en masse, although nowadays, unencumbered by the hindrance of being blind, they were all too frequently observed chasing the petite creatures with cruel exuberance between lessons. Nevertheless, the insignia of the school remained a black sheep in a white blindfold, and was sewn upon the breast pocket of every boy's black-and-white herringbone tweed blazer.

Japes marched jauntily up the stairs to Boreray Wing and down the corridor to the doctor's rooms, which were situated next to the sanatorium. There wasn't a soul about. He rapped on the door and did so again, more loudly, when no answer came within half-a-minute. Then the door opened, and framed within it, arms akimbo, was a smallish but powerfully built woman, perhaps a decade his junior, perfectly turned out in a safari suit.

'Ah, hello. I'm William Japes, physics master, come to see your husband.'

The woman – whom he noted wore not a stroke of make-up, had puffy eyes and was pink around the nostrils as if she were suffering from allergies or a cold – made no answer but merely peered at him.

'I don't have a husband, nor do I ever intend to,' she finally remarked.

Well done you! A woman after my own heart, he thought, but instead said only, 'Oh, I was looking for Lieutenant Commander Ridgeway.'

'I *am* Lieutenant Commander Ridgeway,' she said, putting out her hand. Japes shook it, taking note of her exceptionally firm musculature and grip.

'You?' he laughed. 'This is a boys' school; we don't hire women, except as dinner ladies or secretaries, and they certainly don't sleep here.' He paused a moment to reconsider and added, 'Well, other than occasionally and surreptitiously, perhaps... Does the headmaster know you're a woman?'

'He has, presumably, read my excellent references which, I should imagine, refer to me in the feminine.'

'Hmm, knowing him, I wouldn't bank on his having actually read your references.' He looked her up and down, noting her slightly tight trouser suit. 'Excellent though I'm sure they must be.'

The woman suddenly averted her face and shaded her eyes. 'Perhaps I shouldn't finish unpacking,' she gulped.

At this, Japes realised that she didn't have allergies or a cold, as he'd thought when she had opened the door; she'd been crying. 'I do hope I haven't upset you,' he said.

'No, I was upset already. Come in and sit down,' she stepped to the side. Japes walked into the small, empty flat and took a seat in a tattered, musty-smelling armchair. She sat opposite him and let out a long breath, plainly pulling herself together. 'I'm sorry; this is all new to me – life in civvy street. It's all been a bit of a shock to the system. I've been in the QARNNS for the full eighteen— my whole adult life, really. But it became too... constraining. I wanted to try something different, broaden my experience, not just go straight into an NHS hospital. Do you really think they'll throw me over when they realise I'm not a man?'

'Well, it's certainly going to hit some of the old boys like a rock, but I'll do what I can to soften the blow. Meanwhile, have you got any glasses? You're bound to feel better after a tot of this. Bespoke rum from the dark heart of Guadeloupe; rather like happiness, it cannot be bought.'

'A woman?' Major Cowerd scoffed the next morning over bacon and eggs on the veranda of his Victorian mansion adjacent to the school. His 'fair, round belly' was swathed in a checked, knee-length dressing gown which gaped open showing off to a tee his sagging pectorals. 'A lieutenant commander in the Navy: a woman? Send her back to that damned agency immediately!'

'Major, what does it matter?' Japes smiled. 'It's not as if we have written rules about the gender of our staff. We must keep up with the times, which have changed. It's the age of women in the workplace – and, besides, she's a good egg.'

'No, Japes, no. Tradition: that's what makes a place like this. Other than kitchen staff and secretaries, women have barely set foot in our school for nearly four hundred years. Even my wife has never been *upstairs* into the dorms!' the major spluttered. 'And to add insult to injury, she's a *nurse*, not a doctor.'

'And why ever would we need a doctor?' asked Japes, flicking flecks of Cowerd's egg off his lapels with a napkin. 'It's not as if Blythe ever took out anyone's appendix. He put plasters on the lads' grazes, doled out aspirins for their sore muscles and sent them off to the hospital in town at the first sign of anything serious. Everyone knew he was here because he was unfit for general practice. Why not pay less and have a first-rate nurse instead of a third-rate doctor?'

'Pay less?' Japes had touched a chord. The drive for economy in all matters other than his own salary and perks was the major's principle interest in life. 'Yes, you do have a point there, Japes,' he agreed.

'We haven't quite achieved same pay for the same work, regardless of sex, in this country, have we, Major? And consider that Matron Ridgeway has done eighteen years in the QARNNS. Not only will she be an excellent nurse, she'll have an excellent service pension as well as being accustomed to spartan living aboard ship, largely in the company of young men. I tell you, she's heaven-sent for this school in these lean times.'

'Damn you, Japes, you could sell sand to the Arabs. Alright, she can stay. But I tell you, when the flack starts flying in the Oak Room a fortnight from today, it's you and your friend, the good Reverend Hareton, who'll be in line for it, not me.'

'I can assure you, Major, that the Reverend has fended off worse in his day, not least the poison darts of the Jivaros. As for me, I'm sure I can weather the slightly less toxic barbs of our English master, Mr Fairchild, and friends.'

On the first day of the school year the masters gathered in the

Oak Room, where the staff congregated for breaks and meetings. As its name suggested, it was panelled in that venerable timber, with alcoves at regular intervals for bookshelves laden with the prerequisite leather-bound tomes lined with marbled paper, written by celebrated authors of recent centuries past, the majority of them now languishing in oblivion. On the higher tier of panelling hung portraits of headmasters from Hezekiah Lambton in 1584 up to the present day. As each man had remained in the position for 20 years on average – even taking into account the handful swept off by epidemic and mischance after serving only a brief stint (including one crushed by a team of oxen upon which he was in the act of bestowing a blue ribbon at the county show) – there was still a wall free for the next couple of hundred years' incumbents.

Major Cowerd liked to address the staff from beneath his own portrait – painted, in slimmer days, in his uniform, with its smattering of medals, all of them for distinguished service behind the lines. At the far end of the long conference table sat Bunny and Japes with Matron Ridgeway between them in her full Queen Alexandra's Royal Naval Nursing Service uniform, including pillar-box-red half-cape and cap.

'I do believe we are all arranged, so I shall make a start,' the major bawled over the general chatter and clatter of teacups. 'I trust you've all had a good holiday and I wish you a cordial welcome back. As usual, the boys will be returning from midday today, so be at your posts in case you need to field any questions from parents. They will be gone soon enough so please do try to be gracious with them. It is they, after all, who pay our salaries.

'Now, I'd like to introduce a couple of new faces to you: Tony Tree, who'll be joining the English Department as second in command, and Gareth McKenzie, four years captain of Durham University's Rugby Championship Seven, who joins us as our new Head of PE.

'Lunch will be at the usual time. Anything further from anybody?'

'Yes. I have a question,' the diminutive form of Fairchild, Head of English popped up suddenly. 'Why is there *a woman* seated in the Oak Room?'

'We were just saying we thought she might be an apparition,' chimed in Rollo, Head of History, with one of his sarcastic chuckles. 'Or that perhaps she had been brought hither by Mr Japes, for some philanthropic purpose connected with fundraising for mildly dissipated former servicemen, such as himself.'

Bunny stood up slowly. It took a moment for him to reach his full height. 'It is my privilege to introduce Matron Ridgeway, former Lieutenant Commander in the QUARNNS, our new medical officer and leader of cadets. Doctor Blythe unexpectedly decided to retire over the summer on the grounds of ill health. We are very lucky to have acquired Matron Ridgeway – a highly experienced field nurse, a qualified physical therapist and, I might add, a black belt of the Fifth Dan in judo – at such short notice.'

'And will she be leaving us to be replaced permanently by a male doctor at equally short notice?' drawled Rollo.

'Returning to my initial question, which remains unanswered, *why* is there *a woman* sitting in *this* room?' Fairchild snapped.

A number of the older masters let out a turkey-like volley of 'Hear, hear'.

'Oh, what a gang of boring old fogies you are!' Sebastian Hawker, Head of Art, called out from his leather armchair in the corner. He wore a bright-yellow silk cravat with a paisley pattern, his grey hair swept back in a fine leonine wave.

'Well, Major, one thing's for sure: the parents won't want a female poking around, examining their sons,' Rollo said with another chuckle.

'She was in the bloody Navy, Rollo, where she spent her career poking around dozens of men!' the Major barked, but then realised how badly it came out as the Oak Room turned into a whooping macaque enclosure. Matron Ridgeway bowed her head.

Bunny rose again, a head taller than anyone else in the Oak Room, and waited to speak. 'Well, gentlemen, I see you're in no frame of mind to discuss this sensibly at present. Matron Ridgeway is here;

she has got us out of a tight spot. We will be grateful to her and we will welcome her. Thank you. You are now free to go and prepare your classrooms.'

'I'm so sorry, Marion,' Japes said, putting a hand on her shoulder as the overgrown schoolboys made for the door, jostling each other as if there were chocolate cake on the other side of it. 'They're not always like that.'

But she wasn't upset. She was smiling as if at some fond memories. 'The major is quite wrong, you know,' she said. 'Dozens is quite an underestimate.'

Apart from a few surprised looks, as if they'd just seen the ghost of Florence Nightingale, the boys had no problem with Dr Blythe's successor being a woman. She kept to her sick bay and didn't give the time of day to the elders of the Oak Room, who imitated her military stride behind her back. A faction comprising Japes, Hawker and Bunny supported her at every turn and shot down in flames any derogatory comment, such that the sneerers took to sneering in huddles, out of the earshot of the principled trio.

Charles Sedgewick, although not one to rebuke the scoffers, quietly stood by the matron, in awe of the way she managed the drill and sundry activities of the cadets. Dr Blythe's casual approach had consisted of having the boys put on uniforms now and then, and march into the countryside to have a few smokes and to fry up pans of sausages. Under Matron Ridgeway, the cadets were learning how to march properly, to manage their vintage rifles and to get involved in a bit of mock combat in the form of ambushing each other in teams, with foliage on their hats and deploying the hand signals she taught them like true commandos. Sedgewick enjoyed learning alongside the boys. The first aid classes, delivered by a trained and experienced nurse, were full of anecdotes from her time as a nurse in the Navy. With the numbers in the cadet club having dwindled in Blythe's time to six, they very soon tripled to 18.

Two notoriously disillusioned Lower Fifths, Wood and

McDowell, were among the keenest new recruits. After Cadet Club one evening they spoke to the matron.

'You're a first-rate officer to us, Commander,' said McDowell, using her correct form of address in a military setting. 'Which is why we've decided to approach you for help with certain problems that never seem to get solved.'

'What seems to be the trouble, boys?' Matron Ridgeway asked, assuming her most neutral, consulting-room tone.

'It's our showers, Commander. They're cold – or they are at first, then for a minute or two they get lukewarm—'

'But then they turn cold again!' added Wood. 'And then there's the heating, or lack of it. Commander, a two-bar electric fire cannot possibly heat an eight-bed dorm room with a fourteen-foot-high ceiling.'

'We're also sick of the revolting slop they shovel out in the refectory,' McDowell added.

'Cadet McDowell, you will use appropriate language as a matter of course when addressing an officer!' she scolded.

'Sorry, Commander,' the boy corrected himself earnestly. 'The major promised our parents that it would finally improve this year, but it hasn't.'

'It's not just that it tastes awful, Commander,' said Wood. 'It truly is nutritionally inadequate. Fourth Formers who don't buy meat and veg in town to cook up their own grub on their wings always fall ill by half-term.'

'I agree, school food could be more nutritious, and it's true that it's feeling awfully chilly in the dorms now that autumn is drawing in,' Matron Ridgeway commiserated.

'And have you noticed that we have to skivvy for the Sixth Formers? If we don't do their bidding, they can cane us.' McDowell hung his head.

'No, I didn't know about that,' she said. 'What do they make you do?'

'I'd rather not say but it can be fairly humiliating, and they're just having a laugh,' he answered.

Matron Ridgeway promised to see what she could do, and a few days later managed to secure an appointment with the major.

'Damn and blast them – the impertinence!'

'But they do have a point, Major: the food is a dreadful mush. The vegetables are olive drab and the meat is frequently unidentifiable. Some of them would also like a vegetarian option.'

'What? They'll be asking for a tie-dyed uniform next.'

'And there are more cases of flu every week, what with the cold showers and inadequate heating. There are still four weeks until the Christmas holidays and the san is already bursting at the seams.'

'I don't think you understand, Matron Ridgeway: it's because of such things that our alumni have the fondest memories of this school and regularly reach into their pockets to help keep us ticking over. Hard times are character-building and our old boys attribute their success today to the trials and tribulations of Blindefellows. So, if you don't mind running along, I need to check the cricket scores on the wireless.'

Bunny couldn't offer a solution either, saying his hands were tied by the major with regard to the refectory, and that when it came to the installation of central heating and a new hot water system, there simply wasn't that kind of money in the kitty.

At the end of the next cadet meeting, McDowell and Wood were mortified at the news that nothing was to be done, although the matron promised she'd fashion some draught excluders from her old Navy tights. Later, Sedgewick overheard them talking about raiding the cadet club's ammunition store, kidnapping some prominent personage and holding the school to ransom. Sedgewick conveyed all this to Matron Ridgeway after they'd left; she laughed heartily and reassured him that every gun in their possession was decommissioned.

Still, the seriousness of their tone preyed upon his mind that night and drove him to timorously knock on the major's door after school the next afternoon.

'I do think we need to take them seriously, Major. McDowell and

Wood are unusual characters and I think they mean business, I really do.'

'You, uh, don't think they mean to, uh, capture *me*, do you?' the major stammered, pinkening a little on the tips of the ears and suddenly blinking rapidly.

'I truly couldn't say for sure, but you'd be the obvious choice, don't you think?'

And so the major called for a meeting first thing the following morning with Bunny, Matron Ridgeway and the two boys in question, to get to the bottom of any unsavoury plot that might be hatching in their lurid imaginations.

It was a rare thing for the major to stay at school after 4pm. But he was writing his memoirs and was on a roll with the latest chapter, about the rise of so-called Government Cheddar and its part in easing the mobilisation of rationing. Government Cheddar had been the major's brainchild and, following his en masse closure of the smaller, time-wasting creameries, had dominated cheese production during, and then after, the War. It was thanks to him, he said, that every family in Britain had a block of cheese on their dinner table and he wanted to make sure he was remembered for it, thus securing his place both in military and political history. Brenda, the major's secretary, would type up his hastily written sides of foolscap the next day.

At around six o'clock, the major's wife had popped round with a ham sandwich and a flask of coffee and, since her visit, he'd dashed off another 10 pages. He was preparing to pack up for the night and was putting his papers in order when he heard a faint rustle along a distant corridor. He paused for a moment and craned his ear towards the door. The sound didn't go away, but steadily grew into the footfalls of a multitude, heading in his direction. 'They've come for me!' he choked. He put his manuscript into the desk drawer, scuttled over to lock the door, then ducked for cover under his desk. He could hear the clatter of their footsteps growing ever-closer on the flagstone floor. They were almost upon him, not stealthily advancing but brazenly stampeding towards their quarry! Curling into a ball, his heart pounding, he put his hands over his ears and, soiling himself, died.

The Blindefellows flock of sheep flowed down the ground-floor corridor, past the headmaster's office and onwards in the direction of the grand staircase, the most magnificent staircase in the school, created by master craftsmen sent over from Plymouth. They'd never been inside a building before and were running scared with McDowell, Wood and a handful of other boys, dressed in their Cadet uniforms with camouflage paint on their faces, herding them from behind. The boys drove the sheep towards the library, where they planned to barricade themselves and their hostages within.

At the foot of the staircase, the sheep stopped, puzzled. A plaintive chorus of baa-ing then began. The boys inched towards them, edging them into a dark woollen ball. The leader of the flock was a ram known as Vivian, so-called after the Blindefellows' tradition of giving the chief ram the Christian name of the serving headmaster. Vivian was a bit worse for wear these days, with a few frayed patches and no longer nimble on his pins. He had, in his younger days, been active on the fête-opening circuit, sometimes pulling a tiny antique wagon laden with blooms, but he wasn't really up to that anymore, preferring to languish with his oats.

Vivian placed a shaky foreleg on the bottom stair with more than a modicum of tentativeness. He looked over his shoulder and it seemed as if the faces of his favourite ewes were turned to him with something like smiles of encouragement, their eyes and yellow teeth glinting in the moonlight coming through the mullioned windows. Then he was off, with the entire flock behind him, scrambling, stumbling and occasionally tumbling clumsily on a few worn wooden stairs. At the top of the staircase were two more boys, posted to channel the sheep across the corridor and directly into the library. The flock progressed according to plan and the heavy old doors were closed behind them then barricaded inside with several hefty tables. 'Operation Blackbeard', as McDowell and Wood had christened it, was complete.

Mrs Cowerd called Bunny at 7am to inform him that Vivian – her husband, not his ovine namesake – was missing. His bed hadn't been slept in and he wasn't answering the phone in his office. Bunny put on his trouser clips, threw a long leg over his bicycle and peddled over immediately with the master key, where he made the grisly discovery of the major's corpse cowering beneath the desk. The major's eyebrows were arched in surprise, his eyes wide open and fixed on the door; when Bunny stepped into the major's office, he thought for a moment that the major was alive, insane and staring right at him.

An ambulance was called and the late major, locked by rigor mortis into his final crouch, was positioned upon a stretcher and covered with a white sheet, so it was rather as if the ambulance men were carrying off an enormous baked Alaska.

As Bunny strode over to the head's mansion to break the hard news to Mrs Cowerd, he pondered. What could have given Major Cowerd a fright of such proportion that he'd curled up and hidden under his desk? And, what's more, how would the undertakers manage to fit him into a coffin in that shape? And then came the happy realisation that the top job was now almost certainly his, and how utterly well prepared for it he was. Sitting in the drawing room of the mansion, he couldn't help but take a few quick glances around the room, mulling over one or two new décor ideas while Mrs Cowerd buried her sagging, florid face in her handkerchief. She would be out by the end of the month and he would look upon it no more.

Francis Fairchild, whose post of Head of English was combined with that of school librarian, turned the massy brass doorknob of the neo-Gothic Lambton Library, showpiece of the school, with its carved bookcases and its 20-foot-high stained-glass windows illustrating the blind boys herding the flock, clutching books of scripture they weren't able to read. The library had been built to glorify the school's change of use in the 1900s, from a charitable institution for the blind to a money-making concern. Fairchild opened the door but it stopped abruptly after an inch or two and he received a nasty bump on the forehead. He tried shoving it with his meagre form but it was stuck fast. Putting his eye to the narrow gap, he attempted to ascertain the cause of the obstruction. He saw what appeared to be a blockade of furniture before him and was sure – if his ears didn't mistake him – that he heard the bleating of a lamb…

At lunchtime, Bunny called the staff together in the Oak Room and broke the news of the major's demise, which the assembled masters listened to in stunned silence with open mouths, and the kidnap of the flock, now resident in the library under the care of McDowell, Wood and their associates.

'I have in my hand a list of demands that this group of boys insist be met. They will release the flock piecemeal as we work through the list and they've given us until the end of the week. Still, this is a well-planned operation and they do have the facilities and supplies to remain there much longer. The list is not unreasonable, in my opinion. Today I will put an end to the practice of fagging once and for all. They also request the basic comforts of home: warm showers, the installation of central heating and various other amenities, all of which have been introduced at the more progressive and, I would add, more prosperous public schools during the past decade or so, which is probably the reason why our numbers are starting to dwindle.'

'May I interject, Reverend?' Rollo interrupted. 'Is there any link between the sudden death of the headmaster and the activities of last night? Because, if that were the case, we would have good cause to call in the police and bring this insolent episode to a swift conclusion.'

'I have spoken with McDowell through the door of the library and they did not see the major last night. Moreover, their list of demands is addressed to him and it was evident when I talked to them that they were oblivious of his demise,' Bunny replied. 'I do not, therefore, see these boys as having any direct link to the state of high anxiety that the coroner presently believes brought on the heart attack that caused the major's death.'

Sedgewick writhed in his seat, agonised that it might have been his little chat with the major the previous day that had worked up the old chap to this unfortunate conclusion. His right eye started to twitch uncontrollably. He took off his glasses and rubbed both his eyes, trying to look as if he were wiping tears, while Bunny warned, 'Furthermore, Mr Rollo, I think it will be readily evident to all present that asking the police to descend violently upon a small group of legitimately disaffected fifteen-year-olds for whom we act in *loco parentis* would not have the most positive impact upon our already diminishing student numbers.'

'I wonder if the matron, with her eagerness to give the Cadets their recent commando-style training, could be in any way to blame for this military coup,' Fairchild scoffed. 'Has it not been said for centuries at Blindefellows that from the day a female infiltrates the Oak Room this *institution* – and I use that particular word with intent – would be jinxed?'

Commotion erupted in the Oak Room, with grey heads nodding everywhere and all eyes on the matron. Japes, sitting beside her, glared at them.

'What a load of tosh, Fanny,' Hawker belted out. 'She's been doing Blythe's job better than he ever did and for half his salary! We should all be paying homage to Matron Ridgeway on bended knee.'

'Gentlemen, gentlemen...' Bunny held up his hand calmly and quelled them, slipping with ease into the role of headmaster, which, following a friendly chat with the board in a week or two, would soon be his. 'I'm going to confer with the boys again and see how we can bring this siege to an end in the smoothest possible manner, limiting disruption to school life and avoiding press interest. It may necessitate meeting their demands, which, I hasten to remind you, are all perfectly reasonable. It's no secret that the major and I were at loggerheads about many of the very same issues the boys have raised, such as central heating, and I'll be meeting with our bank manager this afternoon to secure release of funds to start work on this pronto.'

'You mean you're actually going to give in to their demands?' Rollo chortled. 'What kind of message is that going to send out?'

'The message that you don't need to wear a coat and gloves in the classroom for several weeks a year, Rollo,' Japes chortled back.

'I, for one, am mortified that the flock is in the library, more than likely damaging some very valuable volumes, and I won't stand for it!' Fairchild shouted, hot in the face, the froth of grey hair on top of his head shaking and the skin beneath glistening with ire. 'Who will join me in turfing out these hoodlums?'

Commotion reigned again as the majority of the veteran masters followed Fairchild, who grabbed the school megaphone from the cupboard by the door and led them downstairs like the mob storming Frankenstein's castle. Those remaining moved to the window and looked down on the yard where the masters were excitedly gathering.

'Well, thank goodness the rest of the boys are in the dining room – this is an utter embarrassment,' Hawker said, shaking his head.

'It's remarkably crass of the senior masters to carry on like this,' muttered Crane, Head of Classics. Such outbursts of heightened emotion were the epitome of vulgarity to him.

An appalling noise rattled the windows as Fairchild shouted, unnecessarily, into the megaphone, 'You boys in the library, come out of there forthwith! Those sheep are threatening valuable artefacts and you are in breach of the Blindefellows Code of Conduct!'

One of the library windows was flung open and a hail of sheep excrement rained down on the party below, forcing them to make for cover.

'Ah, deploying dirty-protest tactics – now that's clever.' The matron nodded, impressed.

Bunny left forthwith for his meeting with the bank manager to have the frank discussion of the school's finances that had perennially been denied him while the major was alive.

On the third day of the protest, the boys in the library looked down on the yard and watched a plumbing firm carrying in the paraphernalia of a central heating system. An hour later the hammering and drilling started. In response, the boys made good their word and released the first two sheep, a couple of ewes, as a token of their approval that the work had started in earnest. McKenzie, the new Head of PE, found them loitering at the top of the grand staircase, each waiting for the other to place a cloven hoof onto the first polished step. He rugby-tackled them, stuffed one under each arm and manfully carried them downstairs and released them outside.

Bunny was struggling to find a replacement chef at such short notice. Bottomley, the surly chief cook – a great favourite of the major's due to his success in keeping costs down – had made it plain that he had no intention of altering school menus in any manner that would take as much as half an hour more per week of his time. Bunny happened to mention his travails to Sedgewick, who still felt wretched after the major's sudden death.

'Is there anything I could do to help, Reverend Hareton?' Sedgewick asked. 'Perhaps I could try to reason with them. Maybe they'd accept a written promise that the school will undertake to meet all their demands, improvement of school meals included, by next term.'

'Hmm, that might be worth a try, Sedgewick,' Bunny ruminated as the Sex Pistols' 'Anarchy in the UK' blared from the library windows for the fourth time that day. 'Very well, I will prepare a signed promissory letter, accompanied by a few gifts – some currant buns and a fruit basket would go down well at this point, I should think.'

And so, at 4pm on the third day of the siege, with Bunny and Japes waiting in the yard below, Sedgewick tentatively made his way up the fire escape that led to the library with a hefty basket of provisions in one hand and a white flag in the other. The boys watched his ascent from the windows and unbolted the fire exit door for him.

'Welcome, Mr Sedgewick!' McDowell called out cheerily as two boys patted him down for weapons. Sedgewick smiled back awkwardly, trying to get into the spirit of things.

'I come bearing gifts and the olive branch of peace,' Sedgewick recited his rehearsed opening line.

'Looks more like the white flag of surrender to me, Mr Sedgewick,' McDowell quipped. Sedgewick had never seen him so bright and good-humoured.

The boys accepted the gifts but Sedgewick could see they were hardly starving. They had a camping stove set up and a neat stack of field rations taken from the vast stock that had accumulated in the cadet club hut over the years. It was clearly a very well-planned operation and Sedgewick found he couldn't help but be impressed. The flock had also been properly catered for. There were a few large sacks of porridge oats, presumably purloined from the refectory stores, and the little sheep seemed happy enough pottering around the library and occasionally nibbling off the odd bit of leather binding from the antiquarian books that Fairchild had been carrying on about.

McDowell and Wood retreated to read the letter Bunny had prepared. After 10 minutes of quiet discussion, they strode back over to Sedgewick. He thought they looked like they were from some paramilitary guerrilla force and he suddenly felt terribly important by being the mediator.

'We are pleased with the progress thus far, sir,' Wood said formally. 'We have had confirmation from our contacts on the outside that the installation of central heating and improved hot water is genuine and not a ruse. For this, we are truly grateful and will release four of the young rams in the flock as a gesture of good will. We are also pleased to learn that fagging is being addressed.'

'So am I, Wood, so am I.' Sedgewick nodded. 'Though after what you and McDowell have managed here, I doubt that any of the current Sixth Formers would've been likely to try it on with either of you again.'

'Why, thank you, sir.'

'Always a pleasure to be complimented by a fair and reasonable adult such as yourself,' McDowell said. 'However, the issue of improving school food is, according to Reverend Hareton, nowhere near being resolved so we have decided to take you hostage until the Reverend gets his skates on and sorts it out.'

'What?' Sedgewick said, suddenly frightened and glancing about for an escape route.

'No need to be concerned,' McDowell reassured him. 'You will be given adequate food and we have sanitation in the form of the staff toilet just off the librarian's office.'

'However, if you try to escape,' warned Wood, 'we will secure you in the broom cupboard adjacent to that facility.'

'You are now free to wander the library with the flock,' McDowell indicated. 'Dinner will be at eighteen hundred hours.'

'Dinner?' Sedgewick looked at the hay and oats stationed on the bookcase above his fellow captives.

'No, no, not that – you're a VIP: a Very Important Prisoner. You get to eat what we eat: baked beans with mini sausages.' McDowell gestured towards the pile of cans. 'With currant buns for dessert. Thank you for those, by the way – much appreciated.'

McDowell called down to Bunny and Japes, who were awaiting Sedgewick's return, to inform them of the new state of play.

'Something of an adventure for the Shropshire lad.' Japes chuckled.

'Would you find it so humorous, Japes, if it were you they had interned up there? And possibly for some time, too, as I presently have no idea where can I get a decent chef capable of bringing round our refractory refectory for the salary we can afford to pay.'

Meanwhile, Sedgewick was noting that the flock had split into two distinct factions. A group of three young rams stood apart in the theology section. They would, without any visible cause, suddenly stand on their hind legs and drift into a clacking of petite horns with each other, 10 or so clacks at a time, until one of them caved in and went off for a lie-down. The other faction consisted of Vivian and the ewes, who resided in the history section. Sedgewick sat midway between the two groups in one of the library's few commodious reading chairs, having selected from the valuable books a rare signed first edition of the third volume of Gibbon, the one dealing with the actual fall of Rome, to which Fairchild had hitherto refused him access.

Ironically, in this position of rare privilege, he couldn't read as much as a paragraph due to worrying about whether he'd be holed up here for a week or – perish the thought – until Christmas, and about the anxiety he'd be sure to cause his parents when their only child failed to turn up in Bridgnorth for the holidays. He was reminded of the false optimism of 'It'll all be over by Christmas' and it made him shudder.

Vivian arose from the history section and the ewes followed suit, taking a turn around the library, tailed by the young rams from theology at an edgy distance.

The 10 boys responsible for the Lambton Library siege played cards, read the papers and periodically worked themselves up with 'Anarchy in the UK', their so-called anthem, played far too loud. This they would accompany with a form of dancing with which Sedgewick was unfamiliar, in which they would bounce up and down as if on pogo-sticks and occasionally slam into one another.

It brought back to him a memory he preferred to forget of his university girlfriend, Phoebe, whom he had taken for a person as respectable as himself, jumping about and throwing off her clothes to a song aptly named 'Dazed and Confused' after she'd smoked a funny cigarette in the bathroom. He shook his head in dismay at the recollection.

In the evening, after a plate of beans and mini sausages, the boys gave Sedgewick a suspicious-smelling sleeping bag from the Cadet store room and he did his best to settle down at lights-out on the cracked leather seat-cushions of the three reading chairs he'd placed in a row. Unfortunately, they slithered apart on the polished oak floorboards each time he turned over. Moonlight streamed in through the stained-glass windows, illuminating the young blind boys depicted there. *What has become of this school over the course of the centuries?* Sedgewick wondered. Once a kindly place, a refuge for the blind, now a hotbed of anarchy borne out of inadequate heating and sloppy meals. What would Hezekiah Lambton, that humble sheep-shearer-turned-philanthropic-wool-merchant, have made of it all? Had he, Sedgewick, done the school a favour by helping the major on his way and bringing in this new 'Age of Bunny'? Guiltily, he rather thought he had.

The school chapel bell struck 2am. Unlike the boys, who were at the other end of the library, for Sedgewick it just wasn't possible to sleep on the library floor, especially given the regular rising and falling buzz of Vivian's senescent snoring. Sedgewick had tried to sleep on one of the reading chairs but that was also impossible for him, as a rule. He longed for his own bed and fretted over the classes he wouldn't be able to teach the next day. They were up to the reign of the Boy King, Richard II, in the Lower Fourth's medieval history, and he feared that in his absence the Peasants' Revolt would be mis-construed and the boys would wind up misguidedly siding with the peasants. He considered creeping over to the fire exit, ever-so-qui-etly unlatching the door and leaving while the youthful comman-dos slept. It took an hour or so before he was able to pluck up the courage to wriggle out of the rather tight sleeping bag and tentatively start his tiptoeing progress across the library. Vivian's head shot up and Sedgewick froze. The ram's marble eye gleamed at him, his teeth looking disturbingly like an angry leer in the moonlight.

Sedgewick was unnerved but decided to continue – but just as he was about to open the fire escape door, Vivian gave his game away with a hideous rumbling baa. Three boys were on him in no time, and he was tossed into the broom cupboard, the door locked behind him, where he sat miserably atop an upturned zinc mop bucket, bemoan-ing his impetuous folly.

'They're going too far now,' was all Matron Ridgeway could say to Bunny when he told her of the most recent turn of events, as called down to him that morning from the library window. 'Only letting him out for the toilet? He's not tough enough to stand it.'

'I've put out ads, called agencies, but the earliest we can get a chef who has the know-how to run a kitchen of this size, and make a veg-etarian option, is three weeks!' Bunny shook his head in dismay.

'But he won't last three weeks!' she cried. 'Reverend, I'm run off my feet at the moment with the san, but with Cadets Club suspended for the present, what if I try to double up and run the kitchen? I took a few courses in fine cookery in the Navy and think I could possibly juggle the two for a few weeks through to the end of term. If the food were better, we'd soon have fewer boys for me to cope with in the san; I'm convinced the two are linked.'

'What? Are you sure you could do that, Matron?' Bunny clasped her hand. 'Will we end up having you ill in the san yourself?'

'Perhaps, but I think not; I'm made of sterner stuff than poor Charlie Sedgewick.'

That afternoon, the matron slipped a menu for the week under the door to the library for the young guerrillas' perusal. She intended to have the first meal delivered to the boys the next day, via the fire escape, to garner their seal of approval.

Bottomley was a globe of a man in his fifties, with a bald pate, a snub, claret-veined nose and a salmon complexion – all in all, a pig in a chef's suit. He liked to have a pint of stout next to him at all times and ruled the kitchen with a long steel spatula with which he menaced his terrified female subordinates when they went wrong in even the smallest way. On being informed by Bunny that he was, from today, to take orders from Matron Ridgeway, he started shouting and prodded Bunny in the chest with the spatula. Seeing his chance in this act of physical aggression towards him, Bunny laid a calming hand on the seething boar's shoulder, smiled down kindly upon him and fired him on the spot, much to the female subordinates' relief. Later in the day, one of them reported that he had made off with a case of Wüsthof kitchen knives belonging to the school as well as the refectory account book. This meant the police had to be involved and Bottomley was arrested on his doorstep in his pyjamas the next afternoon.

In the kitchen, Matron Ridgeway's job was less trying than she'd imagined it would be. She'd helped out in ship's kitchens far larger than this when they were overstretched at holiday meals and the like. The six refectory ladies were eager to do their best for Matron Ridgeway and were happy to prepare something other than the usual bland slops. The first meal under her new regime was lunch: chicken Kiev, or cauliflower cheese with a crunchy top for the vegetarian option, both served with minty peas and rosemary roast potatoes, followed by apple charlotte with vanilla sauce. Neither the boys nor the masters quite knew what had hit them and there were moments during the meal when nothing could be heard other than the clinking of cutlery on china.

Although Fairchild remained intransigent, Rollo, who relished nothing quite so much as a fine meal, sidled up to Matron Ridgeway and as good as capitulated. 'By Jove, Matron, I'll gladly put up with you in the Oak Room if we can keep you in charge of the refectory.'

Following lunch, the matron and the refectory ladies carried trays of food up the library fire escape and were let in immediately.

'This is just marvellous, Commander Ridgeway,' McDowell said, beaming between mouthfuls. 'I don't suppose I could persuade you to stay with us at my father's place over the Michaelmas break, could I? He's divorced and not bad looking for his age.'

'That's very kind of you, McDowell,' she laughed, 'but I don't think it would be quite appropriate for the school matron to do that now, would it?'

Sedgewick, who at the matron's insistence had been brought out of the broom cupboard to join them for the meal, smiled feebly.

Following the meal, McDowell tapped his tin mug and stood up to make a speech. 'Thanks to the Commander saving the day and meeting our final demand until a permanent school chef is appointed – who will, I trust, be up to your standard, ma'am – I declare this siege over! Mr Sedgewick and the flock will be released and the company will leave the library with me as soon as we have cleared up.'

The boys removed the barricade and herded the sheep back downstairs and outside, where they gambolled about, plainly delighted to be back home on the school lawn.

That evening, they had an audience with Bunny who, although firm, was sympathetic. Each of them shook hands with him before returning to their wings for a shower and a proper bed. Matron Ridgeway helped the stiff and shaken Sedgewick to his rooms and ran a hot bath with bubbles for him. Following his soak, he put on his flannelette pyjamas and she tucked him into his bed with the first-edition Gibbon Volume III, which she'd reassured him he was fully justified in spiriting out of the library for a week or so as fair recompense for what he'd been through, and told him she'd bring him dinner on a tray later on.

By the time the new chef arrived to learn the ropes over the final week of term, the matron had slashed sick bay cases by 50 percent through better nutrition and warmth. On the day the new central heating boiler was officially inaugurated, Bunny congratulated her in the Oak Room, where Hawker and Japes presented her with flowers and chocolates, respectively.

'To say that you've saved the day for us is to put it mildly!' Bunny declared. 'You have been instrumental in improving our school, to the point where it is almost unrecognisable as the archaic institution it was only four short months ago. Please, don't ever leave us!' And all, apart from Fairchild, stood up and heartily applauded her.

Exhausted as she was by the effort of running two full-time jobs, that evening she accepted a dinner invitation from Japes at his house down the hill in the town, but not before she had turned down an invitation from Hawker to come to his house out in the country to sit for a nude painting. After dinner, Japes suggested they make a week-end of it and she stay over in his guest room. 'My room's on the left; guest room is on the right,' he said as he followed her up the stairs of his narrow Georgian terrace house following his customary nightcap. It had been a long, gruelling four months for Ridgeway and she could finally afford to let go. Up on the landing, she didn't hesitate in turning left.

Reverend Hareton sailed through his interview with the Blindefellows Trust's board of governors once they learned of his cool-headed victory in the siege of Lambton Library. And it gradually emerged that the cost of installing the school's central heating and new hot water system would not be all that onerous now that they were no longer paying the incredible sum of a thousand pounds a week in salary and expenses to which the major had increased his remuneration during the general confusion over the conversion to decimal currency a few years earlier. The Age of Bunny had arrived and it would last for the next quarter of a century.

At the far end of the field at the back of the school, a new chief ram, one of the trio from the theology shelves, who would soon acquire the name of Beaulieu, was leading the flock towards the Disraeli Chapel. Vivian rested alone under an aged oak and watched them through half-closed eyes, his forehead bloodied around the base of his horns, too weary to pay any heed to a last battle lost.

3

Of Art and Cheese

Lent and Trinity 1979

Reverend Hareton paused at the door of the art studio and watched as Hawker, the art master, sat before his easel crumbling pencil shavings into dust in his hand. It was 5pm on a chilly January evening and, apart from those who lived on site, the other teachers had long since gone home.

'Burning the midnight oil, Sebastian?'

Hawker jumped, spilling the shavings onto his trousers. 'Good Lord, Bunny – don't hop up on me like that! As a matter of fact, I'm here every day after five. Not a lot to go home to these days.'

'Mm, yes, I suppose so.' Bunny bowed his head sympathetically for a respectful moment then said, 'I've come to see you about a new pupil starting next week, from Turkey. Wants to do art.'

'So your Mediterranean peregrinations have borne fruit and you've netted your first foreign fish!' Hawker stood up and shook his friend's hand. 'I imagine it won't be too long before you sally forth into more new territories and fill the dorms with Asia Minor!'

Bunny had been away for a month on a six-country recruiting trip around Spain, Greece, Turkey, Lebanon, Egypt and Jordan, leaving his new deputy, Roger Swainson, in charge. He had promised the trustees that every bed would be full again by September 1980, which gave him roughly a year-and-a half to restore Blindefellows to its former, pre-70s, glory; capacity had dropped to an all-time low of 68 percent since Bunny had succeeded to the headship. Although this meant only a couple of pupils fewer than in the final years of his predecessor, on whose watch the school had undergone its long, slow decline, the veteran masters preferred to blame it on Bunny's implementation of such shocking, iconoclastic reforms as the installation of central heating and the abolition of the cane. But he knew the simple truth: that it was more to do with the rise of the new comprehensives, which gave upwardly mobile families a free educational alternative to public schools for progeny who'd failed to make the grammar school cut.

'So, is he as intellectually retrograde as the lads you usually send to A-level art?'

'Oh no, quite the contrary.' Bunny glanced at Hawker's easel, which still held the same unfinished, rather muddy-looking painting of a cracked jug of dried flowers that he'd seen on his last visit to the art studio before his recruiting trip. 'He's doing mathematics and the sciences but has specially requested art as a fifth subject.'

'Really? And why is he starting in the middle of the year? Chucked out of some other establishment, no doubt?' Blindefellows had acquired a reputation for taking boys discarded by better schools and whose disappointing exam results were dragging their school down even further. This had led to yet more criticism of Bunny.

'No, no, nothing like that. His father feels his English isn't up to scratch,' Bunny quickly explained. 'He stumbled upon my presentation in Istanbul by chance. I presumed he wanted to sign his son up for next year but he insisted the lad got cracking right away. And who am I to argue when the board expects me to fill every bed?'

And so it was that Kerem Karaman – another boy in another bed – inched Bunny towards his quota. His black-and-white tweed blazer fit him like a glove; his father had had it tailored like his monogrammed shirts. He kept his hand-stitched shoes perfectly polished and carried his books in a splendid calf-leather briefcase. His black hair was always neatly combed with a splash of lavender oil and his fingernails were invariably clean. In appearance, he was a model pupil, whereas most of the other Sixth Formers tended towards raggle-taggle, in spite of Matron Ridgeway's vigilant eye.

When Karaman arrived at his first art lesson, Hawker took him for a quick sweep of the studio, showing him where he'd find the different materials. 'I like to give everyone a free choice so they can get on with what they like and go off in their own direction. I'm going to leave you to it now. Just come and see me at my easel if you want to ask any questions.'

Hawker returned to his tired canvas while Karaman hovered for a moment then drifted over to sit with the three other boys in the class as if looking for ideas. Grouse was cutting a skull design resembling a happy hamburger into a piece of lino, Jefferson was leafing through magazines for a picture of a footballer to copy and Crabbe was drawing a horseshoe magnet, which was a considerable challenge for him.

Twenty minutes later, Hawker suddenly heard something he hadn't heard for over 10 years: the kickwheel whirring into life. He glanced over his canvas and there was Karaman in an apron, working the treadle and wrestling with a ball of clay. Why the lad hadn't used the electric wheel was a mystery to him but it had become his habit not to take much of an interest in anything the boys did and he returned to tinkering with his painting, hoping the boy would clean up the worst of it when he was finished.

Before the end of the lesson, Hawker laid down his brush to check the boys were tidying away. Their rudimentary efforts at this used to irritate him but nowadays he found himself less concerned, their mess giving him something to occupy himself with when he wasn't labouring at his uninspiring artworks, having stayed behind after school. He was surprised to see all the boys clustered around the kickwheel, with Karaman demonstrating. On a sheet of newspaper on the table stood three perfect classical-style vases, glossy and smooth – a krater, a pelike and a genuine psykter.

'Karaman, this is remarkable!' Hawker walked over to the vases for a closer look.

'It's nothing.' Karaman smiled. 'We have a pottery in Iznik and I make a few pots there every summer. My dad makes my brothers and I learn the skills for all the businesses the family has.'

'He's showing us how to do it, sir – so can we stay here next for our free lesson?' asked Grouse, earnestly peering up at Hawker from under his simian brow.

'Yes, certainly, of course you can, and I'd like to watch too.' Hawker pulled over a stool and watched as Karaman got each of them up on the kickwheel, explaining what to do in perfect English that thoroughly belied his father's professed concern.

A few lessons later, Karaman taught them paper marbling or *ebru*, as he called it – 'the cloud on the water'. In his demonstration, he dropped jewel-like hues of the oily liquid onto the surface of a shallow tray of water and the colours swirled and dazzled. Effortlessly, he stretched the ink this way and that using no more than a goose-feather quill. He traced the veins of a petal with a thick black hair he plucked dramatically from his head. A vivid red tulip lay suspended on the surface of the water until Karaman captured it on a sheet of handmade paper. He presented it flamboyantly to Hawker, who blushed at its beauty as much as at the unfamiliar generosity.

The next day, Hawker found Karaman in the studio before the other boys had arrived, casting his deep brown eyes over the art master's unassuming floral canvases that were dotted about the walls. He waited for the boy to say something, finding himself a little embarrassed that they weren't better.

'You love to paint flowers,' was Karaman's rather neutral comment, and Hawker found himself thoroughly downcast.

'Yes, flowers and the occasional nude, but I did my best work when I was young, before I had a family,' Hawker explained. 'I attended Cedric Lockwood Morris's School of Painting and Drawing in the Fifties. Morris was a fine artist; he has pieces in the Tate. I certainly learned more with him than I ever did at the Slade.'

'Can you teach me oil painting?' Karaman asked as he ran his finger over the impasto of a pot of pansies. 'Perhaps after school on Tuesdays and Thursdays? Would you have time then?'

Hawker agreed, but it was generally his way to avoid giving instruction, just like Morris, who preferred his students to make their own decisions and mistakes. When he wasn't tending to his glorious garden, Morris had painted alongside Hawker and the handful of other students. Hawker could still see Morris now, standing among the beloved irises of his house Benton End with his scarlet macaw, Rubeo, clambering about on his head and shoulders. One summer, a colony of wrens had taken up residence under the eaves and they'd flown back and forth over the painters' heads like little spinning spheres.

Hawker, uninspired at the Slade, had taken a two-year break from his course and had gone to live at Benton End on the advice of a tutor in order to find his way – which he did, and on his return to the Slade he had become the golden boy. His previously scrawny form had filled out and bronzed from doing the garden with Morris and he now walked with a confident stride. There'd been his highly fêted degree show, followed by a steady stream of commissions and he'd painted solidly for three years in his rented rooms in Putney. Then he'd met Rose, whom he had painted obsessively right up until their first child was born. When their second came along, they needed a larger, steadier income so he had taken the post of art master at this lesser-known public school in the West Country. They'd got together enough money to buy a half-ruined watermill to turn into their family home and had lived their lives around their children. Eventually Rose had met someone else and the children had grown up and gone away. Now there was nothing left apart from the job and the nights alone in the old mill.

The aspect of his job that Hawker disliked more than any other was the weekly staff meeting Bunny insisted on holding. In Cowerd's day they got together monthly, if the major remembered. Hawker viewed the majority of his colleagues as complacent prigs and buffoons. Each time he was among their assembled number, he felt more keenly than ever that he had also become one, by association.

Today, one item on the agenda was 'The Future of the Flock'. What could that be about? Hawker mused. At the meeting in the Oak Room, the masters assembled around the long table – apart from Hawker, who preferred to observe proceedings from a comfortable distance, in the armchair in the corner, beside the fire, tossing on an occasional log. Bunny and his deputy, Swainson, a solid little boxer dog of a man with close-cropped chestnut hair and a broad nose, sat at the head of the table. With a nod of his head, Bunny invited one of the most irritating and unpleasant men Hawker had ever encountered, Francis Fairchild, to introduce the next item.

'Thank you, Reverend, for finally allowing me to air my thoughts on this vexing matter,' Fairchild began. He was wearing the tweed jacket he'd worn nearly every day of his 30-year teaching career – patched with leather on the elbows and with leather piping on the cuffs and pockets where it had frayed. He had a preference for dull pastel shirts topped off with speckled bow ties. A thin fog of hair swirled on the top of his head and pulsated as he spoke, which was always with a high-pitched fervour, even if he was just telling a boy to empty the waste paper basket. 'I would like to present the opinion of several members of the faculty regarding the function and future of the Blindefellows flock,' Fairchild piped. 'I have been niggled by this matter for the past year or so and have now had the chance to gather the relevant data. The flock currently numbers thirty-three and the annual veterinary fees, cost of annual shearing in spring and fodder in winter averages one-hundred-and-ten pounds per beast, per year. Hence, we are looking at a minimum expense to the school of approximately three thousand, six hundred pounds per annum. As we all know, Blindefellows is currently operating at a deficit through being undersubscribed, a matter which has worsened considerably since the Reverend assumed the helm, so I propose that we make cutbacks by eliminating the most expendable elements of the annual budget, and the foremost among these is surely the flock.'

Crane, Classics, a young man but with the measured mannerisms and the slow speech of someone in his sixties, rose to add his tuppence-worth. 'Fairchild is quite right, Headmaster: are we in a school or in a farmyard?'

Fairchild gave a pert nod of acknowledgement to Crane before resuming. 'The flock are unsightly pests. They mob the parents of prospective students and encourage the boys to engage in foolhardy antics that often make them late for class and resulted in a sprained wrist for Whyte last year, just prior to his exams, in yet another impulsive sheep-vaulting incident. The flock are also a health and safety hazard: how many times have each of us had to pick their wretched droppings from our soles before we step through our front doors of an evening? Moreover, following the damage to the bindings of many of our most treasured tomes that occurred in the Lambton Library during the unfortunate incident there two years ago – which, I might add, was permitted to drag on due to the unfathomable clemency of our current headmaster – it is evident that these animals, though they have been an intimate part of Blindefellows' past, are a menace to its present.'

Fairchild returned to his seat with a flourish and there was a stunned silence. Most masters couldn't imagine the school without its flock. There were a few wishy-washy rumblings of 'hear, hear', mainly from Tony Tree, Fairchild's assiduous acolyte, who was currently growing out an untended fuzz of a beard that rather resembled the floaty wisps on top of Fairchild's head so that the younger man's visage might almost be a younger version of the elder's, but turned upside-down.

'But they crop the damned grass, Fanny,' Japes called out languidly as he stirred his cup of tea. 'Have you weighed up the cost of an industrial lawnmower, its petrol and maintenance costs, in addition to the time our venerable groundsman, Birdwhistle, would spend pushing it round the place?'

'I have indeed, Mr Japes.' Fairchild reached for a pocket notebook within his jacket and licked his index finger with his sharp little tongue. 'We already have a powerful lawnmower stationed in one of our outbuildings: a Ransome drivable – a little antiquated but Birdwhistle says he can probably get it up and running in the next few weeks. It has never been used – an unwanted gift from the Percy family, three generations of gentleman farmers who sent their boys here. While I was casually chatting with Birdwhistle recently about his responsibilities at the school, it became highly apparent he is well under hours. So, Mr Japes, a drop of petrol is all that is needed to keep the grass short and that certainly won't amount to three thousand pounds a year.'

'You've had it in for those poor little sheep, Fairchild, ever since they were let loose in your library,' Hawker called over, his silvery mane glistening in the light of the fire behind him.

'Yes, I most certainly have, Hawker!' Fairchild leaned forward in his chair and banged his fist on the table, making the teacups jump on their saucers. 'I shall never forget nor forgive the havoc created when the flock ran amok in the library. A number of precious works were lost, too, including a signed first edition by Gibbon.' Sedgewick flinched in his seat at the mention of this. He'd been too terrified of being caught out by Fairchild ever to return the volume mentioned, which he had meant only to borrow.

Hawker bent down to ignite a taper in the fire with which to re-light his meerschaum pipe, carved in the shape of a mermaid, and drawled, 'A shame you're incapable of acknowledging that the flock weren't the perpetrators but merely the victims.'

'As was young Sedgewick,' Japes called out, winking at Sedgewick as he pinkened.

'But he didn't chew the books!' chortled Rollo, Head of History.

'But, Mr Fairchild, what of tradition?' Sedgewick blurted out without meaning to, his cheeks suddenly smarting. 'The flock was a gift to Blindefellows from Hezekiah Lambton himself, a prime source of the fortune upon which this school was founded, and its mascot for nearly four centuries now!'

'Hear, hear,' Japes and a couple of others called out, tapping their teaspoons on the table top, as was the tradition in the Oak Room, so that tiny dents pitted its perimeter.

Fairchild's face suddenly took on a puce hue. 'Mr Sedgewick, is it tradition or survival you support?' Spittle gathered at the corners of his mouth. 'Unnecessary traditions, such as the flock, have to go if we are, for instance, going to avoid having to go *co-ed*, which I happened to overhear the Reverend discussing in the corridor with Mr Swainson just the other day!'

The older men around the table shot a glance at Bunny and

Swainson, expecting them to elaborate on this, but Swainson quickly moved in to draw a line under the matter.

'Thank you, Mr Fairchild, let us ponder the flock item over the coming days and take it to a vote next week.'

'Mr Swainson, what will happen to the flock if they are voted out?' Matron Ridgeway enquired.

'They belong to a rare breed, Matron, and will, I'm sure, find a taker if it comes to that – but we will cross that bridge if and when we come to it,' Swainson answered.

When everyone had finally left the Oak Room, Sedgewick sat for a while, alone, before plodding down the corridor to his rooms in Loaghtan Wing. As he passed the high windows on the landing that looked out onto the front lawns, he spent a few minutes watching the flock, in silhouette against the iron gates. They were starting to settle for the night, huddling close together in baa-ing camaraderie, their leader, the fine little ram Beaulieu, letting out the loudest, longest and lowest notes. True, they had something of a forward manner at times, especially if you had a forgotten biscuit in your pocket, but he was fond of the little creatures and would regularly collect all the stale bread from the refectory ladies to strew round for them.

Sedgewick sighed and continued on his way. He unlocked his door and stepped into his rooms. He was free of marking schoolwork and had a few empty hours before him. He hung up his jacket in the wardrobe and noticed Major Cowerd's unfinished autobiographical manuscript squatting upon his nightstand, where it had lain for nearly a year now. Mrs Cowerd had entrusted it to Bunny's care upon her departure following her husband's unexpected demise and Bunny had eventually passed it on to Sedgewick, asking him to assess its historical significance.

Sedgewick had his doubts as to whether an extravagantly self-congratulatory account of the British dairy industry under wartime rationing, culminating in the creation of Government Cheddar, would ever be of significance to anyone. In fact, he had become quite irked by Cowerd's pride in his systematic closure of low-yield cheese producers the length and breadth of the country in favour of the bland government-regulated product which soon became the only cheese available. Many of these old cheeses were now lost: Plumpton Blue, Crackington Haven, Dibden Purlieu and Portwrinkle Pleasant. Cowerd's derogatory descriptions of them 'done up in pathetic little muslin bags, tied at the top with unhygienic scraps of homespun twine and reeking to high heaven' was, in fact, the only part of the dead headmaster's monograph that had piqued Sedgewick's interest. The local supermarket offered a narrow selection of plastic-wrapped cuboids: bright orange Red Leicester, yellow Cheddar and pasty Wensleydale – all variations on Government Cheddar and about as appealing as a bar of soap.

Sedgewick was then struck with a remarkable idea: what if he were to get the flock to pay for themselves by milking them and helping to revive the nearly-lost art of traditional old English cheese-making? He could set up a little creamery in one of the empty outbuildings scattered around the school grounds where the boys liked to hide out for a smoke. He resolved that tomorrow he would go to the town library and teach himself the rudiments of cheese-making from the pre-War books in the farming section that no one ever touched. For the rest of the evening, he was so excited that he finally had to resort to leafing through his microfiche album in order to calm down.

During his lessons with Karaman after school, Hawker painted alongside the boy much as Morris once had with him, but minus the macaw. Karaman had found some early wildflowers in the hedges where the flock couldn't get at them and had brought them along to paint.

'I think it helps you to paint with someone, sir,' Karaman said. 'This picture you're doing is brighter than those on the walls.'

'Perhaps you're right, Karaman.' Hawker nodded, pausing for a moment at the pleasing swirls of light that were emerging from his canvas. 'It's been years since I painted with anyone.'

'Is your wife an artist?' Karaman asked.

'No, she wasn't... isn't... We haven't lived together for some time. Our children are grown up; both left years ago – disappeared into careers in the Big Smoke. I see them a couple of times a year when I go up to London for an exhibition.'

'But don't you go to see your old teacher, Morris?'

'Morris? No, not for over twenty years. Just send him a Christmas card with a few lines.'

'Maybe you could visit him and paint with him again.'

'I don't think he's doing much painting these days. He told me about his declining eyesight last time I heard from him,' Hawker sighed.

An hour later, Karaman was painting in confident strokes and his preference for bright colours was inspiring Hawker. It was like a breath of fresh air and he asked Karaman if he would like to come along on Mondays and Wednesdays after school too.

'I think I could come only on one extra day, sir. Mr Japes and Mr Swainson give so much homework, and now they all say they want me to try for the Engineering Tripos at Cambridge. Art is what I like best, but my father says I must study engineering so I can help run the family business.'

Hawker looked over to the exquisite marbled tulip Karaman had given him, which he had framed and hung above his desk, and frowned as he considered that the most promising student he'd had for years was going the way of engineering.

The day arrived when the fate of the flock would be decided. Fairchild had spent much of the week canvassing, scurrying around the Oak Room at break times with his pocket notebook and pencil, making a list of yeas, nays or those on the fence. Many had promised yea just to get him off their backs.

'It's so dreadfully unfair,' Matron Ridgeway told Japes. 'The flock can't speak for themselves and Fairchild's such a bully.'

'Don't worry, Sedgers has something up his sleeve.' Japes put his hand on her shoulder. 'It's a little radical but he's got Bunny gunning for him, so there won't be any miniature mutton chops on the menu just yet.'

As the faculty took their places around the long table, Fairchild had a smug look on his face. With a miniature pencil in his diminutive hand he and Tree perused various pages in his notebook. Hawker observed this from his armchair and rolled his eyes. There was an uneasy atmosphere as many colleagues now felt press-ganged into voting the flock out, when deep down they knew the school had a spiritual attachment to them. As they were placid sorts, they didn't want to incur what would, no doubt, be the long-lived fury of Fanny Fairchild if they now went with the nays. Bunny arose to commence proceedings.

'Gentlemen; Matron Ridgeway: let us make a start. The first item on the agenda is the future of the flock, which has grazed the greensward of Blindefellows for almost four hundred years. True, they have their drawbacks – one of them being the expense of keeping them in the present lean times – but before we put them to the vote, one of our younger masters has had an idea as to how the flock could potentially pay its own way and eventually even turn a small profit for the school community.'

Fairchild stiffened in his chair and his foetal features congealed into a formation of disdainful disbelief.

'So, without further ado,' Bunny called in the direction of the door, 'would you like to enter now, Mr Sedgewick?'

Japes nudged Matron Ridgeway and all heads were turned towards the door.

After wrestling with the doorknob for a few moments (since he was now wearing latex gloves), Sedgewick made his grand entry. He was dressed in white overalls and an apron, his hair concealed by a white mop cap and a white surgical mask across his face. The Oak Room erupted into raucous laughter. Fairchild, reassured that this was no more than a comic turn, joined in and became a more mellow shade of pink.

'How can Charles make a joke out of the slaughter of those sweet animals?' Matron Ridgeway called to Japes over the laughter, which Japes himself was also contributing to.

'Just wait, Marion, just wait,' was all Japes could manage to say.

Bunny, smiling, allowed everyone to be softened up before getting down to business.

'Well, Mr Sedgewick – what a surprise. Come and stand here
between Swainson and myself at the head of the table.'

'So your solution is to butcher the lot of them and divvy them
up as joints and chops, eh, Mr Sedgewick?' Rollo bawled out. 'All you
need's a carving knife to complete that get-up. I never thought you
had it in you, old chap!'

Sedgewick took his place between Bunny and Swainson, and
removed his cap and mask. The laughter died down.

'Go ahead, Mr Sedgewick.' Bunny patted him on the back as he
and Swainson sat down.

'Matron Ridgeway; gentlemen: as Mr Fairchild pointed out so
persuasively last week, the flock is a drain on expenses. Yet I believe I
have fathomed a way in which they can earn their keep and possibly
even turn a profit. I am dressed like this today for a reason. I intend to
sell to you the idea of the Blindefellows Creamery—'

'The what?' Fairchild shrieked, his mouth hanging open like a
chicken with the gapes.

'The Blindefellows Creamery will be a cottage industry stationed
in an outbuilding in the grounds and will produce artisanal cheeses
such as those for which Britain was as famed as France before the War,
when Major Cowerd and Co. closed the small creameries down as
part of the national rationing scheme, thereby paving the way for the
monotony of Government Cheddar.'

'Government what? The man's barking,' Fairchild yapped.

'Already there is a renaissance of fine cheese-making underway
in this country, but goat and sheep cheese are yet to achieve their
due recrudescence. Blindefellows and the flock will be first to fill
this profitable epicurean niche with our product, which will be sold
both directly from reception at school as well as from delicatessens in
Taunton and Exeter, whom I have telephoned and already ascertained
firm expressions of interest.'

'Ha!' squawked Fairchild, triumphant. 'The equipment needed

for this "udderly" – if I may make that pun – foolhardy enterprise will cost the school thousands!'

'Not so, Mr Fairchild.' Bunny languidly rose. 'The Percy family, of whose gift of the lawnmower you reminded us only last week, has agreed to kit out the entire creamery with equipment formerly used by their goat-milking facility, which is now being enlarged and upgraded. Furthermore, in recognition of Blindefellows' not-inconsiderable efforts in getting Gawain and Geraint, not to mention Griff, through their A-levels, they have generously agreed to provide workmen and materials to renovate one of the shearing sheds. I'm pleased to say they've already been in there for two days, quite unnoticed by any of you, gentlemen. May I thank you, Mr Fairchild, for having mentioned them last week, because it put me in mind of precisely whom I should call when Sedgewick came to me with this charming idea.'

Fairchild glowered. The other masters, however, seemed to be coming around to the idea, leaning forward and nodding to each other emphatically.

'Mr Sedgewick, do you propose to make all this cheese alone?' Rollo snorted.

'My intention, Mr Rollo,' Sedgewick replied, 'is that we model ourselves on Bedales School in Hampshire, who have their pupils engage in farming projects alongside their studies. Once I have mastered the techniques, I shall pass on my skills to an interested group of students. We can even have them design the packaging and suchlike.'

'Bravo, Mr Sedgewick,' Japes shouted, leading a lively burst of applause.

'How are you going to learn to be a damned dairy maid, Sedgewick?' Fairchild sniped, cutting through the appreciation. He'd disliked Sedgewick from the moment he'd first set eyes upon him, Sedgewick being the first non-Oxbridge faculty-member the school had hired since it had transformed itself from a humble charity school to a going concern in the 1800s.

'I am currently studying a selection of books on the subject from Travistock library,' Sedgewick replied, feeling hot under the collar.

'Blast you, man! Books can't teach you how to pull a teat!' Fairchild reared up to his full height of five foot, two inches, and Sedgewick reddened.

'I'm sure we can find an experienced pair of hands to instruct Mr Sedgewick in the art of milking, should the written word fail him,' Bunny interjected, inviting the shaken Sedgewick to take a seat. 'So, Matron Ridgeway; gentlemen: we have a bold solution that isn't costing us a penny. Let's give our fleecy friends a chance! If our enterprise fails, so be it, but for now let us put it to a vote.'

The yeas for the creamery drowned out the nays, and Matron Ridgeway thrust herself between Swainson and Sedgewick to give the latter a hug. 'Charlie, you're a darling, as always. You can absolutely rely on my help in this.'

Hawker came over and shook Sedgewick's clammy hand, 'You leave the label design to me. I'll get the lads in art onto it straight away. We can even produce a job lot for you on our old hand-press.'

Sedgewick thanked them all and trotted off to his rooms to remove his creamery whites. At the high windows he paused once again to look out at the flock, remembering how dejected he had felt last week. 'I'm going to make it work out for you,' he said to himself, and to them, then continued on his way, determined to re-read the confusing chapter on renneting.

The following week in the art room, Karaman was particularly excited to hear about Sedgewick's creamery idea and immediately got to work, designing a label. He put in a few hours over lunchtime, developing his ideas, playing around with the rather peculiar names for the cheeses which Japes had volunteered to come up with.

The evenings Hawker spent with Karaman were the highlight of the boy's week. While they painted, Karaman wanted to hear about Benton End and the spectacular artists' parties they had held there every month, at which everyone had to prepare a dish sculpted or arranged into some artistic form. Hawker told the boy how, at one such party, he had created a lemon meringue pie in the shape of a white duck that had been much admired. In summer, the parties were held outside on the expansive patio, the air thick with night-scented stocks that Morris had planted for just such occasions. Morris's many parrots, their wing feathers carefully clipped by the painter – just enough for them to be given their freedom without any risk of their flying off – perched on the medlar trees surrounding the patio, waiting for tit-bits, like Audubon paintings come to life.

Sedgewick's creamery was soon ready and waiting. The generosity of the grateful Percy family knew no bounds. They had renovated two of the little outbuildings, one where the cheese would be made and the other where the ewes would be milked. The creamery was painted white, the concrete floor tiled beautifully in terracotta and the reconditioned milking machines sparkling. The Percys had installed other equipment from their own long-decommissioned cheeseworks: marble slabs for working the curds and all manner of lined copper vats and drainers. Above the door, Hawker had hung a painted wooden sign hand-lettered in old-fashioned copperplate script by Karaman that read 'Blindefellows Creamery, Charles Sedgewick, Proprietor'.

Gazing up at it, Sedgewick's heart swelled with pride and he felt the hour had come to have his first try at milking. He'd bought himself a pair of green wellingtons to look the part. He coaxed a bundle of ewes into the milking building using a packet of ginger biscuits and closed the lower half of the rustic stable door the Percy family had installed. Three of the ewes settled down nicely to wait in the fresh straw, but one slightly larger one paraded around, baa-ing. Sedgewick resolved to tackle her first since, judging by the weightiness of her swinging teat, she needed urgent assistance. He took another quick look at the milking machine manual, before attempting to hook her up. For the life of him, however, he couldn't fit the necessary parts to the ewe and, after 10 minutes of trying, was about to give up when the top half of Matron Ridgeway appeared at the door. 'How's it all going, then?' she asked him cheerily.

'I'm not exactly sure what I'm doing, to be honest, Matron,' Sedgewick said as he fumbled with the ewe's undercarriage. 'The suction tube just doesn't seem to fit!'

'Ah, Charles,' Matron Ridgeway said, spotting the problem directly, 'that's because you've got a young ram there.'

'Oh, good Lord,' Sedgewick said, straightening up and wiping his hands on the anorak he was wearing. He removed his glasses, cleaning them with his handkerchief before he returned them to the bridge of his nose. He bent down and squinted at the ram who was now butting the door with his head. 'Well, I suppose you'd know all about that – being a former Navy nurse, I mean.'

'Quite.' She nodded and opened the lower half of the door. 'You let him run along now and I'll come in and help you with the ladies – if ladies they are.'

In Matron Ridgeway's no-nonsense hands, each of the ewes in the flock was hooked up, milked and let loose again in under an hour, each one rewarded with a ginger biscuit for its trouble. The little milk vat brimmed over.

The two of them went to the dining room for a spot of lunch, over which Sedgewick expounded upon the cheese-making process with the use of pages he'd bookmarked. 'The milk should be fresh so we need to make a start on it today,' he explained earnestly. 'If all goes well, we could have our first batch of feta – a nice easy one to start on – by next week. Then we can start branching out into other varieties.'

They ambled back to the creamery, changed into the necessary white overalls, aprons, masks, galoshes and caps and started heating the milk, Sedgewick keeping a keen eye on the thermometer. He lowered the temperature and added the rennet, which he had mail-ordered from Crete and paid to have couriered to Devonshire out of his own pocket.

'Now we leave it overnight,' he said, reassuring himself as much as Matron Ridgeway. 'But I'll keep coming back to check on it every couple of hours, just to be sure all's well.'

The following afternoon they returned to strain the yogurty mass, and such was his excitement that Sedgewick was ready to add cheese-making to his list of favourite things alongside Victorian newspapers and Medieval parish churches. Yet after the straining, the mixture had lost none of its sloppiness and he was flummoxed and on the verge of despair.

'Hello, Mr Sedgewick,' came a voice from the door. 'I've brought you my designs for the cheese labels.' Karaman, well aware that he mustn't enter for fear of contaminating the cheese-making process, politely waited to hand over a manila folder of sketches he wanted Sedgewick to choose from.

'Hang on a moment, Karaman,' Matron Ridgeway called. 'We've just come up against an unanticipated technical hitch.'

'Can I be of help?' Karaman asked, craning to see. 'We make cheese by hand on my family's model farm in Turkey and we have a factory that does large-scale commercial cheese production.'

Matron Ridgeway was quick to bring him in and pass him a set of overalls and white galoshes to put on over his clothes and shoes. He took out a new sheet of muslin, doubling it (Sedgewick noted) and tipped a portion of the milky mass into it, knotting it at the top, then hung it from the hook suspended from the ceiling.

'Ah, that's what the hooks are for,' Sedgewick remarked in wonder.

While they waited for the draining, Karaman drew off some more milk, keen to show them how to make two more kinds of cheese. To Matron Ridgeway's astonishment, he poured out a glass of the raw milk, examined it closely, breathed in its rich aroma and then drank it all down, leaving a light, creamy moustache above his top lip. 'The milk from these little ewes is perfect for cheese-making, Mr Sedgewick, just perfect.'

They were there until nightfall and Sedgewick learned so much from the boy that he felt he might as well cast aside the old library books. The next day in Latin Prayer he would stand up and invite five dedicated boys to learn the art of cheese-making, with Karaman as the in-house expert. Perhaps one day, one or two of these boys would start a little creamery of their own and England could, once again, take its place beside France – or, seemingly, Turkey – as a nation of fine hand-crafted cheeses.

In the art class, Hawker took Karaman aside, away from the other boys, deeply unhappy that he hadn't turned up for their lessons after school the previous week.

'I'm sorry, sir, but I saw Mr Sedgewick was struggling with his cheese-making and I felt I had to try to help him,' Karaman explained, his expression sincerely apologetic.

Hawker still felt quite perturbed. 'It seems everyone is pulling you hither and thither. Sedgewick with his dairy, Japes and Swainson with all the work they want you to do for Cambridge – but Karaman, you mustn't neglect your art; you have so much talent.'

'But sir—' Karaman smiled '—you've neglected *your* art, and *you* have so much talent!'

Hawker was taken aback and looked down at his feet. It dawned on him that there was an unhealthy, grasping selfishness in teaching the boy after school that was more about restoring what he had gradually lost over the past 20 years than any notion of helping Karaman. He put his hand over his eyes, excused himself and left the studio, ignoring Karaman, who called out, 'Sir! Are you alright?' behind him.

Without looking back, Hawker moved in the direction of the hedges that encompassed the playing field. He wanted to find the early wildflowers that Karaman had brought to the art room. He used to walk with Morris, finding flowers in the hedges of Suffolk. They'd paint them, and if they found a new variety they'd name it after one of Morris's cats or parrots before submitting the find to the Royal Botanical Society.

As he strode along, he saw the flock clustered around the new creamery building. A small man in a tweed jacket was peering through the windows. It was Fairchild who, armed with a wooden yardstick, was periodically swiping at the little sheep when they came too near to him. Fairchild glanced slyly about him but Hawker was out of his field of vision. Then he stooped to pick up a rock and aimed it at the creamery window.

'I wouldn't do that, if I were you!' Hawker called out.

Fairchild dropped the rock and spun round. 'Do what?' he squealed in mock astonishment.

Hawker walked up to him and seized the ruler. 'Or that.'

'That's my yardstick!' Fairchild shouted in petulant outrage.

'How would you feel if someone struck at you with it, eh?' Hawker poked him in the stomach.

Fairchild, acting as he'd been stabbed, doubled up. Hawker felt strangely satisfied, and gave him a whack across the shoulders for good measure, at which the yardstick snapped and one half whizzed through the air.

'Let this be a warning to you, Fanny Fairchild: desist from your bullying, whether it be of Sedgewick, one of his woolly friends or the little lads in the First Form.' Hawker then proceeded to snap the remaining half in two across his knee and watched Fairchild scuttle off. He felt quite invigorated, and drew in a deep breath.

Three months passed and the school year was nearing its close. Bunny had seen a prime marketing and recruitment opportunity and had pulled out all the financial stops for the grand opening of the Blindefellows Creamery. The mayor, the press, the masters and their spouses had been invited, along with the Percy family, who had now, at Bunny's insistence, allowed a brass plaque to be mounted on the wall of the creamery acknowledging them as its sponsors. A small marquee had been erected and samples of the cheeses produced by the Blindefellows Creamery were cubed, placed on cocktail sticks and carefully arranged on long wooden boards made of elm. The whole cheeses were displayed on plinths, dotted around a number of trestle tables and delightfully swathed in wax or a creamy white muslin with the labels Karaman had designed, based on observational drawings of the sheep themselves but with their prominent teeth aesthetically overlooked. There was a variety of crackers, red and green grapes, along with a modest array of British wines, which were to be poured by a select group of boys hand-picked by Bunny on twin criteria of having a smart appearance and being trustworthy enough not to down what they were meant to be serving to adults. The flock had been sheared and bathed especially for the event and restrained in a little pen to the side of the marquee to prevent them from ambushing either their own product or the crackers upon which it was to be sampled.

Sedgewick was suffering dreadful nerves. He'd tried to get into the swing of everything and had splashed out on a milk-white linen suit, which had immediately begun to crumple and pucker terribly; doused by profuse sweat from the anxiety into which Sedgewick had worked himself.

'Here, Mr Sedgewick, have a glass of wine to calm your nerves,' said Karaman, handing him a glass from his tray, taking care to choose white not red as he noticed that Sedgewick's hands were shaking and he didn't want him to spoil his linen suit.

'But is... is... isn't it for the opening toast?' Sedgewick stuttered.

'Don't worry, sir, you can have another for that, and may I say that your cheese is outstanding – it is the King of Cheeses.'

Sedgewick's heart fluttered at the thought that such an epithet might someday soon be bandied about in epicurean circles in reference to his work. This boy would know, coming as he did from a family who were among the largest producers of cheese in Turkey, a nation, so Karaman had enlightened him, that lines from *The Iliad* confirmed to be among the most ancient cheese-making lands in the world.

Bunny took the podium. 'Your Worshipfulness, Mr Mayor, and Aldermen of Travistock, members of the Blindefellows Board; Blindefellows masters, ladies and gentlemen of the press and public; and especially Mr and Mrs Galahad Percy: welcome to the grand opening of the Blindefellows Creamery, an innovation of our own man in the white suit, history master Mr Charles Sedgewick.' There was applause, which made Sedgewick blush. He wondered whether his hat, a white straw boater with a black ribbon in honour of the flock, would make the right impression. He had seen just such a hat on the head of the chief cheese judge at the Shropshire county show last summer.

Bunny continued. 'Several of the Blindefellows boys have now learned the venerable art of cheese-making and have enjoyed it so much that they are planning to attend the Royal Agricultural College at Cirencester next year. Mr Sedgewick has been assisted throughout by Oxbridge candidate and next year's head boy Kerem Karaman, the first of a new wave of Blindefellows students from continental Europe and the Middle East, whose families are selecting Britain and our school as the best choice for educating their sons. The striking oil paintings of flora on the display boards in the marquee – some featuring members of the famous Blindefellows West Country Pygmy Bearded Blacks, which provided the milk to produce the cheeses that you are about to sample – have been created by the multi-talented Karaman and our art master, my dear friend, Mr Sebastian Hawker, RA.'

Hawker, who was standing beside Karaman, now took his hand and raised it with his own toward the marquee roof, to further applause and cries of 'Bravo, bravo' from Japes.

Bunny paused for quiet, and resumed. 'This afternoon, we are going to sample three tried-and-tested brand-new organic sheep's milk cheeses, the recipes for which are said to be kept so secret that Mr Sedgewick sleeps with them under his mattress. So, without further ado, may I introduce you to Marion's Blue-Veined – that's the larger cheese orb in the pink wax; to Beaulieu's Cullion – that's the small fused double sphere cheese in the muslin bag; and, last but not least, to Stenchy Blindefellow – the runny cheese which, as its name suggests, is our strongest, so hold onto your hats – or rather your noses – with that one. Might I add that all three of our cheeses have been so inventively named by our physics master and prize-wordsmith, Mr William Japes.'

Bunny raised his glass to Japes, who swept the crowd with his most winsome smile and declared, 'I hope you will now join us in toasting the Blindefellows Creamery, and wishing it a prosperous future.'

The crowd drank to the creamery's success and descended upon the tables. The cheese was unlike anything many had ever had – but then many had only known the various Government Cheddar looka-likes in the refrigerated cabinet in the supermarket in town.

Everyone seemed thoroughly impressed – except for Fairchild, who kept out of Hawker's way, hiding behind his deputy, Tree, and whispering to him how 'utterly rank' the cheese was.

Sedgewick was approached by Karaman, accompanied by a dapper man carrying a briefcase. 'Mr Sedgewick, may I introduce Hector Valentine, cheese-buyer? I hope you don't mind that I mentioned our efforts to my father, who took the liberty of inviting him here today. He supplies our hand-made cheeses from Turkey to Harrods Food Halls, and is considering adding the Blindefellows Creamery to his repertoire.'

Sedgewick's eyes opened wide, magnified further by his lenses in their square tortoiseshell frames. There was soon a little gathering around Mr Valentine as he sampled the cheeses and gave his opinion on the them, praising each in turn. From that point on, everyone in the marquee rushed to buy up the whole stock on display. Swainson murmured to Bunny about expanding the size of the flock, while perhaps doing something to resolve their unsightly dental problem by bringing in Ouessant ewes from Brittany.

'To think they considered turning this cash cow into mutton chops!' a triumphant Matron Ridgeway said to Japes. Under the influence of the native wine, she was now feeling more flattered than embarrassed by his homage to her in the cheese-naming and she placed her arm around his waist.

'Well, Fanny, guess you'll be going home with your tail between your legs tonight!' Japes called across to Fairchild, who he spotted skulking out of the marquee with a serviette full of little cheese cubes on cocktail sticks because he was too stingy to buy a whole cheese.

On the first day of the summer holidays, Sebastian Hawker stepped off the bus on Hadleigh High Street in Suffolk and walked through town towards Benton End. Apart from a few new houses and a Spar corner shop, it hadn't changed much with the years. He walked past St Mary's church and the Old Monkey public house where he and Morris had enjoyed many a fine ale with Lett-Haynes, Morris's long-term partner who had died the previous year.

Sebastian knew his way as if he'd been there only yesterday. He carried a canvas pack on his back and a wooden case of art materials in his hand. Morris was expecting him. He flung open the front door and stepped outside as soon as Hawker appeared at the gate. He had lost most of his hair, but his eyebrows had made up for that.

'Sebastian!' cried Rubeo the macaw, his wings waving on Morris's back.

'He hasn't stopped saying that since I told him you were coming!' Morris beamed.

They embraced. Morris was no longer such a tall man, and Hawker had to stoop slightly. Bunny had granted him a sabbatical for a year, or for however long it took. He told him a job as Blindefellows' official artist in residence would be there waiting for him, if he ever chose to return. He never did.

4

A Blindefellows Chronicle

Michaelmas 1983 and Lent 1984

Things were getting out of hand now that Japes was approaching 50. He'd always erred on the side of risqué when it came to his physics experiments but these days he was throwing caution entirely to the wind and an injury, or even a fatality, was almost certainly on the cards. It was his devil-may-care insouciance and his boisterous conviviality with the boys that had cemented his enduring appeal at Blindefellows ever since his arrival at the school. All in all, they saw Mr Japes as one of them, and it ran much deeper than the youthful twinkle in his eye.

'Timber!' Japes's voice echoed across Blindefellows' tranquil lawns, the flock scattering like billiard balls.

'Good Lord, what's he dropping from the top of the bell tower now?' Swainson gasped from the safety of Bunny's office.

'I'm afraid it's the cannon balls again,' Bunny sighed. 'I told him last week to use ping-pong balls or tennis balls, but he says that's not what Galileo used so he's not interested.'

Swainson shook his head in disbelief. 'It's only a matter of time, Reverend, before there's a fractured skull. Those sheep are a damn sight cleverer than some of our boys. I just hope Gosling, our new biology master, doesn't take any advice from him about how one should go about teaching science.'

'And that is precisely why, Swainson, we made you, and not Japes, Gosling's mentor last year!'

An animated group of boys, led by Japes – his academic gown

fluttering in the wind – flowed out of the chapel and huddled around the dropped cannon balls.

'And where did this authentic cannon with original balls come from?' Swainson asked. 'Our Classics master, Crane, tells me Japes always fires it off during his choir practice.'

'Interesting, isn't it, that his trajectory experiments always seem to coincide with the singing, but then he never did like Crane, nor the Latin chanting he wrests from the boys,' Bunny mused. 'And I expect you're wondering, Swainson, how Japes got hold of a rare eighteenth-century trench mortar, complete with a pyramid of miniature cannonballs? Well, when he goes on his jaunts up to London a couple of times a term, he stays with a lovely lady who just happens to be curator of the British Artillery Collection. She apparently has an awful lot of clobber in storage, some of which Japes seems to have on long-term loan.'

'Did he bring the cannon back on the train?' asked Swainson, somewhat alarmed.

'Oh, no, he got her to drive it over.' Bunny smiled. 'You know Japes, with his powers of persuasion.'

'I was thinking, Reverend, is it just a matter of his needing an outlet? I mean, the trustees have landed this 400th anniversary of Blindefellows affair on us: don't you think Japes could take it on, with his fondness for fine dining and a shindig?'

'Hmm, true, he'd enjoy choosing the menu and swanning around with lady caterers, getting a few free samples, no doubt.'

'You mean of the ladies or their catering, Reverend?' Swainson smiled.

'I've seen Japes in action for over thirty years, on and off, Swainson, and you may rest assured that praise of each would be a means to obtaining the other.'

'And he'd probably need to spend a few hours with the lovely Isobel – you know, the angelic-looking lady who does our flowers in the foyer and whatnot – possibly over a lunch or two.'

'Isobel? Ah, yes, I remember. And he'll also have to keep an eye on whatever theatrical offering Tree conjures, as that could lead to trouble.'

'Splendid, Headmaster. If he agrees to all this, we should be able to keep him productively occupied from now until the anniversary, just before Easter break. He'll wind down after that as he always becomes absorbed in his – shall we say – preparations for the summer holidays; ever a time of rampant exertion for him.'

And so it was that Bunny and Swainson cornered Japes one afternoon with their proposal, in the hope of distracting him from his hijinks in the bell tower. It took some persuasion but in the end Japes had something of a smile on his face, though it worried Bunny that it looked a shade mischievous.

Japes's first port of call was Sedgewick, who he thought might be an amusing choice for helping with the entertainment at the anniversary celebration. On Japes's advice, Sedgewick had finally moved out of Loaghtan Wing, where he had resided for nearly 10 years, and bought himself a house in a cul-de-sac just off Travistock town park. Sedgewick had bashfully turned down every single woman Japes had wafted in his general direction, always with the same excuse: 'Sorry, Japes, but I just can't risk it. You know it's strictly against school rules for masters to entertain ladies in their rooms.' Consequently, Japes had badgered him for the best part of three years to move out, and now he had finally done it. Unfortunately, Japes had been away over the summer when Sedgewick suddenly decided to start house-hunting; Sedgewick's newly-widowed mother had suggested it as a diversion from her grief and had looked round the houses with him. Had Japes known, he'd have put off his holiday to steer Sedgewick towards choicer abodes: the tall Georgian terraces, such as his own on St Andrew's Street, or the stylish apartments in the renovated old grammar school building overlooking the river.

In Japes's absence, however, Sedgewick had, alas, swiftly settled on something under the influence of his mother, the tedious Eunice, and Japes was deeply worried as to what it might be as he rounded the corner of Ponsonby Gardens. He promptly saw that he'd been right to be concerned, for parked in the driveway of a dormer bungalow at the far end of the cul-de-sac was Sedgewick's purple Austin Allegro. A dormer bungalow! No! Anything but that! Japes tried not to gawp at the dreadful Dutch-style shingled roof that took up the entire top half of the building, a twin triumph of parsimony and dowdiness in construction. Two oval windows overhung with roofing tiles, like a heavy-lidded pair of eyes peering out sleepily, reminded Japes of Sedgewick without his glasses on. Every house on the street was a dire bungalow of one sort or another. Only Sedgewick's and a couple of others were a little more cutting-edge, having had their roofs revamped into spare rooms for visits from the grandchildren or, as in Sedgewick's case, the widowed mother. Yes, that was probably her insidious plan, Japes thought… Eunice was plotting, under the cover of elderly ingenuousness, to permanently join her ever-obedient son in this awful bungalow she had foisted upon him, thereby scuppering Japes's well-laid plans for his younger friend to finally discover a belated smidgen of the joys of sex.

Japes marched through the gate and up the ruler-straight concrete path towards the house, which sat in the dead centre of the stark plot. Either side of the powder-blue front door, with its obscured glass window, grip bars were fixed at appropriate angles. No doubt Eunice had requested they not be removed, in shrewd preparation for her own imminent decline. The garden was a barren square of patchy grass devoid of flower and feature. Japes shook his head. How would this ever inspire a woman's passion? It was about as romantic as a polling station.

Sedgewick caught sight of him from the window and rushed to the open door as if he thought his friend might burst through it, he was walking with such momentum. Japes stepped inside and recoiled. The entirety of the décor was steeped in the imagination of a woman who obviously considered the most repugnant fashions of the past decade to be the epitome of good taste: Formica, woodchip and tangerine accents.

'Well, what do you think?' Sedgewick smiled broadly, standing in one of his mother's themed aprons, this one featuring 'Teapots Through the Ages'.

'Is she here, your *mater*?' Japes asked furtively, glancing about and making ready for a quick retreat.

'Oh no, she had to go back home last week – finally got an appointment with the urologist at Bridgnorth General. She just left me a few aprons and a cupboard full of ready meals, now that I have to do some cooking for myself.'

'That's a relief.'

'Nice little place, isn't it?' Sedgewick closed the door before Japes backed out of the house, as he could sense his friend's discomfort. 'I feel so settled here I was thinking of calling it "Dun Roamin".'

'Quite,' Japes responded, 'First Shropshire, then Warwickshire and finally here, Travistock. It's been a long haul, Sedgers.'

'Indeed it has, Japes, indeed it has. I wouldn't be surprised if I were here for my retirement.'

Sedgewick was all of 36 and Japes couldn't take any more of this at present. 'Of course, many people select the name Belle End for their retirement bungalow.'

'Oh, that might be good too,' Sedgewick replied in all ignorance, 'with the shape of the cul-de-sac and all.'

They had stood in the cramped hallway long enough and Japes was eager to get the visit over and done with. 'Well, show me around quickly and I'll tell you what you need to do to it to make it bearable, then I'll brief you on an important job I have for you.'

'You wouldn't mind removing your brogues, would you Japes, old chap? Mother opted for a long shag on the carpet and I'm trying to keep it clean.'

'Mm, I bet it gave her a real lift that, being newly widowed and all.'

'It did, Japesy, thank you. And, you know, it cheered me up no end just seeing the look on her face when the carpet man put it all in.'

'Doubtless, it must have. You should be sure to tell Matron Ridgeway all about it next time you bump into her at school.'

They had tea from a mustard-coloured Hornsea Pottery tea set, sitting on a cheap wicker suite in an aluminium-framed conservatory at the back of the bungalow, looking out onto the sagging washing line billowing in the wind. Japes wondered whether he'd wasted his time on trying to shape Sedgewick's life for the past decade.

'… So, if I understand you correctly, your plan is that I'm to provide a sort of historical slide show to accompany the revue Tree is writing on the highlights of the 400-year history of the school?'

'Exactly so!' Japes smiled. 'A multi-media extravaganza! Do you think you'd be up to that?'

'Well, Japes, as you know, I'm quite the whizz-kid in the classroom with my slide projector now. It's a mainstay of my lessons these days. Mother recently gave me my father's old one, complete with carousel, and, as it so happens, I recently read an article in my periodical *Modern History Teacher* which featured a gadget that can synchronise two or more projectors. It's quite exciting, it really is. I shall order it straight away.'

'Wonderful, Sedgers, old man. I knew I could rely on you. You and Tree can have a few pow-wows to get it all straightened out. In the meantime, I'll be arranging the menu with Gigi, a fine figure of a caterer whom I know.'

Gigi, whom Japes had become well acquainted with a few years ago, was astonished that he had the cheek to call her on such affable terms; they'd parted acrimoniously when she had discovered that he had his iron in fires other than her own. On his third call about the anniversary, she begrudgingly agreed to discuss catering requirements, as long as it was strictly business. She was in something of a fallow period and slightly strapped for cash; her teenage son had recently gone off to medical school in Rome and was living beyond his means. This was hard for her because she was a single parent. She had fallen pregnant as a result of a rash act with a rather famous actor in an aeroplane toilet while working as an air hostess, so she claimed, but said she was far too proud to ask him for any contribution because it was 'as much my fault as it was his'.

Japes had asked her to meet him in the Four and Twenty Blackbirds. She'd made sure none of her grey roots were showing, using a kit in her bathroom the night before, and had put on her casual but clinging mint green velour track suit, the zip-up top of which was ever so slightly on the short side, which afforded little glimpses of her toned and tanned midriff. 'Gigi, darling!' Japes waved her over and embraced her. She felt the lighter-flame in her groin, her friend and her nemesis for the past 35 years, click into life.

The next morning, she rose early to make him a first-class breakfast, a delicious egg dish taught to her by her Italian grandmother, before he walked up to school. She would stay at his house for the day, making sample dishes for him to try that evening before they decided on the menu for the 400th Anniversary dinner. Bunny and Swainson had indeed been shrewd in their assessment of potential diversions. The dangerous experiments abruptly ceased and Japes became more subdued, spending his day looking forward to another evening with Gigi.

Meanwhile, Sedgewick and Tony Tree were getting down to another form of business and had met twice already in Sedgewick's bungalow to mastermind the 'multi-media revue'. Tree, English and drama master and descendant of that great pontificator, Sir Herbert Beerbohm Tree, had already informed Sedgewick that he intended to make an impact with the revue that would far outdo Japes's recent experiments with the Georgian portable mortar. Sedgewick was inclined to believe him because, ever since he had joined the school, Tree had put on the annual school play, which was always a veritable medley of melodrama. Japes liked to say that, in Tree's book, a boy wasn't acting unless he was chopping the air as if he were practising some bizarre form of martial art. 'Alright,' Tree would say, 'I know you're just a messenger holding a spear in the background but you need to react to every single word!' Thus it was that, eurythmic-style and frequently in togas, the boys of Blindefellows gesticulated their way through school productions.

Japes was pulling on his overcoat on a Friday after school in the science prep room when he heard Tree's voice bellowing out his name in the lab. He wondered for a moment if he should just lie low until Tree went away but, to his surprise and regret, his better nature got the better of him, and he emerged, smiling. Tree approached and, stooping low into an extravagant bow, handed him a script the thickness of a London phone directory and announced, 'Behold, *A Blinde-fellows Chronicle!*'

'Too long!' Japes said, dropping it onto a lab bench with an echo-ing thud.

'But you haven't read a word!' Tree gasped.

'Don't need to… It's obvious that in its current six-pound version it would run for the duration of the entire anniversary event.'

'But it's covering four hundred years, Japes – it has to be long!'

'So, do we instruct the cheque-book-wielding Old Blindefel-lonians and the Lady Mayoress of Travistock to bring along their sleeping bags?'

'I was thinking we'd perform it throughout the entire event with intervals every two hours for meals or coffee.'

'Perhaps it would be even better if we just hooked the spectators up intravenously to caffeine drips throughout the show, thus elimi-nating the need for coffee breaks?' Japes suggested.

'But then how would they go to the toilet?' Tree asked in all seri-ousness.

'We can have lavatories installed in lieu of seating.' Japes was starting to wish he'd concealed himself in the prep room. 'No, Tree, I'm not being serious, so stop looking confused, but we'll all have our backsides cleaved to the unyielding pews of the Disraeli Chapel, watching your show, so please be considerate of this part of our anatomy. Also, strict instructions from the top: the guests start to arrive at noon and we wrap up around midnight. There'll be class reunions at lunchtime and a black-tie dinner-dance, leaving around two hours max for a matinée in between.'

'But I just wouldn't know what to take out; it's all quite brilliant.' Tree's voice was tearful and his large mossy beard trembled.

'Look, Tree, you and Sedgers wade through it and set the hedge trimmers to work. I shall take a look when it is less than one quarter of its current bulk.' And with that Japes swept out of the room leaving a miserable Tree shambling off to find Sedgewick.

It took three lengthy sittings in Sedgewick's bungalow before Tree's script had shed its superfluous foliage. Tree fretted and clutched his brow, but the script was eventually shaved down to a dozen key dramatic events in Blindefellows' colourful history. Tree's idea was that as many boys as possible should participate, so there were still nearly 100 parts in the end. Three months of rehearsals later, rehearsing three nights a week, Tree was utterly exhausted since he felt he must demonstrate every line, every walk, every tiny mannerism.

After school on a vernal Saturday morning, Bunny gave Japes the seal of approval on the excellent menu he'd put together with Gigi. 'It sounds exquisite, Japes – but not too expensive, I hope. We may be well out of the woods now all the beds are filled but I still need to raise a fair whack for the new theatre.'

'Oh, Gigi is a marvel,' Japes beamed. 'She has a network of local organic producers, and she's taken me hither and thither to visit the most extraordinary farmsteads which charge her next to nothing. Of course, we'll also be using the cheeses of the Blindefellows Creamery so that'll save us a bob or two.'

'And how's it going with Isobel on the décor?'

'Ah, another marvel,' Japes winked. 'I tell you, Bunny, your life of celibacy must be an utter misery.'

Bunny sighed. 'It's just how it has to be, Will, for a man of my persuasion in my position. Not everyone shares your broad views on such matters, as I've been reminding you ever since we met. If we were in London, it might be different, but we're not. This is deepest, darkest Devon and 'Pride', as many younger chaps call it, will take some years to wend its way along the A303 and onward to Tavistock. At least people still have a faint notion that 'men of God' are wont to be celibate so they're not too surprised by my perennial lack of a wife.'

'But you're not telling me everything, Bunny. Surely you have a bit of fun in the summer holidays in South America with your tribal chief?'

'Ah well, perhaps not with him as he's happily married – to three wives just at present – but one does what one can. I somehow doubt I'd match up to your prodigious talents, however.'

'No, probably not,' Japes concluded. 'Anyhow, I've been over to Isobel's a few times to look over her arrangements, etcetera. I'll bring the plans over to you on Monday. She's developed a black-and-white theme in honour of the school colours. There'll be posies of black-and-white miniature roses on every table in anniversary vases she's having made specially. I'm getting a couple-of-hundred extra of those made so we can flog 'em at some grossly inflated price on the night, to help raise funds. There'll be white table cloths with black swags and a huge wicker sculpture of Beaulieu, our head ram, as the room centrepiece.'

'Wonderful, Japes. How reassuring to learn I shall be immortalised as a sheep in wicker.'

Japes patted his old friend on the back and excused himself. He was due to drop in at the chapel as Tree wanted to show him the costumes, all of them the labours of Tree's endlessly patient wife, Tabby, on her Singer sewing machine. McKenzie, Head of PE, would be there too, taking photographs. Dropping in was all Japes could manage as he was due at Isobel's to collect her final drawings for Bunny's perusal next week. It might well turn out to be another all-nighter with her, so he needed to keep fresh.

Ten Fourth Formers with black sheepskins tied to their backs, and their legs and arms clad in black tights, represented the Blindefellows flock. Tree confided that they'd also be painting their faces black for the performance itself but Japes advised that this might be going a bit too far. Tree showed Japes how he was training them to move expressively as a flock – ensemble theatre, as it were – crawling around with them, baa-ing, leading the way in a pair of curly papier-mâché horns. He threw back his bearded head and demonstrated his fine projection with a powerful 'Baaaa!', thrusting out his purplish tongue to hideous effect.

Tabby rushed about sorting out costumes while the motor-drive on McKenzie's Nikon whirred. Next came more Fourth Formers as the chorus of blind boys, complete with walking canes, hamming up the blind walk.

'Do you think they could be a little less bewildered in their movement, Tree?' Japes asked. 'Maybe tone down the sweeping arms and craning necks?'

In the mid-18th century, the training of the blind as musicians had been quite the mode and Blindefellows had boasted a fine orchestra and choir which had attracted the attention of George Frideric Handel, who'd made an honorary visit to the school to conduct the popular middle portion of his oratorio, *Israel in Egypt*, featuring the 10 plagues. For the anniversary play, Handel was being played by Crane, who now posed for McKenzie, clawing the air like some maleficent magus in a pantomime. The cut of his frock coat looked authentic enough to Japes, but the shimmering, mock-metallic fabric struck him as a flight of fancy more appropriate to the wardrobe of Liberace. As he marvelled at the garment, Tabby sidled up and began informing him in a rapt and rapid murmur that it was her *pièce de resistance* because she was mad, *simply mad*, for sequins and loved, *just loved*, to pick up handfuls of them and feel them running through her fingers… to which monologue Japes smiled and nodded, smiled and nodded.

Tabby must have had quite a ream of the sparkly stuff as it kept cropping up – on Cromwell's Roundheads, on Queen Victoria's gown, and even on the lapels of a Luddite leader. In the midst of this, a lone boy was trotted out in the tatty brown Fagin costume, complete with straggly long beard, that Tree had worn in last year's school production of *Oliver! The Musical*.

'And what precisely is Fagin's part in the history of Blindefellows?' Japes asked archly.

'Oh, no, Mr Japes,' Tabby mewed. 'That is Simeon Disraeli, cousin of the then Prime Minister – you know, the converted fellow who changed the school over from a charitable institution for blind boys to fee paying school for anybody who could pay.'

'But Tabby, you can't kit him out in that ghettoised get-up simply because he was of Jewish origin!' Japes reproved as mildly as he could manage, but Tabby shrank away looking crestfallen. He took her small hand in his and patted it reassuringly. 'Tabby, I think you've done a truly wonderful job, but several of Blindefellows' most generous alumnae are Jewish, and Simeon Disraeli, the second most important figure in our school's history, must be dressed like any other well-off English gentleman of the time – and not in a cast-off Fagin suit.'

'Oh, but wasn't Tony marvellous in it last year?'

'He was, indeed,' Japes assured her in his best false-earnest tone, as the great actor himself approached.

'Japes, I'm not sure whether I've mentioned it yet, but I shall be taking on the part of Hezekiah Lambton and, thereafter, in the person of his spirit, I shall narrate throughout the four hundred years,' Tree announced. Tabby clapped her hands excitedly beneath her chin, which Japes took as his cue to make an exit and head off to Isobel's. Half an hour of Tree's dramatic style, even if mostly in tableaux, would take its toll on any man, and he now felt an urgent need for a glass of hock and a younger woman to fortify himself.

As he walked down the hill towards the town, he caught sight of the familiar figure of Matron Marion heading up the hill with a basket of groceries.

'You're leaving school late for a Saturday,' she called over to him.

'Yes, just been in the chapel viewing Tabby Tree's procession of sequined costumes for the anniversary revue, and now I'm off to Isobel's for the décor *exposé*.'

'Isobel now, is it? I thought it was Gigi for a second time round. I know her slightly, Japesy. This town's especially small for well-heeled single women, and we all know each other's business. Tread carefully.'

'Whatever do you mean, Maid Marion?'

'I mean that Gigi, like you, is approaching fifty and, at bottom, so to speak, she's a Mediterranean woman. She's probably hoping to marry you and, while I'm sure you've never made any promises, I'd be willing to bet you haven't gone out of your way to disabuse her of such fantasies.'

'Ah, you know me too well, Marion, flitting like a butterfly from one beautiful, bounteous blossom to the next,' Japes said whimsically and he continued on his way, blithely ignoring her wise warning.

At lunchtime the next day, he ambled home with Isobel's drawings under his arm. He paused and frowned for a moment when he observed Gigi standing on his doorstep, ringing his bell.

'I've been trying to call you all night, Will.'

'Why?' he asked in the most innocent tone he could manage.

'I made a birthday cake for you. Devil's-food cake – your favourite. It is today, isn't it?' she said, proffering a white box.

'Ah, yes, so it is.'

'I remembered from when we were together last. I remember it every year, in fact. But where've you been? You weren't home last night!'

Japes had always considered honesty to be the best policy with regard to his lack of fidelity but with the anniversary event coming up later that month, he felt that he couldn't risk tipping his hot-blooded caterer over the edge and decided to lie. 'I stayed over on Sedgewick's couch. We slightly overdid it with our drinking session, I'm afraid. He was in no state to drive me and I honestly wasn't sure if I'd be able to find my way home.'

'Oh, Will! At your age!' she scolded.

The phrase cut him to the quick but he smiled sheepishly and invited her in for coffee and a slice of the cake. Coffee was not quite what she had in mind once she was inside, having not seen him all week. Her comment echoed around his soul and he found he wasn't up to much – or, in fact, to anything at all. He said it must be the hangover and suggested they see each other the following day. Gigi rolled her eyes and put on her coat to leave. As she was passing the console table, Isobel's drawings – from which he'd passingly congratulated himself for having distracted her attention – now caught her eye.

'These are the sketches you had when you came in. Plans for the four-hundredth, are they?'

'Yes, it's going to look superb, isn't it?'

'Who is it doing the décor, anyway?'

'Isobel, a retired lady who does the flower arranging at school,' he nonchalantly reassured her, despite Isobel being some 20 years Gigi's junior. It worked a treat and, following a brief amorous moment standing on the doormat, she was gone.

The day of the grand event dawned and Gigi was in the school kitchens by 6am, supervising the school chef and his handful of kitchen assistants. Preparations for the grand evening meal had begun in earnest. Matron Ridgeway had volunteered her services, too, as their task was ambitious: they were to serve a five-course evening meal to over 400 guests. Bunny had carefully selected a crew of the best-mannered Sixth Formers to act as waiters, thereby allowing old boys to be charitably impressed by new ones, while saving on catering staff. Also on site was Isobel, arranging her swags and positioning her wicker ram on its podium. Japes, delighting in this infrequent opportunity to wear black tie, was keeping his distance from both kitchen and dining area by keeping himself busy making conversation with numerous Old Blindefellonians and their wives at the entrance to the chapel.

The guests had begun assembling for Tree and Sedgewick's grand revue, and were serenaded by Crane's choir, who were presently singing *Sumer is Icumen in*, the ongoing choruses of which served as a repetitious reminder to Japes of the urgency of keeping his caterer in the kitchen and out of the dining area, and his decorator in the dining area and out of the kitchen. By standing at the chapel entrance, interminably shaking hands, he fortunately didn't have to endure the sight of Crane conducting, which he had often likened to a marabou stork killing an eel. Old Blindefellonians of all ages, from jaunty twenty-somethings to tottering nonagenarians, were taking their pews around the stage, which had been erected in the nave with a white drop-cloth across the back onto which Sedgewick would project his and Tree's 'cutting-edge' multi-media presentation – a twin-projector slide-show with reel-to-reel sound effects. Those pupils involved in neither stage show nor dinner dance had been stringently ordered to make an extra effort, with spotless uniforms, nicely combed hair and neatly trimmed nails. They sat in orderly rows on the balcony level of the Disraeli Chapel with their house masters.

Tabby was having kittens backstage, with needles and threads hanging out of her mouth as she scampered about making last-minute repairs and adjustments. Sedgewick, fairly bursting out of a tuxedo borrowed for the occasion from Japes in order to save the rental from Moss Bros, was seated on a stool at a high table with his two carousel slide projectors – his own and the one he'd recently inherited from his father, with his father's family snaps carefully stored in another part of the carousel. The two projectors were precisely angled at the screen so as not to overlap. The reel-to-reel tape recorder and his slide-and-sound script were at his fingertips but he was feeling more and more flustered as the stream of affluent Old Blindefellonians filled the chapel. His waistband was pinching and his cummerbund constricting. His hands had become clammy and, whipping off his glasses to wipe them when they steamed up as he fumbled through his last-minute tech-check, he lost his balance on the stool and tipped over his projector table onto the floor before him. Many of the slides spilled out of the two carousels and Sedgewick now crawled about, frantically trying to gather them up and reload them in the proper order, shining the pocket flashlight from his key-ring onto one after another.

He had just managed to get everything back in place when he noticed Tree giving the signal that the revue was to begin. It was to open with the melodious baa-ing of sheep, a genuine recording of the Blindefellows flock captured by Sedgewick out in the grounds, microphone in hand. With a little flourish, the suddenly confident Sedgewick clicked the 'play' button on the reel-to-reel, but the volume was monstrously loud and the gentle baas were amplified into gigantic booms. The line of white-haired Old Blindefellonians in front of the stage almost shot off their pew and Sedgewick was quick to readjust the volume.

Tree entered in the threadbare Fagin suit, which had been reassigned to the character of the impoverished Hezekiah Lambton as a young man. He entered carrying a real member of the flock, an innovative touch which provoked a volley of applause. Tree, in the tradition of his progenitor Beerbohm, paused, made a deep bow then intoned his speech about being a pious, itinerant sheep shearer in front of Sedgewick's slide of the rolling Devonian hills around Travistock. There was another burst of applause and Sedgewick swelled with pride at being a part of it all. Tree bowed again and exited for a quick costume-change as the boys-as-sheep came on and sang a song about a sheep's life, to the tune of 'Hi, Diddle-Dee-Dee, An Actor's Life for Me' with jolly new lyrics by Tree, substituting 'actor' for 'sheep'.

Tree then reappeared, still as Hezekiah Lambton, only now he had become a prosperous wool merchant wearing a white ruff and a shiny black hat. The sheep in his arms had been replaced by a swaddled babe, and at his side stood his new wife, Dorcas Ramsay, played by Tabby (she'd been unable to resist adorning her Puritan petticoat and apron with a few well-placed sequins to catch the light). But, alack, all was not well: Hezekiah and Dorcas were weeping with a passion of melodramatic proportions. Their son, they cried, was blind and was going to have something of a dullard's life with no school at which to learn the word of the Lord.

Cue the next slide, intended to be an engraving illustrating the sad fate of so many blind children – begging; but instead up popped a picture of a pudgy Sedgewick aged 11 standing by a swimming pool in turquoise trunks crocheted by his mother, holding up a certificate that read, 'Breast stroke proficiency'. Irrepressible titters from boys – old and new – in the audience were quickly drowned out by the volume of the Lambtons' woe. Sedgewick plucked the errant slide from his father's carousel and the backdrop was glaringly white during half a minute of frenetic fumbling until the correct slide was inserted. He glanced over at Japes, who smiled at him reassuringly. Japes had predicted things might take an amusing turn with Sedgewick on tech.

As news of the free blind school spread, boys from across the West Country made their wary way toward Blindefellows. Tree's next song featured blind boys in hessian sacking carrying meagre bundles. It was an *andante* musical number, incorporating multiple use of the words 'plodding' and 'trudging'. At the song's close, Sedgewick snapped up a slide of a marble statue of Julius Caesar while Tree, as narrator, declaimed that Blindefellows was the first known institution to have had an all-blind cast perform a Shakespeare play. The boys on stage threw off their sacking to reveal that staple of the costume department, the toga. Armed with stage daggers, they proceeded to locate Caesar by his shouts in order to close in and stab him in what resembled a role-reversed game of blind man's buff.

Francis Fairchild, as a diminutive Cromwell, now marched his Roundhead army up the chapel aisle and onto the stage, recreating the episode during which they were invited to rest and recuperate at Blindefellows for a fortnight between the Battles of Torrington and Stow-on-the-Wold. Sedgewick clicked up the next slide, but instead of Puritan military glory, there was his grandmother with her whippet, Nancy, seated in the funicular railway at Bridgnorth. Cheers, quickly silenced by the housemasters, came from some of the boys on the balcony, while Sedgewick fumbled again for the correct slide – Samuel Cooper's 1646 portrait of the soon-to-be Lord Protector, which he managed to throw up on the screen just in time for Fairchild's speech.

Sedgewick froze almost as soon as the irate little librarian began to speak– something was highly amiss with Fairchild's lines.

'It is high time for me to put an end to your sitting in this place...'

What was this? It certainly wasn't in the script, and Tree was looking dumbfounded at his lectern.

'... which you have defiled by your practice of every vice,' Fairchild spat out at the audience, sneering and leering in a shiny helmet and tiny cuirass.

'But that's the Dissolution of Parliament speech of 1653! He's turning history on its head!' Sedgewick said to himself, shaking his head in astonishment.

'You pack of mercenary wretches!' the diminutive man screamed at a full bench of confused-looking elderly men.

Sedgewick now recalled that Fairchild had told Tree he was going to produce a 'most memorable performance' in this, his final year at Blindefellows, before his eagerly anticipated retirement at the age of 68.

'Like Esau, sell your country for a mess of pottage!' he gesticulated at the pale, doughy faces of the boys staring down at him from the balcony.

Sedgewick saw that he must do something to distract attention from this ranting bantam because he knew the speech was about to get far fruitier.

'Gold is your God!' Fairchild raved at a young man in a five-hundred-pound suit, an older and wiser McDowell who'd made a mint in the city.

With lightning-quick thinking, Sedgewick randomly flicked up an alternative slide from his father's carousel in the hope of deflecting the audience's attention. And there he was with his father on the beach at Budleigh Salterton, both of them wearing knotted polka dot handkerchiefs on their heads and kicking up their heels in imitation of the famed music hall sand dance of Wilson and Keppel. Unbridled laughter now erupted. The house masters, appearing to follow Sedgewick's plan, allowed the boys on the balcony to let rip, thus drowning out Fairchild's 'Ye sordid prostitutes, have you not defiled this place?', this time directed at the Lady Mayoress and her entourage. A further slide was randomly thrown up, this time of his parents in Blackpool, his mother doubled up at his father, who was wearing a bizarre hat in the shape of two huge cartoon breasts with 'Boob Inspector' written along the hatband. Fairchild's finale, 'Take away that shining bauble there and lock up the doors', was thus utterly lost in Sedgewick's impromptu memorial to his father that celebrated a lightness of life that Sedgewick himself had never quite managed to achieve.

Fairchild stormed off the stage, throwing down and denting the silver-coloured papier-mâché Roundhead helmet Tabby had made for him at her feet, and charged out of the chapel to be seen no more that evening. Japes turned to Swainson, sitting next to him, and quipped that no doubt the long-suffering housekeeper at Fairchild House would be subjected to his tantrums relating to this event for several weeks to come.

Tree stepped forward with his narrator's script to draw a line under the digression, hastily waving off the boys dressed as Round-heads who'd marched onto the stage with Fairchild and had been floundering throughout the rant, performing the odd eurythmic ges-ture in the manner Tree had taught them in an attempt to react expressively. He gave a hand signal and Crane strode on stage – a defining moment for him, showcasing his sparkly tailcoat; Crane had even allowed Tabby to sweep some shimmery gel over his sharp cheekbones to highlight them. He then grandiosely conducted the blind boys in Handel's second plague air 'Their Land Brought Forth Frogs'. He dearly wished his wife was there to see his shining moment but she seldom accepted invitations to school functions, especially now that baby Ptolemy had come along.

Then there was the recreation of Blindefellows' one and only royal visit, featuring history master Rollo as George III who, in the early throes of his malady, had turned up unexpectedly at the school dressed in a smock, to discover for himself the unique method devel-oped there to teach blind boys how to shear a sheep by touch alone. He had insisted on attempting the feat blindfolded, and had cut him-self with the unwieldy shears nearly as badly as he'd cut the terrified sheep.

A most unfortunate episode in Blindefellows' history came next, but one that Tree insisted be kept in the revue despite Sedgewick's suggesting otherwise. Blindefellows had at the time been a school that attempted to shield its disabled pupils from the periodic upheavals of a fractured world, but a handful of the blind boys had got in with a Luddite agitator who'd armed them with bludgeons and escorted them one night to a factory, where he abandoned them in the door-way for fear of being implicated. They didn't realise that the Luddite had mistakenly left them at the door of the wrong factory and they had bashed up a room full of partially constructed fine harpsichords. Their fate was to be transported to Australia, while their craven provocateur was never captured. 'We've simply got to keep that in,' Tree had stressed to Sedgewick. 'It will serve as a warning to any boys thinking of getting up to anarchic monkey business again.'

Next to enter was Tabby Tree in a walk-on part as Queen Victoria, Tabby yet again showcasing her costume-making skills. During an outbreak of smallpox at the school, the queen had sent relief to 'the poor, dear blind boys' in the form of a royal farthing, which still resided in its original purple-satin-lined box, albeit now faded, in a display case in the school foyer.

There was an interval with refreshments by the entrance to the chapel and Japes went over to shake Sedgewick's hand. 'Quick thinking when Fairchild went AWOL, Sedgers! I was most impressed. By the way, your dad looks to have been quite the party animal.'

'Oh, he was, yes, Japes, a very amusing man; mother is quite lost without him.'

'When she visits you next, you must both come over for dinner,' Japes said, feeling he'd been a bit harsh to judge her on a couple of passing meetings and her choice in bungalows. 'Come along, let's get you a stiff drink and we'll see what it makes you throw up in the second half.'

Simeon Disraeli was first onstage after the break, regaling the audience with the *laissez-faire* tale of how he turned Blindefellows, in its dwindling early-Victorian fortunes, from a charitable institution to a sighted school for the new middle classes, packing off all the poor blind boys to Dr Woodcock's Institute for Unsighted Youth in Portsmouth and opening the wrought iron gates to the bankers, lawyers and Imperial civil servants of the future. Then came the world wars and the roll call was read out of those Blindefellonians who had fallen. A boy stepped onto the stage and played 'The Last Post' on his bugle, during which Sedgewick feared he might sob out loud on his stool. Following this, a spectacle had been strategically placed to lift the mood. It was an 'End of Rationing' extravaganza, with boys wearing body-sized papier-mâché hams, butter packets, flour sacks and sugar cubes or whirling about as generous wheels of Government Cheddar. The potent tipple with which Japes had plied Sedgewick at the interval didn't help him to focus and a slide of his father in a lobster bib, waving an oversized crustacean claw, at a Rotary Club dinner popped up. Everyone cheered him and he intentionally left the image there for a few moments longer, swept away with pride by this other impromptu memorial to his father, before putting up the intended slides of firework displays. To a spirited tune on the tin whistle, the papier-mâché clad boys reeled about the stage in something akin to a traditional West Country fisherman's dance.

At the end of the show, Bunny feigned surprise at being called onto the stage, where Tree presented him with a book: his original, unabridged script bound into a hefty leather volume embossed with gold leaf Gothic script which read *A Blindefellows Chronicle*, amply illustrated with McKenzie's photographs of the actors, Tree in particular. It was a very generous gesture engineered to engender what Tree hoped would be his seamless transition to Fairchild's post as Head of English at the end of the year. Bunny thanked Mr and Mrs Tree for their hard work, as well as Sedgewick for his comic touches, and finally Japes for organising it all. There was rapturous applause from the Old Blindefellonians and the boys in the balcony stamped their feet. When the cheering had died down, Bunny lost no time in getting down to business, giving a speech about the planned state-of-the-art theatre and inviting donations, before everyone headed to the wining and dining in the refectory. Those boys not involved in the event were to have platters of sandwiches in their wing common rooms and there would be videos.

On entering the refectory, glasses of wine were handed out from trays to the accompaniment of the surprisingly good school swing and jazz band. The Old Blindefellonians were keen to show off to each other and were soon queueing up to hand over their cheques to Brenda, the headmaster's secretary, positioned behind a leather-topped desk in a prominent location, with the architect's plans for the new theatre on display on the wall behind her. She also had the task of shifting the boxed anniversary vases at their highly inflated price. As a rule, the more the alcohol kicked in, the fatter the cheques became, and Bunny tended to target those Old Blindefellonians who seemed particularly well oiled, even to the extent of casually escorting them to the donations desk.

The place cards had been arranged to ensure that masters (black cards) were scattered tactically among Old Blindefellonians (white cards). Given that Isobel was the one who'd laid out the cards, Japes found himself at a table with her. He glanced about for an opportunity to switch her, but there she was, suddenly behind him and forcing him into an embrace which he caught Gigi spotting from the serving hatch.

'Who's that with Will?' Gigi meant to say in her head, though it came out of her mouth.

Fortunately, Matron Ridgeway was within earshot. 'Oh, probably the wife of one his students from his early days here. You know how it is at these fundraising dos, the masters are expected to fawn on The Money.'

Gigi went on passing the appetizers out to the boy waiters, but with one eye perpetually on Japes and the pretty younger woman orbiting around him.

Sedgewick, whose blood alcohol concentration was already tipping his scales after two mid-show gin and tonics, followed up by absent-mindedly downing two glasses of white wine as soon as he arrived in the refectory. Joining a group of old boys in raising a third glass to the next 400 years of Blindefellows, he suddenly felt much the worse for wear and plonked himself down in the vacant place on the other side of Japes, almost taking off the tablecloth. As he looked across the flower arrangement, he was surprised to find himself suddenly quite smitten with Isobel, with her luxuriant blonde curls and silky, slinky black-and-white-evening gown. Japes eagerly introduced them, suspecting he was under surveillance by the Anglo-Italian secret service and hoping to divert Gigi with a red herring.

'Healthy turn-out of Blindefelons tonight, eh, Isobel?' Sedgewick slurred.

Isobel chuckled. 'I think you mean Blindefellonians, Charles.'

'Yes, yes, of course: Blindefellations,' he drooled.

'Let me swap places with you, Sedgers, so you can talk to Isobel properly,' Japes interjected, rising and virtually heaving Sedgewick from his current seat and lowering him into his own. Gigi, peeping out from the serving hatch, breathed a sigh of relief, but Isobel was not best pleased. She smiled politely at Sedgewick and promptly turned to her right to have a chat with the old gent sitting there, who told her how much he admired her wicker ram. Japes turned to McDowell, Sedgwick's one-time kidnapper, on his left and raved about how much the school had improved, much of it sparked by his rebellious actions less than a decade earlier. Sedgewick, with no one to talk to, convened with the food, which was delicious.

By the arrival of the fifth and final course, the Blindefellows Creamery cheese and cracker platter, Sedgewick could hardly move in Japes's rather neat tuxedo, but he had an idea up his taut sleeve to wean Isobel away from her old man. He would tell her how the creamery was his brainchild and how he had developed the new cheeses, through trial and error, albeit taking care to omit his early blunder of attempting to milk a ram. 'Have you sampled Beaulieu's cullions, Isobel?' he said as he tapped her clumsily on her bare shoulder.

She turned to him in surprise to see him mouthing a sphere of creamy white cheese somewhat lasciviously, she thought, though he certainly hadn't intended it that way.

'Not lately, Charles,' Isobel said, turning back.

'How about Marion's Blue-Veined?' he said, proudly displaying an entire breast-shaped cheese in his palm under her nose.

'Really, Mr Sedgewick!' she drawled, pushing his hand away. She got up in a huff and went to the ladies.

The jazz ended with a clarinet flourish and the band went off for a break while the coffee and brandy were served. Twenty minutes later they were back and launching into the first number of their second set as a rotating coloured light came on above. No one dared step onto the dance floor at first, as if it were a pond covered with thin ice. Finally, the Trees got up to save the day and, one by one, masters with their wives and Old Blindefellonians with theirs, dipped their toes.

'Would you like to dance, Will?' Isobel popped up from nowhere to ask Japes in a somewhat nettled tone. He promptly agreed without weighing up the possible consequences.

In the kitchen, the dishes were being washed and the surfaces scrubbed down. Gigi took great pride in leaving the kitchens she worked in immaculate. Matron Ridgeway had set the kitchen assistants to preparing packages of extra food to take home for their families and sat down for coffee with Gigi, who was exhausted.

'I should nip out and see Will,' Gigi said, rubbing her eyes.

'Are you sure you want to? It's been such a long day for you and he'll be obliged to dance with one alum's wife after another.'

Gigi looked at her suspiciously. 'Is he still dancing with that curly blonde thing?'

'Knowing Japes, he's probably dancing with every attractive woman out there. That's just how he is, as well we know.'

Gigi wandered over to the serving hatch and, peering out, went suddenly rigid. 'You're mistaken, Marion. He's cheek to cheek with her right now. I'm going out there to ram her into that ram!' She turned and headed towards the door, with Matron Ridgeway rushing after to try and detain her.

'Signora Gigi, I'm so glad you haven't left yet!' Bunny smiled as he entered the kitchens, took Gigi's hand and kissed it.

Gigi took a step back and composed herself as Bunny presented her with an envelope.

'I have to say, that was one of the best meals I've had in my life and it's largely due to you that Brenda is knee-deep in cheques out there. I've just doubled your fee and I want you to do all the important functions at the headmaster's lodge in future. I have something or other happening every month, so we're going to be keeping you very busy.'

Gigi smiled and accepted her bountiful cheque. It was just what she needed. There'd been so much stress about money lately with her son, and only her reunion with Japes had helped to distract her.

'Oh, and here's a little souvenir – a complimentary four-hundredth anniversary vase,' he handed her the box and returned to the party.

'Well, Gigi. That was just what the doctor ordered.' Matron Ridgeway laid a friendly hand on her back.

'It is. I'm alright now. I don't know why I thought Japes would ever have changed. Twice bitten, twice shy, Marion.'

'Oh, I agree completely. We women are all japes to Japes.'

Gigi took a deep breath, gave her dyed-black ponytail a shake and sauntered proudly out of the kitchens to her car, slapping the white envelope against her shapely thigh.

Matron Ridgeway put on the evening gown she had hanging on the back of the kitchen storeroom door and joined the party for its final hours, dancing her way through a plethora of Old Blindefellonians. Isobel was on the dance floor too, getting on with McDowell like a house on fire. Japes and Sedgewick were sitting together, laughing to the point of tears.

'Come, do join us, Marion. Sedgewick is telling me tales of his father,' Japes called to her. 'Tell her the one about the Skegness caber tossing, Sedgers.'

She sat down with a martini. 'You seem to have got off scot-free tonight, Japes.'

'Has Gigi gone?' he said, suddenly looking nervous.

'Yes – for good, I should think. She's had more than enough of you second time round.'

'That's a relief, Marion; it was all becoming rather awkward. You don't think me too much of a heel, I hope.'

'Well, wouldn't I be quite the hypocrite if I did, Will? You're not guilty of any offence with my sex that I'm not guilty of with yours. Meanwhile, it appears you've managed to cut loose from Miss Isobel too, whether you wanted to or not. I only hope you've learned your lesson at last and you can stop showing off to yourself quite so much, now you've turned fifty.'

In a haze of alcohol, Sedgewick grasped for his own words of wisdom. 'You've tied yourself in knots with these... these quatercentenary tergiversations of yours over these past few weeks, Japesy. You need only look at my uncomplicated existence to see how content a truly single man can be.'

'Too right, Sedgers. From tomorrow morn I shall strive to lead the bungalow life and lose myself in microfiche, but first I'd like to tell Marion how lovely she looks in that evening gown and invite her for a nightcap at my place later.'

'Tantalising offer, Japes, but I've promised the last dance to a dashing not-too-old Old Blindefellonian over yonder, who's invited me to house-sit his charming villa in Tuscany come the summer hols, so I must pass on your kind offer for tonight.'

The two men watched the compact yet curvaceous form of the black-gowned Matron Marion recede, each following their own private train of thought. 'What was that you said I'd tied myself up in a moment ago, Sedgers?' Japes asked his old younger friend with a broad smile.

'Sorry, Japesy, it's gone straight out of my head.'

'Quadri-something something-something?'

'Ah, yes, quatercentenary tergiversations!' Sedgewick recalled.

'What a remarkable turn of phrase for two in the morning,' Japes mused. 'Let's finish off this bottle of champagne and see what we can get you to come out with at three!'

5

The Man in the Brown Suit

Michaelmas 1986

Lesley Leggatt was now entering his second month as lab technician at Blindefellows. After finishing his science degree at Sheffield Polytechnic, he had returned to his home town of Travistock and entered the graduate scheme in the Watkins Biscuit Factory, in charge of quality control on the garibaldi line. There he had happily remained for seven years, until something changed in the mix and hives started appearing on his neck.

'Tell me again, Les, what it was that drove you from the biscuit factory? Was it that frightful smell of wet cardboard that emanates from its chimneys?' Japes asked as he dunked another chocolate bourbon into his mug of tea.

'Well, there was no concrete evidence, Mr Japes, but I suspect I became contaminated with Balsam of Peru,' Les replied in a nasally sort of voice, which Japes enjoyed imitating behind his back.

'But you've never set foot in Peru!' called the rotund, flaxen-haired biology master, Toby Gosling, from the wormery.

'It's finding its way into everything these days, Mr Gosling,' Les intoned as he sorted the pipettes, by size, into trays, wearing his latex gloves. 'Pickles, sauces, shampoo... I have to be so careful about what I eat; they often don't declare it on the label. But I didn't do too badly out of Watkins; they gave us a new suit every year, along with staff Christmas parties and other perks.'

Gosling and Japes glanced at each other with wry smiles.

'Ah, the brown suit.' Japes nodded in feigned appreciation.

'Indeed, Mr Japes. Watkins suits are actually modelled on the exact shade of brown of that bourbon biscuit you're enjoying at this very moment. I have seven in my wardrobe. And they're polyester, so they can be thrown in the washing machine and drip dry with no ironing.'

'You have seven?' Gosling marvelled.

'Yes, Mr Gosling,' Les chirped. 'You weren't under the impression I was wearing the same suit since I arrived at Blindefellows last month, were you?'

'Well, I suppose we were, but it's refreshing to discover the truth.' Gosling smiled. 'And isn't it also the self-same hue as your old Travistock Secondary Modern uniform?'

'Not quite, Mr Gosling – that was more of a deep Caramac, whereas your blazer at the Travistock Grammar was a very pleasing mulberry worsted, if I remember rightly.'

'Yes – emblazoned with the looming swan on the breast pocket.'

'But there's no beating a machine-washable uniform. I imagine your gran must've spent a fortune getting yours dry-cleaned.'

'Yes, I suppose she did,' Gosling politely agreed.

'And did you know, Messrs Japes and Gosling, that the humble custard cream is the nation's favourite biscuit?'

'Yes, you told us that one already,' Japes drawled. 'Always fancied it was a woman's biscuit, to tell the truth.'

He threw his academic gown over his head and went out to teach his class. Japes could be brusque towards Les, but Gosling felt one should always make a friendly gesture, even if Les was a tad dull, constantly regaling them with great lists of everything he had to avoid due to his dire allergies, hence his wan complexion. Gosling now suggested Les join him at church for morning service that Sunday and pop round for coffee afterwards. He knew that Les attended a Christian Science group a couple of evenings a week in a dismal little red-brick hall that doubled as a venue for pensioners' bingo. Gosling wanted him to experience a beautiful church like St Peter's, set in a fine old graveyard with yews and cypresses. Les accepted, but said Gosling must instead come to his place for coffee afterwards as he would without doubt be allergic to Gosling's West Highland Terrier, Huxley, so he wouldn't be able to spend more than five minutes in Toby's sitting room.

Gosling arrived early at St Peter's with pink carnations for his grandmother's grave. He took out last week's bunch and put some fresh water in the vase before arranging them nicely. It was the least he could do for her now. At 14, his mother, a nurse, had left the family home for a doctor in Glasgow who then traded her in for a younger nurse five years later. His father, a businessman who sold copper cable couplers in the Middle East, was neither home nor interested enough to look after his son properly. Gosling started dropping in at his grandmother's after school with ever-greater frequency, in particular for a proper warm meal when he couldn't face the potato waffles in the freezer that his dad used to leave for him. He didn't know what to do with himself at weekends in the empty house and mooned around the pick 'n' mix in Woolworths or occasionally wandered over to the park to sit in a deckchair listening to the town brass band playing various themes, from James Bond to *Hawaii Five-0*. Apparently, Les had been in the band on the cornet, but Gosling couldn't recall seeing him, probably because he was often in a daze during that miserable time, forgetting to bathe, his hair greasy and lacklustre. He also lacked the cash to have his woollen uniform dry-cleaned, which led to his friends giving him an increasingly wide berth.

His grandma smelled a rat soon enough and went round to his house with him one Saturday afternoon to investigate: filthy bathroom, unwashed sheets, mouldy food in the fridge. 'Pack your bag and come to my house. That's where you're living from now on!' she ordered. She gave him the top floor of her timbered cottage on Trumpet Terrace (where he still lived now). She sat down to a proper dinner with him each evening and asked about his homework with genuine interest, supplying anecdotes of her own distant girlhood from time to time. On Saturday evenings, they sat in front of the television with fish and chips from Bob's across the road, which Gosling would fetch, marvelling at the dexterity with which Bob manipulated the fish in his withered arm, dipping it into the honey-coloured batter. Later, he and his grandma would play cards on the fold-out tray-table, its top embellished with scenes from Malta. On other nights, he would do his homework and, in this way, he gradually regained his high rank at the grammar school following the disruption from his parents' divorce.

Les appeared at the church door looking tentative, and Gosling gave him a cheery wave and walked over to him. He was out of his brown suit now and wore an Argyll jumper in an orange design, beige corduroys and a duffle coat. They went in together: Les, tall and gangly, and Gosling, short and stout, one fearing most foods and the other embracing all. Gosling was greeted by a congregation of elderly ladies, most of whom had been his grandmother's friends. Cakes had been arranged on the trestle table at the back to accompany the tea and chin-wag after the service, to which Gosling added a golden-topped Bakewell tart flecked with toasted almonds. Baking was a skill he'd learned from his grandmother in her kitchen with its marble worktop and shelves containing a myriad of ingredients, each in their own labelled canisters with her handwritten labels, faded but just about legible – candied peel strips, dates, extra-bitter chocolate chips.

'Hello, Toby, have you brought us a new recruit?' asked an old lady with loose dentures at the door, handing them an order of service.

'Good morning to you, Mrs Belcher. This is Les, our lab technician at Blindefellows. I thought it was about time he experienced the splendours of St Peter's.'

Gosling was pleased to see his favourite hymn on the agenda – 'All Things Bright and Beautiful'. When the time came, he sang it with unbridled joy. Unfortunately Les, at his side, merely mumbled, which Gosling found disheartening.

After the service came the tea and cakes. Tea without milk for Les, with his dreadful allergies, and decorous refusal of offers of cake; meanwhile, Gosling's paper plate proudly sagged, indicative of his sweet tooth. 'Just a sliver,' he'd insist when the old ladies swarmed about him, proffering their wares but he'd amassed a dozen slivers, all of which he felt obliged to finish. Friendly competition between the ladies became intense as Gosling considered which cake he thought the best, the ladies watching his face after each bite he took and making a mental note of how often he made his 'mm' sound. After much deliberation, he announced the winner: 'I'm going for Mrs Gusset's lemon drizzle today, ladies.'

Les's flat was stark white with an ochre lino floor and wooden furniture that was unupholstered (due to his severe dust allergies, he explained), apart from the tautly made-up bed with its khaki counterpane, which Gosling stared at in wonder.

'Ah, you've observed my bed, Mr Gosling; it's no ordinary place of repose. I suppose you are familiar with the scourge that is the excrement of the domestic dust mite? The bane of all allergy sufferers? The mattress of this bed is filled with a unique gel originally designed by NASA. There's no cotton ticking, springs or foam – the squalid metropolis of the dust mite. The counterpane is actually a woven plastic, made by Heathercot's Silk Mill, for very hush-hush military purposes, but I have a Christian Science acquaintance on the inside who was able to procure me an offcut – at great risk to himself.'

'Oh, well done,' said Gosling, looking for an opportunity to leave as soon as possible – but at that moment he noticed something very familiar suspended by strings at the window: two carefully constructed Airfix models. 'Gosh, that takes me back. The Wild Weasel and the de Havilland Vampire, aren't they? You and I are of the same age, Les. We must have both shopped at that little model shop on Basket Parade on Saturday mornings.'

'Ships that pass in the night, Mr Gosling. Do you still have yours?'

'No, I told grandma to sling them once I went up to Cambridge.'

'That's a shame. We could have compared our handiwork.'

'You've put these together marvellously. Mine were a bit on the ham-fisted side.'

Les invited Gosling to sit while he went to make coffee. As Gosling wriggled to make himself comfortable on the Parker Knoll vinyl recliner, he jumped out of his skin when he caught a glimpse of a ghoulish woman standing stock-still, staring at him in the room off the sitting room.

'Good God, Les, who's that in there?'

Les entered with the coffee on a tray. 'Oh, you mean Juno, the Transparent Woman? I acquired her from a science museum that had gone under in East Germany. Brought her back sitting next to me on the overnight coach.'

Gosling went over for a closer look. Juno was a life-size model of a woman encompassed in a transparent layer of plastic skin, beneath which the skeleton, organs, veins and capillaries were all precisely mapped out. Gosling noticed that she even had properly articulated joints, which must have greatly facilitated their bus journey from Germany. 'You should bring her up to school, Les, to show the boys.' She stood in the corner of what seemed to be a sparsely furnished spare room, where anyone staying overnight would have a rude awakening in the morning – though Les never had any guests.

'She is a beauty, isn't she?' Les looked into her face and smiled. 'I've dabbled with members of the opposite sex in the past, Mr Gosling, but they just don't agree with me. I went out with a girl in the brass band for a few months when I was sixteen. A cornet player, like myself, so it should have been a match made in heaven. I don't know what it was about her but whenever she wanted to have a bit of a kiss, I soon developed a terrible red ring around my mouth. I started looking like a clown. I could understand why they were all laughing at me. The same thing happened when we swapped cornets by accident. She ended up with one of the trombone players and my face eventually went back to normal again.'

'Well, it looks like you've found the right woman now,' Gosling jested, but Les nodded back in earnest.

'Do you think I should buy her a dress so she doesn't shock visitors?' he asked.

'Well, maybe you should discuss that with her, Les.'

Following coffee, Gosling walked home along the path alongside the River Tidd. He passed by his old school, Travistock Grammar, a fine 17th-century edifice now converted into smart riverside apartments with granite worktops. He paused for a while, remembering his wonderful time there and mourning the fact it was no longer a school. The modernistic comprehensive, which had been built after Gosling's and Les's school days in the late 1970s, styled itself as a business school, with the children arriving in black suits every morning, like a hoard of undersized undertakers. Gosling shuddered. They even had to bring their books to school in black briefcases.

Les's secondary modern had been bulldozed just after the comprehensive was completed. Gosling had gone along to watch its razing. The flimsy buildings had folded like cardboard as soon as the bulldozer nudged them. The grammar school building had been made of sterner stuff so it was snapped up, as all such buildings seemed to be, by Noctifer, the local property developers. He looked up to the room on the corner of the second floor which had been the biology lab; now he saw it was someone's kitchen, with fancy copperware of all shapes and sizes hanging from the ceiling.

Gosling returned to his eager terrier and had a few hours on the sofa watching nature programmes, digesting the samples of cake, before preparing dinner. All in all, he felt he'd done a good deed, which Les had attempted to reciprocate by suggesting Gosling sit in on one of his Christian Science meetings sometime.

In the evening, Gosling thought he'd do a spot of baking, with Huxley sitting at his feet, waiting for offcuts. Gosling's pastry had a reputation that preceded him – it was even better than that of the ladies at the church, with their decades of experience, and he nearly always won first prize at the annual agricultural fair for his lemon meringue pie, beating down the battalions of WI entries. Today he'd bake an apple pie to take into work tomorrow, which he did on most Sundays, to the delight of Japes and Swainson. Les, who'd always refused a slice of his other cakes, surely couldn't be allergic to apple pie, not with him always snacking on Golden Delicious apples.

Gosling loved the feeling of rubbing the fat into the flour. He relished folding in the splash of icy water to form the pastry, dusting the marble slab with flour and rolling it into a perfect round, then scooping it up and fitting it to his grandmother's pie tin. He also enjoyed adding his individual touches: sprinkling the fruit with a spoonful of Bird's custard powder to thicken the juices, and a generous dash from the little bottle of his grandma's secret ingredient, Angostura Bitters, before crowning it with the pastry top that he would make perfectly fluted around the edges and brush with a deep-yellow egg yolk. From start to finish, just 20 minutes, then into the oven.

The next day, Gosling ambled into the science prep room with his apple pie to encounter a tense scene.

'Christian Science?' Japes was scoffing, 'It's an oxymoron! You think you can pray your allergies away with that mumbo jumbo? You're a chemistry graduate, for God's sake!'

'Now, now, Japes,' Swainson tutted from his chair by the window. 'Each to their own.'

'I suppose you think your allergies are some sort of bewitchment – "malicious animal magnetism", "malevolent mesmerism" or any number of other superstitious tongue twisters!' Japes was flinging his arms about by now, static-charged wisps of hair standing on end atop his thinning pate.

'Mr Japes, I've tried what medicine had to offer and it didn't help, which is why I turned to prayer,' Les pleaded.

'Are you sure you really have all these allergies, Les?' Swainson asked kindly. 'When did you last get them tested?'

'Not since I was a boy, Mr Swainson. Doctors terrify me. They bring me out in a...'

'A rash! Oh good Lord!' Japes spluttered.

It just so happened that, at the back of his filing cabinet, Gosling had an allergy testing kit, and following some gentle persuasion from Swainson and some not-so-gentle persuasion from Japes – who pinned him to the chair – within 10 minutes Gosling had placed 10 adhesive patches down Les's stick-like forearms.

'Nothing. Absolutely nothing,' Gosling announced cheerily as he peeled each patch up.

Les was thunderstruck. 'Oh, I cannot believe that, Mr Gosling. You mean, not one of my allergies is showing up? Not even the virulent one against mouse dander?'

Swainson patted him on the back and left in his academic gown to teach his A-level chemistry class.

'No reaction whatsoever – see for yourself: no angry swelling, not even a tender blush,' Gosling beamed.

'This test never lies, Les,' Japes declared. 'Why don't we all celebrate with a slice of Gosling's fine pie?'

'This is no ordinary apple pie, Les; it contains a hearty splash of my grandmother's secret ingredient, Angostura Bitters, to bring out the flavours. You eat apples, don't you?' Gosling coaxed.

Les politely declined, gently rubbing his forearms. 'Thank you, Mr Gosling, but I can't accept a slice. I don't really know what Agnostic Bitters are and I don't know what they contain.'

'Tell you what I'll do just for you tomorrow, Les. I'll make a totally plain apple pie, nothing but apples, which you'll be able to eat with no adverse reactions,' Gosling said warmly.

Les nodded, mustered a smile and followed after Swainson with a box of chemicals, looking decidedly disheartened after his negative testing.

Gosling served the fine pie to Japes and himself and they ate in silence, appreciating the sheer pastry perfection. Just before Japes had finished his last morsel, he jumped to his feet, closed the door and spoke in hushed tones.

'Here's an idea, Gosling – how about you bring in an apple pie tomorrow with a smidgen of nut dust in the filling and we'll observe his reaction. The fellow's clearly not allergic, the test confirms that. After he's eaten it, you can tell him you put it in by accident and he can eat nuts with gay abandon thereafter. He's got himself into such a tizzy with food, he's wasting away. He'll have to have his brown suits nicked in, next thing. In fact, we could be really scientific about this and make him a mini-pie each day this week and each time sprinkle in a different one of his so-called allergens.'

'So…' mused Gosling as he licked his finger and turned the page of his scientific notebook and started to write. 'Ground almonds tomorrow, cream of tartar on Wednesday, the slightest hint of lemon on Thursday, and rounding off the week with a wee dram of the Angostura Bitters.'

'Excellent. But best not tell Swainson,' Japes warned. 'Too sensible for his own good; spoils any kind of fun.'

The results were heartening from the onset: no reaction whatsoever, with every contaminated apple pie sallying through Les's digestive system with flying colours. At the end of the week, after school, Gosling and Japes would unveil the ruse and, hopefully, convince the man in the brown suit of the unfoundedness of his self-proclaimed maladies.

On Friday, Gosling went down to the Blindefellows dining room for fish pie followed by rhubarb crumble, leaving Les in the science prep room eating the baked potato wrapped in foil that he brought to work every day in the pocket of his brown suit. When Gosling returned, using the lift – as he often did when he'd eaten a little too much – a gurgling noise was coming from the prep room accompanied by Japes shouting, 'Pull yourself together, man!' Gosling stepped in and immediately saw how badly Japes's jape had gone. Les was slithering off a wheeled office chair as Japes repeatedly righted him and fanned him with a textbook.

'Should I fetch Matron Ridgeway?' Gosling asked, aghast.

'I think it's gone beyond that, Gosling. I've loosened his tie and called the ambulance.' Japes dropped the textbook and heaved Les back up into a sitting position.

Les's face had taken on a blueish hue and his eyes were rolling up into his head. Trying to remain clear-headed, Gosling had an idea. 'Let's take him down so we can get him into the ambulance as soon as it arrives. We can simply wheel him into the lift *in* the chair.'

'Yes, and use the side door to avoid a scene, with paramedics charging in through reception,' Japes added. 'Best try to keep mum about all this.'

They started manoeuvring the chair out of the prep room but Les kept slithering down towards the floor.

'There's only one thing for it, Gosling – get the packaging tape.' Japes sounded quite military now and Gosling jumped to attention, fumbling around the rather disorderly desks for a roll of the tape while Japes kept Les upright, bracing his knee against Les's chest. When he finally came across the tape, he passed it to Japes. Then Japes couldn't find the end, and beads of perspiration formed on his nose which sent his glasses sliding to the floor.

'You do it, Gosling,' he said, passing the tape back.

Gosling fiddled for a moment, his hands starting to tremble. When he finally peeled up the end, he returned the roll to Japes.

'Now, Gosling, lift up his arms and we'll tape him to the back-rest,' Japes said loudly over Les's shallow yet rasping breathing.

Gosling did as he was told, leaning slightly so his protuberant belly wouldn't be an obstruction as Japes wound the tape around and around. Japes jiggled the chair to test his handiwork and Les held firm. He didn't bother to cut the tape but simply left the roll hanging.

=

They bounced Les down the steps of the school's side entrance and onto the street outside, Japes and Gosling trying to maintain a nonchalant demeanour, with Japes even waving at someone as he went past in his car.

'Friend of yours?' asked Gosling.

'Yes, it's Spanky, from the Frog and Onion,' Japes replied.

'Retired head of the old secondary modern. Gives me tips on the horses. Big fan of corporal punishment in his time.'

Surreptitiously, Gosling felt the pulse on Les's neck. 'He's fading, Japes.'

At that timely moment, the ambulance appeared. Japes and Gosling both put up their arms as if hailing a bus. Two men in bottle-green suits ran out, loaded Les into the back, chair and all, and sped off without saying a word to them, giving no reaction whatsoever to their packaging tape handiwork, as if it were a common practice.

'I'm sorry, Gosling, it seems my plan backfired a bit,' Japes admitted after a silence. 'I can tell I've given you a terrible fright.'

Gosling shivered. 'If he pulls through, Japes, we can't tell him what we did; he could have us through the courts. And Swainson mustn't get wind of it either.'

'So, it was the Angostura Bitters that did for him in the end,' Japes said, shaking his head in disbelief. 'What the hell is in that tipple that he'd be allergic to anyway?'

'One of Trinidad's best-kept secrets, Japes. Only a couple of people hold the formula, locked within their heads. His particular malady must remain forever cloaked in mystery.'

'I suppose we can't tell him about the *other* days on which all his unfounded phobias were poo-pooed? I suppose he will have to live in fear of food for the rest of his life,' Japes concluded. 'It's a tragedy.'

'Well, it would be for us, but I rather think it makes him happy – provides a purpose and direction to his life,' Gosling said, but they resolved there and then to tinker no further with Les's idiosyncrasies – should they ever see him again.

But Les did return to Blindefellows, one week later, and Japes and Gosling breathed a guilt-laden sigh of relief. He proudly lifted the bandage on his throat to reveal the sutured red wound of a tracheotomy.

'I was entering the final stages of anaphylactic shock; they got to me in the nick of time,' Les beamed. 'I'll be eternally grateful for your quick thinking, Messers Japes and Gosling; especially you, Mr Japes, with the deployment of that packaging tape; truly the mind of the veteran British officer, always level-headed under fire.'

6

Toby and The Tree People

Trinity and Long Break 1989

Providing the weather was mild, on Sunday afternoons Gosling would walk the two miles over to Monks' Wood with his West Highland Terrier, Huxley. As they rounded the brow of the hill, Huxley made a beeline for his favourite watering spot, the 'Majestic Chestnut', as Gosling's grandmother had called it – 200 years old at least, with a trunk in excess of 2 metres in circumference, set at the entrance of what was more of a copse than a wood.

His grandmother had first brought Gosling here as a boy, and it had been one of the places he had most wanted to trot over to visit when he came home from university. These days, he took his pupils on a twice-annual trip there to collect data on the plethora of flora and fauna concentrated into just under two hectares, followed by a picnic lunch. All around the Majestic Chestnut were its offspring, fine trees in their own right, along with a dozen or so fine, healthy beeches and a few patches of scrub oaks where wrens hopped about. Gosling stepped under the canopy of the wood and the sound of the road over the hill was instantly muffled, a dewy moisture filling the air. The path through the wood, a parting through wolfsbane, foxglove and blue-bell – a toxic triumvirate – was beautiful at this time of year, in its haze of budding blueness.

Gosling heard Huxley growling, and he expected to see a squirrel, but the terrier was fixated upon a notice nailed to the trunk of the Majestic Chestnut at the approximate eye-level of a small child. Frowning that anyone could have had the audacity to knock a nail into the ancient tree, Gosling strode through the undergrowth to assess the damage. As he approached, he saw what it was, and gasped – a council notification informing the public of the imminent felling of 'the area known as Monks' Wood', clearing the land to make way for a new shopping centre. Gosling's head swam and he leaned on the old chestnut for support. If it hadn't been for Huxley's growling, he'd never even have seen it. The date for felling was down as 22 July, just over a month away. *Well, they've kept this very hush–hush!* he thought. Not a peep about it in the local rag, *The Travistock Times*, which he read from cover to cover every week. He hastily started back for home, already planning what had to be done to prevent this outrage.

After school the following day, Gosling, accompanied by Japes, walked down the hill to the town hall on the market square, and after a ponderous 10 minutes the clerk located the file and handed it to them.

'Documentation relating to Monk's Wood has been lodged for twenty-seven days and notice of land clearance was posted three-and-a-half weeks ago,' he told them before they asked.

'Yes, posted at crotch height on a single tree trunk in the middle of a wood and discovered by chance by a West Highland Terrier,' Japes quipped. 'All very underhand, if you ask me!'

'The council has followed all the correct procedures, sir,' the clerk called over his shoulder as he closed the filing cabinet drawer and busied himself with untangling elastic bands at his desk.

'As I suspected, it's another brainchild of Douglas Merryjohn's,' Gosling said, tapping the signature at the foot of the paper. 'We wish to appeal.'

The clerk rolled his eyes and found Gosling and Japes a pink form which they filled in there and then. A week later, the curt rejection ambiguously citing the Highways Act, the new White Paper *Highways for Prosperity* and the county council's *Development for Devon* plan, landed on Gosling's doormat. Profoundly upset, he went into overdrive. He canvassed his MP, gave an interview to Mary Creighton, a reporter at *The Travistock Times*, started a petition and got himself booked for a slot on the local radio talk show, *Travis-tock-2-Day* with DJ Steve Appleby…

'We've got Toby Gosling with us today, listeners, biology master at Blindefellows School, who's more than a bit disgruntled about something nasty lurking in the woods that his terrier just so happened to chance upon,' Steve melodiously crooned into the microphone.

'Yes, thank you, Steve. It's about the permission the council has granted to local business magnate Douglas Merryjohn to bulldoze Monks' Wood in order to make way for a new shopping centre to be constructed by his company, Noctifer Development. Monks' Wood is an ancient copse spanning four acres which contains a majestic chestnut tree that's over two hundred years old. It's also an educational resource that has been used by Blindefellows for decades and is now visited by local primary schools too. Last but not least, it is on common land owned by the people of Travistock.'

'So how is it, Toby, that Noctifer can build on it then?'

'Unfortunately, a council has the right to decide what to do with common land in line with what they determine to be the interest of the people. Sadly, this is the last remaining patch of common land within the town limits. They've built on everything else so they claim there's no alternative, although there are ample larger shopping facilities within half an hour's drive of Travistock that are already responsible for the closure of many of the smaller shops in town. Hopefully we, as a community, can put pressure on the council to make them change their minds. I'll be in town every Saturday afternoon, standing outside the supermarket, with my petition, which should acquire enough signatures to demonstrate the townsfolk's preference for this precious patch of woodland over a shopping centre.'

'But are you sure about that, Toby? In my experience, most people would be more inclined to go on a trip to a shopping centre than take a ramble in the woods, beautiful though I'm sure they are. Anyway, let's have a phone-in about that, and Toby here can answer your questions. In the meantime, here's Amii Stewart with 'Knock on

Wood', which Toby is hoping the developers won't be doing with their bulldozers next month…'

Gosling had no idea there was going to be a phone-in and was taken aback; he was also alarmed as this was his lunch break and he'd thought he'd be returning to school in time for class.

'But Steve, I have to go back to school,' he said over the Seventies disco beat. But Steve couldn't take back what he'd said on air.

Gosling nipped out of the studio into the office next door to call the science prep room so he could warn Les he'd be late, and to get him to start the Fourth Form off on their SAVE MONKS' WOOD posters.

Les set up the radio in the biology lab so the pupils could hear Mr Gosling live on air while they made their posters. By the fifth caller, Les had decided to turn the radio off. The callers had been less than sympathetic towards Toby and his cause, the gist of their claims being he was a toff who didn't care about the jobs the shopping centre would generate, or the convenience of having it on their doorstep, and that he was stuck-up with a posh accent and had no idea about the real world.

However, there were a couple of day boys, Ferguson and Tindall, in the class, and they were worried by what they had heard, rendering them barely able to focus on their drawings of the vulnerable copse, or to come up with effective slogans. Unlike the other boys present, they had a vested interest in the area and, like their biology master, had been visiting Monks' Wood as long as they could remember, as had their parents and grandparents. The two boys had become carried away by their felt-pen depictions of the developers, whom they armed with axes and scribbled with untidy beards. On Gosling's return to school, they noticed how pale and shell-shocked he looked, following the onslaught. Les ushered him into the prep room for a sit-down.

'Don't lose heart, Mr Gosling,' Les said as he handed him a cup of tea.

'But there's only a week before the felling and the petition isn't worth much because it's mainly been signed by the old ladies from St Peter's.'

'You've put up a valiant fight and done everything you could,' Les sighed, patting him on the shoulder. 'The summer holidays start in a couple of days and you need to sit back and relax with your feet up.'

'I haven't been beaten yet, Les,' said Gosling, shaking his head resolutely. 'I have one piece of ammunition left in my cannon, but I'm going to need your help.'

A week later, on the eve of the felling, Gosling, Les and Huxley drove up to Monks' Wood in Les's Java green Mini Clubman. On the roof, Les had tied a ladder and a bundle of planks. For the rest of the day they constructed a platform about 20 feet up in the branches of the Majestic Chestnut, to which they attached a frame draped with a tarp. When the structure was complete, a camping mat, a sleeping bag and a holdall of bits and bobs was carried up. They stretched a banner from the Majestic Chestnut across to a slightly less majestic chestnut, with SAVE MONKS' WOOD painted across it. Finally, a rope ladder 'borrowed' from the Blindefellows gym, which Gosling could hoist up to stop unwanted policemen trying to encroach on his picket, was tied to the branch of the mighty tree. Les found it hard to watch Gosling trying out his descent, as he was on the tubby side and characterised by a distinct lack of nimbleness; Huxley yapped this way and that as the ladder swung like a pendulum.

'Are you sure you want to sleep up here tonight?' Les asked, gnawing an apple and nervously tapping the damp leaves off his shoes.

'We must never underestimate the sneaky ways of Douglas Merryjohn, Les. Tomorrow is the twenty-second of July, the felling day. It wouldn't surprise me if his crew turns up at one minute past midnight tonight. In the meantime, you've done more than enough for the cause today. Take Huxley home' – Gosling threw Les the lead – 'and thank you so much for seeing to him.'

'Don't you worry about him,' Les said, taking the terrier's lead. 'His dander may make me sniffle but he'll get three walks a day while you're here. I'll drive over with him every lunchtime so he can see you – and I can bring you a Cornish pasty.'

Gosling watched them drive off and, as dusk gathered, felt truly at peace in his little wilderness. He clambered his way up the rope ladder for his first night in the Majestic Chestnut. Building the tree house must have taken it out of him because the next morning the sun was already high in the sky when he was woken by the sound of vehicles driving up the track to Monks' Wood. The bulldozers had arrived, joined, right on cue, by Mary Creighton from *The Travistock Times* along with a photographer.

'Good morning, gentlemen,' Gosling called down from the tree, providing a front-page photo-op and half an hour of head-scratching before the drivers returned to their vehicles and drove off. He then came down and shared a flask of coffee with Mary and the photographer while she interviewed him about his first night in the wood.

The day after he hit the front page, Gosling was deluged by visitors. He had stirred up an interest in the wood and he was pointed out to children as 'The Tree Man'. With no developers about, Gosling came down from his tree and led groups on woodland walks, adding over a hundred names to his petition. Ferguson and Tindall appeared in their hiking attire with offers to assist Gosling on the guided walks every morning and to run errands. At around 1pm, Mrs Gusset and Mrs Belcher from St Peter's Church arrived with a roast dinner kept warm in an insulated bag and a slice of treacle tart with cream. Thirty minutes later Les and Huxley appeared with a warm pasty, which Gosling politely managed to find a little space for.

'We're going to organise ourselves into shifts, Toby, and bring you something every day – because you'll need a hot dinner living out here,' Mrs Gusset told him, and although his hopes of losing a few pounds in the great outdoors fell by the wayside, he was secretly rather pleased.

It wasn't the developers who woke him the next morning; it was the national press setting up cameras, white screens and spotlights. Mary Creighton was there too, rubbing notepads with them all. Gosling quickly brushed his teeth and combed back his fair hair. He gave an interview from his platform, glowing in the artificial light.

The bulldozers returned, this time with Douglas Merryjohn bringing up the rear in his glossy burgundy Jaguar. They parked at a safe distance and surveyed the scene. Over his pale-grey suit Merryjohn wore a new Barbour jacket– the pristine kind that has never seen the outdoors, in the same way his pallid white skin had barely seen the sun. His full head of dyed black hair grew upwards, giving him the appearance of a pot of cress or, at the other end of the spectrum, Stalin. Looking at his gesticulations, Gosling fancied he was saying something containing expletives to his driver. He stomped towards the tree in his unblemished green wellingtons then, at around about the half-way point, suddenly assumed a jovial gait. At the foot of Gosling's tree, he raised a megaphone to his smiling lips, unnecessary considering the proximity but he enjoyed being heard by all.

'Good morning, Master Gosling, and how are you today?' he called up.

'Ah, Mr Merryjohn, how nice of you to drop by,' Gosling called back. 'Have you met my friends from the press? They've christened me Toby the Tree Man, and, apparently, I speak for the trees!'

'You've made yourself a cosy little tree house up there, haven't you, young man?'

'Yes, it's very comfortable indeed. I could stay here indefinitely.'

'Ah, but Master Gosling, I have in my hand a copy of Mrs Thatcher's white paper *Highways for Prosperity*, and this particular development has even been praised by the Prime Minister herself. Her letter to me is in today's *Times* – the Travistock one, I mean. These trees are due to be felled "By Order of Travistock Council".'

'But, Mr Merryjohn, you can't possibly do that while I'm inhabiting one.'

'True, true, but we can cut down all the trees you're NOT inhabiting, which we intend to do later this week as soon as the press have moved onto a more interesting story. Come, Mr Gosling, it's what the people of Travistock want. I heard your phone-in on the radio. Not everyone's a nature boy like you, you know. Tell you what, I'll have my lads make a lovely wardrobe for you out of that big tree you're in and you can climb on top of it whenever you want to play silly buggers.'

'Well, Mr Merryjohn, it's been lovely chatting but I have to get back to saving the environment.'

'What you're doing, Gosling, is an act of civil disobedience and against the law. You are acting like an overgrown schoolboy.' Merryjohn's smile had given way to an ugly leer. 'I'll be back on Friday with reinforcements if you haven't seen sense by then.' He strode back to his Jaguar, and he and his entourage drove away.

Gosling's heart sank. How could he get more people to live among the branches by the end of the week? The only people who had time on their hands were his faithful followers Ferguson and Tindall, but they were too young to be involved in a protest, and he couldn't ask the old ladies from the church to climb up and down rope ladders and sleep in trees like Barbary apes. Although it was the start of Long Break, Les would never agree to this, with his allergies to pollen and damp leaves. Japes had undergone an operation on his creaky knee that had, to his dismay, grounded him for the summer, and Swainson? Never! It wasn't what a deputy head did, at least not at a private school.

Two days later and no one had yet responded to his plea for fellow tree-sitters – no one, that is, until a decrepit converted double-decker bus drove up with the words 'Mother Nature's Warriors' painted along its sides in letters intertwined among badly painted trees and vines, with hints of some other letters, including a 'Z' underneath that Gosling couldn't quite make out. The antiquated bus laboured up the track in a trail of black smoke. Gosling slowly descended the rope ladder with a strong feeling that this was something more than a group wanting a woodland walk. Behind the bus, a TV crew's van followed, having been tipped off about this new development in the Monks' Wood story.

The bus came to a stop and around a dozen exceedingly unkempt people clambered out carrying ropes, planks and toolboxes. A buxom but bra-less woman with a vast mass of dark curly hair, partially constrained by a red knitted beret, appeared to be in charge. As soon as she spotted Gosling she briskly walked over to him.

'Hail Gaia, Earth-Mother, Toby!' she intoned, giving a sort of circular salute as if she were washing a window. 'We have come to be tree-sitters with you. We saw you on the news and journeyed here from far-off Essex to join you in your fight against fascism. We just finished a stint with the Anti-Nazi League in Berlin and were at a loose end regarding what to do next.'

So, that explained the 'Z': they obviously rather hurriedly repainted their bus according to the protest they were joining. 'I didn't know there was any trouble with Nazis in Berlin of late,' said Gosling sympathetically. 'I'm very sorry to hear it.'

'There wasn't; we were misinformed. Our stint in Berlin was short. We mainly just hung around,' she replied.

She told Gosling her name was Mel and that she and her band lived their lives going from protest to protest, their lifestyle funded by the state and generally directed against it. He watched as Mother Nature's Warriors erected 'twigloos' up in the branches. They seemed wobblier than Gosling's tree-house but would serve the purpose when they faced down Merryjohn's bulldozers.

Vee, Mel's deputy, was a tiny wiry woman with crew-cut orange hair, in a black vest-top and faded, baggy dungarees with a tool belt. She appeared to be very handy with a hatchet, and the twigloos went up at a rate of knots.

Watching the national news that night, Japes was pleased to see another interview with Gosling out in the woods, giving detailed and highly articulate responses. The viewer was then distracted, however, by a dishevelled-looking man sheepishly wandering into the rear of the shot, relieving himself against a tree and giving himself a good shake. Japes, not normally a man easily surprised, wiped his glasses in astonishment. Then, at Gosling's side, a woman in a red beret materialised and ambushed the interview.

'What the hell's going on down there?' Japes muttered to himself as he sipped his gin and tonic.

Accustomed to hogging the limelight, Mel, the red-bereted woman, spoke.

'Monks' Wood is a wildlife corridor, an abundant foraging ground, a bird-rich woodland, a paradise.' She talked right into the camera, her face filling the entire television screen, as if she were trying to ooze into Japes's living room. 'We have a question for the Trivetstock Council—'

'It's Travistock,' Gosling interjected politely.

'Sorry, Travetstock Council. Have you conducted an Environmental Impact Assessment on this land and can we see it, please? Mr Merryjohn is a renegade against Mother Nature and we will not budge from our twigloos in the face of his chainsaws. Furthermore, we are convinced that Monks' Wood has grown up on the site of an ancient monastery, which means there are almost certainly monks' graves here that cannot, by any means, be desecrated. What's more, we have seen evidence that this is a fledgling site for the basically extinct Desmoulin's Whorl Snail.'

Gosling looked at her in speechless amazement as the camera panned onto his face for his response. He knew nothing about ancient monasteries or fledgling snails, and was convinced Mel didn't either. Were these flights of fancy going to sabotage his credibility and the campaign? Japes could read what he was thinking in the shot of his dumbfounded expression and immediately telephoned Sedgewick to get him to research the beret-woman's claims.

Now that Fairchild had retired, Debbie Pilbeam, wife of the head of Modern Languages, sat at the library desk each morning in term time, reading *The Lady*. Sedgewick had immediately struck up a friendship with her and she'd given him a spare key to the Lambton Archive that she'd had cut for his private use. The very idea of Sedgewick having this key would have sent Fairchild raving as, according to him, the manuscripts in the archive were 'crumbling and susceptible to fouling by human breath', a fact he related to Sedgewick in a whispering, hissing angry-librarian sort of voice – itself reeking with the odour of stale coffee and crumpets – even if they were the only two people in the library.

Since Debbie had taken over, Sedgewick had spent many an absorbing evening sitting at the bench table in the archive room, just as he did now, cardboard boxes open, contents strewn around, enjoying a mug of tea and half a packet of ginger biscuits. He couldn't recall ever having seen anything alluding to the alleged monastery Japes had asked him about, and poring over old maps and land records from the time of Blindefellows' founder, Hezekiah Lambton, magnifying glass in hand, there was no sign of a monastery anywhere. There were numerous other delightful documents, however, pertaining to the sale of so many bales of wool to such-and-such a merchant from Flanders, purchase deeds for parcels of land, lists of wages paid to shepherds and shearers, even an archaic sort of veterinary report listing 'a surfeit of wolfsbane' as being the probable cause of the sudden death of 20 sheep and the resulting hiring of men – list of names attached – in an attempt to staunch the pestiferous weed. Lambton really was a man for keeping every bit of paper that was ever given to him, most likely because, having been born a humble shepherd and raised a shearer, he couldn't read well enough to determine what to throw out. And here was the record of his marriage to Dorcas Ramsay, youngest daughter of money-lender, alderman, and eventual lord mayor, Phineas Ramsay, who'd come to own most of Travistock during the reign of Henry VIII. Lambton, having managed to work his way up to being a minor wool merchant, had found himself miraculously elevated to the Elizabethan grand-bourgeoisie when smallpox carried off most of his wife's family. Sedgewick drove home in his new Atlantis Blue Vauxhall Cavalier and telephoned Japes to confirm the absence of any evidence of a monastery.

At the first crack of dawn, Gosling and Mother Nature's Warriors, whom he had begun to call 'the tree people' for practicality's sake, were braced in readiness for the bulldozers, sitting in the trees. The press had returned in force; the reporters and cameramen staying in The Unicorn Inn on the market square had got up early to catch their story. But no developers came. Perhaps they felt they had to tread with more care now the number of protesters had increased. At lunchtime, the old ladies from Gosling's Church turned up, seven of them this time. They'd seen the new recruits arrive on the news and were setting up trestle tables with camping stoves to warm up a delightful lunch of chicken and mushroom casserole accompanied by roasted vegetables with rosemary, topped off with a topical fruits-of-the forest crumble with custard. The old ladies waved the press over and started handing out platefuls of homemade food.

'I don't know what to say, ladies,' Gosling said as he was given his lunch, 'I'm absolutely flabbergasted at your generosity and care.'

'Well, Toby, when you lost your grandmother, our dearest Elsie, you gained a whole churchful of grandmothers.' And Mrs Mungo gave him a hug, providing a touching photo-op for the newspaper reporters.

'More like guardian angels, I think,' Gosling proclaimed.

Vee, speaking for the tree people, stepped forward. 'Ladies, this is a fantastic thing you've committed to, to come out into the woods every day to fuel our protest, but do you think you could provide vegan dishes? Most of Mother Nature's Warriors are vegan. Well, the women are.'

'Does chicken count?' asked Mrs Belcher, her dentures still not quite right.

'No, we don't want chicken; chicken is meat,' Vee explained.

'So no white meat?' Mrs Carrigan ascertained.

'No, no white meat or fish,' Vee continued, starting to show tinges of exasperation, 'The roast vegetable dish is fine, but put some nuts in it next time for protein, please.'

'And we can't eat your crumble as I can taste you've put butter in it,' chimed in Jenny, the youngest member of the group, who had dropped out of the final year of her law degree just a few months ago.

'But butter isn't meat, is it?' Mrs Carrigan consulted with the other old ladies who were screwing up their wrinkled brows, puzzling out these new-fangled notions.

'But it's *from* an animal.' Jenny smiled patronisingly. 'You can make vegan cakes for us. I'll write some recipes down for you.'

'Let's not give the ladies too much work to do, Jenny,' suggested Gosling, who hadn't been able to enjoy his meal with the turn the conversation had taken. 'After all, they are doing this out of their own pockets and in their own time.'

The next day, the old ladies had done their best to follow Jenny's recipes but the tree people complained that the vegan Battenberg was on the dry side.

'Maybe your recipe was wrong – again!' Mel rolled her eyes and Jenny uttered twittering apologies.

'Could I have a word, Toby?' Mrs Mungo beckoned him to the serving side of the trestle table where five old ladies stood.

Gosling approached, embarrassed. 'I'm so sorry about these dietary requirements, ladies. I know it must be extra work and—'

'No, it's not that, Toby, it's this,' and Mrs Mungo pointed to the ground, which was dotted with human excrement and shreds of toilet paper. 'It was quite difficult to know where to place the table this morning and it's none too hygienic.'

'Oh, good Lord!' Gosling shrank back, 'I told them to bury it.'

'And Toby, we're also a bit worried about you starting to look rather scruffy out here in the woods.' Mrs Gusset brushed him down with her surprisingly strong hands. 'You need to keep up appearances for the cameras and remember Elsie – she never allowed you outside without ironing even your undergarments.'

What she said was true. His hair was starting to tangle and he was developing a tide line on his neck despite his daily washing attempts with a sponge at the little stream in the next field. He looked across at Mother Nature's Warriors, wolfing down the vegan fare the old ladies had graciously handed to them. The four men among them were particularly grimy. Pete, the most untouchable, his hair matted into untended dreadlocks, liked to smoke strange-smelling roll-ups incorporating lichen. He spent much of his time sitting on a fallen tree trunk looking depressed and being told off by Mel for not pulling his weight, which was bordering on the obese. Simon, Terry and Graham were a shade cleaner and appeared to serve as floating partners to the lady warriors.

'I have to see this thing out, Mrs Mungo, now that I've started it,' Gosling sighed. 'I know they're not my kind of people but they are deterring the developers for now.'

While Les was visiting that afternoon with Huxley, a new recruit appeared out of the blue. It was as if the mist parted and she was suddenly there, gliding towards them, an elfin slip of a girl, 19 at the most, with sharp green eyes and dimples in her cheeks. She was almost entirely decked out in mossy-hued amateur crocheting. her auburn hair was tucked into another crocheted creation in the shape of an unravelling rose bud on top of her head, and she carried a little basket. She introduced herself to Gosling, who was sitting with Les on a ground sheet. She trilled, 'I am Acorn, the Mystic Wood Being.' Gosling and Les looked at each other as the tree people gathered around, curiously.

'I presume you're here to join us in tree-sitting?' Mel ventured, and Acorn nodded coyly and curtseyed, offering a most engaging demure smile. 'Where've you come from then?'

'Through the door in yonder oak!' she confided.

'No, you didn't,' Vee scolded. 'I just saw you from my tree. You got off the number eleven bus up the track.'

'Anyway, however you got here, it's always good to have an extra pair of hands,' Mel resolved. 'Come with me, I'll show you to your tree.'

And Gosling and Les watched as the tree people walked off with the spritely new member of their pack.

In the days that followed, the male tree people went out of their way to fawn upon Acorn, the Mystic Wood Being, much to the exasperation of the female tree people, who felt her feyness and frailty were a liability. The men held her hand as she descended her rope ladder, gave her extra blankets at night and brought her plates of vegan fare as she perched pixie-like upon a mossy stump. To thank them, she said she would organise a party for Lughnasadh, the pagan festival midway between the summer solstice and the autumn equinox, and she started gathering vines and sweetly asking the men if they could weave them into a web and hang them up for her to create a canopy over the withy-throne, interwoven with bluebells and monkshood, which she was constructing in the centre of the wood. When Gosling saw her, he was quick to scold her for handling the poisonous plants, and told her she was lucky she'd been wearing crocheted gloves, which he then sent her to the stream to wash. Graham was in the vicinity at the time and rushed over to do it for her, for which she rewarded him with a peck upon his grimy cheek. Gosling cringed. He found himself wishing the developers would make an appearance to bring the matter to a head so he could go home and get away from these people.

His wish was swiftly granted, for at four o'clock the following afternoon the bulldozers, accompanied by police vans and Merryjohn's Jaguar, arrived, and the onslaught began. They had waited until the national press had grown tired of hanging around. Only the stalwart Mary Creighton remained, along with a freelance cameraman who had stayed on at Mary's request and who turned out to be a godsend in what was about to be the greatest scoop of a career that had so far been rather pedestrian. She had a few moles hither and thither and had an inkling that today would be the day. In her youth, Mary had intended *The Travistock Times* to be the place to cut her teeth but, 10 years on and approaching 30, the stories of kittens in mittens, dogs in rivers and lollipop lady retirements had all gone on for far too long, and she thanked her lucky stars for Toby Gosling's protest.

The shocking news of the bulldozer's arrival was on national news that evening. Mrs Belcher saw it and ran round to her neighbour, Mrs Gusset, to tell her in high-pitched tones to turn on the television set. They saw specialist climbers brought in by Merryjohn, plucking the tree people from their trees and forcing them down their rope ladders with pointed sticks. 'No, no!' Mrs Belcher cried out. When they got to the ground, the protesters were mobbed by police. Vee, putting up a valiant fight despite her small stature, was dragged through the undergrowth, kicked and punched before being hurled, shrieking, into the police van. Mel was yanked by her tattered Warrior T-shirt and landed in a puddle. When she stood up, the shirt was ripped in half and she ran toward the camera. The two old ladies caught a glimpse of her muddied breasts and almost fainted clean away. When the climbers couldn't manage to pull Gosling out of his tree due to his clever use of a fire extinguisher (much to the delight of the old ladies, who leapt up clapping), the police tore down the banner he had rigged up and stamped it into the mud. Merryjohn himself also entered the fray, trying to stop the rolling of the camera with his square fists and wrangling with Mary Creighton, who had some training in ju-jitsu and swiftly felled him after he gave her a rough shove. Jenny was the last one to be pulled to the police van by her hair, torn-off clumps of which the cameraman captured trodden into the mud. The news feature had shown a few minutes of choice moments, but the actual fracas had gone on for nearly half an hour.

The female members of Mother Nature's Warriors had all been brought down, (apart from Sarah, a considerably larger lady whom the climbers had failed to dislodge), and would spend the next two nights in the cells in Travistock's police station. The men had been able to stand their elevated ground and remain in the trees. As the situation now stood, the trees that were still inhabited were strategically spread throughout the copse, preventing any felling that day due to concerns as to possible loss of human life.

Mrs Belcher and Mrs Gusset were so shaken by the episode that they took to their telephones to invite every church-going old lady in the region to congregate at Monks' Wood the next day from 5am. With the enthusiasm they received, they felt sure their numbers would rival those of the annual Devonshire Women's Institute Convention. They would stand their ground and pelt the developers with last year's fossilised Christmas cake if it came to that. Matron Ridgeway had the same idea as Mrs Belcher and Mrs Gusset and, after watching the news, she too rang around for support, gathering promises from 20 Blindefellows masters to assemble at Monks' Wood at dawn to stand guard alongside Gosling. A group of townsfolk, horrified at the violence, had already driven over with a reel of barbed wire that they were unrolling by torchlight.

When Douglas Merryjohn's entourage rolled up the next day, they were greeted by the return of the national press, half the faculty of Blindefellows, including a gaggle of day boys, Ferguson and Tindall among them, some outdoor types from the local comprehensive, scores of townsfolk and over 300 elderly ladies singing 'We Shall Overcome' with Matron Ridgeway conducting from the front. There was a 10-minute conversation, with the climbers and the police refusing point-blank to use force before returning to their vehicles and driving off, to cheers from the protestors. Pushing his driver to the side and getting behind the wheel himself, Merryjohn turned and sped off, tyres spinning, in a cloud of leaves.

The old ladies had prepared a massive breakfast for the multitude present, and following that there was a meeting chaired by Gosling on how to maintain the Monks' Wood picket, in which groups were established so there would be a continual presence for the next few weeks. Les went around with a clipboard to sign people up.

'Do you think he's going to need "tree leave" come September?' Bunny asked Japes.

'Very possibly, Bunny, unless Merryjohn backs down, but that's highly unlikely.'

As Sedgewick was negotiating a way round the barbed wire, Mrs Mungo called out to him, 'Oh, Mr Sedgewick, do avoid venturing into the undergrowth. It's not just the tree people's natural offerings, it's also the monkshood – very nasty, you know, even if you don't ingest it.'

'Monkshood?' Sedgewick froze to the spot, looking about him in the watery light of the burgeoning day.

'Yes; that pretty blue flower at your feet can kill a man just by handling it.' She stepped a little nearer to point it out. 'You may know it as aconite, wolfsbane, even mousebane. A bane to all animals!'

Sedgewick tiptoed gingerly around the plant as an idea germinated in his mind. As soon as he got into his Vauxhall Cavalier, he headed to the Lambton Archive.

Acorn had played a decidedly back-seat role in the ambush the day before. So back-seat, in fact, that as soon as she had heard the police sirens, she had fled to the far side of the wood and hidden under a blanket. Now that the mood was upbeat, she had announced that her Lughnasadh festivities would take place from dusk on the next day. Gosling graciously refused his invitation and stayed up in his tree, trying to concentrate on a biography of Thomas Henry Huxley. He was up to the part featuring his famed 1860 debate with Samuel Wilberforce on evolution.

To kick off the Lughnasadh festivities, the men were asked to choose a girl to be crowned Queen of the Copse. With the choice being between Acorn and the lumpish and impassive Sarah, the selection was made within a matter of seconds. As a consolation prize, Sarah was given the role of handmaiden, and was assigned the duty of ceremonially placing the crown upon Acorn's head. There, sitting on the throne, they saw the entirety of Acorn's rich auburn hair for the first time, tumbling in swathes over her bare shoulders. Wearing the crown of ivy and wild berries, she resembled some Pre-Raphaelite fantasy. From a communal bowl they ate 'the fare of the forest', including the fungi that Acorn had gathered, even though Gosling had warned her about it. Cross-legged upon her sylvan throne, Acorn incanted the pagan myths of Daphne pursued through the forest by Apollo, his pumping blood brimming with lust; of the Zoroastrian creation of the first man and the first woman from two halves of a tree cleaving together, bursting through the earth; and of the Dryads, the wood nymphs who lived together in trees with no need for clothes.

And so it followed that the next thing they did was to remove their clothes and hug the trees. Gosling perceived that some of these hugs erred far too much on the amorous side, and glanced away from the antics below in horror. Sarah, with slow reluctance, only got down as far as her underwear, to Gosling's relief. Thank goodness the press were back at The Unicorn for the night, probably knocking back a few ales with Mary Creighton, whom he could see was angling to make a few contacts on Fleet Street. He lay back and wished for the festivities taking place below to be over as soon as possible, but they only became louder, as if fertile howler monkeys were calling to prospective mates across the wood, scurrying about in a giant game of hide and seek.

Ten minutes later, peering over his platform, Gosling could see Acorn's fungi taking effect. The tree people's speech had become slurred and their movements tottery. The men fell in muddy puddles as they lunged after Acorn in the manner of Apollo and Daphne, making grabs for her as she slid out of their grasp with excited squeals. Sarah, however, sat on a tree trunk, gulping and heaving. Gosling recalled Jonathan Swift's debauched yahoos in *Gulliver's Travels* and quickly drew up his ladder.

When the women were released and returned to the woods at 9am the following morning, in something of a fed-up state, they walked through the scores of other protesters and into the copse with the intention of climbing up into their trees and purifying themselves with nature and light. In a clearing, they came upon a muddied heap of knotted human limbs. Next to it, in dirty underwear and staring blankly, sat Sarah, on the throne Acorn had built.

'Graham, is that you?' Jenny cried plaintively, peering down into the pile of people.

'Hey, you lot!' Vee prodded various bodies with the steel toecap of her boot and they began to stir.

'We've spent the last two nights in the lock-up and you've been having an orgy in the mud with her?' Mel screamed, and yanked one of Acorn's mud-encrusted locks. 'That's it! That's bloody it! We're going!'

And with that, the women gathered their belongings from the trees, threw a poncho over Sarah and walked her, barefoot, towards the bus.

Terry staggered to his feet, hiding his manhood behind a handful of mulch. 'Where are you going?' he called.

'To Greenham Common!' Mel called over her shoulder. 'We've been talking about it for the last couple of days and, guess what? There are no men allowed!'

The people who were now congregated at the entrance to the wood watched the women load Sarah into the bus and rev the engine. The men staggered after them, pleading with them to stay, largely due to the fact that most of their stuff was on the bus. They were standing naked in full view of the picket line but the bus lurched off, with Mel scowling in the driver's seat and the other women making rude gestures through the open windows. As the exhaust smoke settled, the men gradually shrank away as they became aware of the crowd regarding them with some amusement.

Acorn peered out from behind some bracken. One of Mrs Belcher's new recruits caught sight of her from behind the trestle table. 'Penelope? Is that you?' she called out aghast, and the girl fled, Dryad-like, into the trees.

'Penelope!' Les exclaimed, suddenly remembering. 'I knew I'd seen her somewhere before!'

'Not on the garibaldi line, was she?' Gosling joked.

'Hardly. But she is Penelope Watkins, heiress to Watkins Biscuits. I used to see her from time to time, doing her homework in her dad's office. She's off to university in a couple of months to study business. That's her gran over there. Her ma and pa wouldn't be pleased at all if they knew she was here cavorting in the undergrowth. She's had a very prim and proper upbringing: ballet, piano and all the trimmings.'

'Look, Les, this is no place for a naked young biscuit heiress,' Gosling told him. 'Why don't you tell her you've found her out, bundle her into your Mini Clubman, take her to your place for a wash then drop her back at her parents' manor house?' Twenty minutes later, the Clubman pulled out, with Penelope Watkins wrapped in a blanket and looking forlorn.

The burgundy Jaguar arrived at almost the same time. Merryjohn hoped this would be his final appearance. He had talked the police superintendent, who also happened to be a member of his Masonic lodge, into supplying most of the force on that day to cool the situation off with the use of water cannons, if necessary.

Merryjohn's self-important jaunt as he led the fifty-or-so police in body armour to the woods, followed by the bulldozers, was filmed by the news teams. He had his megaphone at the ready but before he could raise it to his lips, Bunny stepped forward out of the crowd, with his own megaphone aloft, and the television cameras panned over to him instead.

'Welcome back, officers of the law, developers, Mr Merryjohn. I'm Reverend Hareton, Headmaster of Blindefellows School. Before you get started with today's intended proceedings, I'd like to share with you a little discovery my colleague Mr Charles Sedgewick, here, has just made.'

Merryjohn rolled his eyes. 'Come on then, let's hear it. I'll give you two minutes and then we're moving in.'

'In 1670, through his marriage to Dorcas Ramsay, Hezekiah Lambton, founder of Blindefellows School, acquired vast tracts of land in and around Travistock. This land stayed within the family until its eventual extinction in the late eighteenth century, at which time most of the land was sold off to pay the debts of a once-proud dynasty long since fallen into decadence and decline—'

'Please, Reverend Hareton, spare us the history lesson!' Merryjohn gave an exasperated arm gesture but Bunny carried on regardless.

'There was one bit of land, however, unsuitable for any kind of farming – a vexing patch of woodland infested with a deadly plant, wolfsbane, also known as monkshood, which the efforts of generations of pre-industrial labourers could not quash. Hezekiah Lambton lost many fine sheep due to their wandering into this poisonous copse and he finally had it fenced off.'

Bunny paused for dramatic effect, as he often did during his occasional orations at Latin Prayer, and held up a folio ledger. 'You can see here in this book of land records of the area, Lambton has drawn a circle around it and written there in his distinctive block hand – for he came into his fortune only in adult life and was not a wholly literate man – 'Monkshood Wood', which is the name by which Travistock folk referred to this area in the Elizabethan era. As the centuries wore on, this became shortened to Monks' Wood. In his will, Hezekiah Lambton gifted these four ill-starred, if beautiful, acres to Blindefellows, the school he founded, with the notion that they be used for gathering firewood for the school. This was indeed the case for over two centuries, as records in our archives amply show, until the 1880s, when it became more expeditious to use coal, and the connection between this wood and our school was gradually forgotten.

'Lambton saw the place as only fit for firewood, but it has become more than that. It is an outdoor classroom our pupils love to visit whenever they are given the opportunity, as well as an island of tranquillity and beauty for those people of Travistock who have the wisdom to take the time to appreciate it – among them our biology master, Toby Gosling, who was first brought here as a boy by his grandmother. His initiative, although unorthodox, has bought enough time for Mr Sedgewick to figure out this connection and we thank you, Mr Gosling, for your bold and brave action. Monks' Wood is ours, Mr Merryjohn, to be shared in perpetuity with the people of Travistock; it shall not be erased.'

There was a stunned silence, followed by an applause that lifted the crows from the treetops. 'Victory! Victory!' Gosling shouted, tears rolling down his cheeks, and hugging Sedgewick, Japes, Bunny and virtually everyone else there. Bunny strode over to Merryjohn and the chief of police and presented them with the report he had compiled along with copies of the documents to be used as evidence.

'We dropped one of these off at the town hall last night,' he told them calmly, 'which I imagine they're just starting to read now. You may try taking it to court but the evidence is quite incontrovertible; you'd be wasting your money and your time.'

Merryjohn threw the report down, ground it into the mud with the heel of his shoe and stormed off. Bunny, Japes and Sedgewick, along with the school's lawyer, drove over to the town hall and straightened things out at the council, presenting all the original documents.

Gosling, the hero of the hour, went home to soak in the bath for a couple of hours. He had invited Les and the old ladies from St Peter's out for tea and cakes at the Four and Twenty Blackbirds. He was back to his former jolly self, in mustard slacks and a brightly coloured plaid shirt (albeit not in ironed underwear, these days), with his hair combed and a healthy ruddiness to his cheeks after his days in the sun and fresh air.

In the café there was much to talk about. Mrs Belcher and Mrs Gusset astonished him with the details of what had been shown on the television and he told them about the many peculiarities of the tree people, including the story of the mushroom-fuelled naked cavorting, diplomatically omitting the true identity of Acorn, the Mystic Wood Being. Gosling had noticed a few members of the press sitting in the Four and Twenty, and had nodded to them as he came in. Now they could see that that his food had gone down, one of them approached him.

'Mr Gosling, I wanted to tell you how much we enjoyed covering your story,' he said. 'I've had a call from my boss, David Fitzgerald, who produces wildlife and nature shows aimed at schoolchildren for ITV and Channel 4. He's very interested in having you present his new show. Here's his number, if you wouldn't mind giving him a ring as soon as you can manage. He's extremely eager to talk to you.'

'But Mr Gosling already has a job as biology master at Blindefellows,' Les declared on behalf of the speechless Toby. 'I'm his lab technician and best mate!' he added.

'Best mate?' queried Gosling. 'Well, surely, Les, that honour must go to Huxley…' He turned back to the television man. 'Thank you. I shall give Mr Fitzgerald a ring first thing tomorrow, though I couldn't possibly leave Blindefellows in the lurch.'

'Yes, David knows about that. He's hoping to work around your schedule, initially, filming during school holidays. Full-time can wait until next year but I'm sure you'll be a success, Mr Gosling – you're quite the household name nowadays.'

By the time Gosling's TV contract was signed, sealed and delivered in mid-August, a large notice had been erected by Travistock Council at the entry to Monks' Wood. It read, 'Property of Blindefellows School. Open to the public. Beware, poisonous plants!'

7

Cold Foot Farm

Trinity 1993

In the Oak Room at Blindefellows, the headmasters of the past, lining the upper section of the wood-panelled walls, rested their hands upon hefty tomes, imbuing all whom they surveyed with studious intent. The varying conventions of scholarly attire through the ages were on show, starting with bearded chins encompassed by frothy ruffs and black skullcaps and gradually evolving to the clean-shaven, navy-blue three-piece peak-lapel suit of the Reverend Beaulieu Hareton of the present day. What they all had in common was the intensity with which they stared down at the teachers, as if checking they were spending their recreation wisely. Crane, Head of Classics, was doing just this as he sat on one of the uncomfortable Regency-style dining chairs that had been placed in a rigid line directly opposite the fireplace, which nowadays had a gas-powered flame. He thumbed through Burton's *Anatomy of Melancholy*, occasionally nodding to himself over its supremely well-chosen Latin quotations. Two other teachers, however, one in early middle age and the other approaching 60 – Sedgewick and Japes – both unmoved by the painted hard stares, were using the long, highly polished conference table as a football pitch, with the requisite equipment of flat-bottomed stainless steel sugar basins, china tea things and screwed up wads of paper.

'A volley of attacking flair with a scissor kick from Japes United,' Japes commentated as he scored a goal between the teacup posts at the opposite end of the table. 'This fox in the box is out to dethrone the

Sedgewick Wanderers, who appear to have totally lost their centre of gravity. What's up, Sedgers? You're all sixes and sevens.'

'Sorry, Japes, I'm in the doldrums today.'

'Well, put some welly into it, man!'

Sedgewick took a deep breath and tried to pull out of the bag something worthy of his former table-football prowess. He spun the sugar basin into a looping header with such energy that the paper ball arced right off the table and plopped into Crane's cup of tea.

'An X-rated tackle!' Japes clapped his hands, beaming, and what was left of his hair stood up on the top of his head.

'To think you two call yourselves adults!' Crane snipped. 'What kind of role models are you for the boys?' He banged his cup and saucer onto the tea trolley and strode out of the room, gown sweeping after him.

Japes flicked another paper ball straight at the closing door (hitting it directly) then turned to Sedgewick. 'What's up, Sedgers? Anything I should know about?'

'Well, uh, I don't know if I should talk about it just yet.' Sedgewick fiddled anxiously with his rolled-up paper balls.

Japes drew two cups of tea from the urn on the trolley and invited Sedgewick to join him in front of the fireplace. He filled the silence with chit-chat until Sedgewick was ready to spill the beans. 'Nice of the bursar to splash out on the imitation Regencies, but not the most soothing balm to *la derrière*. I personally preferred the squashy old Chesterfields, even if they were bursting at the seams. These don't quite fit, don't you think? Makes the place look like a French bordello.'

Sedgewick stared into his teacup, miserably. 'I'm not quite sure how to tell you this, Japes.'

'Come on Sedgewick, you know you can tell me anything. We've known each other nearly twenty years now.'

Sedgewick couldn't hold it in any longer. He'd kept it to himself for nearly a week of sleepless nights. 'I... I really can't fathom why I did it. It was totally on impulse. I hardly know the gal. I don't even think I'm the marrying type.'

Japes's jaw dropped. 'To which *gal* precisely are you referring?'

'The temporary receptionist – you know, the one who's been bringing me eggs.'

'What, the one with the tam o'shanter of ginger hair?'

'Well, it's more red than ginger... isn't it?'

'You're going to *marry* her?'

'Well, you see, she came over to my place last Sunday. Cooked me a roast dinner with a fresh joint of beef from her family's farm. Her Yorkshire puddings are second to none. Positively pneumatic, even when doused in gravy. I don't know the slightest thing about cookery – you know me, with the ready meals and the pub lunches all the time. She really is a damned excellent cook – whips up her own custard with fresh egg yolks and cream; it's remarkable.'

'I'm flabbergasted! You mean you actually proposed to her on the strength of her Sunday dinners?'

'Well yes, I suppose I did, without exactly meaning to.'

'When you're married, Sedgewick, it won't be Sunday every day, you know.' Japes solemnly placed his cup and saucer on an occasional table. He took off his glasses and wiped them ponderously with his tie. 'You'll recall, Sedgewick, my golden rule, which I've mentioned to you on many an occasion: you don't have to wed 'em to bed 'em.'

Sedgewick was well-versed in this mantra, even if he had never put it into practice, and now he felt like the apprentice bachelor who'd let the master down somewhere in the middle of the roly-poly last Sunday. He now wanted to back-pedal but didn't know how. He had never really developed the knack of talking to women, other than to his mother and Matron Ridgeway – and, of course, there was the odd bit of schoolboy humour with the secretaries. It was only two years since Blindefellows had decided to open its doors to female teachers. The three or four ladies who now frequented the Oak Room tended to stay in their own little coven-like huddle in what was essentially an old boys' club.

Sedgewick didn't know the code of conduct for breaking things off. It had been easy with his short-lived university girlfriend, Phoebe, the only girlfriend he'd ever had and who, after a couple of weeks of bedroom flounderings, simply sent him 'to Coventry' and he took the hint. Japes had to admit that he'd no idea how to renege on a proposal, never having been stupid enough to put himself into that particular predicament in the first place.

'I suppose, Sedgewick, there's also the possibility, if the relationship were to become serious, that she might want a bairn with you. Have you given that any thought?'

Sedgewick hadn't, and shuddered in bewilderment. 'But isn't she past her prime for all that?'

'True. Therefore, you'll need to take precautions or you could find yourselves bringing forth the Exmoor Beast.'

That evening, as he drove home through town, Sedgewick caught sight of Yvonne, the lady in question, standing at a bus stop with a glazed expression amid the hubbub of rush-hour traffic. He had to admit, she'd behaved commendably since his inadvertent proposal, which she'd accepted almost before the words had left his mouth, which just happened to be full of roly-poly at the time. Sedgewick had only intended to ask her for 'More roly-poly please', but somehow 'more' and 'roly' had got mixed up in his mouth, and he'd said something like 'Morry', then something or other mumbled, followed by 'please', which she had taken as a proposal.

To her credit, she had continued to call him 'Mr Sedgewick' when he walked through reception in the morning and she hadn't pursued him through the corridors for further clarifications on his offer. The ball, he felt, was entirely in his court. He thought it wouldn't look too out of place if he casually offered her a lift home to her farm the following day. He might then ascertain how best to proceed – or rather, how not to proceed – with Princess Roly-Poly, as Japes had immediately taken to calling her – in honour, Sedgewick assumed, of her fine pudding.

On the day he planned to casually offer the lift, he dressed in the best he could muster that would serve as suitable country attire: a Harris Tweed houndstooth blazer in autumnal hues, Lincoln-green three-quarter-length cords, beige knee-socks and some brogue boots, an ensemble that had been a great hit with the lads in A-level history.

He was quite looking forward to going over to Yvonne's farm and imagined a cobbled farmyard dotted with chickens, a porch hung heavy with honeysuckle, and jugs of frothy milk straight from the teat, covered over with little bead-bordered cheesecloths. He'd go in for a quick cup of tea with her parents then get the whole matter cleared up with her; it wouldn't mean a thing. And that would be that.

Yvonne looked sheepish when Sedgewick pulled up in front of her in his Vauxhall Cavalier at the bus stop. She gratefully accepted his offer of a lift, clambering in with expected timidity, but she became somewhat flustered when he asked if he could pop in for a cuppa once they got there.

'It's alright, Yvonne, I don't expect everyone running around and tidying up for my sake,' he reassured her. 'I can imagine how things are on a working farm – noses to the grindstone and all that. I'm something of a part-time dairy farmer myself, you know, with our Blindefellows Creamery. The whole thing was my brainchild, you know. Quite a few of the lads who've dabbled in it under my auspices have chosen farming as a career. I must show you our little cottage industry one day.'

Yvonne said she'd like that, and directed him along winding lanes with high hedges. A deer sprang away from the roadside and a rabbit nibbled at the undergrowth. Sedgewick found it marvellous and suddenly regretted all the time he'd spent mooching around his bungalow in the town when he could have been out in the country at the weekends. As they rounded a corner, a silhouetted figure on the crest of a grassy slope came into view. Sedgewick peered up and made out a beanpole of a man balanced precariously on a small pony – no, a donkey – a figure so tall that his feet were almost touching the ground, while he brandished a crop with a flailing arm.

'Why, it's Don Quixote!' Sedgewick chuckled. 'That's what we call him, Japes and I. Comes into the Frog and Onion, one of the watering holes we frequent when there's a game on.'

Yvonne made no answer to this, staring out of the passenger window, but this didn't stop Sedgewick's revelry. 'That beast of burden certainly gets it in the neck after the Don has had a few. He brings the donkey so he can ride home without getting ticketed for drink-driving. I overheard the bar tender talking about it. Incredible! Parks the old nag round the back. The chap's quite a character. Mad staring eyes and grizzled beard. Frightfully gaunt. You should see him up close. Not an ounce of fat on him with his daily liquid lunch. Must be at least six foot. You wouldn't happen to know if he lives in these parts?'

Yvonne turned to him with her limpet blue eyes, which he was surprised to see were now glossy and damp, and murmured, 'He's my father.'

'What?' Sedgewick swerved, nearly hitting the hedge. 'Really? Shall I just drop you at the end of your drive then?'

'But I was so looking forward to you coming in for a cup of tea. Mother will be so pleased too. It's been years since I brought home a young man. Father always frightened them off. I think he'll be different now I'm older though. He's always telling me I should be married and out from under his feet by now.'

In stunned silence, Sedgewick drove them slowly forward towards what he now saw as his dire and inexorable fate.

'It's just here, on the right.'

'Here?' he said as a bouquet of manure piqued his nostrils.

Sedgewick was puzzled by the little pair of red-brick semis stuck in a muddle of corrugated iron structures and a crumbling concrete – not cobbled – yard. 'This is a farm?' he asked, unintentionally sounding incredulous.

'Yes,' said Yvonne, sensing his disappointment.

He read the hastily daubed sign: '"Cold Foot Farm". What an extraordinary name!'

'Oh, yes,' Yvonne brightened at her opportunity to teach him a bit of local history. 'So called because of the stream the farmer – my great grandfather – had to leap across to reach his animals out in the pasture. Occasionally, he didn't quite make the bank, hence the name. That was over a century ago, though. There's a cesspit there now. The cows live in the barn just here, and next to that is the milking shed.'

Sedgewick drove past the barn and caught a glimpse of 30 or more Friesian cows, ankle-deep in their own excrement, following the progress of his car with lackadaisical eyes.

'You can park just there, next to the chicken coop,' Yvonne pointed to a fenced-off area scratched right down to bare earth by a large gathering of foul-smelling fowl, most of whom had exposed angry red neck flesh, courtesy of the monstrous iridescent cockerel, who surveyed his handiwork with pride.

'That's where I get your eggs from,' Yvonne beamed, but Sedgewick's returning smile was blighted by thoughts of salmonella as he glanced at the dishevelled coop. He parked and stepped out gingerly.

'Hello, Turvy,' Yvonne called cheerily to the ancient sheep dog advancing towards them, its rear legs circling like unsynchronised egg whisks. Sedgewick backed away.

'Good boy. Sit.' Sedgewick feebly tried to fend off the decrepit fawning animal.

'Sorry, he's a bit disorientated since Topsy died – that was his sister. She was seventeen years old,' Yvonne proclaimed. 'Please come inside, Charles. I'll introduce you to Mother.'

If her father was Don Quixote, her mother was Sancho Panza, only without the wit. A dumpy sort of wench with a dreamy smile and naught to say other than 'Oh-aye' and 'Er-arr', apart from when she showed him her extensive collection of Wade Whimsies covering every inch of the mantelpiece; she then became impishly animated about a thimble-sized porcelain orangutan, which she told him she'd named Wayne after a distant cousin. Sedgewick had, by this time, resolved to depart as soon as possible, and certainly before the Don appeared.

'Mother, have you seen my straighteners? I've just got to get this kink out of my hair before I go out,' a voice whined from up the stairs.

'Is that your sister, Yvonne?' Sedgewick asked, trying to make conversation.

'No, it's…' Yvonne started to explain, when a huge man with a quiff of red hair, dressed in tight pressed jeans, a form-fitting mauve shirt and a sateen lilac tie bounded into the room. '... Angus, my brother.'

'Didn't you hear me, Mother?' Angus continued, barely registering Sedgewick.

'Angus, this is my friend, Charles.'

'Oh, is it?' Angus raised a sarcastic eyebrow, before turning to his mother again.

'So, where are they this time then?'

'Maybe she put them in the bathroom cabinet again, Angy,' Yvonne suggested gently.

The father suddenly materialised, tall as the chimney breast, swaying slightly, crop in hand. 'Why are you tarted up like that, Angus? Have you milked the girls already?'

'Mother did it,' Angus called over his shoulder as he retreated up the stairs.

'Again?' the father's voice echoed up the stairwell. 'You know she never does it right. They'll all end up with mastitis for the hundredth damn time!'

Sedgewick looked down into his teacup at the now-curdling clumps of raw milk he'd liberally added in a bid to cool his tea so he could drink up and leave as swiftly as possible.

'What a wastrel,' the father muttered through bared yellow incisors. 'Works well with a broom under constant supervision.' He then turned to his wife who sat transfixed by the undulating net curtains. 'Look at that! Damn you, woman! Living with you is like being handcuffed to a ghost.' He stood bang in front of her and clicked his fingers in her face. 'Hey, you there, have you put the dinner on yet?' he asked, his eyes protruding from their bony sockets. The mother suddenly sprang up and scurried off, a beetle in a navy-blue knitted bed jacket.

'And who the hell might you be?' Sedgewick had been hoping the autumnal hues of his Harris Tweed might have made him blend into the mossy decor of the sitting room and had kept as still as he possibly could ever since becoming aware of the father's presence. 'Haven't I seen you before somewhere?' the old man growled.

'No, no, I shouldn't think so,' blurted Sedgewick, who feared being recognised from the pub, where he might have been seen sniggering at the Don with Japes.

'This is Charles, father, a friend from the school.'

'You still working for those posh twits then?'

'Just until the lady returns from maternity leave.'

'Maternity leave? What kind of a daft notion is that? Well, Charles, I must apologise for my son, in inverted commas. Neglects his responsibilities. Seems I called him after the admirable Aberdeen Angus for nothing. No interest in the noble beasts. I have to do everything around here. Anyhow, you two appear to be inhabiting the couch, where I now intend to take my pre-prandial nap, so if you wouldn't mind, kindly shove off and have your digestives elsewhere. I bid you good day.'

'Oh, of course. Sorry. Yes. Thank you. By all means.' Sedgewick quickly made his way towards the door, with Yvonne at his heels.

'I'll walk you to your car,' she whispered.

Outside a sorry sight met them. A grey-speckled donkey stood, lathered in sweat, its gums bleeding from cruel jerking of the bit and sores on its sides from sustained thrashing with the riding crop.

'Oh, Oaty, Oaty,' Yvonne moaned as she cradled the old donkey in her arms. 'I asked for a pony one Christmas when I was a teen and I got Oaty instead. Father was really buying him for himself for his jaunts to town. I do my best to patch him up after Father's had his way with him. He's terribly old now, you know, for a donkey – well over twenty.'

With Sedgewick following, Yvonne led the donkey to a secluded little outhouse with fresh straw on the ground and a bottle of hay in the manger. She gently took off his saddle and bridle, and lovingly covered him with a baize-green blanket that had seen better days. He drank deeply from a bucket of clear water which she had drawn from an ancient and rusty hand-pump in a corner of the farmyard. As she smoothed his sad long ears, Sedgewick found himself moved with unexpected tenderness for Yvonne, and wondered whether he shouldn't be the one to rescue her from this dreadful wasteland after all.

At his car, Yvonne thanked Sedgewick for the lift and he thanked her for the tea. Without entirely meaning to, he gave her a peck on the cheek, then drove hurriedly away. Glancing in his mirror, he noticed she was looking after him, her hand over the cheek he had kissed. He then regretted doing it in case it might, in her mind, have moved them one step closer to matrimony.

In his pigeon-hole at school the next day, Sedgewick received a dinner invitation from Clive, an earnest German-teacher in his mid-thirties who had taught at Blindefellows for the past five years. Stalwarts like Sedgewick and Japes often received such invitations and always attended if it meant the chance of a good meal. Crane, with whom Clive occasionally discussed cricket, was also invited, along with his wife, but she generally made excuses not to attend. The 'Sages', as they were wryly referred to by the younger teachers, were viewed as having influence. Therefore, whenever a promotion was afoot, they were invariably invited to social occasions in the hope that they'd put in a good a word.

Derek Pilbeam, Head of Modern Languages, and his wife Debbie were also invited. Pilbeam was set to retire and was in charge of selecting his successor. This would mean a salary hike for Clive and a shot at a house-mastership that would launch his ambitious wife, Caroline, into the epicentre of school life, putting Clive on the path to headship, to which she had already let slip that she aspired on his behalf.

Japes and Sedgewick generally aimed to be the first to arrive at such occasions, so as to make a head start on the hors d'oeuvres. As they sat munching their way through a platter of devilled eggs, crab puffs and stuffed mushrooms, they couldn't help overhearing Clive and Caroline in the kitchen.

'Do go easy on the wine tonight, Caroline, please, with the interview coming up and everything.'

'I can hold my booze a damn sight better than you can! And are you sure about that shirt? I don't think pig pink with amber cufflinks gives quite the impression of manly leadership qualities we're aiming to convey tonight, do you?'

Japes winked at Sedgewick. 'Looks like we might be in for a few fireworks this evening. How's it going with your cookie anyhow? Any closer to a yea or nay on the marriage dilemma?'

'Oh, it's a nay, naturally,' Sedgewick replied, attempting nonchalance by tossing a crab puff into his mouth – only it missed. 'It's just a question of finding the right time to break it to the gal.'

'And if that time never comes? Will we be seeing you step into the role of gentleman farmer in the not-too-distant future?'

Sedgewick brushed this off with a chuckle. He hadn't gone into details about the shambolic farmstead and certainly hadn't let on about Yvonne's familial relation to Don Quixote.

By the time Crane and the Pilbeams arrived, at the official hour, Japes and Sedgewick had made a large dent in the hors d'oeuvres. However, Caroline, a culinary whizz, had another platter stashed away, which she set out with the admonishment, 'Do try and restrain yourselves this time, boys. There are other guests!'

Dinner was on a game theme and consisted of a home-made foie gras terrine, accompanied by granary bread Caroline had baked herself, followed by a braised rabbit of turkey-like proportions, rounded off with fresh forest fruits on meringue, dolloped with vanilla mascarpone. As usual, Caroline led the conversation, mainly talking about her sons' precocious prowess on the sports field and her future hopes of scholarship places for them at Blindefellows. Clive interjected when he could, but kept slipping in German words even though he'd been born and bred in Faversham, something he did when he was nervous: 'Ja, ja, Derek, the new language lab assistant is doing a marvellous job,' and, 'Ach zo, we have to have more evening revision classes. I'd be happy to do a session every day after school, even at weekends, if we're to raise the bar on results.' Pilbeam, not interested in talking shop outside school, preferred to turn his ear to Japes's stories about his struggles with diarrhoea in the desert while trying to lead a unit as a green second lieutenant during the Suez Crisis. Crane, who disapproved of Japes, found it difficult to chuckle along with the others at anecdotes he felt were unbecoming at the dinner table.

The wine did its work and Caroline inadvertently put a few dents in Clive's bid for promotion. 'Come on, Clive, spit it out!' she scolded when he was ponderously responding to a simple question while twiddling his amber cufflinks. Then, a few minutes later, she snapped, 'No, don't turn the light on all the way over there, Clive; it's easier to go to the light switch in the kitchen!' She glanced over at Debbie Pilbeam and rolled her eyes as if she were a kindred spirit, in that she too was a woman fated to suffer being married to this inept breed. Debbie, not really understanding these subtleties, smiled back politely.

'The man's an automaton!' Japes muttered as he leaned over to pour a glass of Hungarian dessert wine for Sedgewick and himself. 'A finger puppet – and she's the finger. Beware married life, Sedgers, beware married life.'

At the end of the evening, over coffee and brandy in the lounge, Caroline, who was by now slurring her words but continuing to hold forth, recounted a story which served as yet another nail in the promotional coffin for Clive. On one of his few cooking adventures, Clive had dared to go out and purchase a packet of breadcrumbs. 'Breadcrumbs! Can you believe he *bought* breadcrumbs?' she scoffed, laying a firm hand of inebriate camaraderie on Debbie's shoulder, but Debbie wilted away uncomfortably. Japes looked over at Sedgewick, shaking his head in despair. Sedgewick responded by turning his eyes up with a glance at the ceiling. The marital horrors of the evening had set his resolve to wash his hands of the whole business with Princess Roly-Poly at the earliest opportunity.

The next morning, Sedgewick decided to drop a hint to Yvonne by breezing through reception without so much as a glance in her direction. As he did so, he noticed out of the corner of his eye a flushed and florid, tear-stained face. Throughout the day, he was plagued by the sense that he'd been cruel, and felt he should drop in on her before he went home and finish things in an upright and decent manner. He decided to sugar the bitter pill by taking along two cups of tea and a packet of chocolate digestives he'd rooted out of Crane's pigeon-hole from their hiding place behind some Latin text books. When he arrived in reception, Yvonne had lost none of the crimson hue he'd caught a glimpse of that morning. As he approached, he saw the waste paper basket swollen with soggy tissues. She gazed up at him and fresh tears slid down her puffy cheeks.

'Oh, Charles, you saw how sad I was this morning and you brought me some tea,' she gulped.

'Yes, and chocolate digestives as well,' he replied, clumsily putting the cups down and sloshing the tea into the saucers. He wafted the packet of biscuits under her nose, inviting her to take one. She did so and ate it ravenously, followed by a second and then a third. Sedgewick glanced around, checking that no one was witnessing their intercourse.

Through a mouthful of chocolatey crumbs, Yvonne blurted out something that he didn't quite grasp. She repeated it when she saw his dumbfounded face. What he heard the second time was, 'Don Quixote is dead!'

Don Quixote, dead? The old scoundrel! Must have come a cropper with the nag on the way home. Drink-driving got him in the end, so it seemed. Wait until he told Japes!

'No! Dead? I'm so terribly sorry, Yvonne.' Sedgewick sympathetically pulled up a chair next to her, looking forward to hearing all the gory details and then relaying them to Japes in the pub that evening.

'I loved him so much,' she wailed, a little too loudly. 'He was the light of my life. No one cared for him like I did!'

Sedgewick shifted uncomfortably in his chair. This surely was an exaggerated accolade for the Don.

'When I was lonely,' she continued. 'I'd just bury my face in his mane and I'd start to feel a little better.'

'His mane?' Sedgewick didn't like the allusion.

'And I'd feed him special little treats from my hand—'

Sedgewick felt this flow of information had to stop right there and then. 'Yvonne, you really shouldn't be in school when you lose a parent. Why don't we call you a taxi to take you home?'

'No, no, not my parent: my donkey – my poor old donkey, Oaty.'

'Ah, "Donkey Oaty", not Don Quixote?'

'Yes, my donkey, Oaty.' She let out a new volley of sobs. 'He committed suicide!'

Sedgewick was thrown into confusion again. 'Your donkey committed suicide? Are you certain? How is that possible?'

'Father was riding him home from the pub in town and, as usual, he was treating poor Oaty with such cruelty, whipping him to within an inch of his life and digging his knees into his flanks. The poor creature threw himself down an open storm drain in despair. They say animals don't suffer melancholy, Charles, but I think he'd been depressed for years. I believe he was even trying to take father with him to the grave.'

'And the Don—' Sedgewick quickly corrected himself. 'I mean your father – is he alright?'

'No, he's in a coma and they don't expect him to pull through. It took them three hours to recover him from the drain. His legs were wedged between Oaty's sides in the drain shaft. Is it wicked of me, Charles, to say that it's divine justice and a blessing in disguise? He was a cruel, brutal man.'

'No, of course not. No, not at all. I could see that he wasn't exactly a warm chap, the instant I met him. It's better to be honest about these things. I wouldn't blame you if you took the rest of the week off. You're not in a fit state to come to work. You've had a terrible shock. Now, let me know if there's anything I can do to help, anything at all. I'll leave you with the rest of the biscuits.' Sedgewick rose to leave; he felt this was not the time to break the news to her.

'Well, there is something you could do, Charles,' she called after him as he made his retreat. 'It would be so helpful if you could come to the hospital with me after school. It's hard to bear all this alone.'

And, against his better judgment, he did so. As predicted by the doctors, Don Quixote died a few days later. There was a funeral and more tears, with Sedgewick's shoulder to cry on. Over the next few months, he helped 'Mrs Sancho Panza' with selling off the farm. With the proceeds, she was able to afford a trim little two-bedroom semi-detached on the edge of town, where she and Angus would live. Only two bedrooms were necessary at this point because Yvonne, by dint of feeding Sedgewick one superb dinner after another, had moved in with Sedgewick following a low-key ceremony at the local registry office.

With Yvonne conjuring such a cornucopia of delectable puddings, there was no real incentive for Sedgewick to go out and seek nourishment, so pub meals with Japes dwindled to nothing, while Sedgewick's waistline blossomed. His friendship with Japes faded to little more than the occasional game of table football in the staff-room, but without that ebullient conviviality which had hitherto characterised those epic sporting moments. Meanwhile, Yvonne had got him to go out and buy himself a whole new wardrobe under her direction, leading Crane to comment dryly to the Sages – convened around the living flame of the Oak Room fireplace one morning at briefing – that old Sedgers was looking more like the gentleman farmer every day.

8

The Fräulein of Ravensbrück

Trinity and Michaelmas 1994, Lent and Trinity 1995

Clive stood up abruptly and strode purposefully to the toilet. This was his third visit in the past hour. Caroline had insisted on his buying the sleek three-piece pinstripe for the interview for Head of Modern Languages, and the neat waistline was strangling his bladder. Pilbeam, Swainson and Bunny had narrowed the shortlist to two candidates: Clive and a middle-aged woman from Brazil. Caroline had laughed this off: they'd never be organised enough to fly her over; the job was in the bag for Clive and, after all, he'd been there long enough to prove himself solid and reliable – if somewhat lacking in drive, other than when Caroline stepped in and provided it for him. Clive returned to the waiting room outside Swainson's office, where he and the woman from Brazil, Fräulein von Ravensbrück, awaited their interviews and gingerly – as he feared for the stitching in his crotch – sat down.

'I cannot place your accent, Clive,' she asked in her musical Brazilian-German one. 'Is it Danish?'

'Ach no, I'm from Faversham.' He often misled people with what he hoped was a German accent. 'I've taught German so long that I've developed a sort of mishmash of Surrey and Saxony.'

'Extraordinary.' She nodded. 'Then I mustn't come to you to perfect my English accent.'

'Possibly not.' Clive let out a chortle which suppressed a shudder of anxiety at how Caroline would react if this woman were to get the job instead of him.

She smiled at him softly, which showed off her fine facial structure. Everything about her exuded a warm self-assurance: her plum-coloured tropic-wool trouser suit, the long string of opals at her neck with their little sparkles of azure, which matched her large eyes. Her impressive stature was ever so slightly enhanced by kitten heels in a creamy kid leather, presumably handmade in Brazil. Clive felt wooden beside her and wished Caroline had let him wear his favourite salmon-pink shirt and his 'Fall of the Wall' commemorative tie with Brandenburg Gate pictures on it.

When he had first read her letter of application, Swainson had presumed the woman from Brazil to be of noble stock, and wanted to invite her to interview as soon as he'd seen the 'von' in her name. Clive had mentioned this to Caroline, who had immediately researched Ravensbrück and found it to be an out-of-the-way East German backwater with no castle, and therefore, without a doubt, no exiled aristocrats. However, there had been a concentration camp there and the fact the woman had been born in Brazil just after the war was, in her opinion, an incontrovertible indication of 'dodgy parentage'. All of this Caroline had relayed to Swainson at length, as soon as she had heard that they'd gone ahead and invited the woman to interview.

'Goodness me, Caroline, you certainly have an enquiring mind!' Swainson exclaimed when she told him. 'Too late now, though – we've bought her ticket. We'll have to at least go through the motions, which is sure to be an opportunity for Clive to shine.'

Pilbeam and Swainson now entered the waiting area and asked Fräulein von Ravensbrück whether everyone had been looking after her. She extolled the virtues of the head girl, who had shown her around that morning, and of the graciousness of Claudette and Pilar, members of the Modern Languages department who had lunched with her. Then, following the gentlemanly dictum of 'ladies first', the two men escorted her into Swainson's office and Clive was left alone, nervously stroking his goatee.

Although their voices were muffled behind the heavy oak door, festooned with carved heraldic scrolls, if Clive was totally still and didn't breathe, he could get the gist of what was being said. She had worked all over the world – Kyoto, Rome, Tanzania and somewhere ending in -stan. She had returned to Brazil two years ago to care for an ailing relative. Clive heard Pilbeam ask her what she would do as Head of Modern Languages to establish the school as a part of the local community. Clive felt himself start to sweat slightly under the collar. Caroline had brainstormed all possible questions with him last week but that one hadn't come up. An international picnic, Fräulein von Ravensbrück replied, inviting the highest-achieving children in the final year at the local primary schools with a view to scholarship selection, thereby ingratiating the school with the community, and addressing the increasingly loud plaints in Westminster regarding the elitism of public schools. What could he say? An international parade, an international cake sale, an international dog show? He settled on an international cake sale – a couple of trestle tables outside the super-market on the market square. They could even give some free ones to children who looked needy, thus fusing the Blindefellows of today with its charitable past. There'd be cakes of many colours, all stuck with mini flags of the world. Clive felt quite impressed with himself, coming up with something all of his own.

Clive didn't get the job and Caroline ranted for two weeks then simmered, muttering under her breath. Prior to the interview, she had prematurely put the house on the market, ready for the move to the decorous flat earmarked for the Head of Modern Languages, with its moulded ceilings and French windows that opened out onto a little private terrace with a trellis entwined with passion fruit. All through the summer holidays she reminded Clive daily that, thanks to his lack of get-up-and-go, they would now have to stay put in a modern box and keep on paying a hefty mortgage.

Fräulein von Ravensbrück joined the school on a lovely summer evening in late August. The employees of Blindefellows and their spouses were already arrayed on the lawn of the headmaster's res-idence. Drinks and canapés were being served to ring in the new school year. At about 8pm, a fleet of three taxis drew up across the lawn. Soon all heads were directed at the contents being disgorged from the cabs: ottomans, rolled-up oriental carpets, a parrot in an antique cage, wooden trunks, a young blonde in wide gaucho trousers with tassel trims and a red bolero jacket, a sparrow-thin elderly lady of a gleaming chestnut hue in a Bahia dress with turban and cradling a wicker basket, followed by the Fräulein herself, in black leather slacks and matching waistcoat, directing the cabbies, who were carrying her luggage.

'Good Lord, it's the three manifestations of the triple goddess – maiden, matron and crone,' drawled Crane over his champagne flute.

'Or Dr Doolittle newly returned from Polynesia!' Japes ejaculated and polished his glasses for a better look.

'Who do you think the older lady is?' Sedgewick asked Japes. 'Could it be Fräulein von Ravensbrück's mother?'

'Don't be daft, Sedgers, the old girl is ginger-cake brown, Brazilian through and through. The Fräulein is bread und butter at the darkest… a something else through and through.'

'An *Apfelstrudel*?' suggested Sedgewick, who possessed a mind well stocked with baked goods imagery.

Caroline appeared at Swainson's elbow. 'What the hell's all this about then? Three women in a two-bedroom flat? That'll be interesting. Bet you didn't think you were getting three for the price of one. And they've brought pets, too! Flaming Kraut! If you like, Roger, I can go over there right now and tell her, as diplomatically as possible, that there's been a mistake and Clive's going to be Head of Modern Languages. He's totally ready for it; we all know that. She's probably of Nazi stock, of course, which could be very embarrassing for the school if someone were to let that cat out of the bag.'

'And Clive's grandfather marched with Oswald Moseley, Caroline. We all have things in our past that we'd rather forget.' Swainson handed her his empty glass and strode over the lawn to greet the entourage.

'Welcome, welcome, Fräulein von Ravensbrück,' Swainson called amiably. 'We weren't quite sure when you'd be arriving but everything is ready for you. Let me show you up to your rooms.'

'Ah, hello, Roger, how nice to see you again.' She smiled and the parade paused. 'Now you must call me Diana. Let me introduce Missy Baba, who was my nanny and has been with our family for fifty years. And this is my dear Sobrinha.'

Swainson graciously shook hands with the young lady, who was quite lovely, but when he held out his hand to Missy Baba, she did not take it, instead dipping an almost imperceptible curtsy while looking him straight in the eye with an intensity that suggested mind-reading.

'Look at the old lady, what a nerve!' Caroline remarked to Clive, observing the exchange. 'I wouldn't be surprised if that's some sort of voodoo woman she's brought along with her.'

By the time the pupils returned a week later, Diana von Ravensbrück had completely re-imagined the regions of the school that she now inhabited. The walls of her apartment had gone from magnolia to magenta, the soft furnishings festooned with alpaca throws, and a sandalwood frieze had been placed on the wall above the mantelpiece which would imbue the air with a delicate perfume whenever there was a fire burning. The pupils gaped in amazement at the Head of Modern Languages' office, a corner room with windows along two sides, which meant you couldn't miss it if you were turning onto the school's main corridor.

Before Pilbeam's retirement, when it had been his office, it had been beige with a downtrodden taupe carpet and he usually blended into it due to the colour of his well-worn invariably khaki suits, like a plaice on the seabed. The room was so drab, in fact, that one barely noticed it. Now, as the pupils moved along the corridor, a bottleneck occurred as they slowed down and pressed their noses up against the glass. A mist of emerald green created by a dozen potted palms immediately grabbed their attention and the taupe carpet was now covered by an intricately patterned red Turkish rug. The pupils could smell the fresh mint she was growing for tea, which she made in a shiny silver samovar in the corner at morning and afternoon breaks. But perhaps the most exciting thing was Cassandra, a red-spectacled amazon parrot who sat on a perch among the palms.

Cassandra had endured a freak pregnancy after an overnight stay at a Brazilian veterinarian clinic, supposedly to treat a feather cyst, and had rejected the resulting egg. Once a nanny, always a nanny, Missy Baba was quick to take up the gauntlet and had successfully hatched the resulting chick, thereafter tending to its every need. Jonathan, as the fledgling was called, still had the look of a child's drawing of a dinosaur, but all three women were confident he would blossom once his plumes came in. For the present, however, mother and son had to live apart as Cassandra had swooped on him once too often, hence her being confined to the perch in the office until Jonathan – almost constantly in the arms of Missy Baba – was more capable of standing on his own two feet.

Clive, being the last male standing in the department, felt a little isolated. The Spanish teacher, Senõrita Pilar Uxia San Ysidro, the unfortunate acronym of which had become established as her sobriquet among the older pupils, treated Clive like a poor thing. She sorted out his tie in the morning and swiped the pudding off his tray at lunchtime in the dining room, since his increasing girth was one of their topics of conversation. The French teacher, Mademoiselle Claudette Dufort, was less forward but regarded Clive with a compassionate *je ne sais quoi*, which made him feel uncomfortable.

The three ladies switched between French, Spanish and English with the swiftness of a cha-cha, and Clive, only really understanding German as an additional language, withdrew into himself. Cassandra the parrot didn't ease the situation, delivering her first words to Clive in French and Spanish in her brassy voice, for which Pilar and Claudette rewarded their precocious feathered pupil with grapes. Her Portuguese and German were already perfect and she also spoke a smattering of English. Occasionally, Diana would try to include Clive by speaking just to him in German, but she couldn't stop herself trying to improve his home-counties pronunciation. Clive spent more and more time in his classroom, finding the constant feminine animation in Diana's office overwhelming.

So it was that Diana von Ravensbrück, the first ever female head of department in Blindefellows' long history, established herself as an internationally-minded and vibrant presence in the school community. It wasn't long before she was making preparations for her star turn, the Modern Languages Department International Picnic. The date was to be May 1, much to the delight of Claudette and Pilar, who, like their supervisor and mentor, were of a strongly socialist stripe that set them apart from most of their male colleagues, other than Japes, long a professed late-comer to anarchism, who had now largely abandoned his former haunts in the sciences prep and faculty common rooms for a regular perch alongside Cassandra in what he referred to delightedly as 'the aviary'.

Ever since young Toby Gosling had left, five years ago now, to start what had become a very successful television career as the presenter of a weekly nature programme, *Walks with My Dog*, the science prep room had lacked the warmth of his personality – and his home-made cakes. Gosling had been replaced by Dennis Drysdale, who'd proved himself a great ally to Jape's, with each of them allergic to virtually everything and sporting matching tracheotomy scars.

Caroline, however, did not share Japes's enthusiasm for the new *milieu* in the Modern Languages department. Chucking the rest of the glass of red wine she was drinking into a sizzling coq au vin, she sniped, 'Well, Clive, do you think the powers that be have figured out yet that they've hired a loony-left Latin lesbo?'

'Actually, she seems to be a big hit with the pupils and she gets on like a house on fire with Pilar and Claudette,' Clive wheedled. 'She's started going to tango classes with them.'

'I bet she has... What about the old crone?'

'Oh, Missy Baba? She just walks about wrapped in a shawl, carrying the baby parrot. The pupils are in awe of her with her exotic clothing. She never utters a word, you know – just stares.'

'And the teenage girlfriend, what's she up to these days?'

'Who? You mean Sabrina, or Sobrinha, or however they say it? She barely comes out of the apartment. Claudette says she's depressed about something or other.'

'Hmm, I wonder what it could be?' Caroline smirked. 'Probably something to do with the age gap in that relationship... Very unhealthy, if you ask me.'

'So, do you think you could whip up something for the picnic next week?' Clive ventured.

'What? Waste my time on feeding those brats and their scabby parents? I've agreed to three days of supply-teaching next week. I probably won't have time.' Caroline hadn't worked as a primary school teacher since her twin sons had been born 10 years ago and she accepted supply-teaching at their school only so she could keep an eye on them.

'Well, I suppose you could see it as something for Harry and Patrick too. They'll be there soon, after all. Please could you do *something*, Caroline? I said you would and I've told them you're such a fantastic cook.'

'Very well, but it certainly won't be a German dish to honour the Kraut. And do be sure to ask me next time before you make any promises on my behalf – thank you.'

Bunny had gone out of his way to get to know Diana. He had even agreed to officially open the International Picnic with her, when such tasks were normally left to Swainson nowadays. It showed the regard in which he held her, as generally he would appear only at alumni events, where donations were potentially forthcoming.

There was an excellent turn-out for the picnic. Selected Year Six children from the five local primary schools, along with their teachers and parents – including Caroline and her sons – mingled with the faculty and with families of current Blindefellows pupils. The weather was fine and open marquees were placed around the school field, offering an array of dishes donated by staff and day-students' parents, with over 13 countries featured by way of cuisine, each with their own decorated little seating area. Blindefellows teachers, aided by their spouses, stood ready to serve, attired in appropriately themed aprons, or even the national costume of the country they were representing.

The flock were contained in a pen as a centrepiece, for both decorative and marketing purposes and as a precaution, as they could be pushy when there was food about. Beside them was a table covered in little cubes of their own cheeses, which even they were trying to reach with their long purple tongues. The display was presided over by Sedgewick in his milk-white linen suit and his straw boater worn at a jaunty angle, such was his now-familiar outfit on cheese-promotion occasions. Yvonne accompanied him in white knee-length skirt and blouse, her thick, wiry ginger hair under a traditional white mop cap and ready to offer samples on cocktail sticks alongside chunks of pineapple.

In the German marquee, Tree, Head of English, stared transfixed into a giant saucepan bubbling with wiener sausages while his wife, Tabby, sliced salami wafer-thin. Next to her, Clive was making a pig's ear of cutting the somewhat dry and crumbly rye bread. A certain young blonde Brazilian was serving the beer, decked out in a traditional German blouse and a mini dirndl dress, her golden curls falling down her back. Missy Baba wore an ornately embroidered boy's lederhosen suit that entirely encased her tiny torso and thighs in green suede, topped off by a grey felt *Alpenhut* with polka-dot guinea fowl feathers stuck in the band. Japes, manning the Spanish marquee with Pilar, likened her to Pinocchio.

'Come on now, Japes, at least she's made an effort,' scolded Pilar in her flamenco dress as she tossed her paella. 'You're just wearing a sombrero on your head and we don't even have a Mexican tent.'

In the French tent, Claudette opened a slightly rusty old biscuit tin that Clive had left earlier. She'd heard about Caroline's professional dinner parties and was eager to see the contents. Six pale vol-au-vent with a slightly gelatinous mushroom filling looked back at her sadly. After a few moments of bewilderment, she resolved to place them on a paper plate at the rear of the sumptuous delicacies – *tartes Tatin*, *Religieuses au chocolat*, miniature soufflés and crème brûlée – where they could remain in reserve in case everything else was eaten.

The microphone crackled to life as Bunny began his address. Standing next to him was Fräulein von Ravensbrück in a pink wide-brimmed hat that rivalled Japes's sombrero. A sky-blue ribbon had been strung across the podium for Diana to cut when the International Picnic was declared open at noon. The local press and regional radio were poised for a photo and sound bite.

'Good afternoon, ladies and gentlemen, boys and girls. I'm not going to keep you long because, like me, I'm sure your mouths are watering at the culinary scents wafting our way from the little gustatory embassies dotted around our school field. First, however, there is one person who I must introduce to everyone here present – Fräulein Diana von Ravensbrück, who joined Blindefellows at the start of the school year as our new Head of Modern Languages and who is already having a revolutionary impact that befits this beautiful First of May. The International Picnic is her brainchild and she made it very clear from the start who this event was to be for. "Blindefellows shall play host to the young scholars of this town, upon the existence of which it ultimately depends," she told me, "and to their dedicated parents." I wholeheartedly agree with her – that the time has come for schools such as Blindefellows to give more back to the community. One quarter of our pupils are now from overseas, and by enjoying the food of the world together we are showcasing Blindefellows as a centre of internationalism and a place where the children of Travistock can broaden their horizons. So, without further ado, allow me to hand you over to the exceptional Fräulein von Ravensbrück.'

Enthusiastic applause erupted as Diana stepped up to the microphone. Caroline rolled her eyes and turned to Swainson. 'Roger, are you quite sure you want to give Fräulein von Flaming Kraut press coverage? Someone might start raking around in her past!'

'I believe you've already done that, Caroline, and you didn't find so much as a shred of evidence,' Swainson quipped; he was finding her increasingly tiresome.

'Thank you so much for joining us here today, boys and girls of Travistock, with your lovely families,' Diana said, beaming at the crowd. 'Perhaps some of you will enjoy yourselves so much that we will convince you to take our scholarship exam thirty days from today. You have already been singled out by your teachers as the most promising young scholars in Travistock and I feel certain that, if you just give it a go, several of you will be joining our school in

September. The founder of Blindefellows, Hezekiah Lambton, who started out in life as a humble sheep shearer, left twelve annual scholarship places in his will, specifically to the children of this town. Unintentionally, these scholarships have become one of local history's best-kept secrets, with only four children coming forward for the scholarship exam last year.'

'Why on earth is she announcing this to these people?' Caroline hissed to Swainson a little too loudly. 'What's the school going to become if you fill it up with these rough kids? I do supply-teaching in this town and I know what they're like.'

'Come now, Caroline, why not widen the field a bit? You've been cramming your own boys for the exam all year; they're almost certain to be among the lucky dozen.'

Caroline crossed her arms over her chest, turned her back on him sharply and watched her nemesis snip through the ribbon and declare the picnic open, at which point various beelines were made towards the enticing odours emerging from the marquees.

Diana came down from the podium on Bunny's arm, similarly slender and elegantly dressed, and they ambled about the grounds like foreign royalty, each of them being about a head taller than most of the crowd around them. They stopped periodically to chat charmingly with current and prospective parents. Catching sight of them, Japes thought this must be the first time in Bunny's life that he had lavished attention upon a woman not in possession of a fortune, a portion of which she might be considering donating to Blindefellows. Eventually they paused at the French tent, where Matron Ridgeway, in a two-foot-high chef's hat, stood making crêpes at a griddle.

The drama teacher, Tristram Randolph, proffered samples at a wine-tasting counter. As the afternoon wore on, he slipped increasingly into a slurring faux-French accent, giving extra tipples to the more attractive Sixth Form girls, who were getting very giggly indeed. Claudette presided over the once glorious and now very depleted dessert display.

'It's like a swarm of locusts, Diana – I never knew such ravening,' the matron quipped as she bit into the Nutella crêpe she'd set aside for herself on a paper plate. 'Why, I've seen some of them filling doggy bags too – and they were parents from here, not from town!'

Diana moved on to admire the remaining patisserie but her heart sank when she spotted the vol-au-vent. 'Oh, my: vol-au-vent!' she exclaimed. 'I haven't seen them since the Seventies. They haven't stood the test of time too well, have they? They look so out-of-place amongst the rest.'

'Yes, they do look rather insipid,' Claudette frowned. 'I suppose they needed a bit of egg brushed on before going in the oven, to bronze them.'

'And they've got that slippery sort of mushroom filling. Whoever made them?'

'I did,' Caroline snapped from behind Diana. 'Out of a packet of Iceland puff pastry and a sachet of mushroom sauce. A commensurate effort for this dreadful event. Must dash.' She strutted off to find the twins, who she suspected were round the back of the Scandinavian tent, kicking a herring can with some of their unsavoury classmates.

Diana and Bunny went over to sit on one of the long benches in the crowded German tent, which had taken on the atmosphere of a beer hall, with its authentic beer server whom Diana regarded fondly. 'It's so good to see my Sobrinha getting involved in this sort of thing. She was a wreck when we left Brazil,' she informed Bunny. 'She spends far too much time alone.'

A gaggle of young lads from the town gazed up at her admiringly and she enjoyed the attention, an angel serving free beer as oompah music belched out of the rickety cassette player in the corner. Next to Fräulein von Ravensbrück and Bunny sat two boys, Gavin Oldknow and Callum Cropper, from Toad Brook Primary School in the middle of Travistock, who had been allowed to graze at will around the stalls while their parents went for a curry in the India tent. They were now enjoying wieners in baps lathered in both ketchup and mustard.

'How's the food, lads?' Diana asked them.

'It's very nice, thank you,' answered Gavin, who had vivid carrot hair and a blood-splatter of red freckles across his nose. 'We've tried something in every tent.'

'We had this, like, custardy thing in the French tent,' Callum enthusiastically extolled, his mouth full of bap and ketchup, 'and then we had flat spaghetti and meatballs in the Italian tent, then some pudding called Teary Sue that had a bit of booze in, I reckon.'

'Tiramisu?' suggested Bunny.

'And they gave us apple pie and ice-cream in the American tent,' Gavin interjected.

'I hope you lovely boys will think about joining us here next year and come up and take the scholarship test,' Diana said, giving each of their sticky paws a little pat.

'I would but I get nervous when I do exams; I feel sick even thinkin' about 'em,' Gavin confided.

'Well, we'd try to make you as comfortable as possible and you could even bring your mother or father along. We'll give them tea and biscuits while you do the test.'

Gavin's skin suddenly went as pale as Wensleydale cheese.

'Are you alright, dear?' Diana asked him gently.

With a pained expression, he tilted forward and said in her ear, 'I'm sorry but I've just trumped and followed through. It's thinking about exams did it, Miss.'

Puzzled, she turned to Bunny, raising her brows for clarification.

'Ah, I believe it means he's had a little accident in his trousers,' he explained as a heady stench enveloped them. 'Look, boys, there's a line of Portaloos, so you'll be able to sort things out over there, then you'll be as right as rain.'

The boys went off sheepishly, with Callum scolding, 'I can't believe you've done it again, and in a right posh place like this!' while Diana and Bunny left the marquee in pursuit of a breath of fresh air.

The picnic, which had been due to end at 3pm, was still chugging along nicely at 5pm, with everyone getting along marvellously.

'Congratulations, Diana, you have broken down a plethora of age-old class divides,' Swainson said, patting her upper arm. 'The press ate it up... literally. You've really put us on the map today!'

At the end of the month, the scholarship exams commenced with a fantastic turn-out of over four dozen candidates. Fräulein von Ravensbrück had taken Gavin Oldknow under her wing, dropping by Toad Brook Primary a couple of times to give him the reassurance he needed to get through the exam, which he passed with flying colours. She had endowed him with such confidence that, after the exam, he showed none of the Wensleydale colouring that had plagued him in the German tent just a few weeks before. He even said he'd enjoyed it.

Caroline had drilled her sons with as many past papers as she could force Clive to smuggle out of school. She was determined she wouldn't be snubbed again after Clive's rejection last year.

The following fortnight the results were out and, as the standard had been higher than expected, Diana had advised the Blindefellows board to add an extra two free places to the quota. Caroline read the letter, which arrived on a fine June morning, smiled and nodded, then placed it into the drawer of her bureau and set off for town. She had seen just the thing to present to Diana, in the little antiquarian book-shop just off the market square.

Diana celebrated her International Picnic triumph by taking the Modern Languages department, including Japes as an honorary member, out to dinner for her fiftieth birthday at a new Cuban restaurant in the city nearby. It proved a tad exuberant for Clive at times, such as when the proprietor got everyone up to dance the Conga and Clive was placed between Japes and Pilar. He hadn't returned home until well after midnight, by which time Caroline and the boys were fast asleep.

As Diana walked along the corridor to her office the next morning, a little late and the worse for wear after the evening's merrymaking, she was pleased to see a large number of pupils peering through the window. *Cassandra will love this attention*, she thought. She found Japes at the door, with the side of his fist pressed to his lips, as if stifling a laugh, or possibly expressing shock. Swainson stood in front of him looking grave. *Oh no,* she thought, *Cassandra is dead, lying on the ground with her feet in the air*. She rushed forward but the sight that met her eyes made her stagger back. A huge, roughly daubed banner in dripping, shocking pink emulsion had been pinned to her book-case – 'Happy Birthday!' it read. Dangling from the ceiling on red ribbons were dozens of little heart-shaped cut-outs of Hitler's face. In the bookstand on her desk was a large illustrated hard-backed version of *Mein Kampf* with a note paperclipped to it, reading, 'Book of the Week!'

'*Mein Gott!*' was all Diana was able to say.

'Looks as if we've had a visit from *Mein Führer, Mein Fräulein*,' Japes sighed, stepping forwards and putting a friendly arm around her shoulders to steady her.

'Now move along everybody. Somebody has played a wicked prank on Fräulein von Ravensbrück,' Swainson said sharply, and the pupils went on their way with Japes herding them from behind, like sheep. 'I think we'd better draw the blinds, before anyone else has a gander at this.'

'I don't know who could have done it, or why – as far as I know, all the pupils are fond of me,' Diana stammered, trembling as she let down the blinds and turned on the light.

Swainson tore down the banner with a flourish and Diana climbed onto a chair to yank down the Hitler hearts. 'Poor Cassandra, she's terrified.' The parrot was bobbing up and down and sliding from one end of her perch to the other.

Diana stepped down from the chair and attempted to smooth the hackled feathers on the back of the parrot's neck.

'Flaming Kraut!' Cassandra squawked at her, eyes ablaze, and then it came again: 'Flaming Kraut!'

Diana jumped back. 'What? She's never said anything like that before! Where can she have learned it?'

Swainson nodded sadly. 'I know someone who has said it on numerous occasions and I think we need to have a little chat with her in my office after school.'

An hour into the conversation, Caroline, sitting on the couch next to Clive, was still not ready to admit to – much less apologise for

– her actions. Swainson tried again to imbue her with some sense of regret. 'Caroline, what you've done is a criminal offence. You've trespassed on school property at night and with the items you planted in Fräulein von Ravensbrück's office you committed an act of defamation and harassment. I could pick up the phone right now and have you arrested.'

'I don't think so, Roger. It's me who'll be bringing a lawsuit against the school, not the school that will be pressing charges against me,' Caroline sneered. 'Blindefellows has carried out a campaign of victimisation against my family. First, the rejection of Clive as head of department, despite his having been the better candidate; and now, a year later, our sons have high-handedly been denied scholarships.'

'But Caroline,' Clive entreated, raising his head from his hands, 'I never wanted to be head of department – you know that. If only you were a bit less ambitious.'

'And as I've repeatedly told you,' Swainson interjected, 'the people who marked the scholarship exams were from an outside company and didn't know any of the candidates.'

'And even my vol-au-vent were picked on by that Nazi lesbian.' She jabbed the air in Diana's direction without looking at her.

Diana rose to her feet solemnly. 'My parents' beliefs were not passed on to their children... quite the contrary, actually. And just because I am unmarried, why do you presume I am homosexual?'

'Who's that girl you live with then, eh? Sobrinha, or whatever her name is', and Caroline jumped to her feet, put her hands on her hips and glared at up Diana.

'Sobrinha? My niece? "Sobrinha" is the Portuguese word for niece. I've been her guardian since my sister passed away two years ago. I returned to Brazil because my sister was terminally ill.'

Caroline retreated to her place beside Clive on the couch and, after a short uncomfortable silence, burst into sobs on his shoulder. Diana and Swainson decided to withdraw. In the hallway outside Swainson's office, they stood commiserating with Clive and the twins. Diana had an idea about how to resolve the situation with minimal loss of face for her colleague but she would need to make a few phone calls.

Later that day, back in Swainson's office with Caroline safely stowed at home for the time being, Diana presented a possible solution to which Clive readily agreed. King Fahd Academy, an elite boys' boarding school in Saudi Arabia, conducted entirely in English, was looking for a German teacher starting in September. The fantastically remunerated foreign staff lived in detached villas on a deluxe compound adjoining the school with its own outdoor pool, restaurant-bar and sports club. The school did not advertise its vacancies, which were filled exclusively by recommendation to the head, who happened to be an old friend of Diana's. The boys would associate with the cream of Saudi youth and would be kept out of mischief; the school was 20 miles from the nearest settlement, a tiny oasis which was largely a camel bazaar. Clive agreed that this would tick every one of Caroline's boxes. He then stood up and profusely thanked Diana, who had been holding their conversation while leaning against Swainson's capacious roll-top desk.

Full of admiration for the stately Amazonian elder who stood before him, Swainson looked fondly up at her and thought, *When I'm in Bunny's shoes a few years hence, I absolutely must, if she'll wear them, put her in mine… What a fine Deputy Head she will make.*

9

Randolph in the Underworld

Michaelmas 1995

Tristram Randolph, now entering his third year as Head of Drama at Blindefellows, had had little in the way of success as an actor after university and had lived at home in Twickenham for a spell, doing the occasional stint as a relief waiter. One day, after yet another long talk with his parents, he had tossed his dreams temporarily to the wind and gone off to Bishop Grosseteste College in Lincoln to get himself a teaching certificate. By teaching drama, he thought, he could at least keep his hand in until he was ready to return to the theatre – and until *it* was ready for him.

Due to only having boys in his A-level class, Randolph had made do as best he could with his all-male productions. These had, so he liked to tell his Lincoln theatre friends, 'aroused some controversy', such as his 'slightly naughty' production of *Twelfth Night*, when he had included a boy-on-boy-masquerading-as-girl-on-girl kiss between Olivia and Viola, played by his young protégés Hubert Alexander and Nicholas Geike. Of course, the boys in the cast had all been somewhat overshadowed in the end by Randolph's poignantly tragicomic Malvolio. His own wealth of thespian experience meant he was the natural choice for the more mature roles when he came to cast a play.

This year, however, he encountered an entirely new directorial difficulty. Girls now made up half of his A-level drama class. Faced with the head's demand for an annual classic and having already shown what he could do with the Bard, followed by a triumph with

Jonson (featuring himself in the title role of Volpone), he turned to Wycherley's *The Country Wife*. It had a number of juicy female parts and, besides, he had the perfect girl for Margery Pinchwife, the female lead, in Abigail Rathbone-Terry, generally known as Abi. True, she was unfortunately named for one with a speech impediment when pronouncing the letter 'R' but he, 'Mr Wandolph', found her quite adorable, with her cornflower-blue eyes, her rosy cheeks and her chaotic buttery curls, which were normally tethered into two plaits. She often forgot to do up all the buttons on her Blindefellows blouse, revealing her ample *décolletage* or her midriff in a manner befitting her character as the eponymous 'Country Wife'. She was always snacking, she explained, because she was 'gwowing'. 'In which direction?' was ever the riposte to this on the scarlet-glossed lips of Arabella Banks, the girl playing Alithea, the secondary female lead.

Here was a precociously mature young woman, Randolph thought, whom one would not feel amiss introducing into one's theatrical circle in London, if one were to have one. She was always chic and sleek in designer clothes, which Randolph had noticed came mainly from Nil by Mouth, the most costly boutique in the region. She wore her mane of razor-straight, horse-chestnut hair in a glossy, long-angled cut like a Forties femme fatale and she knew, Randolph reflected, just how to show off her jade-green eyes with mascara. The two girls were perfect opposites but both had developed one thing in common that might well undermine the whole production unless he mastered his directorial diplomacy. This 'thing' was, as he had anticipated from the day they had arrived in his class, 'a thing' for him.

Following the first week of auditions, he saw there was nothing for it – he and a couple of other teachers were going to have to step in and save the play. The boys simply weren't worldly enough to play the Restoration rakes. Of course, he, Tristram Randolph, would need to take on the lead role of Harry Horner; Tony Tree, Head of English, could, with about a minute-and-a-half of persuasion, be convinced to take on the part of Jack Pinchwife, the cuckolded husband whose best days are behind him. The trick there would be to get him to trim down that dreadful grey bramble of a beard into a decent King-Charles-the-Second handlebar and chinpuff. Randolph was a firm believer in the dictum that the look of the actor or actress is of primary importance. Never mind about acting ability – that would all fall into place, somehow or other, under his expert direction. Unfortunately, there arose another casting obstacle that he had never anticipated. None of the girls in the class was willing to take on the part of Old Lady Squeamish. Eager though they were to play minor male parts, it seemed that being an old lady of extremely unattractive appearance was anathema to them. He briefly considered playing this part too; it would have made a perfect comic cameo for him. The trouble was that Old Lady Squeamish's best lines were all in scenes with Horner. Playing both parts at once would be a feat even he couldn't pull off.

The solution to this conundrum presented itself a few evenings later when he went out to the Frog and Onion to catch the current round of The Ashes. Each time the Waugh twins racked up a few more runs against England, he'd offer Sedgewick another round by way of consolation. In this way, Randolph had talked Sedgewick into confessing an ambition he never knew he had – to tread the boards. 'Something from the history plays perhaps,' Sedgewick had slurred. 'I could see myself as a Coriolanus or perhaps a precocious Prince Hal.' By last orders, Randolph had him signed on as – as he phrased it – 'something from the comedies', a squeamish Squeamish.

Of course, Randolph could always rely on Tony Tree. Initially, Tree had been miffed at being squeezed out of teaching drama, after Bunny told Swainson about his desire to see 'cutting edge over sawing air' in theatre productions. But Tree had eventually warmed to Randolph, since he always found a part for him in the annual play, which was performed in the Hareton Theatre, with its capacity of 900 and its huge thrust stage, perfect for Tree's magnificent pontifications. Happily, in the case of Tree, who seldom went to the pub, getting him on board took no more than a pot of lapsang souchong served up in finest Wedgewood by his wife, Tabby, as Randolph expatiated upon the matchless dramatic opportunity awaiting her spouse.

'There are so many strong lines for a dramatic actor like you,

Tony.' Randolph beamed. '"Eternal shame on your family! Thou legion of bawds!"'

'Oh, that *is* rather good, isn't it?' Tree enthused, stroking his beard. 'I can just imagine the gestures that would accompany such rage!' He repeated the line, clutching his brow and then flinging his arms wide, almost knocking the teapot off the table, to indicate the sheer size of that bawdy legion.

Tabby Tree leapt to her feet and applauded with passion.

'That's it! Perfect!' Randolph gushed.

Thus was Tree hoodwinked into playing the cuckolded husband, a victory abetted by the fact that he could not quite recall the play's plot, which was why Randolph had withdrawn all the copies of it from the Lambton Library to ensure he would not find out more before committing.

A month into rehearsals, Randolph was already decked out in most of his costume to help him get into character. The costume budget was enormous but most of it was spent on Randolph in the lead role; the items purchased for him to wear eventually ended up in the wardrobe in his flat, lovingly driven there following the run of each play in his restored racing-green MG Midget, and often brought out at weekends to try on again in front of the full-length mirrors in his bedroom.

At today's rehearsal he was wearing a cherry-red velvet coat with a gold brocade trim that he'd had made by a tailor in London, which drew attention to his slim hips. He loved the rich, creamy, antique *broderie anglaise* that spilled out of the cuffs. The knee breeches, the buckled shoes and the white stockings emphasised his shapely calves. The *pièce de résistance* was to be the fair ringletted Restoration periwig, which he now awaited eagerly as he found his balding head increasingly difficult to cope with.

Today was the rehearsal of the scene that Abi had been so looking forward to, where Horner says to Margery, 'Give her this kiss from me'. Arabella was in the room, so Abi was looking forward to gloating. It was most unfortunate, however, that Randolph, at the very moment when he should have been saying the line, happened to glance out of the window at the building opposite his classroom, where he beheld one of the most glorious women he had ever seen. Upon a terrace overhung with bright orange passion fruit arose Botticelli's *Primavera* in a translucent pearlescent flowing dress that played about her perfect body in the breeze, her honey-coloured tresses loosely restrained in a blue ribbon: a ship's figurehead sailing into his heart.

'Mr Wandolph, you're supposed to kiss me now.' Abi was unable to hide the disappointment in her voice as Arabella sniggered cruelly.

'Ah, yes, hang on a min, where were we? Oh, yes,' Randolph stuttered. 'You, Goodson,' he called to a lackadaisical mousy-haired boy playing Sparkish. 'Stand in for Horner. I have to get something over there.' He made an exaggerated arm gesture in the direction of the goddess and sped off, making a beeline for the terrace opposite, with Abi and Arabella pretending not to watch him through the windows, striding across the grass. He had heard about Diana von Ravensbrück's beautiful niece who was so private, so solitary, that she barely came out of the apartment. By the time he came upon the terrace and looked up, Botticelli's muse had evaporated, and was replaced by what was, to all intents and purposes, a pirate. Missy Baba stared down at him, the young parrot on her shoulder tilting its head towards him. She said something disdainfully in an incomprehensible language and her gold molar glinted, making Randolph squint.

'Sorry, wrong way!' He feigned confusion and turned tail back to his rehearsal, only to bump into Japes, directly behind him.

'Yes, quite the Lady of Shallot we've got up there, isn't she, but a few months shy of her twentieth year.' He grinned. 'Do you suppose old Missy Baba is there to guard her virginity from young rogues like you?'

'Really, Japes, I caught sight of her on her balcony and was simply trotting over to introduce myself,' Randolph protested.

'No need to dissemble with me, Randy, my dear boy. I'm a fellow sportsman in that respect, as well you know. The difference between us, however, lies in our respective approaches to the game. Based

upon what I've heard of her from her aunt, I don't think she'll play –
or at least not with you.'

'So, you don't think I have a chance with her then? You know,
if I were to show you some photos of my ex-girlfriends, Japes, you'd
soon change your tune.'

'You needn't present me with evidence, Rambo. I'm not doubt-
ing your charms generally, only your odds with "*a sobrinha divina*".
No need to fret, though. As the saying goes, "There's an awful lot of
coffee in Brazil."'

Randolph turned on his heel and strutted back to the theatre,
with Japes in warm pursuit, delightedly whistling the tune of the
Frank Sinatra classic of his youth, the refrain of which he had so
instructively quoted for his ambitious colleague.

From that day, Abi and Arabella were bound together in mutual
envy of the object of their beau's wandering eye. He, meanwhile,
devised a cunning 'student empowerment strategy' that allowed him
to have more opportunities to slope off in rehearsals: each student was
now assigned a scene to direct, thus leaving Randolph with virtually
nothing to do. Whenever he espied the obscure object of his desire
out on her terrace – which was frequently, as it was proving to be
the finest Indian summer in years – he simply had the cast switch to
a scene that didn't require his character so he could nip out. Unfortunately, 'the Beauty' always appeared to be talking to someone, wearing earphones and reclining in a hammock, her ethereal face to the
sky, which meant he was unable to attract her attention, however
much he hailed her with his lace-trimmed arm. He was puzzled by
her conversation in a forced, faux-English accent, which he loitered to
catch as he nonchalantly ambled past: 'I would like the oysters tonight,
my dear. I have heard they are the best in town,' and, 'I'm afraid I
don't like this lingerie; it is the wrong colour for my complexion.'

After many a failed attempt, he finally managed to catch her
eye as she was lying on her side, and bowed to her extravagantly in
an exaggerated Restoration comedy style. She sat up curiously and
removed the headphones.

'*Bien le bonjour mon belle mademoiselle...* Alas, we've never been introduced. Sabrina, isn't it? I'm Tristram Randolph – the drama teacher,' he called up amiably. He had his periwig now and was feeling extremely confident.

'Why does everybody call me that here?' She screwed up her face, annoyed but no less beautiful. 'My name is Mafalda.'

'My folder?' He laughed.

'No, I know what a folder is and I am not a folder. Try to say it with a Portuguese accent: Ma-fal-da.'

He did as he was told but with an exaggerated generic foreign accent.

She laughed. 'You say it with a bit of a German accent, but that's okay; I grew up in Novo Hamburgo, Brazil, where half the people will only speak German.'

Missy Baba suddenly appeared – Randolph could not think from where – as if she'd sprung up through a trap door. She stood exactly between Randolph and Mafalda, who said something to her in a reassuring voice so that she retreated slightly.

'You seem to be on the phone a lot.' He tried to sound casual, as if he weren't prying.

'No, not the phone. I'm making my English better. I repeat the tape. It's very boring here so I do this, then maybe I can get a good job.'

'So you don't have friends yet?'

'I have my aunt and Missy and Yonathan.'

Randolph sensed a rival. 'And who might Jonathan be?'

'He's my little *papagaio!*'

'Your what?'

She turned to Missy Baba, whose lips he saw move.

'Baby parrot.'

On the spur of the moment, Randolph hatched a plan. 'Do you fancy coming to London with me next weekend? My cousin's given me two tickets to Monteverdi's *L'Orfeo*. Do you like classical music? My cousin's in it – plays the lute.'

'London? I would love to go to London!' Mafalda jumped up excitedly and Randolph almost fell backwards as, beyond a shadow of a doubt, she was in nothing but her own golden skin beneath her translucent dress. Missy Baba gave her a stern look that wiped the smile off her face. 'I will have to ask my aunt first,' she sighed.

'Oh! Well, be sure to tell her we'll be staying over with my parents. You'd have your own room. Speak to you about it tomorrow, Mafalda. Got to get back.' He gave Missy a reassuring nod and trotted back to his classroom, knowing his parents would be away all next week on one of their French wine tours and that he had their spare key on the ring in the pocket of his knee-breeches at that very moment.

An unfortunate sight met Randolph's eyes when he returned to the classroom. Tony Tree was there, acting the letter-writing scene with Abi, which Arabella was directing in the most savage manner, with the other students huddled around, astonished. Tree was puce and glossy-browed, pointing a very sharp pencil between Abi's eyes. 'Write as I bid you, or I will write "whore" with this pen-knife in your face,' he said through bared teeth, standing over her.

'Steady on there, Tree! I'm not you sure you should be doing it quite like that,' Randolph interjected.

'Well, she's the director.' Tree nodded towards Arabella. 'And I rather like her vision of Pinchwife as dangerously unbalanced. Plenty of opportunities for real acting there.'

Abi, in very real tears, took this distraction as an opportunity to slip away backstage and compose herself. Arabella tracked her with her gaze, her upper lip curling slightly.

That evening, a strained conversation in the German Riograndenser Hunsrückisch dialect of Brazil's far south was to be heard taking place between Mafalda and her aunt, Diana von Ravensbrück.

'But, Mafalda, I still don't understand: which teacher asked you to go?'

'What's his name, Missy? Tristing Adolf?' Missy sat silently regarding her, with Jonathan doing the same on her shoulder. 'The one who wears clothes for a play.'

'You mean Randolph!' Diana was unable to mask her surprise.

'He's ten years older than you and a shameless flirt with the Sixth Form girls. Absolutely not!'

'It's not like that, Auntie; he's just being friendly. We will stay over with his parents after the concert. Please let me go to London! We've been here a year and I've never asked to go anywhere.'

'Alright, alright. I will consider it. Let me talk to him first and go over his plans.'

The following afternoon, Diana von Ravensbrück appeared at the open door of the drama office just as Randolph was pulling on his knee-breeches for a rehearsal. He tried not to blush to the scant roots of his remaining hair as she held him fast in a firm stare as she enquired about the intended trip.

'Oh, it'll probably be a bit dull for her, Diana – hardly a rock concert. Then it's over to my parents for a spot of supper and a good night's sleep in the spare room. Everything above board, naturally. I heard from Japes about her mother – your poor sister – and just thought she might be cheered up by a change of scene.'

'You know, Tristram, she's not yet twenty, hardly older than the girls in your play. My sister was very over-protective and—'

'You needn't worry about a thing, Diana; she's in safe hands,' Randolph said, patting her elbow as he strode out of the office, as if to make his entrance upon the stage as Horner. In fact, he was going to the lavatory to splash cold water on his face; he found Diana von Ravensbrück strangely difficult to lie to. Japes's blurred reflection suddenly appeared in the mirror as he walked past the lavatories. He was singing, in a fair impression of Frank Sinatra, 'A language teacher's adopted daughter was accused of drinking water and was fined a great big fifty-dollar bill… Oh, there's an awful lot of coffee in Brazil.'

'Japes, is that really necessary?' Randolph pleaded, stepping into the hall.

'So you've freed the princess from her tower, but will you be able to locate the key to the chastity belt?' Japes grinned.

'Look, she's just going to an early-music concert with me in London. Nothing else!'

'Naturally, Random; it'd be beneath you to have designs on an ingénue of such proportions.'

'Exactly, Japes. My intentions toward her are entirely honourable. She's a stranger in a strange land and finally on the mend from mourning her poor mother. This is an act of chivalry, no more, no less.'

'Mm... an act... no more, no less,' Japes chuckled as he wended his way. 'Well, break a leg, Rudolph.'

Ten days later Randolph was sitting on the train next to Mafalda, hardly able to believe his luck, but on edge as he still felt the heat of Diana's stare. He wore his tweed cap at a rakish angle along with tight black cords, leather ankle boots and a vintage Aquascutum trench coat. He felt he'd achieved a theatrical look in addition to being naturally dashing. How could she resist?

A strand of her honeyed hair lay by chance on his shoulder and made him prickle with excitement. He inhaled her frangipani-blossom perfume deeply and felt the warmth of her turquoise cashmere jumper next to his upper arm, her leg, in tight denim, millimetres from his.

'Which name you like better, Tristram or Randolph? My aunt always calls you Randolph.'

Coming out of his reverie, Randolph explained. 'Oh, that's just a private-school thing, using surnames. It's more normal in the UK for people to be on first-name terms, so it's just Tristram.'

'Randolph is like dolphin,' she announced.

'Yes, I suppose it is.'

'You're a little like a dolphin with your bald head and small eyes,' she observed, regarding him with eyes the same hue of blue as her aunt's.

A vein throbbed in Randolph's temple. He had discovered 'Dolphin' to be the pupils' sobriquet for him and now he suddenly felt it might be inspired by more than his name alone.

'But you're still a good-looking man with a good body,' she continued.

Randolph reddened slightly and gave a demure smile. 'Why, thank you, Mafalda; you're not too bad yourself.'

His plan was going beautifully but, owing not only to Mafalda's exceptional loveliness but also to his betrayal of his pretences to her aunt, he was sick with nerves. When that happened, he often broke wind; he did not know why. He had previously attributed this tendency to his lack of success at auditions. He felt he could probably hang on for a time, until the trolley went by with the hot bacon, lettuce and tomato rolls, when the two vile odours would mingle and, with luck, no one would be any the wiser.

In London, Randolph wanted the wide-eyed and wondrous Mafalda to himself, so he opted for the expense of a taxi rather than take her down into the limbo of souls underground. It was drizzling and the multifarious lights of the city glittered in the droplets beaded on the taxi window. She peered out, placing her hand gently in his, and said something under her breath in Portuguese that he thought must've been something like, 'I can't believe I'm in London at last', and he smiled fondly at her. When they arrived at St Martin in the Fields for the concert, people were already starting to take their seats. It was a staged production and there was a huge, vividly painted fibreglass mouth of hell in the centre of the church's slab-stone floor. Randolph looked over to the dozen musicians seated at the side of the stage area, playing an early-music medley as the audience entered. He immediately saw his cousin, Leonardo, whom he hadn't clapped eyes on in four years, when shortly before his 18th birthday he had gone to study at Europe's top early-music conservatory, somewhere in southern Germany. It appeared that Leo was now rather surpassing him in looks. He leaned over his lute like Fiorentino's 'Musical Angel' on the altarpiece of Santa Maria Nuova in Florence, but with the child cherub's features replaced by those of some sinuous Renaissance youth with, to Randolph's supreme chagrin, thick, loosely curling auburn locks.

'Which is your cousin?' Mafalda asked.

'The one you're staring at now,' Randolph jested, a jealous gall rising.

'He's gorgeous!' was all she could say.

'Yes, but married to his music,' Randolph declared. 'Only has eyes for his lute.'

The opening night of this rare revival of the first-ever opera passed without a hitch, as one would expect from the Academy of Early Music at St Martin in the Fields. Randolph thought the hell's mouth used to particularly powerful effect, with the chorus of Infernal Spirits, in sackcloth and covered in ashen body paint – writhing inside it. He leaned toward Mafalda and whispered his approval of various dramatic touches, at which she appeared to nod appreciatively. During Leo's long lute solo, when he said, 'That's our little papagaio!' she furrowed her lovely brow and shushed him.

Leonardo had invited Randolph to the after-party, held in the church. Once the general public had all cleared out and the musicians had stowed away their instruments, Randolph strode forward to shake his young cousin's hand. 'What a triumph, Lenny, my lad!' he bellowed in his most theatrical voice.

'Tristram! Thanks so much for coming! It's great to see you after so long!' Leonardo then caught sight of Mafalda and nodded to her politely at which, unnoticed by Randolph, she blushed deeply.

'Well, it seems as if I'm finally a hair taller than you, Tris! How've you been keeping?'

'Fantastic, fantastic thanks, Lenny. I'm taking a breather from the stage for the moment to pass on my love for theatre to the cream of the West Country's youth... Let me introduce you to my friend Mafalda.' The two shook hands and Mafalda held on for longer than was customary.

'She's Brazilian,' Randolph chuckled by way of explanation. 'Grew up in Novo Hamburgo!'

At this news, Leonardo burst into Portuguese and Mafalda was thrilled, chatting away with him for five minutes before Randolph, with forced jollity, cleared his throat.

'Oh, sorry Tris! I had a friend at the conservatoire from Portugal. Went over there for a couple of summers and learned the basics. Great to see I can still converse. Let's get a drink and I'll introduce you and Mafalda to the cast.'

After a few stiff drinks, Randolph was holding forth to sundry cast members about how he'd stolen the show at the Lincoln Theatre Royal playing The Golden Fly in Offenbach's *Orpheus in the Underworld,* wearing gold spandex tights and leotard, with silver wings. After a few more rounds, he was even able to recreate for his crowd of admirers the famed 'Infernal Galop' around the Hell's Mouth to the tune now more familiar as the 'Can-Can', which he belted out as he galloped. While granting his audience an intermission in order that he might visit the toilet, he suddenly realised that he hadn't seen Mafalda and Leonardo for some time. Maybe, he thought, they should be getting off to his parents' place about now. He didn't feel he'd be able to negotiate the underground so he resolved to whisk her off in another hackney carriage as soon as he reached the end of what was panning out to being an astonishingly lengthy spell before the urinal.

When he returned to the nave, the musicians and performers had thinned out, while the group of admirers he'd been entertaining had all left without his having had the chance to bid them *adieu.* The only light still on was the green glow of the exit sign, which had a group of chorus-members still in their sack cloth underneath it, reclining on prayer cushions, pushing out the bar for total inebriation. He thought he heard Mafalda laugh but couldn't locate the source of the echo. There it was again, towards the vestry. He tripped over a prayer cushion and muttered, 'Impudence!' at it. He swung through the door, into what had been set up as a simple dressing room, with garments hanging on rails and full-length mirrors. There he caught a glimpse of Mafalda in profile, in his cousin's well-toned arms, passionate among the Orphic costumes. With an unexpected burst of energy, he charged towards her. Seconds later he was on the floor – he had crashed into a mirror, thinking he had been going in her direction. He looked behind him to see Mafalda, giggling and running out of the room, hand in hand with Leonardo. Recovering himself, he slunk after them, his head reeling, into the dimness of the church.

'Mafalda!' he yelled up to the rafters, and a pigeon fluttered upwards. 'Where are you? Come on, Mafalda, my parents await. Lenny, you thief of love, you blackguard! I brought you here, Mafalda! Please! Please! Alright, ignore me. You're a baggage, Mafalda, a filthy damned baggage!' And with that he keeled over. The sack-clothed people milled around him, helped him over to their cushions and offered him a glass of something green... *Absinthe? Or just some dreadful mix of spirits imbued with the colour of the exit light?* He didn't know and he didn't care. He drank it down, then had another and then a third. The Infernal Spirits smiled at him, now with missing teeth, peeling flesh and partially exposed eye sockets. He didn't remember that kind of realistic corpse make-up in the opera. Their faces were alarmingly near to his now, but he was stuck to the floor, gazing blankly back. Now the floor began to rotate and nausea welled up. He began to pant and then, with a sudden wrench of his whole body, to retch. The Infernal Spirits were on him now, writhing around him like eels in a mud-hole, their ragged hands moving all over his torso, holding him upright. Their fingers slid up his body to his neck and onto his face. 'Keep still!' he wanted to say, but words failed him and they eased him down into the mud and covered him.

When Randolph awoke, alone in the church, the bright midday light was smudging colour over his face. Above him, the fibreglass of the Hell's Mouth loured, beautified with stained-glass light. He didn't remember how he'd ended up in there. Someone had placed a large piece of sacking over him and left a plastic cup of water by him, which he drank down in one. Collecting himself, he wasn't so much miffed, now that Mafalda had gone off with Leonardo, as panicky about not bringing her home – and her aunt's reaction. He'd noticed a payphone in the foyer of the church the night before and, after 20 minutes searching with a pounding head, he found his jacket with Leo's number in the pocket. There were 10 rings before his cousin answered with a languid 'Hello'.

'Leonardo? Is that you, Lenny?'

'Tris, hi. Are you better now? Back in the land of the living?'

'Just about. Hangover headache but I've only got myself to

blame. I was just wondering about Mafalda. I'm hoping to God she's with you.'

'Yeah, she crashed here last night. You seemed to be in for an all-nighter, Tris, and she was ready for bed.'

'Yes, I can imagine... The thing is, Leo, she's meant be going back to the sticks with me today. I promised her aunt I'd look after her. I don't want to return empty-handed.'

'Well, she's still asleep, Tris, so you'll have to go home *sans baggage* and make your apologies.'

'Ah, yes, sorry about that. Booze talking. She's nothing like a baggage at all. I don't know why I said that.'

'No worries, Tris. I'll get her to call her aunt as soon as she gets up. I've asked her to hang on here with me for a few more nights and she's accepted. We'll see the sights of London town during the day.'

'Right, yes, splendid idea. Great show last night, Lenny. Thanks so much for the tickets.'

'No probs, Tristram. See you again in a few years, I hope.'

'Yes, righto, bye for now.' And he put down the receiver.

As he walked to the nearest underground, Randolph muttered some of his favourite Restoration insults under his breath: 'Odious beast, filthy toad, wretch, incredulous chit, magpie, drivelling idiot.' Much as he wanted to pretend he was addressing these to Leonardo and Mafalda, it was himself he was excoriating.

Sitting on the train back to the 'Mild West', he ordered a black coffee and a BLT, now purely for reasons of hunger, as his nervous tummy had been replaced by a devil-may-care one.

Back at school, he assiduously kept out of Aunt Diana's way, avoiding the staffroom for the next week. When, finally, she did pass him in a corridor, she was, to his astonishment, full of smiles.

'I want to thank you, Randolph, for introducing Mafalda to your cousin. He's an absolute star and I can't wait to meet him. She's having a wonderful time in London. This is the happiest she's been since before my sister fell ill; perhaps the happiest she's been ever.

You've given her the opportunity to step out into the wide world as a woman.'

'Oh, of course, good, I'm so glad. It's all turned out better than I'd ever hoped,' he lied.

'She's decided to stay on there until the end of the run of *L'Orfeo*,' Diana enthused. 'Then Leo's coming back with her to stay here for a few days. And how were your parents?'

'No idea, they're still in Fr—' Randolph stopped himself. 'Fromages. Didn't even get to see them as I arrived after they'd gone to bed, after seeing Leo and Mafalda safe. When I woke up, they'd gone off shopping for *fromage*. They're totally mad on French cheese these days. Not really the best thing for people of your – I mean, their – age. Then I had to be on my way before they got back... Anyhow, rehearsal awaits!'

Diana watched him recede down the corridor, hoping his cousin would prove easier to follow.

Following six more weeks of rehearsals, with the captain now back at the helm for all scenes, *The Country Wife* began its three-night run. Every student in the school was set on attending as word had got round that Mr Sedgewick, in the role of Old Lady Squeamish, was wearing a mop cap and starched pinafore smock-dress, which Japes had told everyone made him look like the spitting image of Toad as the washer woman in *The Wind in the Willows*. Mr Tree, meanwhile, had fine-tuned his part such that Pinchwife bore more of a resemblance to Bill Sykes from *Oliver Twist* than to a comically cuckolded Restoration husband. The production proved to be a touch unconventional in other ways as well. Randolph had decided to do the infamous 'China Scene' with Sir Jasper Fidget delivering his allusive line – 'My Lady Fidget, he is coming into you the back way' – in a spotlight downstage, while Lady Fidget moans back – 'Let him come and welcome, which way he will' – in a compromising silhouette with Horner.

When news of this reached Bunny, who had passed his entire adulthood being utterly discreet about his own intimate life, he was sufficiently perturbed to attend the school play for himself, rather than leaving it to his trusty deputy, Swainson, as had been his habit from time to time. Unamused though he was by the silhouette, it faded into insignificance in the light of events unique to the school play's final performance. Knowing full well that this was her last chance to act upon the crush that had, for an entire term, been consuming her adolescent soul, Abi Rathbone-Terry took the performance into her own hands. On Horner's line, 'One kiss more', which had, on previous nights, been followed by a peck on the cheek, Abi now quickly turned her face to Randolph and grabbed his ears, pressing his lips onto hers with such force that his periwig came off and his thinning pate gleamed in the spotlights. An audible collective gasp rose in the auditorium, followed by a lunatic giggle from Abi, who stared past Randolph at Arabella Banks's powdered, bony face glaring at her from the wings.

When the time came for the curtain call, Randolph found himself hoping, as he peered out into the stalls, that Mafalda might have made it to this final performance and that she, made aware of the effects of his talents and charms upon Abi, would regret her choice, if only for a moment. Alas, she was not present. As the applause died down and the students, faculty and parents (thankfully few in number by the last night of the show) began to file out, Bunny remained in his seat, tall and dignified as ever, left leg crossed over right, his long hands resting one upon the other upon his long shank.

'Tomorrow, Swainson,' Bunny began, 'could you bring Mr Randolph to understand that this is to be the last Blindefellows school play in which staff act alongside students. We've boys *and* girls to play all the parts now, so it's just a question of choosing our scripts prudently.'

'Hm, Reverend, I'm not sure how that'll go down with Randolph.'

'Should he hesitate to comply, Swainson, then tell him I shall expect him to present himself in my office by the end of the school day.'

'Well, I think that will probably settle it there and then. Should I convey the same message from you to Tree and Sedgewick?'

'I don't imagine that will be necessary. I believe they're as much victims in this as Miss Rathbone-Terry.'

'Yes, I rather thought that myself.'

'Very good, Swainson. You know I rely on your perspicacity and our likeness of mind.'

At this, Bunny rose and gestured to his destined successor to precede him out of the theatre. As they left, they spotted Japes heading backstage to enjoy a slice or two of pizza and a discussion with his old crony, Sedgewick, on the jolly subject of Mr Toad as one of the truly great fools in the English literary canon.

The students were all still in the dressing rooms, removing their make-up and getting into mufti for a last night party. Randolph, who felt no urgency to remove his costume, makeup or periwig, stood by the refreshments table, tucking into a slice of pepperoni pizza.

'Randolph, my boy!' Japes bellowed. 'Haven't seen you around school in ages! Well done tonight!'

'You know how it is, Japes. They're all-consuming, these bloody school plays.'

'Especially, I think, for those drama teachers who cast themselves in the star role in addition to directing,' Japes quipped, handing Randolph a plastic cup of Fanta. 'I must say, I particularly liked one of your character's witticisms: "Bubbled of his mistress as of his money."'

'Not too much money. Just a few train and taxi fares,' Randolph admitted. 'I've learned my lesson, Japes: don't go to them, let them come to you.'

'Bravo, Randolph, that's how I've always played it and I've never been left high and dry.'

Abigail Rathbone-Terry emerged from the dressing room in a tiny black party dress cut slightly lower and vastly higher than the Restoration number from which her plump form had just been liberated. She descended upon the pizza, plucking up the largest slice of the as-yet-untouched triple-cheese pie and bit off the tip. Masticating fiercely, she turned to her idol, rested her free hand on her ample hip and asked him, 'Mr Wandolph, will you dance with me later?'

Japes answered on his younger colleague's behalf. 'Certainly not, after your fanciful improvisations in the Third Act in front of the entire school. Off with you now, and dance with Goodson. I hear he's mad for you.'

'Ooh, is he?' she yelped and teetered off on her black patent heels.

10

Gone with the East Wind

Trinity and Michaelmas 2001

Head of Classics, Aristarchus Crane, or 'Starchy', as he was referred to by the pupils, sauntered into his study next to his bedroom to catch up on his contributions to *Ask an Alum*, a forum for prospective students of his old stomping ground, Oxford University. He generally found the internet irksome, but he had given in to his son's demands. Now he felt he had to make some use of it, hence his agreeing to sign up for this service to undergraduates. Tedious was too mild a word for it – the youngsters seemed obsessively concerned with trivialities such as mixed showers and vegetarian diets; quite different from the higher thought of his day. It had been over a month since he had last 'logged on' and he skimmed over nigh on 30 posts needing answers.

One particular question piqued his interest. It was from a young lad destined to follow in Crane's own footsteps with an offer from Brasenose to read Classics. The boy had all kinds of questions about the set books for Michaelmas, which he had already read, and now sought additional materials he might 'look over'. Crane leaned back in his Chesterfield swivel-chair, splayed fingertips touching in front of his long chin, and considered which scholarly works might inspire this promising young man. After five minutes of slow contemplation, he leaned forward and scrolled down to give his response, which would be quite a trial for him because he could type only with his two index fingers... But the words, 'You are a twat!' struck him in the face. Aghast, he perused other recent responses beside his name and his carefully chosen, affable photograph. They were equally crass and similarly characterised by allusions to private parts.

'Clarissa. Clarissa!' he wailed in the direction of his wife, who was curled up on the sofa downstairs reading the Sundays. She entered the room with her usual patient, helpful expression, which generally had a calming effect on her husband – but not today.

'Look! Look at this! I... I... I would never! I can't believe it!' He stammered apoplectically, clamping a sweating palm to his ashen cheek. Clarissa calmly leaned over to decipher the words towards which her husband was so frantically gesticulating... and laughed.

'Why are you laughing?' he squawked, his voice shrilling to its top octave. 'Did *you* do this?'

'Of course I didn't. I don't have your password,' she reassured him firmly. 'Perhaps it was Tom having a giggle; he's the computer whizz in this house.'

'Would you *stop* calling him that? He's nearly eighteen, for goodness sake – he ought to be referred to by his full name. In the meantime, where *is* Ptolemy, so I can ask him how to get rid of this?'

'He's out. But it's quite simple, just click on each reply and press delete.' She leaned over him to demonstrate, her cream silk dressing gown softly brushing his face but failing to soothe him in the slightest.

'Did you say that Ptolemy could have done this? Why would he do such a thing?' Crane flung himself out of his desk chair, stalked over to the window on his stork-like legs and peered out, as if hunting for a newt in the garden. 'Some of those messages are two weeks old. Hundreds of people must have seen them by now. I'm a prominent Old Brasenosian! What will people think?'

Clarissa quietly lowered herself into the Chesterfield to complete the deletions. She sat, focused on the task, while Crane awaited reassurance, his eyes fixed on her.

'There we are. All done now.' She smiled at him pacifically and rose to resume her consumption of the Sundays.

'You know, Clarissa, I've just remembered: someone at school has been hacking into staff email and using remarkably similar explicit vocabulary. Swainson made an announcement to the boys at Latin Prayer the other week that anyone with a clue as to whom it might be should come forward. I'm going to have to inform him, as I now suspect we may well be sheltering the culprit beneath our very roof.'

Clarissa turned and looked her husband in the eye. 'You can't do that! Tom's A-levels are next month! Boys will be boys, Aris. If they expel him, he's had it – he'll lose his university place.'

'My reputation at Brasenose is what has had it. It's about time someone halted Ptolemy in his tracks, and Swainson's just the man to do it. That boy doesn't care a fig for a thing I say and you've indulged him for too long. Anyway, an offer from a former polytechnic to study sport science isn't worth tuppence ha'penny.'

'It's the only offer he wanted and it's the only one he's got. Would you really risk taking that away from him?'

Clarissa gathered her silk dressing gown around herself and left her husband to mull over whether his allegiance was to his only child or to the two educational establishments to which he had devoted most of his life, but she already knew in her heart what the outcome would be.

In Swainson's office the following morning, Ptolemy Crane – or Tom, as he preferred to be called, in defiance of his father's wishes – blithely confessed and showed very little remorse. After careful consideration, Swainson and Bunny decided they had no other course than to expel Tom, but agreed to allow the lad to sit his exams at Blindefellows, for which Crane thanked them both obsequiously. Tom, for the sake of a quiet life, went through the motions of apologising for his miscreant behaviour. Something inside him, he explained, had finally snapped during his last term at Blindefellows, a school he'd never felt particularly comfortable in and whose stuffier traditions had always chafed him. In addition to the hacking lark which, in order to shield his accomplices, he insisted that he'd carried out alone, he admitted that he was also the one who'd been dropping burning trainers out of windows onto the heads of some of the teachers – 'but only when they were wearing their mortarboards'. This had culminated in one falling onto Sedgewick while wearing his academic gown. Matron Ridgway, fearing the hapless history master would go up like a Roman candle, had rugby-tackled him and rolled him along on the grass, while Crane had stood by, drawling, 'You want to put that out quickly because his gown's from Warwick, which means it's basically polyester, unlike the silk-linen blends in which we Oxbridge masters robe ourselves.'

That evening in Crane's study, rather than any frank discussion of Tom's state of mind, either leading up to or following on from his 11th-hour expulsion, there were instead the usual recriminations over his lack of academic prowess. From his accustomed perch on the Chesterfield swivel-chair, Crane repined, 'Both your mother and I are Oxford Classics graduates and my father was a don there. Yet your sole offer is from a former polytechnic to read sport science. Where have we gone wrong with you, Ptolemy?'

For his part, Tom bemoaned his father's ever having forced him to attend Blindefellows, as well as having chosen such a silly name for him – 'They called me Lobotomy all through the first form!' – followed by his customary announcement that he would change it to Tom by deed poll when he reached his 18th birthday. Meanwhile, Clarissa's final words to her husband on the matter – 'I'll never forgive you for reporting Tom and just before he takes his A-levels!' – drew a line under Crane's oft-repeated justification of his actions. On the bright side, however, mother and son were now able to spend more time together and enjoyed one another's company throughout the school day in the absence of Crane's lofty presence. They went out to the Four and Twenty Blackbirds, where she helped him revise over sandwiches, cream cakes and coffee. Often, they would save their crusts and walk over to the riverside where they would feed the swans, as they had when he was still a small boy and she a young woman. She held onto every moment, knowing her time as a mother was draining away and that she faced a cold future alone with Crane.

After the exams were over, Tom went off for a fortnight of unbridled merriment in Ibiza with his mates from the Sixth Form at the local comprehensive, a journey that Crane thoroughly disapproved of and towards which he refused to contribute a penny.

Clarissa began ponderously gathering his things in the spare room for his long-anticipated trip to university, in Brighton. Occasionally she would ask him if he thought he might need some superfluous item like a potato masher or an apple corer. She neatly wrote out simple recipes for him in a little notebook and amassed dry ingredients to accompany them. The items mounted up and she packed them with Jenga-puzzle precision into labelled cardboard boxes, unpacking and repacking when a packet of macaroni or a tub of raisins wouldn't fit properly. Crane kept to his study and out of her way. His *Ask an Alum* account had been suspended pending investigation. He felt certain that once the boy was gone, Clarissa's state of mind would improve and they could move on to other things. Perhaps they might get out a bit and join the Ramblers' Association. In the meantime, he sought solace in the epics of Quintus Smyrnaeus, writing up a list of anachronisms in the poet's depiction of the Trojans and Achaeans.

The day came to drive Tom to Brighton. Crane offered to come along to carry boxes but Clarissa assured him that the welcome committee at the university provided this service. She'd stay over in Brighton for the weekend in a guest house, just in case Tom needed anything. On her return, Crane heard her walk into the hallway and stifle sobs. He waited diplomatically in his study to allow her time to acclimatise to the change. In the following weeks, more often than not he found her inhabiting Tom's bed in the mornings. Sleepily she'd tell him he'd been snoring in the night so she'd moved. She often slept until midday wearing one of Tom's over-stretched T-shirts which he'd thrown into a bag for recycling. It was as if, Crane thought, she was becoming Tom. She'd even got herself a short 'mod' haircut like Tom's, which somewhat alarmed him with its lack of femininity. She didn't put any time into the cooking, as she had when Tom was there. She no longer made everyone's favourite, fisherman's pie.

Crane confided in Swainson, explaining he was at a loss to know what to do, and could he perhaps give Clarissa a role teaching English to the Chinese pupils, to take her mind off Tom?

'Yes, good idea, Crane – distract her from her fledged young. Either get a job or get a Labrador like young Cadbury here, is what I say!' He slapped the fleshy sides of the ottoman-shaped chocolate lab panting beside him. 'She can start right after half term. We'd be happy to have her on board.'

Clarissa generally had her nose in a book, and it was Crane's life-long habit, passed down from his own father, never to disturb anyone absorbed in reading. This made it difficult for him to start conversations with her, which is what she intended. Finally, over a supper of microwaved frozen pizza, he explained that the Chinese pupils needed a spot of extra help with their English, and would she mind giving up a few hours of her time each week until the Christmas holidays. After a few hours of thought, she agreed to take it on.

Over the next few weeks, Crane found himself surprised at the enthusiasm with which Clarissa threw herself into her new post. Indeed, on several evenings she went so far as to bring it home with her in the form of a gaggle of Chinese boys in the Third and Fourth Forms to whom she even offered use of their private bathroom facilities, including towels, which they would leave on all the radiators to dry, filling the house with steamy dampness and leading Crane to imagine himself living in a Chinese laundry. Following the showers, they would gather in the kitchen, where Clarissa gave them free reign to prepare home-cooked Asian meals, all of which appeared, to his befuddlement, to involve Pot Noodle.

She went along fairly buoyantly until Tom rang one day to announce that he'd be away for some of the Christmas holidays as he'd been invited to Hogmanay at a new friend's hunting lodge up in the Scottish Highlands. Picking up on the distress in his mother's voice at this prospect, he added, 'Term's over by mid-December, Mum, so not to worry, I'll still be at home with you for the first couple of weeks.'

Crane tried to comfort her to the best of his abilities, handing her a twenty-pound note together with an invitation he'd received to the upcoming Rotary Club Christmas Ball and declaring, 'You can go out and buy yourself a new dress.'

He also shared the exotic news that a Maori rugby coach had arrived and would be working at Blindefellows until the end of term. He was on a teacher exchange scheme with McKenzie, the Blindefellows' Head of PE and rugger coach, known to the boys as 'Bollocks McKenzie' for reasons Crane had always hesitated to enquire, although he had picked up that it was something to do with a malfunctioning bathing suit.

'The boys tell me he'll be demonstrating a *kaka* on the stage in assembly tomorrow,' Crane declared, trying to be as chipper as possible.

'I think you mean a *haka*, Aris,' she corrected him.

It was Friday afternoon and the Maori rugby coach, who had taken up his duties earlier that week, was to be formally introduced at a whole-school assembly by Swainson. There was an air of nervous anticipation, as there was a general belief that the Maori teacher was about to appear naked, or almost naked, on stage. Japes, with his love of all things anomalous was on the edge of his seat, his unkempt hairs bristling with static electricity in the direction of the ceiling. Sedgewick, beside him, was, however, slightly more reluctant. Public displays of semi-nudity by either sex, or even the prospect thereof, were inevitably unsettling to him.

Crane was surprised to see that even the secretaries had been drawn out of their crannies and now stood clustered shyly in the entrance way to the auditorium. The female teachers in the hall were, he noted, behaving abysmally. They had quickly shaken off their initially demure conduct when they started working at Blindefellows, and had gradually turned quite crass. Not one of them was Oxbridge and he suspected that they had all been to comps. They were making grotesque tribal gestures, guffawing and doubling up. Crane was grateful Clarissa was not in their vicinity although, he reassured himself, she would never participate in such vulgar antics.

Swainson appeared at the lectern and the pupils were instantly attentive.

'It's not every day that a teacher travels more than eleven thousand miles to come to work. Nevertheless, that is what our Mr McKenzie and New Zealand's Mr Amiri of the Benjamin Greenfield School for Boys in Auckland have done this month. They have embarked on a teacher exchange scheme in order to promote a more global outlook that is surely good for us all, as we can see in the international community that our school has become. As such, they each set off last weekend and, like planes that pass in the night – somewhere over Thailand, so I'm told – they took up their respective posts at one another's school on Monday morning.

'Mr Amiri, who tells me his name means "East Wind" in the Maori tongue, is one of the most gifted coaches active in New Zealand Under-18s rugger today, and I have already been hearing reports of the magic he has been working this week with our team, the Blindefellows Black Sheep. It is now my pleasure to introduce him formally to our community in this whole-school assembly. Many of you already know the *haiku* from your television screens, where you will doubtless have seen it performed shortly before the All Blacks thoroughly trounce one or other of our British national teams.'

Sitting in the audience, Tree furrowed his brow trying to work out why this whimsical form of poetry would be performed at the start of major international rugby matches.

'However,' Swainson continued, 'I imagine that precious few of you have had the opportunity to witness a live performance of this ritual war dance which, in times not-so-long past, was used by Maori warriors to terrify their enemies prior to battle. Though the display we are about to see may strike some of us as a smidgen unorthodox, I trust that everyone among us will refrain from any impolite sniggering. So, without further ado, I present to you Mr Amiri performing his *haiku*.'

Ecstatic applause accompanied by hoots – from one of the female staff, Crane suspected – were heard as a strapping Maori man approaching middle age assumed his position centre-stage. He wore nothing but a knee-length skirt of some fibrous material and had inky spirals drawn onto his face. Crane already felt a welling discomfort as soon as the fellow stepped onto the stage, but the *haka* shocked him to the core. The harsh slapping of thighs and forearms seemed inordinately loud, but then this was a man built like a rhinoceros. If, Crane thought, he himself were to attempt antics like these, surely no more than a muffled pat would be audible and they would be sure to result in dreadful bruising.

As Mr Amiri played the fierce tribal rhythm on his rippling musculature, he barked an accompaniment in his native language, his eyes periodically popping and his tongue shooting forth like some obscene cuckoo clock. All of a sudden he sank down, his hands wavering, his voice now a tad softer as he called up to the heavens like some incanting shaman. It was at just this moment that Crane shifted in his seat and caught a glimpse of Clarissa sitting with the Chinese students, reddening to the roots of her fair hair. It just wasn't right that Swainson had thrust this on respectable people.

The Maori man then arced into a graceful turn and all was then revealed: what he was wearing wasn't so much a grass skirt as a grass apron which exposed his intricate buttock tattoos. There was an audible intake of breath from the auditorium that was quickly dispelled by Japes leaping to his feet and shrieking, 'Bravo!' This seemed to break the ice and got most of the pupils jumping up, whistling and whooping. The noise, Crane thought, was appalling, but it was the sight of Clarissa joining in with the commotion and leaping – yes, leaping – up and down that fairly made him swoon.

'Sit down!' he called in her direction, and the boys immediately to his left returned to their seats – but his wife didn't hear him: or perhaps she did, but was no longer listening.

Swainson returned to the lectern, his eyes glistening. 'Marvellous, Mr Amiri, just marvellous!' The racket subsided and the audience returned to their seats. 'I think I can confidently say that that was the most remarkable display that has ever, in four hundred years, taken place in these hallowed halls.'

Mr Amiri bowed courteously. 'Thank you for giving me the opportunity to share the *haka*, sir. The Blindefellows Black Sheep are looking forward to learning the routine themselves, and will try it out with me at the start of their match against Swineforth Hospital next week.'

'Fabulous!' Swainson beamed. 'It's about time we gave the Swines a good roasting. And will you be eating them when you defeat them, in the grand old Maori style?' Mr Amiri laughed politely and shook his head.

At dinner that evening, Crane asked his wife how she could ever have behaved in such an indecorous manner at a school assembly. 'I don't know why I did it,' she replied, her green eyes glowing. 'It just made me feel… well… liberated.'

'Why would watching a half-naked man stomp about like that make you feel liberated?'

'I simply couldn't say,' was the extent of her reply.

'Well, thank goodness he'll be gone by Christmas.' Crane picked up his plate and walked into the kitchen to put it in the dishwasher. 'I only hope his uncouth example doesn't encourage those boys to get tattoos on their behinds. And did you see Japes? Hardly the choicest role model, as usual, and we're supposed to be the ones with the clear heads.'

But when he turned he found he was talking to the four walls. Clarissa had gone up to bed and had left her plate for him to clear away.

All the next week, Clarissa stayed behind after school. She told Crane to go home without her as she had orals to do and she'd walk back later. Crane found himself looking out of the window at the setting sun.

One day, she bustled back after dark, looking flushed and flustered.

When he woke up one Sunday morning, he heard her busying herself in the kitchen and hoped she might be preparing them a cooked breakfast with smoked kippers, something she hadn't done since Tom had gone. He went into the bathroom and combed his hair. He put on his casual weekend clothes – his old cricketing slacks and a tan turtleneck that served to cover his Adam's apple, which was beginning to look particularly sharp these days. It had become impossible to shave around this pointed protuberance, such that Crane had developed a sort of trimmed version of a turkey's tassel.

On entering the kitchen, he saw Clarissa was indeed busy, but she was placing everything into Tupperware containers: lamb stew with dumplings, sliced mango and freshly made bread rolls. She was wearing her red wool duffel coat with all the toggles done up.

'Morning Aris, must dash, got a message that Mr Amiri is very ill. This cold climate doesn't suit him at all. He's a North Islander, you know: "the Coast of Coromandel, where the early pumpkins grow", as Edward Lear wrote. Thought I'd take him all this, with the food being a bit sketchy at school on a Sunday. He's got a match coming up and he's insisting on getting out of bed to coach the boys! Can't have him catching pneumonia, you know.'

'I thought you might be doing brunch, like in the old days,' Crane mumbled.

'There's some of that muesli you like, with the dried mulberries, and there are a couple of those pizza baguettes in the freezer you could have later, for lunch.' She placed the last Tupperware in her basket and sped out of the house.

Twenty minutes later, Clarissa strolled into school and passed Japes, who had been visiting Matron Ridgeway. He greeted her warmly. 'Well, hello, Clarissa. You look like Little Red Riding Hood off to visit Grandma with provisions. Or perhaps you're visiting– dare I venture to say it – the wolf?'

'Oh, yes, the wolf – but he's really a lovely beast, you know.'

Full of admiration, Japes watched her walk off jauntily towards the staff quarters. He'd always felt she was wasted on a cold fish like Crane.

Passing Crane on the stairs the next day, Japes asked him where he might find Clarissa.

'Sorry, Japes, haven't seen her all day,' Crane replied languorously.

'Gone with the East Wind, perhaps?' Japes called after him, grinning – and he registered Crane take a few faltering steps before resuming his usual languid, long-legged progress.

In his empty classroom, Crane quickly closed the door and malfunctioned, putting text books out on the desks and then collecting them in again, sharpening pencils, opening and closing his blinds. Four words kept going around his head and he whispered under his breath: 'Clarissa, please *Abstineo, abstinere, abstinui, abstentus.*' He wrote them on the blackboard in copperplate, again and again, before collapsing in his chair, his bony frame wracked with sobs.

The bell brought him to his senses. He sprang to his feet, mopped his tear-stained face with his monogrammed handkerchief and patted down his hair. At the door, he could hear the pupils starting to line up. In a moment, he would have to let them in. He took a deep breath, drawing solace from the portraits of the classical philosophers he had hung at regular intervals above the wainscoting when he had taken up residence in the classroom upon his arrival at Blindefellows a quarter-of-a-century earlier. He gazed at the pictures until his breathing was regular again, before opening the door.

The pupils took their seats with the usual decorum. Crane left the door open to allow for a through-breeze as he still felt agitated. He had never wept like that in his life and it pained him to think he could lose control like that. He told the pupils to open their textbooks at chapter three. As they were doing this, Hipkiss raised her hand and asked him the meaning of the verb on the board. Crane convulsed inwardly as he realised it was still there and his heart was laid bare in front of the class.

'It means 'to refrain from' and you will be learning the conjugation of this verb today, Hipkiss.'

Hipkiss persisted. 'But why did you write it about twenty times?'

'Because you will be repeating it twenty times in order to learn it, of course.' Crane's crisp tone put the idea of any further questioning out of anyone's head. 'Right, open your notebooks and recite the words.' The pupils chimed in with '*Abstineo, abstinere, abstinui, abstentus*,' again and again. About half way through this recital, Clarissa walked past, leading her group of Chinese students to the library, and looked into the room. His beseeching expression was met with a serene smile from her, as if to say, 'The deed is done; let us move on.'

When Crane arrived home that evening, he found Clarissa in bed with a mug of Lemsip. She'd developed a high temperature and had been driven home by Swainson who, it seemed, had forgotten to inform Crane that his wife had gone home sick.

'There's something going round.' She sniffled hoarsely. 'I haven't even got Tom's bed made and he's coming back tomorrow.'

'Don't worry; I can do that,' Crane reassured her. He had decided this was an opportunity to prove himself to her. He brought her hot instant soup and, later on, tea and toast with honey on a pretty tray, after which he watched her sleep and occasionally dabbed her clammy brow.

By Christmas day, Clarissa was fit enough to make dinner after Crane had been sent on several shopping trips to gather ingredients. Since Tom had returned two weeks earlier, he had been at his mother's side, talking quietly with her and giving her what appeared to be reassuring hugs. No longer were they avoiding Crane, but asking him to sit with them and doing their best to include him in their conversations. It wasn't easy, but everyone tried. In the back of his mind, Crane knew what they knew – this was their final Christmas together. He was tempted to become angry and petty but he called up the images of the philosophers hanging on his classroom wall and compelled himself to remain calm. The incident in the classroom had alarmed him. That person wasn't him.

When Tom left, Clarissa left. She said she was taking the taxi to the train station with him but Crane saw the extra cases going into the boot. From the window, he watched the cab retreat down the long, straight road until it was nothing more than a yellow dot. Then he went into the kitchen to read the note. She was going to New Zealand and she was sorry. Crane wavered for a moment, feeling his throat tighten. His Adam's apple rose and fell, but then he nodded to himself resignedly, breathing deeply until the feeling passed. After several hours of careful consideration, he resolved what he must do: he would get a cat – a Siamese perhaps, flaxen and lithe. It would be enough.

11

A Farewell from Fairchild

Lent 2004

Fairchild was dead. The obituary in *The Travistock Times* took up a half-page spread with a large photograph of the man himself, taken seven decades earlier, capturing a rare smile. 'Francis Eugene Lafayette Fairchild, treasured son of Lionel and Madeline Fairchild (deceased), passed into the light on 22 March 2004 at the age of 88. Loved and cherished by all who knew him. Funeral at St Peter's Church, Travistock, Wednesday 31 March, 2pm. White lilies only.'

'I suppose we'd better put in an appearance at the funeral, those of us who "loved and cherished" him,' Bunny said to Swainson. 'I'll ask Brenda to spread the word.'

As was to be expected, given Fairchild's age and temperament, the Blindefellows' turnout was thin. Bunny stood in the church porch with Swainson, Japes and Sedgewick, sheltering from the wind stirring up the leaves.

'Surprised to see you here, Sedgewick,' Japes said, 'After Fairchild's perennial animosity towards you for saving the flock.'

'Well, I thought I should tag along; there's often a meal laid on after these services, in the Travistock Grand or The Unicorn.'

'No such offering will be made in this case, Sedgewick,' said Swainson. 'Not even soup and sandwiches in the Frog and Onion, such was Fairchild's spirit of generosity.'

Four black geldings with black plumes on their heads pulled an ornate carriage hearse towards St Peter's. The glass-sides revealed Fairchild's ebony coffin, topped with white lilies. In the course of his 30 years in Travistock, Sedgewick had never seen a horse-drawn hearse. The vehicle and, most likely, the animals pulling it must have been specially brought in from Plymouth or Exeter, at enormous expense. Swainson had forgotten about the stipulation in the memorial notice and placed his bunch of yellow chrysanthemums on a bench in the corner of the porch.

Behind the carriage walked a petite woman with a black translucent billowing veil, giving a glimpse of a deathly pallor and dark eyes beneath. She was flanked by six pallbearers in top hats.

'However, Fairchild appears to have spared no expense on his final journey,' Swainson corrected himself.

'You'd never have thought it, for all his miserly ways, but Fairchild's family was one of the wealthiest in the West Country in the nineteenth century,' Bunny chipped in.

'Who's the woman?' asked Japes.

'No idea,' Bunny replied. 'He was unmarried, so a sister, perhaps, or a professional mourner, like the pallbearers.'

Without glancing in their direction, the woman followed the casket into the porch. She wore a knee-length black velvet dress and a waist-length black wool cape. There was some kind of small fur clasped close about her neck and Sedgewick shuddered at the bead-like eyes in its head, which he felt were peering at him nastily, reminding him of Fairchild's fiendish little face. In the hand at her breast she clutched a bunch of white daisies.

The four schoolmasters went in at a respectful distance behind her as she moved at the stately, measured pace of a bride walking down the aisle. They sat down in the middle of the empty church, the only people present apart from a roughly-dressed burly fellow with greying red hair, sitting right at the back.

The vicar delivered his eulogy, which dropped in some of Fairchild's accomplishments: photographer, archivist, scholar, poet, playwright, landscape gardener; and humanitarian and philanthropist – at which all four glanced at one another in disbelief. They then said the '*Dixit custodiam*' followed by the '*Domine, refugium*', whereupon the vicar announced that the recitation of 'Corinthians 15' would be omitted at the request of the deceased. Suddenly, as if from nowhere, a full choir stood up in the gallery and, to the accompaniment of St Peter's massive organ, sang 'Come Thou Fount of Every Blessing'. This was no local choir; they too must have been bussed in from some cathedral.

The grave diggers hung back in a decrepit shelter topped with a rusting Victorian wrought iron cross, having a smoke while they waited for the vicar to finish off the graveside patter. The shabby-looking man from the rear of the church stood with the grave diggers, shyly cadging a cigarette. In a quavering, high voice, the chief mourner chanted the prayer to be recited at the graveside.

'Man that is born of woman hath but a short time to live and is full of misery...' Without lifting her veil, she threw her bunch of white daisies onto the coffin then walked away quickly before the first spade dropped its load of soil. As the vicar recited the prayer for the casting of the earth upon the coffin, Sedgewick looked across to the shelter and noticed that the red-haired man had gone.

'The Lord's Prayer' had hardly finished when a croaking voice behind them said, 'Is one of you Reverend Hareton?'

They turned to see a small, bald, hunched man in his sixties at the very least, wearing a navy-blue rain mac and carrying a beaten-up black briefcase.

'Yes, I am Reverend Hareton.'

'I am Osbert Harty, junior partner of Hole and Harty, Solicitors. I wonder if you could drop by our office for twenty minutes as the senior partner has some information to impart that may be to Blinde-fellows' advantage regarding the last will and testament of Mr Francis Eugene Lafayette Fairchild.'

Bunny was taken aback. Could Fairchild truly have had a lapse in his spitefulness and arranged a bequest? Without wasting a moment, he left with Harty, while the remaining three went off in the opposite direction, to The Unicorn, to raise a glass to their late disagreeable colleague – or rather to his passing.

Hole and Harty had their offices in a bowed Elizabethan cottage in an alley called Scrag End just off the market square, where the firm had been located for more than 100 years. In its former days, this alley had been a shambles for butchers' shops and slaughterers. The evidence was still there in the form of a gutter running down the centre of the cobbles to catch the blood, and substantial iron meat hooks still in the beams above the windows. Bunny ducked gingerly through the low office door and moved warily beneath the uneven ceiling that varied from two inches to half-an-inch above his crown. Fortunately, he still had a good head of hair to serve as a buffer.

Rolled up scrolls tied around with black ribbons were piled up on every surface of Harty's chambers, including the windowsill, and were heaped in the corners on the floor. Bunny wondered how Harty knew what was what. The man himself was as unkempt as his office. He took off his rain mac to reveal a threadbare plaid suit and a rotund belly which had popped off some of his shirt buttons. He was out of breath after the short walk from St Peter's and wheezed as he gulped from a cup of cold milky tea left among the scrolls on his desk.

'So, what of this mystery bequest from Fairchild, Mr Harty?' Bunny asked, as ill at ease in the musty, dusty ambience of the room as with the shabby figure who inhabited it.

'Oh, no, Reverend, no. I do not impart details to clients in matters of this kind. I merely chaperone them to Mr Hole,' said Harty, with a drip of the milky tea on his chin. 'On occasion, I do go through some of these papers, but I never seem to make much of a dent in them.'

A phone rang and Harty, taking a moment to dig it out, placed the grimy receiver to his ear. A nervous twitch played at the corner of his mouth. He didn't speak, he only listened as if he were momentarily hypnotised. He put down the receiver and spoke.

'Reverend Hareton, the senior partner will see you now. His office is just across the hall.'

Harty indicated the direction with a stubby finger, smiling and frozen in this attitude – rather like Tweedledee, Bunny thought.

Bunny tapped on the door bearing the brass name plate 'Hole' and a muffled caw beckoned him inside. The office and the man in it were opposite in both situation and presentation to what Bunny had just experienced in Harty's office. No scrolls tossed into corners, and the polished walnut desktop was clear apart from an inkwell, a pen stand and two manicured bony hands with long interlocked fingers resting upon a shagreen document wallet. The hands belonged to Hole, in a black suit of an early Sixties cut and a crisply ironed sepia-coloured shirt. If Harty was Tweedledee, then Hole was the monstrous crow. Bunny wondered if the cadaverous man behind the desk was smiling faintly or if his jaws just happened to be set that way. His hooded, dust-coloured eyes regarded Bunny with something like remorse.

'Do take a seat, Reverend.' And Bunny did so. 'I am so sorry for your loss and for my sending Harty out to summon you here with such haste. A year ago, the late Mr Francis Fairchild made an appointment with me to rewrite his will and I have some news to your school's advantage. It is not entirely straightforward, however, and I will now endeavour to explain. It was my esteemed client's wish that Fairchild House and all its contents pass to Blindefellows, his former place of employment, but only if certain conditions are met.' Hole opened the shagreen document wallet and intoned, "The deceased, Francis Fairchild, requires that a vault be built on the grounds of the school to commemorate his life and work there as librarian and archivist. Said vault, to be named *The Fairchild Archive*, shall house the Hezekiah Lambton papers and all other historical documents pertaining to Blindefellows School, along with the rare books currently situated in the Lambton Library." Such was Mr Fairchild's concern for the longevity of these artefacts. I have here the exact requirements bookmarked in the document, if you would care to peruse them? I, as the deceased executor, will scrutinise the works once they are completed, prior to releasing the benefaction.'

The long, bony fingers proffered the wallet. *A vault?* Bunny mused, and he opened the bookmarked page entitled 'Conditions'. The many instructions were meticulous and pharaonic. For instance, in the antechamber of the vault there should be a gold-plated bust of Fairchild on a marble plinth that would have a strategically angled shaft of sunlight of a precise diameter cast upon it every day at midday, from an opening constructed above it. The bust itself had to be commissioned from none other than the sculptor to the Royal Family, Lady Cecilia Stirling, RA.

Bunny shook his head and sighed. 'Well, Mr Hole, it's certainly an interesting notion but – and I can see this immediately, just glancing over a few lines – it is clearly going to be hugely expensive. With the architect's fee and the construction of such a specialised edifice, along with the sculptor's commission, would it really be worth our while? I don't mean to be ungrateful but Blindefellows has a very narrow profit margin and putting up this kind of money would be quite a feat. We have to tread with caution, and besides, I know virtually nothing about 'Fairchild House and all its contents' so I haven't the slightest notion whether we would break even, at the very least.'

'Neither have I, Reverend, neither have I,' Hole said, suddenly a touch theatrical, his ivory palms held up to the ceiling. 'Naturally, I had anticipated your reservations and have had a conversation with the late Mr Fairchild's housekeeper, Miss Berry, who holds the keys to the entirety of the property. I can arrange an appointment with her for you, if you wish.'

Bunny agreed to this and took his leave of Mr Hole, who by now had returned his hands to the interlocked position atop the shagreen wallet and was gazing out of the window at the magpies, which he fed every morning, scavenging on the windowsill.

Walking back through town, Bunny glanced through the window of The Unicorn and noticed Japes, sitting alone at the bar. He went in and told him about the alabaster-lined subterranean vault.

'With that golden bust of Fairchild at the entrance it sounds like the Batcave,' Japes jibed. 'Does the head tilt back to reveal a keypad?'

'Well, if it does, we're not allowed to give the code to Sedgewick. He was specially mentioned as *persona non grata* with a restraining order not to go within ten yards of the vault.'

'Ah, the man may be dead, but the rage goes on!'

'Speaking of death, Japes, the Board has asked me to retire.'

Japes was astonished. Bunny might be approaching 70 – which was, it had to be said, one of the later retirement ages in the Blindefellows faculty – but the man was invaluable! He had saved the school and built it up, turning its eight-bunk frigid dorms into pleasing, carpeted en suites with radiators and double glazing. He had hired a chef who was an expert in nutrition. He had diversified the place, filling it with multiple nationalities. Over time, the school had crept up the league tables to its current position in the top 20. They now had an entrance test and offered places only to those with high scores (hence the considerable concentration of students from Hong-Kong in the school) rather than just accepting anyone who could pay.

'And of course, with our being the same age, it's something you need to consider too,' Bunny added.

Japes hadn't considered it or, rather, if the thought had flickered into his consciousness, he had drowned it out with a quick gin and tonic.

'One becomes so settled in a place that leaving it is akin to leaving the body; a drifting sensation until another purpose is found,' said Bunny ponderously. 'I thought I would stand for Mayor of Travistock, to supplant what I've grown accustomed to, and perhaps keep a tortoise.'

Japes ordered a gin and tonic and drank it down.

'Of course, Swainson is ready for it,' Bunny continued. 'Quite literally chomping at the bit. He's been a good deputy to me. And Diana is lined up to step into his shoes.'

'Diana? Mm, good choice,' Japes mused.

'So we leave the place in good hands,' Bunny concluded. They put on their coats, walked into the street, shook hands as if they had reached an agreement and made their way to their respective homes.

Three days later, Swainson was driving Bunny over to Fairchild House, 16 miles from Blindefellows, amid rolling farmland.

'Reverend, I'm really not sure about all this,' Swainson began. 'Fairchild never came to a single school function once he retired. No one heard a peep out of him. Didn't give a damn about the school or anyone in it, so why this bequest? He had all his marbles, so we've been led to believe, so what provoked this sudden U-turn? Are we to trust Mr Hole?'

Bunny thought for a while. 'All I have to go on, Swainson, is what is written in a legal document; that the house and contents are ours providing we build Fairchild's vanity project. These West Country piles are worth a mint with the city bankers et al wanting their weekend boltholes. If I can sell it for a couple of million, then we shall make a tidy sum which can serve as my *coup de grace* upon retirement.'

Hole had given them directions. They were to turn into the driveway opposite Folly Foot Farm and drive up to the house, where Miss Berry would meet them. The long driveway was lush with the dark green leathery leaves of rhododendrons. The house loomed ahead; an impressive biscuit-coloured mansion with a slate roof and mullioned windows in the Victorian Gothic style. The exterior was immaculate and Bunny almost rubbed his hands together with glee. Rising out of the middle of the roof was a tower housing an original striking clock by Cornelius Tyte, which Fairchild had enjoyed boasting about in the Oak Room. To the rear of the property, beyond the formal gardens, Bunny had heard there was a picturesque lake set in a valley, which was part of the estate. They walked up the wide stone steps, pulled the ringer and a solemn bell echoed on the other side of the door. No answer came so they tried again and waited. It was eleven o'clock – the time they were expected. They rang one last time before turning to go, but then heard a rustle of scampering footsteps on the inside. The door was opened a crack and the pale face of Miss Berry peered out.

'Make haste, dash inside, before Francis gets out,' she whispered.

Before really thinking about what she had just said, which Bunny thought he must have heard incorrectly, the two men quickly slipped inside and the enormous door was closed behind them. They found themselves in a cavernous hallway with a curved staircase with its original handrail and spindles. An antique grandfather clock in tip-top condition was chiming eleven o'clock.

Once Bunny had made a favourable first sweep of what he was about to inherit, he turned his attention to Miss Berry – and what a curious creature she was! What was she wearing? A Victorian nightgown, it appeared – floor-length, white, trimmed with dreadfully snaggled lace, possibly due to contact with her long, sharp, yellowed toenails at the end of her bare feet. Her greying hair was all done up in those torn white rags they used to sleep in to form ringlets. Her face was as pale as her gown and had a powdered, crumbling texture.

'Oh, I do hope he didn't get out just now,' she said, her tadpole-black eyes darting about the skirting boards.

'Who, my dear?' asked Bunny.

'Why, Francis, of course. I've been looking for him all morning. He can be such a naughty thing, you know. Gets up to all sorts of preposterous tricks.'

Swainson surreptitiously checked to ensure there was no concealed weapon inside her nightgown. 'Miss Berry, Francis has died. I'm so sorry for your loss.'

'What? Did you run him over when you came up the drive? How could you do such a thing then stand here in our hallway chatting so nicely?'

'No, no, we didn't run him down,' Bunny said soothingly. 'He died two weeks ago; we were at the funeral with you. The lilies were beautiful.'

'Not that Francis, sillies, I mean Francis Ferret!' she said with a giggle and a shiver. 'When darling Francis was informed of his own imminent demise, he went over to the pet shop in Travistock and got me Francis Ferret as a replacement. You know, to ease the pain. I always wanted an otter, with my name being Otterly, but he said there wasn't one there so he got me the ferret, which is sort of a lesser otter in its way, you know.'

She spoke in small, halting little gasps, with 'you know' like a little tic, and glancing back and forth from Bunny to Swainson.

'Miss Berry, Mr Hole sent us, to have a look around.' Bunny was ready for things to move on.

'Oh, did he?' She looked blank. 'But would you mind first helping me to find Francis? I'm sure with the three of us we'll be able to root him out very quickly indeed, you know. I'm going to look in the conservatory and you two split up. You know, together we'll catch the little imp.'

She floated off, calling to the animal. Swainson was about to follow suit in the opposite direction, but Bunny grabbed his arm. 'Swainson, let's conduct the tour on our own. I don't think we need concern ourselves with the ferret.'

Going in the opposite direction, Bunny and Swainson took a quick survey of the house. A library, a music room, a drawing room, a grand dining room were all stuffed with tasteful antique furniture that was going to fetch a bomb. Bunny felt sure one of the many fine paintings was a Gainsborough. The kitchen was clean and functional, with some up-to-date appliances. Six bedrooms and three bathrooms upstairs, with much of the fine furniture covered with dustsheets. In the master bedroom, which had clearly been Fairchild's, a painting of the Jacobean playwright John Webster hung over the bedstead. The book he had been reading, *The Monk* by M.G. Lewis, still lay on the nightstand. Bunny opened it at the page before the bookmark and glanced over what was probably the last thing Fairchild read:

'The Monks terrified his young mind by placing before him all the horrors with which Superstition could furnish them: They painted to him the torments of the Damned in colours the most dark, terrible, and fantastic, and threatened him at the slightest fault with eternal perdition. No wonder that his imagination constantly dwelling upon these fearful objects should have rendered his character timid and apprehensive.'

So, thought Bunny, *comforting thoughts on the eve of his demise.* Swainson ventured to peep into the mahogany wardrobe to see two neat rows of Saville Row suits and wondered why he'd only ever seen the man in one tatty tweed jacket with leather piping.

'Oh, he won't be in there!' Miss Berry's face was suddenly at the back of his neck making him jump. 'He can't open doors, you know. Did you see the photographs Francis took? It was one of his passions, you know, photography. That one just there is me when I was eight, you know.'

Bunny and Swainson walked over to take a look at a collection of framed black-and-white photographs on the tallboy, among them a little girl coyly posing with a daisy chain in her hair.

'He'd come home from Oxford, quite despondent, you know, due to his being second in his year in literature,' she explained. 'And there I was, the housekeeper's darling daughter, so fresh, so alive. The little sister he'd always wanted! Let me show you the nursery where we used to play.'

She led them, skipping slightly, down the corridor to a room still in use, without dust or dustsheet. A jigsaw puzzle of the Prague astronomical clock lay half-done upon a table, a rocking horse positioned in the bay window had Fairchild's old tweed jacket draped across it like a horse blanket and toy soldiers were set out in attacking formations on the floor.

'I've kept it just as he left it three weeks ago.' She smiled serenely, then suddenly cried out, 'Ah-ha!' and she picked up a large antique wooden jack-in-the-box, brightly painted on each side with a different Punch and Judy character, and started frenetically winding it up. She nodded her head rapidly to the twinkling notes of 'Pop Goes the Weasel' and then – pop! – the lid snapped open and out flew a furry snake that wrapped itself around her neck. Bunny and Swainson took a step back and perceived how what they thought had been a snake now metamorphosed into the missing ferret, long and sinuous, hiding its face in her hair. 'Ha! He's done that before, you know!' Miss Berry tittered.

'Quite.' Bunny smiled, impressed by the extent of the woman's lunacy. 'You had a fur like that around your neck at the funeral, I think.'

'Yes, it was Francis; he goes everywhere with me, don't you, Francis?' She kissed the ferret on his two yellow incisors and Bunny decided it was time to say farewell.

'Thank you, Miss Berry, so much, for allowing us in for a tour but we have to be getting back,' and they hastily made their way down the staircase.

'But first I must show you the garden. It is a sweet-scented and tranquil haven of birdsong!' she called after them whimsically from the landing.

They kindly refused and retreated up the driveway.

'Do you think the bequest comes with complimentary house-keeper?' Swainson asked.

'I would prefer to think it does not, Swainson. Let us hope so, anyhow.'

Driving home, Bunny approximated the sale of the contents at auction and how much the house itself could be put on the market for with Pickerings, the upmarket estate agent in town which also had offices in Mayfair and the like. As soon as he returned to school, he had Brenda phone architects to invite them for visits to make quotes for the vault. She also managed to get Lady Cecilia Stirling on the phone. Bunny talked to her at length about the commission, explaining the curious challenge the school had been set to earn its bequest so as to pique her interest, yet taking care to mention how it would be difficult for them to put such a hefty sum up front. His charm worked and she said she was keen to help. She promised to see what she could do with regard to reducing her fee and that she or her PA would get back to him with a figure by the end of the week.

Meanwhile, Japes had told Sedgewick about Bunny's meeting with Hole, which Sedgewick mentioned to Yvonne over a fine cottage pie with green vegetables.

'I know Mr Fairchild's house – it's opposite Folly Foot Farm, which is next door to where my family's farm used to be,' Yvonne told him. 'Angus and I used to sneak onto the Fairchild estate to pinch apples from the orchard. Sir Lionel was still living then. We were often hungry as children. They had a gardener who used to turn a blind eye to us, a terribly shy, sweet man. He would leave us chocolate in a little hole in a certain tree, and sometimes little model animals fashioned using fir cones. There's a public footpath which passes alongside the lake in their grounds, which I know angered your colleague when he was younger – he tried for years and years to get the council to close it off. You can get a fine view of the big house from there.'

Sedgewick decided he'd like to go and take a look at the bequest for himself, perhaps date the house or even identify the architect for Reverend Hareton, which would give him a better idea of what it might be worth. And so, the following Sunday he and Yvonne drove over there with a small picnic hamper.

Yvonne looked towards the place she was brought up, the land having been bought by Folly Foot Farm. She was shocked to see the sign had gone and the house and farm buildings had been razed. 'Probably for the best,' she said, holding back the tears over all the misery she'd endured there.

They parked in a clearing just off the road. Sedgewick changed into his wellingtons and breathed in a lung-full of country air. The council had constructed a very nice path down through the valley, ending at a picnic spot on the far banks of the Fairchild Lake. Once at the lakeside, Yvonne started arranging brunch on a yellow gingham tablecloth she'd laid on one of the wooden tables. Everything was homemade: bite-sized pork pies with mustard, crispy coleslaw, smoked salmon on slices of baguette, all topped off with a pair of fine apricot cobblers.

The lake was certainly large enough for the Fairchild family to retain their privacy, Sedgewick thought, given that the footpath was on the other side of their house and gardens. What appeared to be an ornate wooden boathouse was sagging into the water opposite, so there were some signs of neglect.

With his binoculars, Sedgewick peered up at the house on the hill, which was slightly obscured by trees. 'Oh, very nice,' he said aloud to himself. 'Mid-Victorian, I'd say – Gothic revival lancet windows, couple of finials.'

A movement somewhere below the house caught his eye and he tilted his binoculars downwards. A tall figure with a loping gait, carrying something limp and brown, was heading along the lakeshore, then disappeared into the trees. Sedgewick, aware that he wasn't doing anything wrong by being at this designated council picnic spot, still had a sudden pang that he was in trouble as he was on Fairchild land, as if Fairchild himself might pop his head out of the water at any moment and, with a sodden and algaed hand, grab his ankle and say something like, 'No, you may not borrow it,' in that horrible hiss he used to use in the library. Sedgewick gave his head a shake to free himself of the apparition and resumed his survey of the house.

'Nice scalloping at the eaves, hood mouldings too. All looking very good.'

Yvonne walked off to the edge of the water and started tossing crusts from a bag of stale bread she'd brought specially for the flotillas of hungry ducks she knew to frequent the lake. Something swept across Sedgewick's line of vision, as if a duck wing or a hand had wafted in front of him. He lowered his binoculars and checked them, polishing the lenses with his scarf.

'Could I... could I have a bit of that there bread?' said a male voice, slowly and shyly.

Sedgewick turned about to see a tall man in ragged clothes with a large hunting knife about his waist and a dead pheasant in his hand.

'I can... I can give you this here pheasant in return. I'll... I'll chop off its head and feet if you're preferring it that way,' and his hand moved to the knife.

'Erm, just a moment,' Sedgewick yelped. 'Yvonne, you give this chappie the rest of that duck bread and come and stand with me. We don't need the pheasant, thank you; you can keep that.'

Yvonne did as he said, handing the bag of bread to the man at arm's length. He sat down on a nearby rock and wolfed it down. As Sedgewick and Yvonne watched, they inched closer to each other.

'He's terribly hungry,' Yvonne whispered.

'He's got a large knife,' Sedgewick replied.

'Yes, but he's been hunting; maybe he's a gamekeeper.'

'Or just a passing murderer.'

'I don't think so, Charles. I believe he might be the man who worked here when I was a girl, the one who let us take the apples and left us chocolates,' she said, and before Sedgewick could stop her she was walking towards the fellow and offering him an invitation to their repast, which he demurely accepted. It was then that Sedgewick realised he'd seen the man before – he was the red-haired chap at the back of the church at Fairchild's funeral.

Twenty minutes later, Rufus, in the hesitant, broken monotone that was his voice, had told them that he was Mr Fairchild's gardener. He'd not had his usual seven pounds a week since Mr Fairchild had passed away. Miss Berry had refused to give him a penny, so he'd been forced to seek game in the woods. The man was famished and it was lucky Yvonne gave him her cobbler, thought Sedgewick, because he didn't at all want to go without himself. She then told him she'd lived across the way as a child, and had picked apples in the orchard.

'I... I... I remembers you and your brother,' the big man said, nodding slowly. 'You was skinny and you... you... both had red hair and was scared like me. When I had extra money, I got you some chocolate and left it in... in the tree.'

Yvonne's eyes filled with tears and she thanked him, taking his huge hand in hers.

'Where do you live, Rufus?' she asked.

'In the house, yonder,' he replied.

'What? The big house?' Sedgewick asked, astonished.

'No, I's never allowed in there,' Rufus shook his head emphatically. 'I... I... I lives in the house on the lake.'

'But that house is water-logged!' Yvonne gasped, looking over at the subsiding wreck.

'It be sinking into... into the lake. That is... that is why I only lives upstairs,' Rufus was proud to tell them of his innovation.

'May we look inside your house, Rufus?' Yvonne asked gently.

'Well, perhaps that's intruding a little, Yvonne,' Sedgewick suggested. 'And Rufus would probably prefer we didn't.'

Rufus, however, was all too pleased to show someone around, and five minutes later they were scurrying after him, trying to keep in pace with his long strides, despite the fact he was older than each of them. *An outdoor man*, thought Sedgewick, *used to tramping about the woods and foraging for a meal*. A far cry from his two perimeters of life – in the classroom and in his dormer bungalow with Yvonne, having choice meals set in front of him on both sites.

They entered the house via a plank of wood. The lintel had collapsed and Sedgewick didn't want to go in but Yvonne insisted. She suspected the worst and felt driven to have it confirmed. Sedgewick would have preferred to go home. The fact that they'd given the man a meal surely was enough. Various lumps of fallen mortar served as stepping stones through the ankle-deep water of what was once the hallway. Some ducks swam around them and there was a stagnant smell. The staircase was eaten away by termites and crumbled with every step. Clearly it had been quite a smart little place once, looking at the chandeliers.

'That's my room. I... I sleep in there. There's the stove I cook on,' Rufus walked into what would have once been a master bedroom but was now reduced to a horsehair mattress in a corner. Upon this lay an old Jack Russell who put up his head and wagged his tail when they entered. There was a pot-belly stove, a table and chair at the window and a chaise longue that was losing its stuffing and faded to a mottled shell-pink.

'Well, this is a cosy little room,' Sedgewick said after a silence, which he hoped would reassure Yvonne enough for them both to depart back to their warm car and drive home.

'No, it isn't, Charles. It's dangerous and unsanitary,' she replied, horror-struck. 'How long have you lived like this, Rufus?'

'I has always lived here. I were a boy here. My mother lived here, but there were no water on the floor downstairs then. She were Mr Francis's auntie, she were. They didn't like her. They told her she were a bad woman because... because she had no husband. But she were always good to me.'

'So, Mr Francis was your cousin!' Sedgewick exclaimed, astounded at the polarity of the two men – one highly educated, miniature and vicious; the other highly uneducated, gigantic and softly spoken.

'Rufus, you are going to come and stay with us for a while until we can find you somewhere safe and dry to live,' Yvonne said decisively.

'Is he?' Sedgewick gasped.

'Is it warm there? Because I... I can't find any dry wood for my stove, and I'm always so cold,' Rufus asked.

'It is very warm, Rufus,' she said reassuringly.

'But... but can I bring Jeremy?' he asked, picking up the old bundle of a dog in his arms.

'Of course you can.' She smiled.

'Yvonne, are you sure?' Sedgewick whispered.

'We can't possibly leave him here like this – it's inhuman, and that poor little dog!'

It was a picnic Sedgewick sorely regretted suggesting for they had now acquired two new members of their household.

'Oh, what a ruse!' Japes hooted in the Oak Room at morning break the next day. 'You've adopted Fanny Fairchild's bastard cousin and his aged mutt!'

'Now, now, Japes.' Swainson tried to keep order.

'It was all Yvonne's idea; I was powerless,' Sedgewick sighed in despair. 'The bathroom still smelled of algae when I left this morning. He'd bathed his dog in there using my anti-dandruff shampoo. Yvonne's out shopping with him today, getting him some clothes, then they're off to the council office to fill in an application for a council flat.'

'Oh, it can take months – years even – to get a council flat,' said Matron Ridgeway.

'Really?' Sedgewick looked alarmed.

'You're in for a long innings, old man,' Japes laughed. 'He's for life, not just for Christmas.'

'Do you think Fairchild left the house to the school to spite this poor man?' Matron Ridgeway asked.

'It's true: this cousin isn't mentioned in the will at all,' replied Swainson. 'The housekeeper is taken care of somewhere, though – she gets something or other but I'm not exactly sure what; it's rather vague. She'll probably have to go into an institution though – mad as a March hare. On a happier note, Reverend Hareton has sorted out a decent price for the bust and hired the best architects in Exeter for the vault. He thinks he can have it all done for under quarter of a million, a fraction of what the school will get for Fairchild's place.'

Japes chose not to comment. He still had his reservations about the credibility of the Fairchild bequest, but didn't want to put a damper on Bunny's plans for his parting gift of Fairchild's endowment to the school before retiring.

When Sedgewick returned home that evening, he felt he should probably explain to Rufus that Fairchild had left him no provision and perhaps he needed to go with Yvonne to the benefits office. The poor man wouldn't have the faintest idea what this was, relying for his survival all his adult life only on bits of pocket money parcelled out by Fairchild in return for tending those vast gardens, day in and day out, year after year.

'But Charles, if Rufus is a Fairchild, how can the school be getting Fairchild House?' Yvonne asked, stroking Jeremy, who was lapping up the attention in her lap.

'My house is going to a school?' Rufus asked wistfully.

'Yes, Rufus, I'm afraid it is,' Sedgewick said.

'Do… do you mean they will move it from the lake and… and put it in a school? Can I live in it again then?' Rufus asked. 'Because Fairchild House is going… going to sink if they don't move it away from the lake.'

'No, it's the house on the hill that will be given to the school,' Sedgewick explained.

'Fairchild Hall?' Rufus asked, puzzled.

'Fairchild Hall? What's that, Rufus?' Yvonne asked.

'Mr Francis's house is Fairchild Hall,' Rufus told them.

'So, then what is your house called?' asked Sedgewick.

'My house is called Fairchild House,' he replied.

'Oh my goodness!' Sedgewick said slowly.

'Charles, do you think Fairchild left the wreck to the school?' Yvonne put her hand over her mouth.

'I knew it was too good to be true! A philanthropic bequest from Fairchild! It was always an absurd notion.'

'I think you'd better call the Reverend straight away, Charles.'

Three days later, Bunny and Swainson were driving over to Fairchild Hall, this time with Hole and Harty in the back. Hole had acted surprised when Bunny had confronted him about this turn of events. Whether this was genuine or feigned was impossible to say. The will had left Fairchild House and all its contents to Blindefellows, and 'the remainder of the estate' – the slyly unstated Fairchild Hall and surrounding land – to Miss Berry. Miss Berry was expecting Hole and Harty to call round for some routine signatures.

The door opened and there stood an impeccably dressed older lady, in a rust-coloured two-piece and court shoes, her hair combed and drawn back neatly. There was still one thing very strange about Otterly Berry's appearance – the ferret coiled about her arm.

'Why have you brought the Blindefellows men?' she said in some alarm, staring at Hole.

'Please, Miss Berry, we won't take up too much of your time,' Swainson said, striding in with the others following. 'Let's go into the drawing room and get this matter settled.'

Miss Berry perched on the edge of an armchair as if she might fly off at any moment. Hole and Harty sat together on the sofa, trying to look hale and hearty but appearing pale and sickly. Bunny and Swainson stood at the fireplace, framed by the ornate mantelpiece.

'Miss Berry, might I say that you are looking so much better than when we last met,' Bunny said courteously.

'Well, yes, I have funny turns sometimes,' she pouted.

'Funny turns that render you incoherent, thus distancing those around you from the truth?' Swainson scolded and Miss Berry looked down and smoothed her ferret.

'I wouldn't know,' was all she said.

'It's quite a ruse from the grave you've been abetting Fairchild to perpetrate,' Bunny began. 'But let us not dwell upon that any longer and cut to the chase. It is fortunate for us and for you that only time was wasted on this false enterprise and that no money had, as yet, changed hands. But, in a sense, that too is beside the point because Swainson and I are here today on behalf of Mr Rufus Fairchild—'

'The illegitimate imbecile?' Miss Berry scoffed in astonishment.

'If you'd like to continue, Mr Hole?' Bunny smiled.

Hole struggled to get up from the sofa and Harty stood to assist

him in his clumsy manner, bringing him out in an instant sweat. Hole
then joined Bunny and Swainson at the mantelpiece, physically con-
firming his rapid change of side.

'Miss Berry, we would like to resolve this – erm – situation as
swiftly as possible,' Hole began. 'The Trustees of Blindefellows have
contested the will in favour of Mr Fairchild's last remaining relative,
the last of the Fairchild bloodline—'

'No, no, no!' She rose and the ferret dropped to the floor and
scuttled under the chair. 'He was not, is not, and never shall be
allowed even to set foot in Fairchild Hall!'

'Ah, that's another thing,' Hole continued. 'The appalling cruelty
and neglect to which Rufus Fairchild has been subjected over the
years puts you in a very precarious position, Miss Berry. It could lead
to criminal charges being preferred and very likely to a prison sen-
tence of several years' duration. If I were you, I would hear out Reverend Hareton's offer, take it and keep quiet.'

She resumed her position on the armchair, but now leaning back,
deflated. The ferret gave her some comfort, jumping into her lap and
stretching itself to its full extent.

'So, yes, we do have documents to sign today, Miss Berry, but
they are not what you were expecting. This is the gist of what they
say...'

As Hole summarised, Harty laid out the documents on the coffee
table in front of her and held out a silver fountain pen. 'You are agreeing to accept Rufus Fairchild as the true heir to the entire estate of
Francis Fairchild,' began Hole, 'which comprises both houses therein,
all their contents, gardens, and land etcetera, as well as all securities
and bank accounts in the late Mr Fairchild's name. In gratitude for
your long and loyal service to the Fairchild family as housekeeper, a
role which you stepped into in the wake of your mother, who also
kept house here, provision has been made for you from today in the
form of a single room with board at The Maples, an exclusive new
retirement residence on the banks of the River Tidd in Travistock
town. This will be made available to you for the rest of your life, along
with a modest allowance to meet any sundry needs.'

'But what about Francis Ferret?' she almost whispered.

'We selected The Maples with this in mind, as pets are permitted,' Harty reassured her. 'Now please sign here and here and here, Miss Berry.'

'And it might interest you to know, Miss Berry,' Bunny added, 'That Rufus Fairchild wished to leave this house to Mrs Sedgewick on his demise, since he saw her as his saviour after she found him starving on the banks of the lake down there and welcomed him into her home. Mrs Sedgewick will hear nothing of it, however, so on her suggestion he is now gifting the estate to the Blindefellows School Trust in an arrangement whereby it will pass to us automatically upon his death and until which time we will manage it and protect him by serving as his guardians. I shall simply take it as given that you are in agreement with this arrangement and will raise no legal objection to it.'

Miss Berry's only reaction was a slightly more wavering signature on the final document.

She was given two hours to pack four suitcases of her possessions to take with her to her new life at The Maples, while Bunny and Swainson celebrated with a bottle of first-class champagne from Fairchild's wine cellar. At the appointed hour, a taxi drew up to remove Mrs Berry from the premises. At the same time, the Sedgewicks drove up with Rufus in the back. As the two cars passed each other, Miss Berry glanced away – Bunny hoped, in shame.

Rufus had to be coaxed into the house on Yvonne's arm, and insisted on taking his boots off at the threshold. Despite being attired in new clothes, he tried to put down a piece of newspaper to sit on when they went into the drawing room and looked about him with wide, wary eyes. Jeremy, immediately at home, found a perfect spot on the Persian rug in front of the fireplace.

'Now don't you be tempted to go down to the house on the lake, Rufus,' Yvonne patted his shoulder. 'You'll be sleeping upstairs in the master bedroom tonight and from now on.'

Sedgewick and Yvonne stayed with Rufus for a month until he was accustomed to his new home and a reliable live-in helper could be appointed to keep house and provide companionship for him. He insisted upon continuing to do the gardens, though. Fairchild House was demolished to prevent any misunderstandings in future. By way of compensation to the local waterfowl, Rufus constructed an ornate duck house on its site that was better suited to their needs and served in memory of his mother.

The 'Age of Bunny' had reached its grand conclusion and he retired at the end of the school year with the belated bequest in place and taking a reluctant but resigned Japes along with him. They would live together in Japes's house in town, at least for the time being, like the old days at Cambridge. What lay in store for Japes, no one, not even Matron Ridgeway – who understood him best – ventured to predict.

12

Japes Abroad

February 2011

Japes had left Travistock five years ago and found himself a job at Our Lady of Perpetual Succour, a Catholic girls' school in Zamalek on the Nile island of Gezira, a stone's throw from downtown Cairo. Bunny, who'd been staying temporarily with Japes since their joint retirement from Blindefellows, ended up remaining at Jape's place as a more or less permanent house-sitter. This morning there was a letter on the doormat bearing an Egyptian postage stamp. It wasn't like Japes to send a letter; he generally sent a postcard every couple of months but that was the extent of it. There was always a short message relating some quirky detail or other, which was enough to reassure Bunny that his friend was in fine fettle. He reached down to pick up the letter and walked into the sitting room to put on his reading glasses. It wasn't Japes's hasty block lettering on the envelope, either, but a meticulous, sloping cursive on a vellum-like envelope. Bunny unfolded the letter within – just one sheet of costly stationery yellowed by time at the edges, folded into precise quarters and bearing a brief, perfectly centred missive:

Cher Père Hareton,

Monsieur Japes is unwell. He sustained a head injury in the recent upheavals and is hospitalised at present. He has said always he has no family other than you. I am the owner of the building where he resides and his particular friend. Please advise me the best course of action. You will find my telephone number and address above.

Meilleures amitiés,

Mme Mona Abban

Bunny had been watching the protests against the Mubarak regime on the news. He had tried to call Japes but phone lines in Cairo were always either dead or overwhelmed. He'd scrutinised the footage of protesters in Tahrir Square – mainly young men, many of them strikingly handsome in their ire – half expecting to spot Japes among them. Now his fears were confirmed by this letter. In spite of his age, the old soldier had been out there in the thick of it.

Bunny phoned Egypt Air, bought a ticket for the day after next and picked up the phone to call Mona Abban with his flight details. It would be one o'clock in the afternoon there now, late enough even for an older lady of leisure to be up and about. After a few attempts, a loud crackle interrupted the wavering ring tone, signalling an answer. This was not in Arabic, as he had been anticipating, but in French. He followed his life-long custom in circumstances of Francophony and announced, '*Bonjour, Madame. Je suis Reverend Hareton. Pardon, je ne parle pas Français.*' Madame Abban politely assured him in English that it was her pleasure to speak with him at last and that she had heard so much about him.

When he asked about Japes, she said, 'He had quite a knock to his head', her slow, gravelly delivery making it sound vaguely as if she might have suffered the same herself of late. 'The girls who brought him to the hospital say they can identify who did it but there's nothing to be done.'

'But, Madame Abban, how is he now?'

'It's hard to know, Père Hareton. He's come round but he's... confused. There were some lucidity issues before but now it's much worse.'

'You keep addressing me as Father Hareton. I hope that doesn't mean you think he needs a priest?'

'No, no, it hasn't come to that yet, thank heavens. I'm only thinking about his future. It's no good for him to be here any longer, now we have all this trouble in Egypt.'

Bunny flew out to Cairo two days later on what was a largely empty flight. Swainson had urged him to wait until half term, when he could accompany him, but Bunny wanted to be there as soon as he could. Mona had arranged a car to collect him and told him the driver would hold a sign with his name on it in arrivals. He finished his meal and wiped his hands on the 'refreshing towel' inside the little sachet provided by Egypt Air, settling back to appreciate the sunset through the clouds.

Bunny had enjoyed his retirement thus far and hadn't missed his daily routine at Blindefellows at all. He still went up the hill to school from time to time, for alumni dinners and board meetings, but he'd confidently handed the gauntlet over to Swainson and Ravensbrück, who were doing sterling work. Within a year of leaving, he had been chosen as an alderman of Travistock, and was so capable that he'd been elected mayor the next year, a post he'd held until the end of 2010. Now he was ready to properly retire – well, after this trip to Cairo.

Japes, however, had been at a loose end since leaving Blindefellows. He'd got himself a motorcycle licence, then gone and bought a Royal Enfield Silver Bullet, no less, and charged about the West Country lanes in a manner more becoming of T.E. Lawrence. 'Watch out for the trees,' Bunny had warned.

Japes had threatened to invest in a sidecar to take his old friend about on his aldermanly duties, which Bunny politely declined. Japes kept a handful of his relationships simmering: the curator at the British Artillery Collection in London, a French woman from the Riviera, and, of course, Matron Ridgeway, when she was free. But when speed or passion weren't in his life, he floundered. He hadn't shared Bunny's interest in coffee and papers in the Four and Twenty every morning, and no more matches were shown in the Frog and Onion, which was now attempting to metamorphose into a wine and tapas bar, with a new clientele of estate agents and primary school teachers' hen parties.

Japes had given retired life with Bunny a year, at the end of which he announced, in the summer of 2005, that he'd landed himself a job with the only woman left who'd really want a man like him at his time of life, Our Lady of Perpetual Succour in Cairo. At the back of his mind, Bunny wasn't surprised at all.

Gingerly making his way down the aeroplane steps to the Tarmac at 10pm, the first thing Bunny noticed as he arrived in Cairo was the hint of burned plastic on the air, which caught in the back of the throat and made his eyes water. He was waved over to an ornate minibus, festooned inside with rather dusty faux flowers, which drove him and the handful of other passengers to arrivals. There were no seat belts and the driver headed off the runway at a rate of knots.

'He has to get to arrivals over there before the next plane lands on us – that's why we have to make a run for it!' a jolly Egyptian businessman explained to Bunny. Bunny looked skyward as a jet came into view and roared over the bus.

Progress through customs was swift with so few people entering the country, and Bunny wheeled his suitcase through the sliding doors into arrivals and loitered near the door, looking for his name. The terminal was jammed as there appeared to be a mass exodus taking place, and the air was potent with sweat. It looked as if all those Egyptians who could scrape together the money to do so were getting out of the country, but their money did not seem to have stretched to suitcases as most were carrying cardboard boxes tied up with string. Nearly every woman he saw was fully covered in swathes of black or brown polyester, with children hiding in the folds. Their husbands led the way, waving the tickets and the passports. A life-size model of a biplane hung precariously from wires above the crowds of travellers, slightly wafting this way and that.

'Bunny! Bunny! Over here!' Japes was suddenly in front of him, with a black eye and a bandage around his head into which the wound on his temple had seeped.

'Good Lord, Japes, should you be out and about?' Bunny gaped at the injuries as he shook his friend's hand.

'Discharged myself yesterday. Bored stiff sitting in bed. God-awful hospital anyhow. Blood and guts up the walls. Many injuries far worse than mine for them to deal with. The police are tossing bricks and concrete blocks down from the rooftops onto protesters, who have nothing more to protect themselves with than baguettes and empty plastic bottles tied to their heads. It's dreadful!' As he spoke, he ushered Bunny through the crowd and hailed a rickety black-and-white taxi. 'Here you go, Bunny. Jump in and I'll throw your case up top.'

'Please, let me help you,' Bunny begged, worried about Japes's exertions, but it was too late, for the case had already been tossed onto the roof rack.

'*Zamalek, min fadlak, Ahmet Heshmat Street*,' Japes called to the front, as the exhausted looking taxi driver dropped his foot onto the accelerator and they sped away.

Japes looked thinner and older with a weariness about the eyes. The corners of his mouth were turning downwards and his hair was now entirely gone on the top. He explained what had happened to him.

'I'd just gone down to Tahrir Square for a shufti, not looking for trouble, when I saw a couple of the girls from Our Lady – my school – in a spot of bother, men massing around them. The girls are mostly Christian – no headscarves, you see – so the men were hectoring them, calling them whores and whatnot. This revolution is increasingly being hijacked by Islamists, you know. Anyway, the girls were terrified, though doing their best to hold their own. Naturally, I bounded over. I was waving round an antique walking stick I'd brought along just in case, and started giving these chaps what-for in my limited Arabic. Next thing I knew, someone smashed me in the side of the head. One of them slung a brick at me, so I'm told, which set the girls screaming like billy-o and brought over a couple of soldiers from a nearby tank who scattered the gang. The girls, four of them, picked me up and carried me between them to the nearest hospital, where I was stuck until this morning, for my good deeds.'

Bunny, who was on tenterhooks merely listening to Japes's story, was made considerably more tense by the taxi driver who, constantly yawning and with his window wide open to keep him awake, swerved in and out of unbelievably small gaps in the traffic in improvised lanes. Women clutching babies or dragging tiny tots periodically ran across the road laughing and no one slowed down for them. In spite of the revolution and the late hour, everything was still open: ironing shops, car repairers, bakeries, barbers. The driver frequently took his eyes off the road and peered into the grubby, fluorescent interiors of these establishments, as if he thought he might see an acquaintance within one of them. Eventually he did and, as he pulled over, a fellow ran out to his cab and gave him some kind of croissant and a glass of hot mint chai which the cabby then balanced with one hand atop his steering wheel as he drove along. A motorcycle passed with a whole family astride its seat – father driving at the front, his arm about a toddler perched on his thigh, an older child behind him and the mother at the back, her *abaya* flapping dangerously near the rear wheel spokes. Then there was a decrepit pick-up truck filled with scrap metal and a goat in the passenger seat that regarded Bunny's surprised face with nonchalance. A donkey cart laden with ears of corn, with a sort of improvised oven in one corner, laboured down the road the wrong way, weaving in and out of the oncoming traffic and driven by a stooping, one-eyed man.

It took an hour to reach Japes's building, a three-story Art Nouveau pile with louvre shutters and carved stone balconies. It was set well back from the pavement with a surrounding wall and garden. The street lamp before the place cast giant shadows of Jurassic vegetation – rubber plants and banana trees – onto the building's front facade.

'I imagine you'll be wanting to get to bed, or did you want to go out for a spot of supper?' Japes enquired as he led the way up to his flat. 'Everywhere's open 'til after midnight.'

'Another night, perhaps, Japes.'

On the third floor, to which Bunny ascended laboriously, lugging his case, Japes fumbled at length to get his key to fit in the lock in the semi-darkness, when suddenly the door was flung open from the inside and a tidy little moustachioed man in a peach-coloured dressing gown with an ornate *passementerie* waist-cord stood smiling amiably. 'Why, Mr Japes – will you be joining us for a late-night cuppa again?'

'Damn and blast, Ali, you made me jump out of my skin!' Japes was genuinely shaken. 'How did you get in here?'

'You've overshot your floor again, darling.' Ali stood smiling at length and another man appeared at his shoulder, tall and bearlike, also in sleepwear, except his outfit comprised full-length tartan pyjamas.

'Well, good evening, Mr Japes. How's your head and who's your friend?' the new man enquired affably.

'Hello, Ashraf. My head's on the mend and this is the highly respectable ex-headmaster of my old school, and sometime mayor of the English market town of Travistock, the Reverend Beaulieu Hareton,' Japes rattled off.

The two men shook hands with Bunny, who accepted their invitation for dinner later in the week, before he and Japes backtracked a flight of stairs to Japes's sparsely furnished apartment with its high ceilings hung with antique chandeliers. With the ornate ceramic tiles of the sort seen in fine old Edwardian houses, their voices and footsteps were amplified, making Bunny feel the need to whisper and tiptoe. Japes led Bunny into one of his spare rooms and was surprised to see the bed had been made up. 'Can't remember doing that – Mona must have sent her cleaner in. I must introduce the two of you. Splendid woman; known her nearly as many years as I have you, old chap.' And then he said his goodnights to Bunny, who lay awake another hour listening to distant gunshots.

Japes, up early, showered and with a clean bandage, brought Bunny to the balcony where he'd laid out a typically Egyptian breakfast which he'd just had delivered – *ful medames*, falafel, salad, white cheese and warm flatbread accompanied by watermelon juice. Bunny sat and ate in his pyjamas, delighted with the sunshine and warmth after the West Country winter, and relaxed as much as one can in a city in turmoil. After this, they went over the Nile to Tahrir Square, the epicentre of the revolution. They passed blackened, overturned cars and a smouldering concrete edifice that had been the headquarters of Mubarak's ironically named National Democratic Party. Tank

drivers sat waiting for occasional orders, drinking tea with the protesters, and youths paraded by, asking Bunny, who still stood a head
or two taller than all of them, to take their photograph.

'You should come and live here with me, Bunny. You're certainly getting a lot of attention.'

'That's all very well, but I've got Horace Walpole to think of
these days.'

'Who?'

'Horace, my tortoise.'

'You have a tortoise?'

'I had him before you left. He was the object of perpetual raillery
from you.'

'Yes, I imagine he was. So, you've named the beast?'

'Naturally.'

'I imagine he'll outlive you. Have you made provision for him in
your will?'

'Of course, Japes – he will go to you.'

Japes was keen to go to Café Groppi, as it had been there when
he was attached to the embassy in Cairo. 'Very grand, in the style of
the great Parisian patisseries,' he told Bunny. 'It was bombed in the
riots in 1952 and César Groppi was sorely tempted to leave the sinking ship and return to Switzerland but his staff begged him to perse-
vere. It was quite a place when I frequented it in the Sixties. It'll be
interesting to see how it's fared fifty years on.'

They walked in and Japes frowned. The old café still had the
original marble tables, Art Deco light fixtures and ornate glass-fronted
cabinets but cobwebs hung from the ceiling, flies buzzed, trapped
among the cakes, and there was only scant provision of tables and
chairs. The place was empty and a solitary waiter, wearing shabby
black pointed lace-up shoes that looked far too long for his feet, eventually approached their table.

'About time, César,' Japes said, winking at Bunny.

'Sir, I am Walid. What can I get for you today?'

'Let's simply say any cake as long as it's fresh today and two coffees.' Japes watched the waiter retreat and turned to Bunny. 'You

know, my friend, there are plenty of young men like that in Cairo who'll do anything for a tube of hair gel.'

'Really, Japes, I couldn't care less these days. I'm quite content with my tortoise and a mug of cocoa.'

'Hmm, the tortoise again, an interesting choice of pet, with that suggestively shaped retractable head – says something about the life-long inhibitions of the owner, too, wouldn't you say?'

Bunny bridled inwardly at having rushed in panic to Cairo to be confronted with this. The waiter returned with a dirty tray and presented them with coffee and two slices of white-frosted cake with tiny marzipan carrots on the top, 'Coffees and carrots cakes, sirs.'

'They say carrots cake because there's more than one carrot in the recipe. It's the same with lentil soup. It's always lentils soup here as there's more than one lentil involved. Highly logical, really.' Japes suddenly looked up at the waiter with a wanton leer that Bunny didn't like the look of at all. 'Hail, César, what do you think of my friend here?'

Bunny was mortified and the waiter stepped back, shame-faced. 'Welcome in Egypt, sir,' was all he said, before bowing his head and returning to the counter.

'Japes, do please calm down,' Bunny urged, though he found it difficult to keep his own voice calm. 'We're both a bit long in the tooth for these sorts of games, aren't we?'

'You've always been long in the tooth, Bunny – and when did you *ever* play these kinds of games? They make you as uneasy now as when I first met you at Cambridge.'

'Precisely, Japes. It wasn't my cup of tea then and it certainly isn't now, at the venerable age of seventy-seven. I thought you'd given up on these sorts of high jinks after all your failed attempts to turn Sedgewick into your protégé.'

'Ah, good ol' Sedgers!' Japes smiled and rolled his eyes exaggeratedly, his wounded head lolling back. 'Still married to Madame Carrot-Mop-Top, is he?'

'Yes, but not for much longer, I'm afraid – she's terminally ill.'

'Well, I'd better dash back and take him under my wing again, hadn't I?'

'Look, let's head off. This place clearly hasn't had the best effect on your mood. The cake tastes like… well, cake – I think they only did put one carrot in it, so their referring to it in the plural is, in fact, inaccurate. And the coffee they've brewed up in the pot tastes nine days old.'

They walked back along the Nile and over the Kasr El Nil Bridge with its two grand basalt lions guarding each side, now covered in chalk-scrawled revolutionary slogans in Arabic.

Japes had calmed down and assumed a melancholy air.

'I came down here a few weeks back, bobbing along with a group of teachers from my school,' he recalled. 'They reckoned this first march would be the last – just the sheer size of the crowd would be forewarning enough to show the government they weren't wanted. Anyhow, we were cut off by a blockade of riot police right where we're standing now, preventing us crossing the river and congregating in Tahrir Square with the rest of the protestors. They were popping canisters of tear gas at us, but we were kicking them into the Nile. Then they charged at us. I stood my ground, legs astride, in the middle of the road, folded my arms and looked them straight in the eye, and I've never felt braver as when they careered towards me, riot batons aloft. Do you know what happened then, Bunny? They ran around me, pursuing the younger men instead. That was the day I realised I'd become old, well and truly bloody old.'

They walked to the middle of the bridge and paused; riding the waves and decked out in flashing coloured lightbulbs, a wedding barge was riding the waves, the women aboard ululating to goblet drums.

The following day, Japes took Bunny on a circuit of the island of Gezira. The embassies had upped their police presence in light of recent developments – the prison gates had been flung open on the orders of Habib el-Adly, Minister of Interior and Master of the Secret Police, so as to create pandemonium. Japes took Bunny into a pet shop to see the Egyptian tortoises, small and sandy-coloured for desert camouflage.

'Lovely to see so many of these endangered tortoises, but they are living in rather cramped conditions here,' Bunny sighed.

'Wait 'til you see this,' said Japes as he opened what appeared to be a hidden cupboard in the wall panelling with a door knob on it. Out waddled a full-grown pelican. 'The keepers at Cairo Zoo are selling off the stock on the sly. I was offered a joint of zebra meat the other week – still had the stripes on it.'

The pelican shuffled out onto the street where one of the young men working at the pet shop put it on a lead and fed it a dead goldfish.

'What's going on here, Japes?' Bunny asked, drawing his friend's attention to a glass case of long-eared desert hedgehogs foaming at the mouth.

The pet shop owner came over, smiling, 'Oh, they're fine. They just need fresh water,' as if fresh water were a cure-all, even for rabies.

In another case, chameleons were standing on the decapitated heads of two myna birds. 'Ah, yes,' Japes said. 'The myna birds were looking a bit peaky in the window last month. Such must have been their fate – for their dead heads to tempt flies for the chameleons.'

They continued on their way, to meet Mona at the Gezira Club, passing en route through Fish Garden, with yet more well-cared-for creatures in the form of mummified seals and crocodiles held together with clumsy stitching. Inside glass tanks where aquarium fish once swam, there now stood tall flasks, each containing a pile of fish suspended in formaldehyde.

'But everything in this aquarium is dead!' Bunny said.

'Yes, but they need to show fish in some form or other so they can still call it a Fish Garden and sell tickets at the gate,' Japes explained. 'One of the girls at Our Lady won the British Council's essay competition last year, writing about this place as a metaphor for Egypt under the rule of the late regime.'

They met Mona in a room filled with *mah-jongg* players at green baize tables within the old colonial buildings in the Gezira Club, another place Japes had frequented half a century ago as a young officer in the Royal Engineers. Mona, a woman of approximately 70, had immaculately painted orange fingernails, dyed brown shoulder-length hair and sported a wide-lapelled satsuma trouser suit, circa 1974. She wore half-glasses on a gold chain and a tawny death mask of foundation make-up with sky-blue eyeshadow and lipstick to match her nails. She was playing with octogenarian twin spinster sisters in headscarves who, as Japes whispered to Bunny, were Catholics like Mona but donned the scarf as they were both bald as coots. He went off to buy a round of coffee and biscuits at Mona's request, while Bunny sat and played.

'Thank you again for coming, Father Hareton,' Mona said in the gravelly voice he'd heard on the phone. 'How do you find Mr Japes?'

'Certainly more active than I'd envisaged. We've been out and about all over the place since I arrived. We had coffee in Groppi's yesterday – he barely recognised the place since his days in the Forces.'

Mona smiled and shook her head slowly. 'Father, he was there with me before Christmas for mulled wine and mince pies. We've probably been down to Groppi's twice a year since he came back to Cairo.'

'Do you think the head injury has damaged his memory?' Bunny asked anxiously.

'My worry is more that it will make matters worse,' she sighed. 'For the last six months, he's been trying to pay me his rent a few times every month. When I tell him he's paid, he's embarrassed – humiliated, even – so I don't tell him anymore; I just slip into his apartment and put the money back in his bureau. Is it just forgetfulness or something more? He discharged himself from the hospital because they wanted to do an examination, a kind of dementia questionnaire. There was a neurologist there trained in England who wished to help. Japes doesn't want to know, Father, but deep down, he suspects something.'

'It's your turn, Padre,' one of the old ladies said, laying a crinkly hand on his sleeve.

'What should I do?' he whispered to himself as much as to Mona.

'He will need care, sooner or later. That kind of treatment isn't reliable here any longer. He needs to go home. You know, Sister Hanuna, director of Our Lady, told him before the Christmas Holidays that the time had come for him to step down. All last semester he was mixing up calculations at the blackboard, forgetting what he'd taught in the syllabus and confusing the girls' names. They tried to cover it up because they are fond of him, with his tales of Blindefellows and life in England before they were born. But word got out eventually, as it will.'

'And one frothy coffee for you.' Japes had reappeared and was handing out the coffees. For a moment, Bunny couldn't look at him and stared at the *mah-jongg* tiles in his hand. He felt ashamed that he'd been satisfied with an occasional postcard as a means of measuring the welfare of his oldest friend. Japes, perhaps sensing something was amiss, patted Bunny's shoulder. 'If you like, we can nip next door and watch Omar Sharif playing bridge and destroying a mathematical genius from Cairo University, if you'd care to see an old mind still as razor sharp as ever. There's hope for all of us when we see the master at work.'

On the way home, Bunny tried to talk to Japes about his injury and having a follow-up appointment, but he didn't want to discuss it, changing the subject by pointing out this and that. They passed the 'courtship garden', as Japes referred to it – a park by the edge of the Nile which afforded just a modicum of privacy, with each bench surrounded by bare trellis adorned with pink bows. Couples sat together, holding hands at the most, chatting and smiling coyly. No doubt the revolution was not a topic of conversation, despite the slight irritation to the eyes from tear gas on the breeze coming over from Tahrir Square.

Dinner that evening was to take place upstairs with Ali and Ashraf. On the way up, Japes turned to Bunny: 'Of course, Mona won't set foot up here. They're sitting tenants, left over from an antiquated agreement struck with Ali's grandfather. It's known as rental under the 'Old Law'. Their rent is a few pounds a month. Mona has them give it straight to the *boab* – the doorman. He gets his bread with it.'

Bunny set foot in the apartment with some trepidation, in light of his new knowledge of the law-abiding but plainly unscrupulous nature of the residents. The furniture hadn't changed since Ali's parents had taken over the apartment in the Sixties and decked it out with the priciest imported pieces of the day, all of which had been made to last: Ercol tables, Cadovius rosewood wall cabinets, Eames lounge chairs. Ali, well-toned and in a sleek track suit, was a concierge at the Four Seasons across the Nile. Ashraf, creased and crumpled in a lumberjack shirt with saggy jeans, earned his living from the last of the string of souvenir shops he had inherited from his father...

'There are no tourists now, Reverend; it's barely worth getting up in the morning to open the shop,' he sighed languidly.

'Please, Ashraf, you have no retailing know-how – you've barely sold a thing for ten years!' Ali sniped. 'You just sit on the street playing backgammon and drinking tea with the guys. If not for my job, we wouldn't have two ha'pennies to rub together.'

'I must take you over to Ashraf's emporium, Bunny. Never before will you have seen such a dust-fest!' Japes laughed. 'And a veritable jumble of crass stock left over from his father's day.'

'But the kiddies like it,' Ashraf offered.

'Yes, if they like disintegrating sun-bleached Smurfs that have been left in the window for a few decades,' Japes answered.

At dinner, Ali politely asked Bunny if he had grown up children. Japes jumped in before he could open his mouth.

'One of Blindefellows' best kept secrets, isn't it, Bunny? The pelican in the cupboard! Talking of pelicans in cupboards, Bunny, I must take you to this bizarre pet shop I drop into from time to time.'

Bunny stopped himself from reminding Japes that they'd already been there, recalling what Mona had said and not wanting to embarrass him.

'Of course, here in Cairo,' continued Japes, 'men walk down the street hand-in-hand in what they profess is brotherly love, but is more akin to the sexual frustration brought about by the interminable engagements to their no-shagging-before-marriage fiancées.'

As he spoke, the others noticed a spot on Jape's bandage spreading like the blossoming of a crimson rose in fast motion as his face drained to a greyish white.

'Mr Japes, how are you feeling?' Ali asked anxiously.

'Absolutely fine, if a little ragged with all this sightseeing with Bunny. Why?' he asked, surprised.

'Japes, your wound seems to be bleeding again,' explained Bunny. 'I think we need to get you to a hospital.' Bunny stood up abruptly, his chair scraping on the tiled floor.

Japes jumped at the noise and looked up at Bunny with a frightened expression that startled his old friend. 'No, please, I couldn't go back there. I'll be alright in a minute, really I will.'

'Mr Japes, how about I call my cousin – do you remember Mariam? She's a nurse at the private hospital,' Ali suggested in his most polite and reassuring concierge voice. 'She's home right now and she lives just on the next street. We can have her over here in a jiffy.'

Japes finally agreed to this and while Ali made the call, Ashraf half carried Japes downstairs to his bedroom. He then tried to help him get into his pyjamas, with Bunny standing in the doorway.

'Look, I can do it myself!' Japes snapped, going from frightened to irate in a matter of seconds. 'And what are you looking at?' he suddenly spat at Bunny, as if he were a complete stranger. 'This isn't some peep show, you know.'

Bunny withdrew and leaned on the wall for support, taking deep breaths, his own head spinning. By the time Ali came into the room with his cousin, Mariam, Japes was sitting up in bed sipping a glass of sweet tea. Ashraf was standing by the window and Bunny had cautiously re-entered the room and was sitting in an armchair.

'Hello, Mr Japes. Do you remember me?' Mariam asked in the nurse's voice she used with children and old people.

'No, I don't, but you're very welcome,' Japes said, resuming his charming manner. 'It's been far too long since I've had an attractive woman in my room.'

Mariam laughed and sat on his bed, unwrapping his bandage as Japes stared at her in awe. Bunny saw the livid gash on his temple and tried to remain composed, smiling reassuringly.

'Oh, it's not too bad, Mr Japes. Some of the stitching has come loose, that's all.' She smiled. 'But we can see if a few of these butterfly strips can bind it in the meantime. I'm going to clean it first, though, so be prepared: it may sting a bit.'

It did sting and Japes, who formerly would never show pain, now screwed up his face in agony and whimpered.

'I'm sorry, Mr Japes, but it will help to make you all better.' Mariam smiled.

'Damn you, woman!' He was angry with her now. 'I should never have brought you home with me. You smell like a hospital! Get out!'

Ashraf looked over at Bunny and shook his head very slightly, his eyes weighted with sorrow. Bunny knew for certain, at that moment, that his friend would diminish, would slip away into oblivion, and he was the only one there able to take responsibility for him.

Mariam dressed the wound, unfazed by Japes's outburst, turning his anger around by chatting about this and that. When she stood up to put away her things, Japes smacked her behind lightly and she mock-scolded him, before settling him on extra pillows to keep his head elevated. Ali and Ashraf stayed with him while Bunny walked to the door with Mariam, thanking her for popping round, before asking her the serious question: 'Mariam, in your professional opinion, how long will it be before we lose all trace of Mr Japes?'

'It might be a few years, if you're lucky, Reverend, or a few months if you're unlucky. You will need to have a scan done back in England to see the extent of the damage. The best course of action is for someone to live with him or for him to go into a home. He can't live alone any longer.'

Japes spent much of the next day sleeping, with Ashraf taking the day off from sitting outside his souvenir shop, rallying round with take-away *kushari*. In the night time, however, Japes was awake and restless. He dressed and told Bunny he was going out for a stroll around the island.

'But, Japes, it's eleven thirty at night in a revolution-torn city – and besides, there's a curfew. No one's been out on the streets for over an hour,' Bunny said, alarmed at his friend's plan. 'How about we just sit out on the balcony?'

But Japes would have none of it, saying he was stiff after lying in bed. He breezed out in his brass-buttoned blazer, with Bunny loping after him. At the gates to the embassies, the watchmen were dozing in their shelters, one of them resting his head on the muzzle of his shotgun. Japes jovially related to Bunny that the same scenario had caused one of them to accidentally blow off his own jaw a few months ago, which didn't help put Bunny at his ease. They walked to the Nile, leaned on a railing and looked across at the mainland. In ancient times, explained Japes, suddenly tranquil and lucid, the east of the Nile, where the sun rose, had been the land of the living, while to the west, where it set, lay the land of the dead; that was why all pyramids were over there. Zamalek, of course, lay between the two.

All was quiet that night, with only an occasional muffled gunshot. Little rowing boats were moored, bobbing along the shore, covered over with blankets under which people had turned in for the night. Out of the corner of his eye, Bunny saw a pale shape descending to the water's edge. He peered over and made out a boy, 16 at the most, shoeless and wearing nothing but boxer shorts, walking as if in a dream.

Bunny nudged Japes and pointed. 'Surely that lad can't be going for a swim.'

Japes squinted. 'Good God! I know him – and no, he's not going for a swim.' He sped over and dropped down the bank with surprising nimbleness, firmly taking hold of the boy's arm.

'Hey, laddie, you don't want to go down there.'

The boy looked at him vaguely through a long, ash-blonde fringe, then gazed around at his whereabouts with a slow bewilderment.

'You're the boy I found sleeping in the shop doorway, aren't you?' Japes asked. 'Your mother's English and you live on Ahmed Heshmat Street like me. What do you say, my friend, shall I walk you home?'

'Yeah, can you help me find where I live? Because I'm feeling a bit lost,' the boy answered in a drugged drawl.

Japes and Bunny walked with the fair-haired boy between them. They made their way through narrow backstreets and alleys to stealthily return him home without attracting attention, checking all the time he wasn't going to step on glass or excrement, human or otherwise. Japes tried to talk to the boy, who glided as if sleepwalking and who occasionally answered in a low monosyllable.

'Do you remember when I brought you home last time? You'd told your parents you were staying with a friend for the night and you didn't even remember how you'd got to that doorway I found you in. You stank because someone had urinated on you as you slept there. Whatever it is you're smoking, it's messing up your brain, young man. You may think hashish is a natural product but what they put in it these days to keep you buying it certainly is not. It's bad enough, believe me, that my old head's in a state through no fault my own, but I can tell you, you don't want to be joining that club before your time.'

The dazed boy let out a slow, sleepy, 'Yeah.'

'Sorry about yesterday, by the way, Bunny. I have an inkling of what happened and, yes, we need to talk about what to do next.'

Bunny nodded sadly and they walked the boy up to his front door, just across from Japes's own building. They rang the doorbell and, after a time, his mother answered, befuddled by sleep and in her dressing gown. She thanked Japes for saving her son again, putting her arm around the slumping boy, and quietly shut the door.

Bunny awoke the next morning to another Egyptian breakfast on the balcony and Japes waiting for him. 'Do sit down, old boy. I have a splendid plan. I'd like to take a holiday with you. Possibly my last – who knows? No point in dwelling on it. In a few days, when I've got these bloody bandages off, we're going to catch the night train south to Luxor where we'll board a five-star cruise ship on the Nile. The tourists have all fled the country and the few boats that are running are desperate for custom. We'll go to Karnak, then on to the Valley of the Kings, the Temple of Seth at Kom Ombo and of Horus at Edfu, then to the low dam at Aswan – Imperial Britain's greatest feat of civil engineering – and the island temple of Philae. I saw all this with Mona, just after I arrived here, and now I'm going to take you. And then you know what we'll do?'

Bunny waited on edge for the impossible suggestion of a trip up Lake Nasser, through the Sudan and into Ethiopia to the source of the Blue Nile, but Japes, still ever one to surprise him declared, 'We'll return to Travistock.'

'That sounds splendid, Will.' Bunny breathed a sigh of relief. 'Let me first just check with Marion. She's been going round to the house to look in on Horace Walpole every few days. He's in semi-hibernation but I thought he might still require a watchful eye.'

'Marion, ah, Matron Marion, how I've missed her,' Japes sighed as Bunny rose and went indoors to the phone.

'Chin up, Bunny, it'll all be alright,' she said from her telephone in the san. 'You do this trip together then bring Japesy back here where we can all care for him.' She paused a moment and then added, 'But not a word to Charlie Sedgewick. He has enough heartache with his wife in the hospice. And, by the way, should Japes become disorientated again and try to change the plan, just tell him you both need to be getting back as term's about to start at Blindefellows – that'll get him packing his suitcases.'

13

A Droplet of Cream

Spring 2014

After living alone as a widower for three years, Sedgewick had moved into The Maples, 'an exclusive residence for retired professionals', where some of his ex-colleagues from Blindefellows now passed their remaining years. The Maples was, as its brochure proclaimed, 'perfectly situated on the banks of the River Tidd and only a few minutes' stroll from the centre of the picturesque market town of Travistock'. It was an imposing group of conjoined Georgian townhouses decked out in a colonial style that aimed to recreate the atmosphere of a gentlemen's club – framed prints of old maps and Mughal elephants, Chesterfield armchairs, faux–Turkish carpets and daily broadsheets – strictly *The Financial Times* and *The Telegraph*. At least, Sedgewick thought, it had to be better than the state-funded old folks' place across town, all vinyl wingbacks and plastic flooring, the easier to mop up little accidents, with sing-along sessions on Wednesday afternoons involving tambourines and maracas. It was, he fancied, rather akin to the difference between Blindefellows and the local comp, the infamous 'Travvy High'.

In the next room to Sedgewick lived Crane, former Head of Classics, with his doddery, mushroom-hued Siamese cat, Primrose. Both Crane and Primrose closed their eyes when someone spoke to them as if slowly absorbing every word. Sedgewick found this characteristic irksome, along with the way Crane pronounced certain words, such as 'demeese' for demise. He had managed to avoid Crane for most of his long career at Blindefellows, but now that they were neighbours he suddenly found he had to make small talk with him, which was a chore. Sedgewick wished he had Japes as his neighbour but Japes had gone abroad after retiring and Sedgewick hadn't seen or heard from him since before Yvonne's death. He was forever resolving that he absolutely must get back in touch with the old chap.

As a widower, Sedgewick had lapsed back into bachelor ways and the care he gave to his house, garden and meals gradually declined into the slapdash. His marriage had been a comfortably domestic interlude that had gone by in a haze of good dinners, cleanliness and summer holidays in St Ives. For two decades he hadn't had to buy a single frozen ready meal and had filled out magnificently.

Yvonne never demanded a thing from him. She had all she desired simply by having more than a neglected donkey to care for. She made his house their home and their garden a cul-de-sac Eden of ornamental fishponds, birdbaths, herbaceous borders and a lawn manicured to within an inch of its life. Sedgewick liked to watch her, out in all weathers, from his armchair in the lounge where he did all his marking, occasionally sneaking a look in her *Daily Mail* to enjoy for a moment the grotesqueries of the 'Great Unwashed'. Yet, as her obituary notice read in *The Travistock Times,* 'after a long illness, Yvonne Sedgewick fell asleep', this time without her husband at her side. He had been out for a pub meal with Tony Tree and Tristram Randolph and it had been a couple of hours before he had picked up the hospice nurse's phone messages informing him the end was nigh.

And so it was that Yvonne and her splendid puddings were laid to rest. The lawn became scraggy, as did the toenails that he could no longer reach to cut, owing to the obstruction of his belly. Neither did he any longer possess sufficient manual dexterity to use the extra-long-handled toenail cutters sold to him for an outrageous price by the local pharmacist. The ornamental fishpond filled with clumps of brown leaves and he just couldn't be bothered to refill the birdbath or put out the birds' nuts. With no wife and no job for which to make himself presentable, he soon slipped into shabbiness. His hair, now uniformly grey, was like the hedges in the garden, untrimmed and stuck up at odd angles. His jumpers sagged at the neck, bagged at the sleeves, and usually had splashes of instant soup on them. Occasionally, an ex-colleague would drop by and try their best not to stare at the heaps of tabloid newspapers that he'd never got round to cancelling, or the accumulation of ready-meal packaging in the kitchen.

One of these visitors noticed that matters had got to such a pitch that Sedgewick had taken to using his academic gown – the very gown he had worn every week to Latin Prayer – as a rag to dry his hands on in the downstairs toilet because he couldn't muster the energy to wash and dry the towels. Later that week, Swainson had telephoned him for a friendly chat to see how he was getting on. He casually mentioned The Maples as being quite the up-market place to retire, not only for suitable company but also good grub and a colonial milieu on the banks of the Tidd. A week later, Swainson drove Sedgewick over for an appointment and helped him with the paperwork once he made the decision, while there, to 'give it a go'.

All in all, Sedgewick felt he'd made a good decision coming to The Maples. Meals were regular and tasty, although they didn't quite match up to his late wife's efforts. When the bridge tables were set out at 7pm after dinner, he generally played a game or two. He'd quickly got into the swing of things and learned the routine. Breakfast 8am until 10am, then a look over the morning papers. At 11am he would see the Reverend Hareton walking his tortoise, Horace, past the French windows. That was Sedgewick's cue to take himself for a stroll – doctor's orders. He'd then saunter over to the market square for a pot of tea at the Four and Twenty Blackbirds, often accompanied by a slice of coffee cake – against doctor's orders. He might amble into the library next, or the bookshop to keep a hand in his subject, before heading back to The Maples in time for lunch at 1pm sharp.

Today he was greeted by Linda the day manager, a throaty-voiced woman with a straw roof of bleached hair and tiger-print nails, and toasted to a rich sienna by her sun-bed addiction.

'Hello, Mr Sedgewick, and how are we today?'

'We're *all* well, thank you, Linda.' (She never picked up on his subtle corrections.)

'Fish Friday today, followed by gooseberry fool,' she crowed after him, as if an old man's life revolved exclusively around mealtimes – and perhaps, he thought, it did.

Meals at The Maples were dignified, with Wedgewood crockery, linen napkins, silver-plate cutlery and intelligent conversation. Sedgewick had been heartened to find that none of the residents ever needed help with eating and all appeared to be completely unaffected by dementia. 'Must be the nature of a life of higher thought,' he ruminated. 'Wards off the brain-rot,' and again he commended himself on his decision to move here, to this exclusive residence for retired professionals.

There was no specific seating arrangement but Sedgewick always aimed to sit with Marion Ridgeway, his long-time protector and sometime bedfellow of his old pal Japes, that inveterate bachelor. Sedgewick occasionally thought of asking her if she knew how the old lad was keeping, but he wasn't sure how it would go down and invariably chose to keep mum.

Today Marion announced that she was about to acquire a beagle by the name of Peanuts, as her sister was going into sheltered housing where pets weren't allowed. 'Damn silly name to be calling out across the park,' she guffawed, her mouth full of fish like an over-zealous seagull. Crane, who had, unfortunately, plonked himself down at their table today, responded with an encomium upon the cat as the superior animal due to their independence, intelligence and ability to walk themselves. During this monologue, Sedgewick found himself staring out of the high windows of the dining room, past the pale curtains billowing serenely in the breeze, behind which a silhouette emerged of a statuesque woman with magnificent curves cradling what appeared to be a small pewter ewer. She held her head inclined towards him, as if looking curiously into his soul, as he lost himself in a cleavage of almost unfathomable depth. The chatter around him stilled to a whispering sea breeze and his feet felt like they were sinking into wet sand.

'Would you like that I should cream your fool?' she asked in a lilting voice as silky as the cream she was proffering. Sedgewick looked up, alarmed. She was there, above him, her curved vessel poised. Behind long, thick lashes, her vast brown eyes sparkled, penetrating him to the quick. All he could do was bow his grizzled head in boyish shyness at the marvellous surfeit of rounded beige thighs and forearms and her figure-hugging, cream dress. Like a crack of a whip, Linda's voice brought this momentary reverie to too swift an end. The curvaceous apparition jumped and a pearl-shaped droplet of cream landed upon her finger.

'She means would you like some cream with your *gooseberry* fool, Mr Sedgewick. Lola's here on a trial. Hungarian; just come off the boat. We'll have to see how well she acquires the language.'

'Well, erm, yes, please – just a little, doctor's orders and all that.' He attempted a witty laugh, which came out instead like a monstrous, wheezing gasp. Lola poured a little cream onto his dessert with a shaking hand. He managed to pull himself together enough to give her a reassuring nod, the one he had always used with pupils just before they picked up their pens to start an exam. She smiled at him and breathed a sigh of relief, the warmth of which he felt rapturously upon his cheek.

For the next three weeks, Sedgewick spruced himself up every morning in anticipation of interactions with Lola, whom he thought of almost ceaselessly. He tried to busy himself with history in the library and the bookshop, and often came back to The Maples with a book to continue his studies in the comfort of his room, which helped to distract him a little. He could not remember ever having been so taken with a woman and, now in his sixties, he was somewhat miffed that it had come along so late, particularly as she was some 20 years his junior. If only he'd felt like this during his young and vigorous days under Japes's tutelage! But now, and at his age, what would people think? And without Japes to advise him, how should he proceed?

As he brushed up on the Soviet occupation of Budapest in 1956, he sought to convince himself that he was merely in thrall to a 'smellusion'; that it was her natural musk alone, rather than her mellifluous voice or incomparable figure, that had led him to this state, so that it was, consequently, a matter of pure animal biology and thus entirely out of his hands. When she was anywhere near him, his deflated loins gave a slight quiver in her direction, something that he had never experienced before with any woman, and over which he found he had no control. Perhaps, he thought, he finally knew what it was to be Japes, and what might drive a man who was ever in pursuit of this overwhelming sensation.

'Good morning, Mr Sedgewick, and how are we today?' Lola asked as she flung open the French windows to let the spring warmth into the reading room.

'Now, now, Lola, I've told you about that one.' He folded the newspaper that he wasn't really reading and put it down on the table. 'The word *we* is plural and – to my delight – I am here alone with you. Hence, you need to say, "How are *you* today?".'

Lola perched on the ottoman at his feet, her legs folded to one side. 'How are *you* today, Mr Sedgewick?' she repeated pertly, fluttering her eyelids. 'You are a very kind and caring teacher; you help me keep my job.'

Matron Ridgeway was out in the garden instilling discipline to her elder sister's terrified beagle, 'Peanuts, come here this instant! Get out of that bush and come here! Peanuts! Peanuts!'

Lola looked shaken, 'Why is the old lady calling her dog Penis? I don't understand.'

Sedgewick blushed and tried to enunciate the difference between the two words when Linda strolled in and stood over them, aghast. Lola jumped up from the ottoman and began plumping the sofa cushions.

'I do hope Lola's not distracting you from your paper, Mr Sedgewick.'

'No, no, not in the least. Just giving her a few tips on the finer points of English pronunciation. Once a teacher, always a teacher, you know, Linda,' and again he made a terrible attempt at a chuckle, which instead burst out like the twanging of an industrial elastic band.

At lunch, Crane detected a certain look about Sedgewick whenever Lola wafted by. 'Sedgewick, you might try not to let your tongue loll so whenever the Hungarian woman's in the vicinity. It's rather animal, you know.'

'How can I help it?' replied Sedgewick, emboldened. 'Having her around is like having chocolate cake two times a day.'

'Even so, you might want to try and contain yourself, for your own sake. You don't want to be like Japesey, the lecherous old goat.'

This quite truthful quip about his old friend suddenly made Sedgewick quite indignant: 'And good on him for it, Crane,' he snapped. 'William Japes had more life in him at sixty-two than you had at twenty-six.'

Sedgewick had made up his mind. He would intercept Lola on her way back from the market, whither she was sent every Thursday morning to buy fresh farm eggs and vegetables. He would escort her to the back of his tearoom and propose. He couldn't contain it any longer and cared not a whit for what anyone might say. Sedgewick felt quite sure Japes, his mentor, would have approved of Lola, even if he, Japes, wasn't the marrying type – certainly more than he had of Yvonne, anyway. Perhaps he and Lola could meet up with Japes in Egypt and go on a Nile cruise. Sedgewick smiled, imagining Lola, bikini-clad and coconut-oiled, upon a lounge chair atop the deck of a paddle steamer as it churned rhythmically, rhythmically up the fertile valley of the Nile. He envisioned pink ibises, suddenly startled, fluttering out of the reed bed.

After breakfast, instead of reading the papers, he showered and shaved, singing some of the old wartime songs he had once taught the boys – something he hadn't done for years. He dressed himself up in a silk Ascot, pressed slacks and his best houndstooth worsted sports jacket in the lapel pocket of which, with a twinge of guilt, he placed Yvonne's old engagement ring in its original box. He flattened down his hair with Old Spice hair tonic, took one last look in the mirror, straightened his glasses, and sallied forth.

He caught sight of Lola standing in line at the egg stall, already bearing two fine, full baskets of fresh vegetables. He loitered at the cheese stall, too nervous even to try the free samples, until she had been served. As soon as she went on her way, he appeared at her elbow and gave her a start.

'Mr Sedgewick! I don't recognise you out from The Maples! You are looking so handsome today! Are you meeting a lady?'

'Yes – you!' he answered smartly, which made her laugh. Her teeth were marvellously white.

'Come and have a cup of tea with me.'

'Well…' she hesitated, nervously looking up at the market square clock. 'I suppose I could have a quick cuppa, as you teach me to say, but Miss Linda expects me back by half-past eleven.'

He gallantly took her arm and escorted her into the Four and Twenty. He didn't have much time and saw that he was going to have to grasp the heifer by the horns. He was filled to bursting point with a nervous energy he'd never known before. He ushered her to a table at the rear, where the tearoom was usually free of customers, calling out his order of a pot of Darjeeling as he passed the counter.

Unfortunately, today there were two elderly ladies sitting at the back with their scones. He picked a table he hoped would be out of shot of their hearing aids.

'This is very nice café, Mr Sedgewick,' Lola purred, admiring the décor with its multiple tea strainers hanging on the walls. ' Is it – how do you say – your local?'

'Please, Lola, I'd like you to call me Charles,' he gasped.

'Oh, Miss Linda isn't liking us calling the residents by the first names at all, but I suppose I can say it now, when I am outside from The Maples. When the cat is avay, the mice, they vill play!' she winked at him like Zsa Zsa Gabor and he turned to jelly.

The old ladies didn't say a word but looked at each other ominously over their lapsang souchong.

The waitress brought the tray of tea things and ponderously laid each item in its correct place as Sedgewick jiggled his knee in the uncomfortable silence, trying to muster the courage to do what he had dressed so nicely for.

'Shall I be mother?' Lola said as she picked up the teapot. Sedgewick couldn't quite take this in at that moment, and looked about, flustered. 'Oh, have I not chosen the correct expression?' she asked with concern.

'I have something for you, Lola,' Sedgewick blurted out and almost threw the little box onto the table as Lola poured the tea. She stared at the box as tea spilled over the rim of the cup, before quickly putting down the pot. The two old ladies, in frozen gestures with their scones, their eyes on Sedgewick and Lola's table, awaited the outcome.

'It is something for me?' He nodded nervously. She slowly picked up the box and eased back the lid. The pearl sent a glow into her eyes. 'It's beautiful!'

'You see, I think it was a sign, on that first day, the droplet of cream on your finger – it just looked so perfect there, and it stayed with me, that image, and then I understood why and I remembered Yvonne's ring, which I'd stowed at the back of my sock drawer, and wondered if you would one day wear it, the ring, I mean.'

'Yvonne is your wife?'

'Yes – *was*, not is. Eighteen years we were together, eighteen wonderful years, but she became ill. She really knew how to look after me. More like a mother than a wife, sort of... in a way... you know.'

'So, she was like me. She liked to care for people. That's what she liked to do too?'

'Yes, yes, quite similar, but a bit different too. You see I'm a little overwhelmed by you, if you can catch my drift. I'm very, very attracted to you, Lola. I... I... I've never felt like this before. It's over-whelming – I mean, marvellous – but I don't know what to do about it. My best friend at the school would have known. He knew all about this sort of thing. If only he were here, he'd tell me just what to do, but he's been far away for a long time, Lola, so I have to just bumble through on my own as best I can.'

'But I am thinking I am not having a job at The Maples if I am marrying the residents.' She closed the box gently and placed it in front of him.

'But you wouldn't need a job. I can stop renting out my bungalow and we can live there together. You can have everything you like.'

'But Mr Sedgewick – Charles – it's not working just for money.

It's what I like to do, what I am needing to do for my spirit. In Hungary, sad things have happened for me and it makes me feel better to care for many people. I think it will be a waste if I care only for one person alone.'

'But wouldn't you want to live in a smart house just off the park? Where do you live now? It can't be very pleasant.' It struck him now that he had never, until this very moment, thought of her as existing beyond her interaction with him.

'I am sharing a pretty little house with other women from Hungary also working as carers. It is very nice. We're all happy together. My daughter comes to live there soon. She is finishing her studies as mental health nurse in Szeged. I send her money for university. She is very good in English and can go straight to work for the NHS.'

Sedgewick didn't know what to say, and busied himself with adding milk and sugar to his tea to buy himself a bit of time to ponder. A daughter? He'd never heard about a daughter. Maybe she'd move in with them in his dormer bungalow, possibly have boyfriends calling round, staying the night. Next, Lola's parents, camped out in his sitting room. Perhaps even some long estranged serf of a husband would turn up looking for handouts. And soon enough he'd find himself imprisoned in his own home, surrounded by an extended family speaking a language he couldn't understand, the air thick with the heady scent of a goulash gravy.

'The tea is very nice and the café is also very nice,' Lola said.

'Would you wear my ring anyway, Lola, as a gift?' Sedgewick asked, recovering himself and recollecting his youthful passion.

She smiled and nodded, looking sated somehow, as he sunk back in his chair, a small, portly, dapper old man with a tall, tawny, brawny brunette who could have veritably swallowed him up in her thighs. 'Okay, Charles. I wear it… just for you.' She reached over and took the pearl ring out of its box, slipping it onto her little finger, the only one it could possibly have fit. Sedgewick paid and followed her out of the café carrying her baskets, suddenly feeling horribly downcast that he had betrayed Yvonne, who was always so dear, for this flight of fancy. The old women made no attempt to hide their opinions as their eyes followed him out. He felt like a fool.

From the kitchen window of The Maples, Linda watched them coming up the gravel drive, saw Sedgewick carrying the baskets, and heard Lola calling him Charles. From that moment, she resolved to change Lola's duties. Indeed, a week passed and it was as if Lola had completely vanished from The Maples. *Had she simply left with his ring?* Sedgewick wondered. *Had Linda seen her wearing it and sacked her for trying to marry the residents?* He wanted to explain to Lola that it was all a terrible misunderstanding, that he had realised he could never replace his wife, and could he have her ring back in memory of her, please? He hung around in the reading room after breakfast every day and waited for her. When Bunny walked his tortoise past the French windows at 11am, struggling to keep up with the reptile, Sedgewick lingered on instead of taking his morning constitutional. He went to lunch but Lola was never there either. He leafed through his history books in the lounge, rather than in the comfort of his own room, but still he didn't see her. He felt too nervous to ask Linda in case she thought something fishy was going on.

On the eighth day, he caught sight of Lola at the end of the corridor in front of his bedroom. She went through the drawn velvet curtain where he had assumed there was one of those Georgian false windows. He realised, then, that there must be a staircase there, as he heard her footsteps ascending. He followed her through the curtain and up a two-flight stairway to a corridor of doors. Peeping out from behind the stairwell doorway, he watched as she came out of one door and into another, then appeared again in the corridor only to disappear through another door. He ventured forward and read the names on the doors, one of them, Miss Otterly Berry, seemed familiar but he couldn't quite place her. The other names he didn't know and he thought he knew everyone in The Maples by now. And then there it was: 'Mr William Japes'.

Japes? Japes was here and not in Egypt? Japes! Japes! Excitedly, he tapped on the door. 'Just a moment,' called Lola's voice from within. What was she doing in there? Japes, that old dog, had probably cast his spell over her and she was spending hours a day in there, massaging him with essential oils. Without losing another moment, he burst in to savour the sight of his old hero tête-à-tête with the woman of his dreams.

'Mr Sedgewick!' she said brightly as she fed a shrivelled-looking old man a tiny portion of mush from a spoon, carefully making sure none of it spilled on his paisley pyjamas.

Sedgewick stood agog. 'Japes?' he asked tentatively. The old man looked at him as if through a cloud.

'You know Mr Japes? Come and sit down, Mr Sedgewick! He can remember, now and again, things from a long time ago.'

Sedgewick entered and sat down on a lavender-coloured vinyl wingback on the other side of the bed. The room was smaller than his, with a few old photos from Army days and Blindefellows on the wall and a crucifix above the bed. There was a television but no books or newspapers.

'How are you, Japes?' Sedgewick asked awkwardly. Japes opened his mouth for another spoonful, unaware. 'We worked together at the same school for thirty years,' he told Lola, by way of explanation more to himself than to her. 'I didn't even know this corridor existed.'

'They are moving the residents up when they have the dementia very bad, Mr Sedgewick. We do what we can for them before the end.'

'Moving up?'

'Yes, moving up, like towards heaven, maybe.' Lola smiled as she gently dabbed Japes's chin with a paper napkin. 'Mr Japes, Mr Sedgewick from your old school has come to visit you.'

Japes said something that sounded like a muffled 'Sedgewick' and Lola nodded at Sedgewick excitedly.

'How're you doing, Japes? Always got the better of me at table footie, eh? You won't believe who's downstairs... Starchy Crane. Same old stuffed shirt as ever. Remember when his wife, Clarissa, went off with the Maori rugby coach? Didn't surprise either of us, did it, Japesy? And remember the head, your Cambridge room-mate,

Bunny Hareton? He's here. Can't keep up with his tortoise nowadays. And your old flame, Marion Ridgeway? She's here too.'

'Marion?' Japes croaked faintly, followed by a blank smile.

'Yes, that's her! She's got a beagle,' said Sedgewick, his voice cracking and his eyes filling with tears. 'Always shouting for it: "Peanuts! Peanuts!"'

'Poor Mr Sedgewick. I think he was your very good friend. I am so sorry for you,' Lola said softly.

His breath trembling, Sedgewick replied in a hoarse whisper, 'Yes, he was my very good friend.'

After a few more minutes of Sedgewick trying to recreate memories for Japes, Lola settled the hollowed-out old man on his pillow. Sedgewick tried to connect this shell with the Japes he first knew. An image from more than half his life ago came into his head, of Japes sitting at breakfast in a hotel in France, immaculately turned out with a lovely French woman opposite him, her stockinged feet gliding over his polished brogues.

'He'll sleep now. You should ask Linda if you can visit again. Reverend Hareton visits every morning after walking Wallace Horpole. He reads him little things from the daily paper. Miss Ridgeway used to come but it makes her very sad and she doesn't want to anymore.'

'Bunny and Marion knew he was here?' Sedgewick said, choked up again. 'Why didn't they tell me?'

Lola, observing his trembling chin understood immediately, 'Perhaps they were protecting you because he was dear to you. He's looking at you. I think maybe he remembers you.'

'Do you think so?' asked Sedgewick, brightening slightly.

'Oh, and here's your ring,' Lola said, prising it from her little finger and passing it to him over Japes, lying on the bed, his eyelids now closing in a dream of a beautiful, nameless feminine face, a composite of many, partially obscured by her soft dark hair. Lola put the pearl ring into Sedgewick's palm and gently closed his fingers over it. 'I meant to give it back before but Miss Linda sent me upstairs. Also, I didn't know right words to be sure I would not hurt your feelings. I am so happy you let me wear it but it is for you to keep, to remember your wife by.'

Back downstairs in his room, Sedgewick returned the ring to its box at the back of his sock drawer, glanced heavenward to the upper floor and, sighing, said quietly to himself, 'Where be *your japes now*? Your gambols? Your songs? Your flashes of merriment that were wont to set the table on a roar?' He resolved to visit Japes every morning with Bunny and the newspapers, and sat down to read his history books while he still had a mind that was able. He felt he'd had enough of the Hungarian repression and decided to move on to the Prague Spring.

Acknowledgements

Thanks to all those who splashed out on patronage, Unbound for agreeing to give it a whirl and my editors who helped make it better.

Patrons

Julie Andrassy
Anna Androulakis
Richard Appleton
Youssef Arif
Adrianna Astle
Ezgi Atay
Mohammed Bably
Nicole Bagarella
Anas Baghdadi
James Barton
Bassem Bassily
Nader Bassily
Federica Basso
Johan Bel
Melanie Bell
Manon Bevan
Robert Bradshaw
Dave Brandt
Roz Broodryk
James Cartwright
Rebecca Chamberlain
Alex Clark
Michael Coffey
Peter Coffin
Martha Cohn
Shona Connell
Tony Connor
Joni Costello
Ariane Danut
Victor Dare
Tim Dilnutt

Julia Eisele
Salem El Sayed
Ahmed Elkharbotly
Rick Elya
Nehal Ezz
Wilhelmina Fessenbecker
Porl-Cumberland Forever-Ferguson
Sally Fulker
Yvonne Gainford
Heather Gatley
Sara Abdel Ghany
Heidi Gleb
Courtney Hagins
Gilan Hassan
Denise Holmes
James Holmes
Diane Hughes
Valeria Karbovski
Elena Kaufman
Tamara Kellermann
Hilary Kidson
Shona Kinsella
Maddy Knight
Mavis Le Page Leathley
Cheyenne LeFever
Sarah Lennox-Hilton
Joe Lingle
Greg Lipinski
nabila lotayef
Linda Lucyk
Mohammed Mabrouk
Karl Machin
Isabel Mack
Susan Mack
Anne Maclachlan

Joan Mallett
Hanna Mawla
Declan Mcdonald
Robert McGregor
Jon McLeod
Claudia Medoza
Carlos Alberto Bolaños Mena
Nicole Mensik
Debs Miles
Kyle & Grace Minner
Alfredo Molinas
Lena Naassana
Katerine Niedinger
Santiago Olábarri Oriol
David Owen
Rebecca Painter
Aitor Parada
Louise Perrin
Shauna Petrie
Gill Pinnington
David Pinnington
Chris Poole
Jeffrey Poon
Richard Pope
Annabelle Priest
Gregory Reid
Colleen Reilly
Karla Reilly
Kitty Reilly
Gill Roscoe
Jason Rushworth
Hana Shaltout
Terry Shave
Linda Sloan
Hala Soloducha

Elizabeth Stanley
Marcella Steinbauer
Jenny Storey
Helen Taylor
Mike Scott Thomson
Ann-Marie Thornton
David Tindall
Sue Tindall
Gerard Tolsma
Christina Ulfsparre
Rebecca-Rose Waldron
Melanie Waldron
Bryony Waldron
Joseph Welch
Leon Welchman
Gregory Wellman
Helen White
Marjorie Wiebe
Greg Williams
Derek Wilson
Liz Wood
Alona Yildirim
Nicole Zabbal